MORE THAN A
SKELETON

MORE THAN A
SKELETON

A Novel

PAUL L. MAIER

THOMAS NELSON PUBLISHERS®
Nashville

A Division of Thomas Nelson, Inc.
www.ThomasNelson.com

Published in Nashville, Tennessee, by Thomas Nelson, Inc.

Publisher's Note: This novel is a work of fiction. Most characters, plot, and events are the product of the author's imagination. Most characters are fictional, and any resemblance to persons living or dead is strictly coincidental.

Library of Congress Cataloging-in-Publication Data

Maier, Paul L.
   More than a skeleton : it was one man against the world : a novel /
Paul L. Maier.
     p. cm.
   ISBN 0-7852-6238-5
    1. College teachers--Fiction. 2. Jesus Christ--Resurrection--Fiction.
3. Miracles--Fiction. I. Title.
PS3563.A382 M67 2003
813'.54--dc22   2003016349

To Dan and Edie Marshall

OTHER BOOKS
BY PAUL L. MAIER

Fiction

Pontius Pilate
The Flames of Rome
A Skeleton in God's Closet

Nonfiction

A Man Spoke, a World Listened
The Best of Walter A. Maier (ed.)
Josephus: The Jewish War (ed., with G. Cornfeld)
Josephus: The Essential Works (ed., trans.)
In the Fullness of Time
Eusebius: The Church History (ed., trans.)
The First Christmas

For Children

The Very First Christmas
The Very First Easter
The Very First Christians

PREFACE

Most of the characters in this book are fictitious, but some authentic personalities do appear. So that they might not be thought to endorse everything else in this novel, I have not sought their permission. All are famous enough to be "in the public domain," and will, I trust, find their portrayal in these pages appropriate and congenial. The reader should know, however, that the dialogue I supply for them is mine and not theirs. While this novel follows *A Skeleton in God's Closet*, it is complete in itself and does not require a reading of the prequel, which is referred to only as "the Rama project" in these pages without any divulging of the plot.

Special appreciation is due attorneys Elizabeth Meyer and Gregg Stover, as well as Professors Judah Ari-Gur, Karlis Kaugars, Walter A. Maier III, Samuel Nafzger, Walter Rast, and David Thomas for technical assistance. They should not be faulted, of course, for any opinions in this book that they may not share. A grateful word goes also to Marion Ellis, Monica Nahm, Susie Donnelly, and Robert E. Smith.

P. L. M.
Western Michigan University
March 1, 2003

It was the event for which believers had been waiting twenty centuries. Even skeptics knew that the second coming of Christ—if it ever happened—would certainly be the number one news story of all time. But what if that arrival were dimensionally different from what had been expected, with none of the Rapture, Tribulation, Antichrists, beasts, horrors, and demonic forces predicted by the prophecy specialists? Jesus said He would return when least expected. But could that return also be in a manner least expected?

PROLOGUE

Of the twenty archaeological digs taking place in Israel and Jordan, Sepphoris was *the* place to be. Perched on a lofty hillock in Galilee, the site was a paradise for excavators. In previous seasons they had uncovered broad colonnaded streets flanked by beautiful mosaic sidewalks, a four-thousand-seat theater cut into the side of a hill, an aqueduct, subterranean water systems, two baths, imposing remains of public buildings crowning its acropolis—in short, everything to enthrall those who uncover hard evidence from the past.

Jenny Snow, an ancient history major from Wellesley, easily fit that profile. She was spending the summer digging at Sepphoris as a student volunteer—a smart move, she thought: not only would it look good on her résumé, but there was a certain thrill in finding new paths into the past, courtesy of a trowel. More than half of the other student volunteers at the dig were men, some of whom were taking as much interest in Jenny with her honey-blonde hair, sculpted features, and shorts and tank tops, as in the excavations. Coolly, she ignored them, finding much more interest in what her spade or brush was uncovering.

Many of the archaeological greats had conducted digs at Sepphoris—Ehud Netzer, Eric Meyers, Ze'ev Weiss—but this season James F. Strange was back in charge. The famed University of South Florida professor had a glittering track record at Sepphoris. Jenny recalled his opening remarks at their orientation session earlier in June, when he introduced his staff to the twenty-six newly arrived students and other volunteers from eight different nations. They were sitting in Sepphoris's excavated semicircular theater—much as spectators had done two thousand years earlier.

A stocky, bearded figure in field khakis, who seemed to have freshly arrived from the Australian outback, Strange had walked to stage center. Adjusting his jaunty leather hat—its broad brim turned upward on one side—he announced in commanding tones, "Hello, all of you! I'm Jim Strange. Welcome to the most exciting dig in Israel!"

Jenny had discounted his statement as a bit of friendly bluster, but not for long. Strange proceeded to give a brief history of Sepphoris, but in that short overview, jagged peaks of importance jutted out of the landscape of the past. Two millennia ago, Sepphoris had been destroyed by the Romans for refusing to accept Rome's census, but the place was magnificently rebuilt by Herod Antipas, the most successful son of Herod the Great, and became the capital of Galilee. Josephus, the first-century Jewish historian, called the city "the ornament of all Galilee."

After the destruction of Jerusalem in the year A.D. 70, the ruling council of the Jews—the Sanhedrin—moved to Sepphoris. It was here, too, that the earliest portion of the Jewish Talmud, the Mishnah, was compiled.

"Are you impressed?" asked Strange rhetorically, although some were nodding and even answering in the affirmative. "Then answer this question: who was the most famous resident of Galilee twenty centuries ago?"

Jenny shot up her hand. "Jesus of Nazareth," she replied.

"Yes, indeed! And where do you suppose His mother, Mary, came from?"

"Not . . . Sepphoris?" she wondered.

"According to earliest church tradition, yes, Sepphoris. And where did Mary, Joseph, and young Jesus live? Answer all together now . . ."

"Nazareth," came the general response.

"Correct. And where is Nazareth? Less than four miles that way!" He pointed to the southeast. "We're in exactly the area where Jesus grew up."

Gene Hopkins, a preppy sort from Princeton who was sitting next to Jenny and trying hard to impress her, raised his hand and asked, "Is there any chance that Jesus ever came here?"

Strange smiled, took off his hat to wave away some flies, and said, "Not just 'a chance,' as you say, but an overwhelming probability—say 999 out of 1,000. In fact, He *must* have visited here frequently. We know that young Jesus was a carpenter's apprentice for Joseph, so if Joseph, say, broke a saw blade, he'd probably send Jesus to get a new one here at Sepphoris. Nazareth was only a tiny village in those days, while this was the big city."

A buzz of discussion arose until hushed by Strange's next question. "By the way, what was Joseph doing up here in Galilee in the first place? The man most probably came from Bethlehem, didn't he?"

No one responded.

"Think, team! I've already told you the answer ten minutes ago."

Jenny raised a timid hand and said, "I think you said Sepphoris was rebuilt by Herod Antipas, didn't you? Maybe . . . Joseph was up here . . . to help in that?"

"Bravo, young lady! Bull's-eye! Joseph is called a *tekton* in the Gospels, which is not just a carpenter, but anyone in the construction trades, such as a mason or stonecutter too. It took Antipas only a dozen years to rebuild the city, so he'd need all the skilled labor he could find across the land."

"Yes, but Joseph and family lived in Nazareth, not here," objected Hopkins, the Princetonian.

"Of course," Strange agreed, with a patronizing smile. "Joseph obviously parked his family in the safety of a suburb like Nazareth while he made the short commute to work here each day, probably taking Jesus along as He got older."

Louder discussion welled up from the bottom rows of the stone theater. Strange went on to regale the dig personnel with other intriguing possibilities lurking under the unexcavated overburden at their site. In closing, he said, "So, team: it's by no means a flight of fantasy to suggest that the very stone benches on which you're now sitting could have been cut out of the living rock by Joseph . . . or even Jesus. This is the dig that could help part the curtains for a better look at the so-called 'silent years' in Jesus' life, the time He spent growing up. At the very least, we'll understand His environment better.

"So much for our opening orientation. We'll now move on to

archaeological methodology, and tomorrow we'll survey our target for this season's excavations: what we think are some shops just south of the synagogue."

Jenny adjusted quickly to life at the dig: the spartan accommodations at the tour house where they lived, three or four to a room; the early morning schedule of digging before the heat of the day set in; washing pottery finds in the afternoon; hearing lectures at night.

Slowly, some of the commercial district south of the synagogue at Sepphoris was reemerging into the Mediterranean sun, thanks to the careful use of pick, spade, trowel, and brush. Wheelbarrow loads of overburden were removed, sifted for artifacts, and then dumped.

At break time one morning, Jenny walked over to look at the excavated floor of the synagogue along the northern edge of their sector. A beautiful menorah—the seven-branched candlestick that often served as a symbol for Judaism—was the central mosaic on the tessellated floor. After admiring it for some time, she was walking back to the others when she noticed a low spot in the ground bordering the synagogue pavement. It had rained the night before, and the constant dripping from a column that stood over the area had evidently burrowed a small hole into the center of the declivity. A shaft of sunlight illuminated the hole, and as Jenny bent over she saw a glint of what looked like a piece of mosaic at the bottom. She ran for her trowel, knelt down, and started scooping away the surrounding overburden.

"And just what, pray tell, do you think you're doing, Jenny?" James F. Strange was looming overhead with a vast frown warping his otherwise friendly features. "What did we say about *not* touching any areas of our excavations that aren't on our agenda?"

"I'm . . . so sorry, Professor Strange," Jenny replied, face reddening and tears starting to fill her blue eyes. "I think there's a piece of mosaic down here, and I just wanted to look at it. I . . . I forgot about the rules."

"Where? Show me."

She pointed, then quickly added, her voice choking a bit in emotion, "I can easily put all the dirt back again, and no one will ever know. I'm really . . . terribly sorry."

Strange ignored her. He had taken Jenny's trowel and was on his knees, clearing off more of the seven inches of muddy crust in obvious violation of his own rules. "Please fetch me a pail, Jenny," he said, in a tone any uncle would use with his favorite niece.

While Strange loaded trowelfuls of excavated dirt into the pail, his eyes were brightening. Now he asked for a broad brush. Jenny hopped over to her quadrant and returned with the item. Strange carefully brushed dirt away from the surface of whatever he had found, and his mouth parted in a smile. "Come look, Jenny," he said.

Peering down at a flat surface about eighteen inches in diameter, she exclaimed, "It's a mosaic, all right! And it has some kind of lettering on it, doesn't it?"

"It does . . . yes. Would you mind going over to our trailer and bringing me a canteen of water? There's a good girl."

Happy that she was not banished from the dig, Jenny returned with the canteen. Strange promptly dumped its contents across the mosaic. As if by magic, the mosaic took on color, contrast, and clarity.

Both stared at their find in amazement, speechless for some moments. Finally Strange said, "The inscription, I think, is in Hebrew . . . *Hebrew,* Jenny! We've found a few bits of writing in Aramaic and Greek here at Sepphoris, but never Hebrew."

"What does it say?"

Strange studied the text for some moments, then shook his head. "Pieces of the tessera are missing, so it's difficult to make out. And I can't really be sure it's Hebrew. But if it is, it would have to be an early form of it, since the letters are archaic."

He lifted off the 35-mm Nikon camera that was dangling from his neck and used a whole roll of film in photographing the inscription from every angle, with a whole range of f-stops. Then he flashed a grin at Jenny and said, "You and I now have a decision to make: either we call all the dig personnel over here to see what you discovered . . . or we cover this up again to protect it while we try to decipher the inscription first."

Jenny thought for some moments, then shook her head. "It's your dig, Professor Strange," she said. "You'll have to make the decision, obviously."

Strange nodded and said, "Well, let's look at some supporting considerations for both options, shall we? Morally, I feel obligated to let all our personnel see what you found. The inscription may have little significance, or it could be important. If it's the former, we shouldn't hold out on the others. But if it's the latter, word might leak out, and the whole context here could be trampled over by the curious. But we just don't know which at this point."

"I think we should do what's safest and best for the artifact, Professor Strange."

He unleashed a broad smile and said, "I was hoping you'd say that! Can you keep our secret, Jenny?"

"Of course," she said, smiling.

"All right, then, here's my plan: I have a friend at Harvard University who knows Hebrew and Aramaic inscriptions as if he'd learned the languages in kindergarten. He's also a trained archaeologist, and he'll be over here in late summer to teach at Hebrew University. His name is Dr. Jonathan Weber, and I want him to see our mosaic . . . *in situ* . . . and then help us translate the inscription."

"Oh . . . I've heard of him, I think. Isn't he the one who unraveled that terrible skeleton mystery in Jerusalem a few years ago?"

Strange nodded. "The same. Now help me shove all this dirt back into place, Jenny."

"Am I forgiven then, Professor Strange?"

He merely gave her a happy hug.

Was it Confucius who said, "The journey of a thousand miles begins with a single step"? The mighty Mississippi starts with droplets of water in northern Minnesota. The Dead Sea Scrolls, a discovery of truly "biblical proportions," began when a Bedouin lad, looking for his lost goat, threw a rock into a cavern at Qumran.

Jenny Snow would soon join the ranks of those whose tiny acts led to stupendous results. Her trowel scraped far more than seven inches of the earth's crust. It skewered the earth itself, for the mosaic she uncovered would soon become a crucial link in a chain of events that would fetter the world.

ONE

Some weeks earlier, Jonathan Weber was enjoying the morning drive to his office at Harvard. It was May Day in Massachusetts—though hardly a distress call, he mused, in one of his less successful attempts at humor. He was piloting a blue BMW Z4 convertible through balmy air along the Charles River; the car was the one big luxury he had allowed himself since his book *Jesus of Nazareth* became an international best-seller. *But should a man holding the distinguished Reginald R. Dillon Professorship of Near Eastern Studies at Harvard University be sporting about in a transportation toy that better suited a pampered college undergrad?* his Lutheran conscience inquired.

Ah, there it is, he reflected, the proper sense of guilt so befitting a Lutheran. No one celebrated divine grace and forgiveness better than Lutherans, but the celebration was always more exquisite when preceded by a decent dose of guilt. When an adoring coed remarked that the blue of his BMW perfectly matched his eyes and that he looked like a maturing Robert Redford, Jonathan Weber worried that he may innocently have flirted with her. Still, he had finally learned to talk back to his nagging conscience and enjoy more of life on its own terms.

That morning, the drive to Harvard from his home in suburban Weston had taken exactly a half hour—right on schedule. Crossing the Charles River, he headed northward on J. F. Kennedy Street, carefully maneuvering through the trademark traffic radiating out of Harvard Square. His Beamer was doubly safe, he knew, because of its superb German engineering and his own meticulous care while driving. Not the faintest scratch had marred its enameled surface since he took delivery. At Mount Auburn Street, for example, he gave no thought whatever to outrunning the light that had just flashed yellow, but braked defensively to a stop. And that may have been his undoing.

Brakes shrieked, and a shattering crash from behind hurled Jon into his cream leather seat, then whipped him forward in reaction. Fortunately, he was wearing a seat belt and was only stunned, not injured. The same could not be said of his Z4. The rear-ending had driven its tail end into a configuration not intended by the engineers in Munich.

Storming out of his car, Jon saw a lanky, red-faced lad climbing out of the gray PT Cruiser that had assaulted him. A woeful look of anguish twisted the young man's features—and, of course, his grille. Before any confrontation, Jon walked to the rear of the Cruiser to record its license number. It was then that he noticed a large white sticker with red lettering on the back end of the car just above its plastic bumper: WARNING: IN CASE OF RAPTURE, THIS CAR WILL BE LEFT DRIVERLESS!

"So," Jon snapped at the driver. "Apparently your car is driverless: have you just been raptured? And if so, what in blazes are you doing back here on earth?"

"I'm . . . awfully sorry about this," the youth drawled. "I was looking over at the river—it's such a beautiful day—and I just . . . couldn't stop in time."

After exchanging the usual insurance information, Jon tried a few pleasantries to calm the shaken fellow, obviously a university undergrad. He really wanted to ask him why anyone would buy such an ugly imitation retro as a PT Cruiser, but thought better of it. "That bumper sticker of yours," he said. "Do you really believe that bit about being raptured out of your driver's seat?"

"I sure do!" The lad brightened, adding, "I've read all the books in the Left Behind series, and I think that—"

"But they're fiction!"

"Yes, but they're based on fact—on what Christians believe will surely happen during these end times."

"Not this Christian!" Jon objected. "Here's my card. Why not come to my office sometime and we'll talk about it?"

"Love to," the young man replied, finally managing a sheepish smile. "Again, I'm awfully, awfully sorry about this!"

By the time he reached his office, not far from Harvard's immortal Yard, Jon was angry—less about his wounded BMW and more about how end-times mania had beset the minds even of university undergrads, or at least one poor driver among them. He was scheduled to have an interview with a journalist from *Newsweek* later that morning, during which he had every intention of being cool, dispassionate, and tolerant. Now he wondered if he could actually manage it.

At exactly ten-thirty there was a knock on his office door. There stood the tall, distinguished figure of Kenneth L. Woodward, *Newsweek*'s veteran religion editor, who had come to Cambridge to interview Jon for a cover story on the end-times mania sweeping the nation. The two were well acquainted from previous interviews.

"You know the drill, Jon," said Woodward, while opening his attaché case, pulling out a tape recorder, and placing it on a small table between their chairs. "I'll let you see my copy before we publish. We hardly ever do that, but I make special exceptions in the case of persnickety professors!"

Jon chuckled. "Just be sure you translate my comments into English, Ken!"

"Always difficult in your case!"

"I'm sure! But why me? How do you think I can help your story?"

"Well, isn't that obvious? Aren't you The Man Who Saved Christianity by exposing that 'skeleton in God's closet' several years ago? The Christian world's been grateful to you ever since, so your input on our story should have rather strong impact."

Jon held up his hands to object. "I've never known you to exaggerate, Ken. Why start now? But let's unpack what you have so far."

Woodward cleared his throat and began. "Well, you can guess where we're going with our end-times feature, and I'm sure you know the stats: millions upon millions of copies sold in the Left Behind series and end-times fanaticism abounds."

Woodward paused for effect, then continued, "There hasn't been a flurry like this since Hal Lindsey's *The Late Great Planet Earth*. That book, you'll recall, was the number one international bestseller throughout the 1970s—after the Bible itself.

"What we want from you, Jon, is a critique of the whole end-times thinking—fact *and* fiction. The authors of Left Behind based their series not only on their own nonfiction works on prophecy, but also on the writings of Hal Lindsey, John Walvoord, and other prophecy specialists."

"Okay, I'll have at it," Jon said. "But you may have to tone down what I say. You know I have an overactive tongue in an overopinionated mouth."

"Don't worry. We'll run it by our lawyers."

Jon proceeded to summarize the popular claims of the prophecy enthusiasts as fairly as he could. At the start of their end-times scenario, so they taught, true believers would be physically taken up to heaven in a Rapture that would leave their non-Christian relatives and friends behind for a second chance at genuine faith. A seven-year period of Tribulation would follow, during which terrible things would afflict the new believers and unbelievers alike, many of them caused by an Antichrist figure at the summit of a one-world government with a single currency, who would lord it over subjects branded with "the mark." (Other prophecy specialists argued that the Rapture would take place in the middle of the seven-year Tribulation period or at its end.) Next, a final, horrendous battle at Armageddon would follow, and only then would Jesus return in His second coming, bringing on the Millennium—a thousand-year period of His reign—ending with the Final Judgment. The whole scenario would also be peopled with mysterious witnesses, beasts, demons, and apocalyptic figures mentioned in such biblical books as Ezekiel, Daniel, and Revelation.

"Christians agree on the Second Coming itself," Jon continued, "but they disagree on the rest of these claims. They're really based on overliteral interpretations of what's clearly symbolic material in the Bible. Much of that material published these days is also mistranslated, misunderstood, or misapplied by projection from the first century into the twenty-first. Just a second, Ken . . . see if this helps."

Jon walked back to his desk, pulled out a large plastic card from the center drawer, and handed it to Woodward. "You really can't keep the prophecy claims straight without a scorecard."

"The version on top—what's called dispensational premillennialism," Jon continued, "is the current rage, with most of the prophecy specialists teaching that chain of events. Those farther down, in my estimation, get more and more biblical until we come to amillennialism—nonmillennialism. This is arguably the traditional view of

Diagrams of Millennial Views

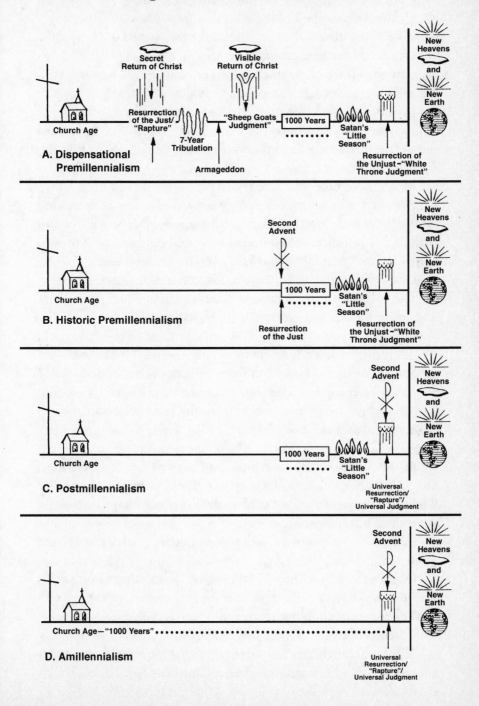

A. Dispensational Premillennialism

Secret Return of Christ · Visible Return of Christ · Resurrection of the Just/"Rapture" · 7-Year Tribulation · Armageddon · "Sheep Goats Judgment" · 1000 Years · Satan's "Little Season" · Resurrection of the Unjust–"White Throne Judgment" · Church Age · New Heavens and New Earth

B. Historic Premillennialism

Second Advent · Church Age · 1000 Years · Satan's "Little Season" · Resurrection of the Just · Resurrection of the Unjust–"White Throne Judgment" · New Heavens and New Earth

C. Postmillennialism

Second Advent · Church Age · 1000 Years · Satan's "Little Season" · Universal Resurrection/"Rapture"/Universal Judgment · New Heavens and New Earth

D. Amillennialism

Second Advent · Church Age—"1000 Years" · Universal Resurrection/"Rapture"/Universal Judgment · New Heavens and New Earth the church ever since its founding: the belief that 'the thousand years' is merely symbolic for the age of the success of Christianity. But take it literally? Why? A thousand years is just a drop in the bucket against the background of eternity!"

"Can you attach numbers to those views, Jon?" Woodward wondered. "How many Christians believe which scenario?"

Jon thought for a moment, then shook his head and said, "I can't give you exact figures, but the great majority of Christians across the world believe in the uncluttered version at the bottom: amillennialism."

"Really?" Woodward's face registered surprise.

"Roman Catholicism will have no part of millennialism, and that's a billion for openers, half of Christendom. Nor will Eastern Orthodoxy, another 350 million. Nor will Lutherans. Nor will Episcopalians or Reformed or Presbyterians. Nor will—"

"Okay, point taken. By the way, is it true that some prophecy specialists have actually changed their earlier predictions in later editions of their books after their forecasts failed?"

Jon nodded.

Woodward frowned for a moment, then asked, "Well, what's the antidote? Why don't you write a book blasting such shoddy tactics?"

"Already been done. There are a number of excellent books out that skewer the more bizarre claims on the basis of proper biblical evidence and sound scholarship."

"Such as . . . ?"

"Anthony Hoekema's *The Bible and the Future*, Gary DeMar's *End Times Fiction*, and Jerry Newcombe's *Coming Again—But When?* for openers. And, of course, the prophecy mania doesn't do too well in my book on Jesus."

"Has Christianity always had these alternative views about the end times?"

"Oh, anything but! Dave MacPherson's *The Rapture Plot* shows how dispensationalist Rapture theology is only a recent novelty when it comes to church history."

"Recent?" Ken pursued. "How recent?"

"A little Scottish girl named Margaret MacDonald claimed a revelation in 1830, and a traveling evangelist named J. N. Darby took it as his own and marketed it successfully to the nineteenth-century American church—to our detriment ever since, in my opinion. An American preacher, Cyrus Scofield, edited a Bible that amplified Darby's views—and many evangelicals have yet to pull out of this eschatological blind alley. I guess they figure the church had it all wrong during its first eighteen centuries!"

Both men chuckled. Then a lingering grin crossed Ken's face as he asked, "What about that southern evangelist with the big following, Dr. Mel Merton? You haven't mentioned him."

"Melvin Morris Merton!" Jon groaned. "Three Ms for the Master! He's the one who called *me* the Antichrist during the Rama crisis in Jerusalem! Merton Ministries has made a cottage industry out of the end times: syndicated TV, radio, books, journals, tapes."

"In Merton's latest book, he claims that you deny the Second Coming of Christ."

"No, just Merton's timetable for the same. That's a standard response from the prophecy crowd whenever you question their scenarios. Most of them begin with the dire things Jesus predicted on the Mount of Olives while overlooking Jerusalem and claim they will soon take place, probably in our generation. Wrong! They already *took* place when the Romans conquered Jerusalem. '*This generation will not pass away until all these things are accomplished,*' said Jesus around A.D. 33. Jerusalem was indeed destroyed thirty-seven years later in the year 70. Perfect fulfillment! But the prophecy pack transfers most of this from the first to the *twenty*-first century! You have to interpret all biblical prophecy passages in their historical context, and not project them two thousand years later."

"All right," Woodward probed, "if the bad things Jesus prophesied took place when Jerusalem was destroyed, what about the good things He predicted for believers—salvation, a new heaven, and a new earth?"

"All of them, including the Rapture, are part of the general resurrection of the dead at the end of time when Jesus returns. The church has always had it right in the Creed: 'I believe in the resurrection of the body and the life everlasting. Amen!' There it is: pure, sublime, and simple . . . no additional clutter necessary from overactive imaginations in the last two centuries."

"What about Merton's prediction that the Rapture will take place on New Year's Day three years from now, and that Jesus will return exactly seven years after that?"

"Not worthy of comment. They had false prophets in biblical times, and we have false prophets today. Someone has counted 1,338 predictions of Jesus' 'imminent return' across church history, all of them wrong, obviously. Remember, it was Jesus who said, 'Of that day and of that hour no one knows: not the Son—not modern doomsday prophets—but the Father.'"

"One of those phrases I don't recall from the Gospels," said Woodward, with a wink. "So, would 'false prophet' be a good label for Merton?"

"Of course! But if you quote me, better make that my *opinion,* not my statement of fact. Otherwise Merton may sue my pants off. He once called me 'the Apostle of Arrogance'—though he could well be right about that!"

Woodward chuckled and said, "Well, Jon, I certainly have enough material here. Any final thoughts?"

"Just this: ordinarily, I'm very tolerant of differing biblical interpretations among genuine scholars, but not in the case of a pseudo-prophet like Merton. His kind hurt Christianity—in several ways. First, people get so hung up on apocalyptic predictions that they panic and prepare for the end when there is no end. Remember the lunacy that took place toward the close of 1999? Even some respectable Christian leaders warned believers about 'the great Y2K menace,' advising them to store up survival supplies. And in the Ruby Ridge tragedy in Idaho, a lot of alarmist prophecy literature was found inside the home of Vicki and Randy Weaver after the FBI raid—"

"Which may explain their doomsday outlook," Woodward commented, while scribbling on his notepad.

"Okay, that's one couple," Jon resumed. "But how about whole movements, like the 'Israel First Millennialists' who are totally pro-Israel and anti-Arab, even though most Christians in the Holy Land are Arab? They want to see a new Jewish temple built in Jerusalem so that the Antichrist can sit inside it. This will supposedly bring on the last days and Jesus' triumphant return. As though poor Jesus needs us to help Him along!"

"Fair enough. Other reasons?"

"Secondly, what happens when prophecy believers see such prophecies fail? Some become disillusioned and abandon the faith entirely, all for the wrong reasons. Thirdly, the heart of Christianity—the gospel of Jesus Christ—gets displaced in favor of amateurish forecasting of the future. And finally, most of these wrongheaded prophecies are an insult to our intelligence. What thinking person can believe in a god who gleefully watches airliners crash because he has raptured Christian pilots out of their cockpits? Or credit a scenario in which Russia attacks Israel, yet its bombs explode harmlessly? Or believe that the United Nations headquarters will be transferred from New York City to Babylon, the archaeological ruin in Iraq? Or find millions destroyed by demonic—"

"All right, all right!" Woodward held up his hands. "*I* didn't write that stuff!"

"Sorry, Ken! I got carried away." Jon chuckled. "I'll stop preaching to the choir!"

Woodward smiled, put down his notepad, and said, "By the way, can you think of anything positive to say about the prophecy crowd? Just to balance the record?"

"Sure," Jon said, nodding. "I believe they're all genuine Christians, after all. And people like Lindsey, LaHaye, and Jenkins have more than proved that Christian authors are no longer limited to some evangelical ghetto, as used to be the case . . . not when their books reach the number one spot on secular best-seller lists!"

"True enough. Well, I think that's a wrap, Jon."

"Good. Oh, and by the way, this time you don't have to send me copy first."

"Thanks for that note of confidence! And for the interview, of course."

Three weeks later, the *Newsweek* story appeared. "Near the End?" was featured in bold lettering across the top of the magazine's cover, with artistic sketches of beasts, monsters, the Antichrist, exploding volcanos, falling stars, assorted demons, and the faithful in tribulation. Woodward had done a masterful job in writing up the story, Jon thought, citing authorities both for and against the current prophecy claims. With a touch of personal vanity, he was pleased to note that his own comments formed much of the core of the article. Woodward had reproduced his critique accurately, though without any colloquial references to Melvin Morris Merton.

Over the next few days, phone calls, voicemails, e-mails, faxes, and letters streamed into Jon's office, nine to one in favor of his views. One of the earliest responses was a call from his father, Erhard Weber, pastor of Saint John Lutheran Church in Hannibal, Missouri. A slender, white-haired patriarch, Erhard scoffed at any idea of retirement. Fortunately, his congregation agreed that the ever-active cleric should remain in harness despite his septuagenarian status, and even refused to accept his offer to retire. Proud of his son Jon's accomplishments, the elder Weber was still ready to criticize anything he found amiss in Jon's theology or practice.

"Thanks, Jon, for the way you took on the prophecy crew!" he said on the phone. "I've really had my fill of them!"

"Getting tired of end-times mania out there, Dad?"

"Yes! Ever since 9/11 and the other terrorist attacks across the world, the Tribulation-Rapture fever is higher yet—even among some of our members who ought to know better. Last Sunday I preached on 'Last Days Lunacy,' and even so hard-core a Lutheran as Irma Fischman tried to argue about it with me after worship. She's been attending an interdenominational women's Bible study group, and some of the ultras there started the contagion."

Among the chorus of affirmation that Jon received, a few discordant notes were heard. Those who disagreed with him often began their letters with an amiable "Dear Spawn of Satan," "To the Sacrilegious Scoffer in his Citadel of Unbelief," and other endearing phrases. At least a solid majority of normal Christians were out there, thought Jon—enough consolation for someone who wasn't particularly looking for any solace.

What he *was* looking for was a word from Shannon Jennings, who had held him in thrall from the moment she stepped into his life at an archaeological dig in Israel several years ago. She was a brilliant excavator, a delightful friend, a passionate lover—in a word, a genuine soul mate.

Shannon was back in Israel writing an addendum to the final report on an excavation she and her father had conducted at a site north of Jerusalem called Rama, the same dig that uncovered a 2,000 year old skeleton and catapulted Jon and Shannon into a very harrowing experience. Jon had told her to pick up a copy of the overseas edition of *Newsweek* when it hit the stands. Finally, a note appeared in his e-mail that revealed she hadn't forgotten.

> Why didn't they put *your* picture on the cover, Jon, rather than all those dreadful beasties?! What's one demon, more or less?! I'm glad you put the "prophets" in their place, although I think you were too easy on them. For instance, I would have called them sensationalizing seers or odious oracles. Maybe pathetic prognosticators? I'm sure, though, that they're crying all the way to their respective banks. I just can't understand why anyone with an IQ over 65 buys their stuff in the first place.

It was sad, thought Jon, that Shannon was so reticent about her opinions. If only the girl would speak her mind!

Several weeks later, a squat, swarthy individual with an augmented waistline appeared at Jon's office door. With a forced smile, he asked if he was addressing Dr. Jonathan P. Weber.

"I confess: I'm Weber," Jon replied.

The man plopped two documents into his hand and said, "You have just been served with this summons from the First Judicial Department of the State of New York, as well as the attending complaint. Good day, sir!" The process server quickly turned about and left.

Jon opened the documents: Melvin Morris Merton was suing him and *Newsweek* for libel, slander, and defamation of character in the amount of $38 million.

TWO

Merton's lawsuit called for $5.5 million in compensatory damages and $32.5 million in punitive damages. The former was for actual losses Merton claimed in reduced book sales present and projected, canceled speaking engagements, and terminated subsidiary rights due to "Professor Weber and *Newsweek* making me out to be a laughingstock," Merton told the press. Punitive damages would serve as a public warning against "further attacks on those who truly declare to the world the great prophecies in Holy Scripture, and alert people to the imminent return of our Lord and Savior Jesus Christ."

The legal department at *Newsweek* called to allay Jon's anxiety. They would file an immediate answer and defend both the magazine and himself against Merton's lawsuit. Since the case involved the freedom of the press, they would move ahead with all flags flying. First, of course, they would try to have the case thrown out of court, which they assured Jon was the simplest, least expensive, and most justified strategy.

Obviously he was grateful that the magazine's celebrated stable of legal beagles would be in his corner, but he found it hard to ignore the gnawing anxiety that would hit anyone sued for $38 million. Even in the worst-case scenario, of course, Merton could never collect that entire sum. But how much might he walk off with if he won? While *Newsweek* likely had deep pockets, his own were shallow enough.

The case would be heard in the First Judicial Department of the State of New York at the Manhattan Supreme Court, which was not at the top of the judiciary rankings, but merely the regular venue for civil cases. A preliminary hearing was set for mid-July. Representing Merton was a flamboyant attorney from Mississippi, Harrison

13

Pomeroy, well known in legal circles as a notorious leech with a hobby of squeezing blood out of stones. The series of high-profile and lucrative victories Pomeroy had won for his clients did nothing to calm Jon's concerns.

For the defense, Alan Dershowitz of Harvard, Jon's academic colleague, had offered his services. It was a gesture much appreciated by Jon, who would have hated seeing Dershowitz on the other side. But for now, *Newsweek* decided to go with its own legal department. "That's what we pay them for," Kenneth Woodward explained. That team was commanded by S. Fletcher Stanwick and Associates, which had an able track record in defending the magazine.

Presiding Judge Paul W. Parker, a silver-haired sage of middle height and age, opened the preliminary hearing on a steamy Wednesday morning in July. Fletcher Stanwick, all six feet, four inches of him, immediately stood up for the defense and moved that the case be dismissed. Deeming the case a frivolous lawsuit, he challenged the allegation that the plaintiff had suffered any damage to his reputation. As a well-known leader among fundamentalist Christians, Dr. Melvin Morris Merton was "in the public domain" and therefore subject to public comment in accordance with the freedoms of speech and press. Finally, Stanwick stated that the damages sought were "an outrageous example of legal adventuring, since they are out of all proportion to the alleged damages sustained."

When the judge turned to Harrison Pomeroy for the riposte, Merton's stubby, rotund attorney shook his hairless head sadly and got to his feet. In a thick southern accent, he drawled, "Reverend Dr. Melvin Morris Merton is highly regahded not only in what we're proud to call the Bible Belt in the South, but among true believahs everywhere." Pomeroy asserted that the attacks by "skeptical scholahs in the Nawth" against Dr. Merton—including using such language as "prophecy fanatics" and "false prophet"— undermined his client's leadership and defamed his reputation. Claiming *Newsweek* magazine equally liable for such libel, he urged the judge not to dismiss it. Then, wiping his forehead in the oppressive heat, Pomeroy sat down.

Judge Parker looked down from the bench, touching the tips of his fingers together. He paused for several moments, as if still unsure of his ruling. Then he nodded and said, "This court well realizes the importance, even the sacredness, of the freedom of speech and the freedom of the press. Ordinarily, I would indeed dismiss this case on that basis. However, I have serious concerns about whether the exemption from filing suits for defamation on the part of public figures applies here. I certainly find Professor Weber 'in the public domain,' but I regret to say that I, for one, am not convinced that the Reverend Dr. Melvin Merton is as public a figure. Accordingly, this case will proceed as filed."

Stanwick stood up to object. "But, Your Honor—"

"My ruling stands," said the judge. "We will now turn to our calendars, set a date for the trial, and proceed to the discovery phase."

Both sides agreed on a trial by jury two months later, and the preliminary hearing ended. Melvin Morris Merton, who had not said a word, stood up, flashed a dark smile at the table for the defense, and gave his lawyer a mighty hug. Pomeroy winced just a bit in Merton's embrace, as if hoping it would be brief.

As they emerged from the courtroom, Stanwick told Jon, "I really thought Parker would dismiss the suit. Can't understand why he's going ahead with it."

"You don't suppose he'll try to make a test case out of this, do you?"

"I doubt it. There've been others like this . . . though not with such high stakes involved. But one thing's clear: Parker is no fan of Merton, or he would have considered him a public figure indeed. Probably he's a secularist who may never even have heard of the man."

During the discovery phase in the intervening weeks, Stanwick and Associates subpoenaed copies of everything Merton had ever published, as well as royalty statements from his publishers. They also learned that Merton had originally hoped for a class action suit against Jon and *Newsweek* for $88 million on the part of all prophecy proponents who must certainly have felt as maligned as himself. But he had found no one else to join him in the suit, except for several publicity-seeking opportunists whom Jon and *Newsweek* had not even named in the article.

"I'll say this for Merton," Jon told Stanwick. "At least he or his attorney had sense enough not to include such parasites. What did they get from us?"

"The usual record of all your publications and addresses, as well as royalty statements from your publishers. Probably the biggest bill in this whole case will be the duplication costs for all your material!"

"Sorry about that," said Jon sheepishly.

"Not to worry: all that paper will probably confuse the plaintiff! Well, stay tuned. If we need anything else, we'll get in touch with you in Cambridge. Sorry that you have to delay your trip to Israel because of this . . . unpleasantness."

When Jon called Shannon with the news, she was, predictably, even more emphatic in her disdain of Merton. "That buffoon wants to sue *you?* The creep who publicly called you the Antichrist and almost got us killed in Jerusalem? Look at his track record, Jon: he predicted Jesus would return to the Mount of Olives on Easter Sunday several years ago, and he got a hundred thousand pathetic pilgrims to join him there. But Jesus pulled a no-show, of course."

"Well, regardless of what we think, the judge didn't throw the case out of court . . . so I won't be joining you in Israel until this is over."

"Well, only Jews have a proper name for what Merton is trying."

"What's that?"

"*Chutzpah.*"

"Exactly: brazen insolence and—"

"No," Shannon objected. "*Chutzpah* is when a man murders his father and mother, then begs the judge for leniency on the basis that he's an orphan."

"Perfect definition!" Jon laughed. He thought for a moment, then brightened and added, "That gives me an idea for the case, darling. Once again you've proven that I just can't live without you."

Pacing his office, he recalled his own definition of *chutzpah* in the case of the man who would one day become prime minister of Israel. In 1982 Ariel Sharon, then commander of the Israeli forces invading Lebanon, had orders to limit the invasion to a buffer zone twenty miles inside the Lebanese border. Instead, he defied his orders and invaded all the way into Beirut. This set the stage not only for the Sabra and Shatila massacres of Palestinians by Christian Phalangist militiamen, but indirectly led to the deaths of 241 American marines and 56 French paratroopers in the truck bombing of their barracks at Beirut Airport by Hezbollah terrorists. But when *Time* then published a story critical of Sharon, he filed a $50 million libel suit against the magazine. Now that was chutzpah!

Jon called Stanwick and suggested that they had a remarkable precedent in the Sharon lawsuit, which had ended in *Time*'s favor.

"Excellent idea, Professor Weber," Stanwick replied. "We'll certainly follow it up. Meanwhile, of course, I trust you'll not be commenting publicly on this case."

"Certainly not."

At the beginning of September, the case of *Merton* v. *Weber and Newsweek, Inc.*, as it would be called in future textbooks, was underway at last. The stakes were high enough, quite apart from the damages specified, since once again freedom of speech and freedom of the press seemed in jeopardy. Many news magazines, wire services, and major newspapers sent reporters to the trial, as did the broadcast media. If Merton won, it looked to be a bland future for American journalism.

On the morning of September 10, at the Manhattan Supreme Court on Twenty-fifth and Madison, a court crier announced in stentorian tones, "All stand! *Oyez! Oyez! Oyez!* All who have business in this court, the Honorable Judge Paul W. Parker presiding, now draw nigh!"

When Parker called for the plaintiff's attorney to introduce his case, Harrison Pomeroy stood as erect as his five-foot, five-inch frame would permit. "Your Honah, ladies and gentlemen of the jury. For all its impawtence, this is not a very complicated case. In fact, it's a simple issue of right versus wrong. Mah client, the eminent Christian churchman and scholah, the Reverend Dr. Melvin Morris Merton, has spent his lifetime doin' what is right. No one has studied the Bible more than he. No one has bettah found in it God's own, inspired prophecies of what will come to pass for both believahs and unbelievahs in the near future. A vast numbah of Christians have heeded those warnin' signs and prepared themselves, and all because of what Dr. Merton has done *right!*"

Pomeroy now turned from the jury and walked directly over to face Jon, who was sitting at the table for the defense with Stanwick and Kenneth Woodward. "But othahs," Pomeroy continued, "like Professor Jonathan P. Weber here, have done *wrong!* In total disdain of God's holy, inspired Word, he has not only ignored the prophecies our Lord has so generously included in Holy Scripture, but has also attacked and libeled and defamed the messengers of prophetic truth, like Dr. Merton, as 'prophecy fanatics.' He has called mah client a 'false prophet,' and thus impugned his entire ministry."

Noticing a rising murmur in the courtroom, Pomeroy paused for effect, then continued, "As if this weren't enough, a great national newsmagazine like *Newsweek* should have had more corporate sense than to publish Dr. Weber's slandah, but publish that slandah it did, and so has aided and abetted Professor Weber in such grievous wrong-doin'. This, ladies and gentlemen of the jury, has severely compromised Dr. Merton's reputation in the believing Christian world and led to losses in sales of his books, canceled public addresses, and acute mental distress for mah undeservin' client. I am sure that, in utter fairness, y'all will find our claims for compensatory and punitive damages not only justified, but modest in the extreme."

As Pomeroy sat down, a murmur of approval rose in the courtroom. Judge Parker banged his gavel in warning, then called for the defense to introduce its case. S. Fletcher Stanwick stood up, itself an act of intimidation, thought Jon, due to the man's imposing height.

After greeting judge and jury in the accepted manner, Stanwick smiled and began. "Right and wrong certainly *are* involved in this case, as in all others. The defense, however, respectfully submits that the wrong cited by the plaintiff's attorney is not *Newsweek*'s publication of Professor Weber's criticism of the theological position of a scholarly colleague, but that the Reverend Doctor Merton should ever have pursued this litigation in the first place.

"For reasons that he has spelled out in great detail in his book *Jesus of Nazareth,* my client finds many of the prophetic claims made by Dr. Merton and those who share his opinions to be extravagant and unjustified, both in their biblical context and according to all canons of theology and even common sense. He feels that untold numbers of people are being misled about how traditional Christianity regards the future, and so he felt compelled to speak out."

After further arguments, Stanwick walked over and faced the jury directly. "Ladies and gentlemen, the spirited exchange of differing viewpoints is the very lifeblood of true inquiry and scholarship. If this free exchange is in any way muzzled for fear of litigation, then hopeless constraints will be placed on human progress, and we will have surrendered our freedoms of speech and press to a perhaps dictated and legalistic conformity."

Jon was delighted to note a slight sprinkling of applause following Stanwick's opening statement, although again Judge Parker's gavel quickly terminated it.

In launching the principal phase of his case, Pomeroy seemed to take every negative syllable in Jon's opinion of recent prophecy from his book on Jesus, his reported public comments, and the *Newsweek* article, and then tried to demonstrate how much these had wounded Merton. He had been portrayed as a "clown," a "buffoon," and a "laughingstock," according to Pomeroy—words that were libelous if ever there were anything called libel. Jon winced at each term. He, his colleagues, and his wife had used them all in characterizing Merton . . . but only among themselves and never in public or in print, thank God!

Stanwick replied for the defense, cataloging Merton's failed prophecy claims, particularly the Easter event at the Mount of Olives in Jerusalem several years earlier, in which he had lured almost one hundred thousand people into believing that Jesus would triumphantly return in His Second Coming that very Easter.

"Does this, or does this not," Stanwick asked the jury, "demonstrate that the plaintiff is a false prophet? And yet my client was careful to state, '*In my opinion* he is a false prophet.' People are certainly entitled to their opinions! But I, for one, would hardly have been so reserved! I would have said, 'This *proves* the man is a false prophet!'"

Pomeroy leaped to his feet and bellowed, "Ah object, Your Honah! Counsel is venting a terrible personal bias against mah client, and I—"

"Objection sustained," interposed Judge Parker. "Counsel will avoid such comments in the future. You may continue."

Stanwick now cited prominent legal precedents in which juries had thrown out suits for damages in parallel media cases, and then he concluded with a brilliant peroration on the great issue of freedom of expression. A rumble of approval heartened the defense and, of course, offended the judge and his gavel.

The principal witnesses were then sworn in and placed on the stand.

For the plaintiff, leading members of the American prophecy fraternity testified on Merton's behalf while dropping acidulous comments about Jonathan Weber. In cross-examination, Stanwick was able to show how often Merton's witnesses disagreed among themselves regarding "the clear prophecies of the Bible." They were at variance as to when the Rapture would take place, the identity of the Antichrist, the nature of the Beast of Revelation . . . in short, on most of the prophecy claims.

As witnesses for the defense, Jon had conscripted a phalanx of biblical scholars who testified ardently on his behalf, some barely concealing their contempt for Merton and his claims. Adjectives like "unfounded," "arbitrary," "delusionary," "fallacious," and even "irresponsible" filled the courtroom. This consumed the rest of the day.

The next morning, Merton himself took the stand and was sworn in. The very image of injured innocence, he answered Pomeroy's questions with an obviously rehearsed precision. When his lawyer asked if he had truly suffered damage from the *Newsweek* article, Merton replied somberly, "Professor Weber has effectively ended my ministry."

"Why is that?" wondered Pomeroy.

"His vicious attacks have discredited me. Here, as a faithful Christian, I was only trying to alert the world that Jesus will be coming again soon, when I was maligned not by an atheist or agnostic or Communist, but by someone who claims to be a Christian himself!"

"Objection, Your Honor!" Stanwick called out. "Such comments impugn the defendant's Christian faith, which is certainly genuine, as his biography of Jesus clearly demonstrates."

"Objection sustained. The defendant's own religious beliefs are not on trial here. You may proceed."

Pomeroy continued. "Dr. Merton, do y'all really think your ministry is 'effectively ended,' or at least compromised?"

Merton thought for a moment, then replied, "Perhaps *ended* is too strong a term. But *more than compromised* would be an appropriate phrase, as our statistics show."

Pomeroy then produced several charts allegedly supporting this claim and handed them to the judge as Exhibit A. Parker directed that these be handed on to the defense and to the jury.

After several other questions and prompts, Pomeroy smiled at his client and said, "Thank you very much, Dr. Merton, for your very helpful testimony." Then he turned to Stanwick and said, "Y'all's witness."

In cross-examination Stanwick demonstrated that deposit records from Merton's *Points of Prophecy* television show revealed very little reduction in contributions. True, publishers' royalty statements on Merton's books showed a decline in sales for the past three months, but that was the case every summer. The statistics, therefore, proved little or nothing. Jon was almost sorry that the *Newsweek* article seemed to have had less effect on the reading public than he had hoped.

Merton gave measured responses in his cross-examination until Stanwick walked over to him and asked, his head just inches from the plaintiff's, "Dr. Merton . . . isn't this case a superb example of the shoe being on the other foot?"

"I don't understand."

"Think back to Easter in Jerusalem several years ago, when you addressed a mass meeting of your followers on the slopes of the Mount of Olives. Did you or did you not publicly call Dr. Weber 'the Antichrist' on that occasion?"

"No, I certainly did not!"

"Correct, Dr. Merton. But a week earlier, during a Palm Sunday procession into Jerusalem, did you or did you not call Dr. Weber 'the Antichrist' on *that* occasion?"

Merton coughed, shifted in the witness chair, and said, "Well, ah, yes, I suppose I did. But that was only for . . . for rhetorical effect. It had no significance whatever."

"Didn't your statement so inflame your followers in that parade that they rioted, grabbed Professor Weber and his friend, Miss Shannon Jennings, hoisted them up in their arms, and started carrying them into Jerusalem at the head of their procession?"

Commotion filled the courtroom. Again Judge Parker banged his gavel.

"Ye-es," Merton admitted. "But I ordered my people to stop, and Dr. Weber and Miss Jennings were soon released."

"Only because the Israeli police arrived and saved them from possible lynching, Dr. Merton. Isn't that true?"

"I . . . don't believe it would have gone that far."

Stanwick placed an aging copy of the *Jerusalem Post* in front of Merton. On the front page was a report of the riot, with a photograph of Jon and Shannon being carried at the head of the crowd, a look of stark terror on Shannon's face. He then submitted the newspaper to the judge as Exhibit B, requesting that copies be given both to the plaintiff and the jury. One of the headers in the story ran "Archaeologist Called Antichrist," which only compounded Merton's embarrassment.

Stanwick excused Merton and called Jonathan Weber to the stand.

His first question, after Jon was sworn in, picked up on the Jerusalem incident. "Professor Weber, do you recall exactly what Dr. Merton said in Jerusalem on Palm Sunday when he called you the Antichrist?"

"Yes. One tends to remember hazardous events."

"What were his words?"

"Dr. Merton pointed in my direction and shouted, '*He* is the Antichrist named Weber.' Then he pointed to Shannon Jennings and added, 'And *she* is the daughter of the other devil named Jennings!'"

Rumblings of surprise and shock surfaced in the courtroom.

"Did you then bring suit for libel against Dr. Merton?" asked Stanwick.

"No, I did not."

"Did you ever contemplate doing so?"

"No, certainly not."

"Why not?"

"That episode in Jerusalem was driven by high emotion. I don't think it happened with malice aforethought . . . or on the basis of reason."

Stanwick frowned, wishing that Jon had provided an answer less congenial to the plaintiff. Jon sensed as much, so he added, "Theological opinions differ dramatically. Martin Luther used to speak of the *rabies theologorum*—the madness of theologians. Passionately argued differences over the Bible and its interpretations come with the territory, whether in the sixteenth century or the twenty-first. Suing for libel and defamation just isn't in the picture when you do theology."

Stanwick smiled and turned Jon over to Pomeroy for cross-examination.

"First," said Pomeroy, "Ah should like to remind the court that the Israeli justice system was open to Professor Weber if he felt that mah client's statements in Jerusalem constituted libel. Clearly he did not, since he did not bring suit. Therefore, Ah would ask the jury not even to consider this evidence and move that it be stricken from the record."

"Objection, Your Honor," Stanwick interposed. "The evidence is indeed very relevant to this case."

"Sustained. Please continue."

Ambling over to Jon, Pomeroy bent down and asked, "Among those who champion biblical prophecy, Professor Weber, who is the theologian you least respect?"

"Your Honor, I object," said Stanwick, jumping to his feet. "The prosecution is on a fishing expedition, and this question has no value for this case."

Judge Parker frowned, thought for a moment, then replied, "Objection overruled. Knowing the mind of the defendant may indeed be important to this case. Please continue."

Again Pomeroy pressed his question. Stanwick was about to advise Jon, but he replied, "Among the prophecy advocates, only Dr. Merton has attacked me publicly, so it might be thought that he is my 'least respected' candidate. But I'm alarmed that not only Dr. Merton but all those cited in the magazine article in question have warped biblical views of the future in serious detriment to the Christian faith. Besides their publications, many of them have radio

and television programs as well as video and motion-picture production facilities. Consequently many, if not most, non-Christians
assume that their bizarre interpretations of biblical prophecy are the
norm for our faith, and they are not!"

And so it went on for several more days of a sweltering September
trial deep inside the concrete canyons of New York City. The defense
presented a parallel precedent in the case of *Sharon* v. *Time, Inc.*, the
litigation Jon had suggested as ammunition for their side.

An entire day was spent on the question of whether or not
Merton was a public enough figure to prevent his suing for libel.
Pomeroy seemed to backtrack on his opening claims of mass support for Merton's ministry. Now he recast Merton as a solitary seer
"strugglin' to be heard in a cacophony of cynicism from Ivy League
scholahs."

Stanwick quickly shot back, "Anyone who can attract one hundred thousand followers to a mass meeting in Jerusalem is certainly
quite famous, quite public!"

Finally came the day for summations. Harrison Pomeroy pulled
out all his rhetorical stops, portraying Merton as a courageous
"voice cryin' in the wilderness," a modern-day John the Baptist
heralding the imminent return of Jesus Christ. "And just as Noah
of old was spurned by his contemporaries when he warned of the
approachin' flood"—here Pomeroy flashed a look of incandescent
disdain at Jon—"so Melvin Morris Merton is spurned by those who
teach in our citadels of unbelief and godless universities today. But
the deluge came all the same! Even so Jesus Christ will return, and
soon!" After further discourse that castigated the media for
"besmirching the reputations of innocent individuals," Pomeroy
shook his head sadly and sat down, wiping his brow.

Stanwick stood up, walked over to the jury box, and defended
Jon's opinions and the ethics of the editorial and legal staff at
Newsweek. He asked the jury not to "bury our sacred doctrines of
the freedom of speech and the freedom of the press."

Judge Parker gave his traditional instructions to the jury, adding,
"Because of the wide interest in this case, and to avoid any possible
intrusion into your privacy, I shall now order that you be
sequestered until a decision is reached. If you have any questions

regarding this case in the course of your deliberations, please write them down and hand them to the bailiff, who will deliver them to my office."

As the jury filed out of the courtroom, Jon and Kenneth Woodward joined in thanking Stanwick and his staff for their conduct of the defense. "It looks rather good for our side," said Stanwick softly. "No promises, of course, but I look for a quick decision."

Since it was midafternoon, they went out for some refreshment and then returned in case there was an early verdict. At six o'clock, however, they left again for a bite to eat, returning to the court at seven-thirty.

Two hours later, there was still no decision. The jury foreman, in fact, asked for clarification on several points in the instructions from the judge, who sent his replies through the bailiff.

The night wore on. At eleven o'clock both the plaintiff and the defense called it a day and returned to their respective hotels. Jon had difficulty falling asleep. A quick decision by the jury should have gone in their favor, but this was no quick decision. Inevitably, his thoughts turned to the worst-case scenario. If found liable for damages, they would certainly appeal, and perhaps appeal as often as necessary. But that prospect demanded far more time, effort, and expense than he cared to think about.

And what if, in the worst of all cases, they were found liable on all appeals? He had not even discussed with *Newsweek* what his share of the damages would be. Probably in the low millions, he thought, in which case he should probably buy a book or two on bankruptcy law.

The next morning, both parties in the case returned to court along with a throng of media reporters and again awaited the jury's verdict. Hours passed, but still there was no verdict. Lunchtime came and went: no decision. The afternoon wore on. Jon and the defense speculated over what the jury could possibly be discussing.

At 4:15 P.M. the clerk of the court summoned both sides to return to the courtroom. Again there was the drama of Judge Parker calling the court into session and warning the media crowd to make less noise. "Ladies and gentlemen of the jury," the judge intoned, "have you reached a verdict?"

"We have, Your Honor," said the foreman, a slender, balding high school coach from the Bronx.

"The clerk will deliver the written decision to the bench," said Parker. This done, the judge unfolded the piece of paper, nodded, and asked the foreman to announce the jury's decision.

"We, the members of the jury, find the defendants . . . *not* liable for alleged defamation in this case, and find no basis for an award of monetary damages against them," said the foreman, with some emphasis and a slight smile.

"So say you?" asked Parker. "So say you all?"

Members of the jury nodded.

"Do you wish members of the jury polled?" Parker asked the plaintiff.

Pomeroy stood up to reply in the affirmative, but Merton shook his head and restrained him. Just as in the movies, reporters and media stringers jumped up and fled the courtroom as if it were ablaze.

Waves of elation splashed over the defense. Jon embraced Stanwick, Woodward, and his legal staff. Or did they embrace him? No matter. At the plaintiff's table, however, Pomeroy was trying to console Merton, who sat in woebegone silence. Finally he groaned, "I think we should appeal."

Pomeroy patted the broad shoulders of his client and said, "Yes, Ah suppose we could appeal, Dr. Merton, since the defense can't claim double jeopardy, as they could in a criminal trial. But Ah do believe it would be a waste of time and money."

"Why's that?"

"Well, our case was tried before a jury, and a court of appeals rarely reverses a jury decision in civil cases. Ah'm . . . very sorry, good doctor. Ah certainly tried."

It was only later that Jon learned why the jury had taken so long. Very early in their deliberations, all but one juror had voted for acquittal. The exception was a slender, aging blonde from Queens who operated a beauty shop and faithfully contributed to several television prophecy programs—a fact that she had carefully concealed during jury selection. The other members of the jury had spent hours trying to convince her, but she would not give in.

Finally, when they threatened to expose her deceit and recited the penalties that would follow, she quickly changed her mind.

The nation's legal system, for all its problems, had succeeded. Freedom of speech and freedom of the press were alive and well in the United States of America. No one was more grateful than Jonathan P. Weber.

THREE

For the next two weeks in October, Jon fielded a happy flurry of congratulatory messages arriving from far and wide. His father called from Hannibal with the cheery advice, "Glad I didn't have to bail you out of debtors' prison, Son! But try not to get sued again, okay?" Merton's followers sent the expected bundle of nasty messages—he had organized a letter-writing campaign against Jon—and these focused on the predictable theme: "Just you wait, scoffer— God will prove Dr. Merton right!" Yet most of the responses expressed gratitude that Jon had done his part to safeguard the freedoms of speech and press.

But suddenly the climate changed; it seemed that Melvin Morris Merton might have the last laugh after all.

An extraordinary cyber event hit all computers that happened to be on-line at the time. It was not the effect of a virus cooked up by some deranged hacker, aiming to destroy the data on computer hard disks like the notorious "Love Bug" that caused billions of dollars in damage in the year 2000. Nor was it an insidious worm that tunneled into servers and computers like "Code Red" the following year, infecting others on the mailing list of each computer and morphing into even more deadly versions that replicated themselves.

This phenomenon was entirely different in two ways. First, whereas in previous cyber incursions only some fraction of the world's computers were infected, this time, incredibly, *all* computers on-line at the time were hit. And second, this cyberevent seemed to be entirely benign. All it did was to overlay an extraordinary bulletin on computer screens—much like the always intrusive pop-up messages—no matter what program was running at the time. Majestic trumpet flourishes heralded a rich background of shimmering magenta that filled the screen, over which the following message scrolled slowly in gleaming silver lettering:

"JESUS OF NAZARETH IS RETURNING!
PREPARE FOR HIS ARRIVAL!"

After two minutes of scrolling in a continuous loop, the message disappeared, and all the world's affected computers returned to the programs they were running before the incursion.

Jon himself was on-line at the time and saw the announcement, but he assumed it was only a local phenomenon. After it had vanished from his screen, he e-mailed Shannon what he had seen. To his astonishment, she replied that she had seen the same thing at the same time, though with this difference: in Israel, a Hebrew version had preceded an English translation.

Jon passed it off as a shrewd hacker's outlandish practical joke, or perhaps a sophisticated production by prophecy-loving computer nerds, maybe working for Merton and providing him a face-saving gesture to help restore his reputation. Whatever. The world was full of cyberanomalies; it was nothing to be concerned about.

Watching television that evening at his home in suburban Weston, however, Jon found NBC *Nightly News* opening with a story on "The Phantom Prophecy." Tom Brokaw reported that the baffling bulletin had hit computers not just in the United States and Israel—obvious targets for American-style prophecy zealots—but computers throughout the world. Even more astounding, the bulletin appeared in French in France, German in Germany, Russian in Russia, and so on, using the vernacular for the twenty most spoken languages across the globe. As if optimally timed to reach a maximum audience, it appeared during the waking hours in the Israel-to-Hawaii hemisphere and twelve hours later in the other half of the globe.

Brokaw interviewed American Internet authorities, but they were at a loss to explain how the global phenomenon could have happened. They planned, however, to investigate immediately and trace down the source, along with their colleagues overseas.

Jon's phone started ringing incessantly. Media religion editors and the wire services wanted to know his take on the "Jesus Bulletin," as it came to be known. CBS pleaded with him for on-camera comment via its Boston affiliate, but to all such inquiries

Jon simply replied, "I know nothing more about this than you do—in fact, probably less. It's really a high-tech problem for the web people. They're the ones you should be interviewing."

"But could the message be genuine?" someone asked.

Jon paused, smiled, and replied, "I really can't tell you how much I doubt that!"

Exactly twenty-four hours later, the same cyberphenomenon appeared again. This time the Jesus Bulletin had a background of fluorescent royal purple, with golden lettering even more dazzling than before. A whole chorus of trumpets continued the previous musical theme with a glorious augmentation. Those on-line at the time sat spellbound in front of their computer screens.

Cyber sleuths in both hemispheres were appalled that no one had thought to engage special equipment to track another such message, were it to occur. After the next twenty-four hours of frenzied preparation, however, they were ready in case of a third.

It never appeared. The two, however, seemed enough to rekindle mass speculation about the end times in all computer-literate nations. Although only words were scrolling by on the monitors of the world, prophecy mavens took them very seriously indeed, and, Jon noted with chagrin, Melvin Morris Merton never managed to turn down a television interview.

"I do believe that the Lord Himself is vindicating me!" Merton told ABC on *Good Morning America*. "All those Ivy League agnostics will rue the day they made sport of genuine Bible prophecy!" He paused. "'*Maranatha*—come, Lord Jesus' was the cry of the ancient church, and today's as well." He spread his arms wide, assumed a cherubic smile, and looked heavenward, crying, "Come, Lord Jesus! Come quickly! Amen!"

Jon turned off his TV, hoping no media frenzy would develop and the quirky phenomenon would soon be exposed, explained, and die a quick electronic death. But when he arrived at his office the next morning, Marylou Kaiser, his dedicated secretary, told him, "We now have twenty-three interview requests from the media, Dr. Weber. As usual, I promised only to relay their messages."

"Well, it's time for Rod Swenson," Jon told her, as he punched in Swenson's phone number at MIT.

If Rodney C. Swenson had not exactly invented the Internet, he came rather close. Colleagues at the Massachusetts Institute of Technology, just downriver from Harvard, had given him the moniker "Web Daddy," and he was centrally involved in building the powerful new Internet superhighway for use by the academic and scientific community. Hackers the world over hated him, since he was one of the preeminent cybersleuths who had ferreted out some of the cleverest in that arcane and repulsive fraternity. In their cryptic communications, they referred to Swenson as Hacker^2, meaning "the hackers' hacker."

"Rod? Jon Weber over at Harvard."

Swenson laughed. "Somehow I thought you might be calling, Jon."

"Okay, once again I see you're in sync with the situation! So what's your take on the Jesus Bulletin thing? How did they ever bring it off?"

Swenson was silent for some moments. Then he replied quite solemnly, "I don't think 'they' were involved at all. I think we're talking the real thing here, Jon—a totally miraculous communication from the divine dimension. After all, Jesus and His angels can do anything . . . and we mortals certainly can't explain it scientifically."

Now it was Jon's turn to be silent.

"Jon?" asked Swenson after some moments. "Are you still there?"

Finally Jon muttered, "Get serious, Rod."

Swenson belted out several guffaws and said, "Who said that Swedes don't have a sense of humor? Okay, Jon, we've all been working on it over the last twenty-four hours. I mean everybody: the FBI; the NIPC; the System Administration, SANS Institute; the CERT Coordination Center at Carnegie Mellon, not to mention Microsoft and the antivirus people, as well as my whole staff here at MIT."

"An impressive alphabet soup! What do you have so far?"

"Nothing."

"Nothing?"

"Not a blooming thing."

"Why nothing? I mean, why weren't all these web people ready for another message the second time around?"

"Well, it didn't do any damage here or anywhere else, so there was no sense of urgency. It seems like . . . a quirky production cleverly cobbled together by some holy hacker—which is still my best guess as to how it happened."

"Mine too."

"But we'll find him—or them—for sure. In fact, we now *have* to find out how it happened."

"Why's that?"

"Well . . . several reasons. For openers, we have to know how it hit all computers on-line. That's never been done before—not even close. Think how someone, especially an enemy, could use this as a perfect tool for cyberterrorism! Or, for that matter, what if the creator or creators of the Jesus Bulletin plan to send others that may not be so harmless, this being just a trial run? Or, worst-case scenario, what if the two bulletins—harmless as they seem—may already have infected the world's computers with a virus or worm that comes to life some time in the future and does horrible damage?"

Jon whistled softly. "Wow! This gets more serious by the minute, Rod—which means I shouldn't take up any more of your time. The sooner you and your cybergeniuses get to the bottom of it, the better."

"Amen to that!"

"Do stay in touch, won't you? Especially when you have something solid?"

"Of course."

"I'm leaving for Israel day after tomorrow, but Marylou Kaiser, my secretary, will know where I am on most days. You have my e-mail address, of course?"

"Right."

"Thanks, Rod. Good hunting!"

Jonathan Weber left for Israel a month later than planned, but several extra sessions had been added to his class schedule to make up for the time missed. For the remainder of this semester and the next, he would finally assume his visiting professorship at Hebrew University in Jerusalem, where the administration had been more than understanding about his necessarily tardy arrival. He would see his beloved Shannon again shortly.

Before boarding his jet at Logan Airport, he picked up a copy of *USA Today* and read it en route to JFK, where he would switch to El Al for the nonstop flight to Tel Aviv. The front page updated the Jesus Bulletin story, comparing it to other historic web incursions, but with no further information on how it could have happened. When Jon got to page two, he groaned so audibly that adjacent passengers looked to see if he were in distress. One of the headers ran "MERTON: JESUS BULLETIN AUTHENTIC." Under a photograph of the prophecy evangelist, his right index finger pointing toward heaven, the story listed Merton's reasons for believing that this was a genuine notice of Christ's return.

The signs told it all, according to Merton: another earthquake in Chile, renewed fighting in the Balkans, fresh threats from Al Qaeda, a blazing meteorite over India, the existence of the Trilateral Commission, and wider acceptance of the Eurodollar—all were markers pointing to the end. The only scrap of logic Jon found in Merton's remarks came at the close: "And why couldn't some modern-day John the Baptist alert us to Jesus' Second Coming through the use of the most sophisticated communication medium yet developed?"

At JFK, Jon boarded an El Al 747 for the transatlantic flight. He felt confident that this was an airline with the best security. Long before the terrorist attacks in New York and Washington, El Al had done the obvious in preventing any hijacking of its jets: it had mightily reinforced the cockpit doors on its entire fleet. Had other airlines done that, the tragedies of that fateful September 11 might not have happened.

As Jon drowsed off during the evening transatlantic flight, his last thought was, *At last I can leave Merton behind on the other side of the Atlantic. Amazing space . . . how sweet the sound . . .*

Jon easily picked out Shannon among the welcoming crowds at Ben-Gurion Airport the next morning. There she was, he thought, with those sparkling sapphire eyes designed by God and lustrous brown locks arranged by the angels, her innocent loveliness always setting a whole new standard for beauty. Rushing over to her, Jon almost felt a stab of regret: if only a given sum of charm existed in the universe, how many women had been denied because Shannon was so radiant?

She wrapped her arms around him and squeezed him tightly. "Can't tell you how much I've missed you, Jonathan," she whispered.

"And I you, little darling." They stood locked in that pose for several moments, exchanging a long, fervent kiss. Then he added, "Thanks for not bending one of your legs upward during our kiss, the way they always do it in the movies for some reason."

She gave him a little jab and laughed. "You flew across the Atlantic to drop such a . . . profound comment as that?"

"Yes, and lots more. Let's go get my luggage."

Jabbering on the way to Jerusalem, they covered their months of separation in short order. Although Jon hoped she wouldn't bring it up, Shannon asked about the Jesus Bulletin before they were halfway to the Holy City. "It's caused a big flurry of excitement over here," she said. "Not among Orthodox Jews, of course, who dismiss it. But the Messianic Jews and the evangelical community are all agog. Even the Roman Catholics and the Greek Orthodox are showing interest, especially because of Joshua Ben-Yosef."

"Because of who?"

"Joshua Ben-Yosef. Haven't you heard about him back in the States?"

"No. Not at all."

"He's becoming something of a media celebrity over here. It reminds me of the way young Billy Graham got started: in 1949, hardly anyone had ever heard of him; in 1950, everyone had."

"How would you know?" Jon laughed. "You weren't even a gleam in your daddy's eye."

"How indeed! I read, you know. They're called books."

"Okay, okay. Tell me about this character."

"Well, he's Jewish, obviously, probably in his early thirties. Comes from somewhere in the north country. A very nice-looking fellow with lots of charisma and charm. Extremely bright too."

"So?"

"He's an incredible speaker, and he has a big following."

"Your description fits lots of people over here, including your old flame, Gideon Ben-Yaakov. Speaking of whom, have you made any visits to the Israel Antiquities Authority?"

"Suspicious man!" She poked him in the ribs. "Gideon's happily married, obviously, and besides—"

"Okay, I'll stop! So what makes this Joshua so different from the rest?"

"I don't know, but you've really got to hear the man speak. Whether he's giving a public address or just teaching some students, can he ever *communicate!* I've heard him just once, and he was speaking in Hebrew, so I could only gauge his impact by looking at his crowd of hearers."

"And he made that big an impression on you? Is this guy married?"

"Ah . . . no, I don't think so."

"Should I—maybe—be jealous, then?"

Shannon laughed, tried to tickle him, and said, "You can be a real dork at times, Jon!"

Jon's academic hosts had rented a spacious apartment for them atop French Hill in Jerusalem, very near the Mount Scopus campus of Hebrew University. Shannon had moved in weeks earlier and could hardly wait to show Jon their new digs. He was impressed with the apartment, but when she took him out on their veranda, he fairly raved at the view. Directly ahead of them was the Mount of Olives, festooned in greenery, with the Brook Kidron at its base, sites saturated with both sacred and secular history. Adjacent to the Kidron Valley, the Old City of Jerusalem rose triumphantly to the west, surrounded by the massive, sixteenth-century walls of Suleiman the Magnificent. Crowning it all was the golden Dome of the Rock where the great temple once stood, not to mention the dozens of other domes, spires, steeples, minarets, towers, and ramparts that identified this as the religious capital of the world, home to the three great monotheistic religions. Although Jon and Shannon had seen Jerusalem dozens of times, their first view of the Holy City after an extended absence never failed to induce a tingle of delight.

Shannon herself had the same effect on Jon. "Let's go back inside," he said. "You haven't shown me your bedroom yet."

She gave that light, airy laugh that had always held him captive. Then she grasped his hand, led him down the hallway, and opened a door. "It's not *my* bedroom, darling," she whispered. "It's *ours.*"

Jon circled her softly with his arms, and they shared another lingering kiss. There were kisses and then there were kisses, thought

Jon, in his growing passion: this one, after so many weeks' absence, totally suffused him. Very carefully, he unbuttoned her blouse and slipped her arms out of it. Then with gentle urgency, he tugged off her skirt. They tumbled onto the bed in a nimbus of exhilaration, and the culmination that followed was one of frenzied abandon. Afterward, they lay together for a long time in each other's arms, not saying a word. Finally Shannon looked over and saw tears in Jon's eyes. "What's wrong, my darling?" she asked.

"This was like our wedding night all over again, but somehow even more intense. I think I'm shedding tears for all those who will never experience such bliss."

She gave him a kiss, laughed lightly, and said, "Our wedding! I'll never . . . ever forget that wonderful day in Hannibal. What was it, 75 degrees—not a cloud in the sky? Remember how your father was beaming as I came down the aisle at St. John's . . . and how you stood there with your arms hanging down, grinning like a boy who'd just raided the cookie jar?"

Jon laughed. "Dear old Dad. His wedding address was . . . was like the mercy of God: it seemed to endure forever."

"Do you remember it?"

"Hardly a word."

Jon laughed, hoping she would not zero in on the worst gaffe he had ever made in his life. But in vain was that hope, especially when he heard her chuckling softly.

"But oh . . . how you ever *blew* your lines, Jon!"

"Please don't, Shannon . . ."

"When we came to the place in the Lutheran ceremony where we recite our vows, your dad says, *'Please repeat after me: I, Jonathan, in the presence of God and this assembly . . .'* But eager-beaver you say, *'I, God, in the presence of . . .'*"

"I simply wanted to die on the spot."

"Well I, for one, was waiting for blue lightning to strike you down for blasphemy! And then your dad says, 'Son, let's try that again.'"

"Yes, while the rest of the congregation was in stitches!"

"I've always thought 'Freudian slip' would be the best explanation for that: the great Jonathan P. Weber, professor, best-selling author, savior of the Savior's Christianity, finally flashing His divine credentials!"

"You take no prisoners, do you Shannon?"

She laughed and said, "Wasn't our reception something else? I don't think the Hannibal Country Club ever saw anything like it—my uncle and aunt flew over from England, your Harvard colleagues coming from Cambridge. . . . I can't believe that Gideon and Naomi actually flew over from Israel!"

"Glorious weather, great music, dancing under the stars, and, of course, the *Delta Queen*."

"Just *perfect* for our honeymoon! How you ever got that fabulous Mississippi paddle-wheel to dock at Hannibal I'll never know—"

"With God, nothing is impossible!"

"*Monster,*" she cried, giving him a playful kick.

"Remember our Honeymoon Suite on board, just back of the wheelhouse on top deck?"

"How could I *ever* forget that!" she tittered softly.

Jon shared her chuckling and said, expansively, "So here we have this magnificent couple, *finally* giving ultimate expression to their great love for one another. But can they then fall asleep in each other's arms? Not a chance! The blasted boat's *steam whistle* blew directly over their heads, shattering our couple's serenity, and —"

"Oh, don't be such a fuddy-duddy," she interposed. "the *Delta Queen* was merely saluting our joy!"

"Hmmm," he murmured. "I like your take on that better than mine. I just can't tell you how much I love you, Shannon."

FOUR

While Shannon worked to finish her supplement to the Rama report, Jon plunged into his duties at Hebrew University. The prime responsibilities of his Ezra Bernstein Distinguished Visiting Professorship were to offer a graduate seminar and conduct whatever research he felt appropriate to his discipline—just the sort of open-ended ticket professors dream of.

Jon's academic sponsor was Professor Mordecai Feldman, the university's Jewish specialist in Christian studies. The two had been close academic friends for years, and both had studied under David Flusser, the preeminent patriarch in Jewish-Christian studies, now deceased. Whenever Jon wanted an informed Jewish opinion on items in his research, Feldman was always his first contact.

Not one to shy away from controversy, Jon had set "Jews and Jesus" as the theme for his graduate seminar. But it was so quickly overenrolled that it had to be converted into a general academic symposium for all interested students and faculty, who now convened in a new theater-style lecture hall with three hundred seats. Jon lectured in English, which was no hindrance to anyone in Israeli higher education, including the many international students at the university.

The broadest ranges of religious backgrounds and beliefs regarding Jesus would be welcome. "In fact," said Jon in his opening lecture, "I'll dismiss only one opinion as unworthy of our discussion or our time: namely, that a man named Jesus of Nazareth never lived. Only a handful of craz—I mean, pseudoscholars hold that position, and you can count them on the fingers of one hand.

"Now, having said that, it would be helpful to learn where we all come from in our opinions on this extraordinary Jew. We have the nonreligious and religious of all stripes in this symposium: Jews and Christians, as well as Muslims and representatives of other beliefs and nonbeliefs. Let's first do that familiar word-association test: I'll throw out a word, and you report the very first thing that comes to mind. It may seem trite, but it works."

Jon looked out at his audience. "The word is *Jesus*. Quick now, what are you thinking? Anyone."

For some moments, not a single hand was raised.

"The first response always takes the longest," said Jon.

Several more seconds intervened. Had he misjudged his audience? Jon wondered. Then a hand shot up from a rangy, carrot-topped, American-looking student who seemed to have just stepped off the prairie. He stood up and announced in a bold tenor voice: "Jesus? He was—and is—the Christ, the Messiah. He's the Son of God and Savior of the world. In this very city His own countrymen brought Him up for trial before Pontius Pilate. Then He was crucified, died, and rose again."

A loud drone of discussion erupted, and a dozen hands shot up. Jon recognized one of them, a tanned Jewish student wearing a yarmulke, who stood up and said, "Jews didn't prosecute Jesus—the Romans did! In fact, as Justice Haim Cohn wrote in his book *The Trial and Death of Jesus*, the Jewish high priest, Joseph Caiaphas, was very likely Jesus' dear friend, who was trying to keep Him out of trouble with the Romans!"

This time, the buzz of reaction was even louder. Jon held up his hands, restored order, and commented, "Fine. There we have two very contrasting versions on how Jesus was brought to trial. Jews were directly responsible—or Jews were not involved at all. Let's hear more opinions."

A cascade of other views on Jesus made this one of the liveliest symposia at Hebrew University that academic year. Toward the close of the session, Jon said, "What we'll try to do in this series is to check out all the evidence—sacred and secular—regarding Jesus and Judaism in the first century. We'll use both biblical and nonbiblical sources. We'll weigh everything from the rabbinical traditions to the latest archaeological finds and historical interpretations. We'll search for the truth wherever it leads us. See you on Wednesday."

In the next days and weeks, Jon's symposium would plow

through all the evidence on Jesus from the Nativity to what did or did not happen when He stood before Pontius Pilate on the other side of Jerusalem two-thousand years earlier. One morning, a brilliant Jewish student from the Negev pointed out that Jews had always had their so-called miracle workers. "Besides Jesus," he said, "there was also Hanina Ben Dosa and Honi the Circle-Drawer." He paused, brightened, and added, "For that matter, how about today and our Joshua Ben-Yosef?"

A flash of commotion suddenly filled the auditorium, as all eyes fastened on the professor for his response.

Jon was on the spot. All he knew about Ben-Yosef was what Shannon had told him the day he arrived in Israel. But he was quite literally saved by the bell: the hour was over, and he dismissed the class with, "We'll take this up next time."

Clearly, he himself would have to take it up with Mordecai Feldman, his academic host. The next day they had lunch together in the university's faculty club. After some delicious matzo ball soup, Jon asked, "Mort—what's the current fuss over this Joshua Ben-Yosef fellow? His name's surfaced several times in my symposium."

"Ah, yes—Ben-Yosef," said Feldman, a pleasantly chubby professorial sort with twinkling green eyes that matched his natty blazer. "A very interesting fellow—in fact, so interesting that we've asked him to speak at the university here . . . though he has yet to accept. Heard him once—a real spellbinder, with a message even Hillel would have appreciated. Extraordinary insights. Brilliant ethics. Words poured out of him off-the-cuff as if he'd worked on each of them overnight."

"*Bons mots,* eh?"

"Yes, all of them *bons mots.*"

"But what did he talk about? What's his specialty?"

"Spiritual issues, and how they impinge on politics, society, and culture today. And in the questions afterward, he met every challenge gracefully, supplying answers that fairly rippled with wisdom."

"But surely you have a lot of people doing that. What's so special about Ben-Yosef?"

Feldman took a long sip of iced tea, then replied, "It's rather hard to explain. He speaks—and people listen, listen as they've never listened before. What a way that man has with words!"

"One of my students mentioned him in the same miracle-worker category as Hanina Ben Dosa, Honi the Circle-Drawer, and even Jesus. Is this guy also a . . . a faith healer of some kind?"

Jon expected Feldman to shake his head, laugh, and say no. But he merely scratched the side of his gray thatch and said, "Well, you may find this hard to believe, Jon, but there *have* been reports of people he's healed. Or helped—whatever. Personally, I've not seen any, but as I said, there are reports."

Jon's perplexity was interrupted when Feldman suddenly smiled and said, "By the way, I should have told you this earlier. Jim Strange up at Sepphoris has been on the phone to me every other week, asking when you planned to arrive in Jerusalem. He seems to have discovered something very interesting up there."

Instantly, Jon's mental antenna shot up. For years, he had been scanning any archaeological reports involving Sepphoris, knowing well enough that if ever a site might yield more information about the hidden years of Jesus' youth, it would be Sepphoris.

"What did he find?"

"A very curious mosaic at an outer corner near the floor of the synagogue. And there are words inside it."

"In what language?"

"Seems to be Aramaic, or even Hebrew."

"What does it say?"

"That, my friend, is why Strange was asking about you."

"Is Strange still up there? I thought he'd be gone back to South Florida at the close of the dig season."

"No, he's taking his sabbatical here in Israel, and still spends much of his time at Sepphoris."

Jon thought for a moment, then asked, "When's your next trip up to Galilee, Mort?"

"Leah and I are planning to drive up there weekend after next."

"Oh-ho—coincidence! So are Shannon and I. Any chance we could meet?"

"Why not? Where would you like?" Feldman had a twinkle in his eye.

"I think you already know." Jon was smiling.

"Fine. Friday after next? I'll get in touch with Strange. Why don't we all have lunch at the Grand New Hotel in Nazareth—which, of course, is neither grand nor new."

"Love it. Done!"

The drive up to Galilee was a delightful reminder to Jon and Shannon of a similar excursion they had taken several years earlier, a trip that had so surprisingly found them in each other's arms for the first time. For this reason they had declined, with thanks, the Feldmans' invitation to join them on the drive north. Romantic memories had to be visited in private.

For security reasons Jon and Shannon took the Jordan Valley perimeter route northward to Galilee, rather than up and down the hills of Samaria. The latest version of an Arab-Israeli truce had only partially taken hold. As they neared Tiberias, they dropped phrases like "Remember when we . . ." and "Here is where we . . ." like some sort of antiphonal chorus. Skirting the southwestern shoreline of the Sea of Galilee and then heading westward to Nazareth, they arrived at the Grand New Hotel in time to join the Feldmans and Strange for lunch.

The professors greeted each other with predictable enthusiasm, while on the other end of the table, Shannon and Leah Feldman chatted amiably in getting to know one another.

"So how did you discover this mosaic?" Jon asked Strange, firing the first in his salvo of questions.

"Credit where credit's due. I didn't discover it: it was one of my student volunteers, a very bright girl named Jenny Snow, who turned out to be a real gift to our dig. I think she had some kind of radar—or maybe an archaeological angel on her shoulders telling her where to dig, because she also found some beautiful pottery pieces, coins, and such." Strange described how Jenny and he had found the mosaic while the others at the table sat spellbound.

After the salad course Jon extracted a piece of paper from his pocket, thrust a pen into Strange's hand, and asked, "How about a simple sketch of the find area, Jim?"

"You'll see it in an hour or so."

"I know, I know, but I just can't wait that long."

"Okay, an artist I am not, but it looks something like this." A few swift strokes of the pen produced this sketch:

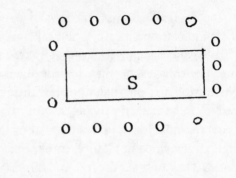

X

"The circles are the synagogue's column bases, of course," Strange explained, "with a drum or two stacked on top of each. Not all the columns are there: I just wanted the sketch to look pretty! Anyway, X is where the mosaic was found."

"What does the inscription itself look like?"

"You'll have to see for yourself, my friend."

"Any of this published as yet?"

Strange shook his head. "I wouldn't think of publishing until I know exactly what the inscription says. Mort, here, has studied several of my photos, and we both have some hazy ideas. But we figure if anyone could tease out the actual message, it would be you."

"Uh-oh. A command performance! What happens if I fail?"

"Then your world reputation as a Semitics linguist will be shattered forever!" replied Feldman with a wink.

"Shannon," Jon remarked with a grin, "I think we should head back to Jerusalem."

The five hurriedly finished their lunch. No one thought of lingering for dessert.

The Feldmans left their car in the hotel parking lot and joined Jon and Shannon in their Peugeot. An eight-minute drive following Jim Strange's Land Rover across the Beit Netola Valley brought them to an abrupt rise named, by the Israeli Park Service, Zippori. "That's how they spell Sepphoris today," Jon told Shannon.

"I know that," she replied.

Jim Strange unlocked the gate and waved them through. He first gave his guests a guided tour of the principal discovery sites, then took them to the excavated synagogue and its remarkably preserved, tessellated floor.

"Isn't that mosaic menorah spectacular?" said Shannon. "It should have been on the wall of the synagogue, not the floor."

"Then we'd probably not have it at all." Strange chuckled. "The walls are gone, but the floor remains. Note that we have mostly geometric designs here and just a few nature motifs. That's all because of the warning against engraved images in the Second Commandment, of course."

"Where do you peg the synagogue time-wise, Jim?" asked Jon.

"We think that it's early first century C.E., most likely part of Herod Antipas's reconstruction of Sepphoris. His dad rebuilt the great temple in Jerusalem; Junior did the job on the synagogue here."

Nice first-century New Testament horizon, thought Jon. *Jesus could have attended here as a lad.*

While Shannon stooped down to examine the floor of the synagogue in closer detail, Jon paced its southwestern perimeter, looking for the mosaic. Trying hard to stifle his mounting impatience, he decided to feign composure instead, knowing full well that Strange would identify the object of their quest in his own good time.

At last Strange announced with a playful grin, "But I suppose you may want to see the new mosaic. We've left it *in situ,* of course." He paused, then continued with mock pomposity, "I awaited the arrival of Jonathan P. Weber and his linguistic, historical, and archaeological skills, of course."

In the same lofty tone, Jon responded, "In which case you may well have waited in vain, my friend."

Strange walked over to where Jon had been searching and crouched down over nothing more than plain, apparently untouched ground. Grabbing a trowel, he carefully lifted off several inches of dry, sandy overburden, and the mosaic came into view. He brushed it clean.

Shading his eyes from the surrounding brightness, Jon dropped to his knees to examine the piece. There was the design, there was the lettering, but his first attempt to decipher it, let alone read or translate it, went nowhere.

"Here, I'll help things along," said Strange. Unstrapping a water canteen from his shoulder, he poured its contents over the mosaic. Again, the artifact suddenly took on color and life.

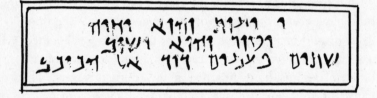

The outer perimeter was of bluish stones, the inner of red or carnelian. Inside, against a buff background, were lines of lettering in black.

"There, Jon," said Strange, almost proudly. "Have at it!"

After studying it for some moments, Jon nodded and said, "It certainly looks to me like Hebrew rather than Aramaic. And very likely a . . . late biblical form of Hebrew, maybe even from the Herodian era, judging by the lettering. But pieces of the tessera are missing, obviously, and some of the black has faded to gray. Hmmm . . . we'll have to check the calligraphy carefully and reconstruct parts of it. The mosaic format also tends to garble the letter shapes somewhat."

He looked up and asked, "Any clues during your dig as to date, Jim? How's the elevation? Same as the synagogue floor?"

"It does seem contemporary with the synagogue," Strange advised. "I measured the elevation of that piece carefully, and it's on the same level as the floor."

"Fascinating! Both would seem to have a first-century provenance then."

"But what does the mosaic say, Jon?" asked Shannon.

"I thought you'd never ask," he trifled. "I don't know yet. I'll try to translate . . ."

The inscription was not in the conventional Hebrew lettering that students learn, but in a much earlier style, further complicated by the missing bits of tessera. After jotting down notes and scratching his head for some minutes, Jon finally shook his head. "I can't make much sense out of it," he confessed. "The first line I can't make out, but the second is about going and coming. The third line also baffles me . . . although . . . *yes* . . . there's the name David! And it's the best-preserved word on the mosaic! This is *fabulous,* Jim and Mort, just fabulous!"

"Then we were right about the word 'David'!" exclaimed Feldman. "The only time David's name has ever been discovered archaeologically was Avram Bihran's find up at Dan!"

"Up to now!" Strange added, grinning wildly.

"I really have to work on this," said Jon. "May I take some photos, Jim?"

"We already have some that you can have. But sure, snap away with your own camera. I know you'll guard the prints carefully and won't publish them or report anything about this find for now."

"Goes without saying! You're the only one who has the right to announce this." Jon shook his head in wonder, adding, "David's name: the second time he shows up in stone!"

"Oh yes, one more thing," said Strange. "Make sure I'm the first to get your translation, Jon—well ahead of Mort here."

Feldman chuckled, "Of course. You know I'd publish first!"

They all laughed and left the dig, though not before Strange had carefully recovered the mosaic with its sandy camouflage.

Jon and Shannon drove back down to the Sea of Galilee and the hotel they had booked for their weekend in the north country, the Plaza in Tiberias. The place was saturated with euphoric memories: it was over a candlelight dinner here that he had fallen helplessly in love with her. They had taken a swim in the Sea of Galilee afterward, during which they had exchanged their first rapturous embrace, followed by a hail of passionate kisses. One of the great romances in all of history, Jon would later style it, in his own (occasionally pompous) fashion. However they would age in the future, the memories of that wondrous night along the moonlit sea would remain young, fresh, indelible.

After dinner that evening they tried to recap the event by strolling along the beach.

"Do you think it's a sign of aging, Jon?" she asked. "Our not taking a 'memorial swim'?"

"Bite your beautiful tongue, sweetheart!" He laughed. "It was hot on that night of nights; now it's October cool. By the way, how's your supplementary report on Rama coming?"

"I'm not nearly as far along as I'd like. No wonder some archaeologists take years to publish their results."

"And, of course, you have to get your father's input too."

"And surprise, surprise: the great Austin Balfour Jennings is being cooperative!"

"Who wouldn't want to cooperate with you, darling? In fact, I'd love to do some cooperative snuggling right now. Shall we head back to the hotel?"

"I thought you'd never ask."

The next morning—mesmerized by Shannon, refreshed, emboldened—Jon did something far less romantic: he plugged in his laptop to check his e-mail. Finally, a message appeared from Swenson at MIT about the cyberphenomenon announcing Jesus' return:

> Hi, Jon! You're probably wondering why I haven't gotten back to you on the Jesus bulletin. It's just that I wanted to give you something hard and specific before e-mailing. Unfortunately, that doesn't seem to be feasible as yet.
>
> The most that all of us can come up with is this: using our best technology, we're now reasonably certain that the originating message came from somewhere in Israel. Yes, Israel! We still don't know where in Israel it started, or how, but we're checking with their best people. One consolation: it doesn't seem to be cyberterrorism at all. We've had no reports of any computers being adversely affected. Now if you get any information on-site there, be sure and pass it on to me, okay?
>
> Best wishes, Rod

"Come here, Shannon," said Jon. "Check this out." While she was reading Swenson's message on the laptop, he commented wryly,

"*Of course* it would have to be Israel as the source of the Jesus Bulletin, wouldn't it? Where else would a modern version of John the Baptist live?"

Shannon shook her head in amazement. "For your sake, Jon, I only hope Melvin Morris Merton doesn't learn about this!"

FIVE

Lunching at a garden table along the shore of the Sea of Galilee in the carefully groomed grounds of the Plaza, Jon and Shannon were startled to hear loud shouting and whistling from the street in front of the hotel. It was so noisy, in fact, that they got up from their table and hurried to the wrought-iron fence surrounding the Plaza to see what was going on. Jon asked a cheering bystander what the fuss was all about.

"Ben-Yosef's here!" the man cried.

"You mean *Joshua* Ben-Yosef?" asked Shannon.

"Yes! He's on his way to Tabgha. He'll be giving an address on the hillside there."

"When?" asked Jon.

"Around three o'clock in Hebrew, at four in English."

They thanked the Israeli and returned to their table, finishing their coffee in silence. Shannon finally broke it: "We're certainly going there, aren't we, Jon?"

"As the French would say, 'But of course'!"

A pleasant, fifteen-minute drive along the western shore of the Sea of Galilee brought them to Tabgha, a secluded seaside spot nestled at the base of the Mount of the Beatitudes between Kibbutz Ginnosar and Capernaum. They got out of their car to look around.

"Up there," Jon said, pointing, "is where Jesus is supposed to have delivered His Sermon on the Mount."

"I know that, Jon. I've spent more time in the Holy Land than you have! But do you think this actually *was* the place?"

Jon shrugged. "It's probably as close as we'll come to any identification, solid or otherwise. Don't look for any bronze plaque that

51

says 'Jesus Spoke Here.'" Then he added, "It's funny, though, that Ben-Yosef should have chosen this spot."

Shannon looked up. "See that domed affair on top of the hill? Isn't that the chapel Mussolini built?"

"Ah, yes. *Il Duce* did better here than in Italy. But where the heck is Ben-Yosef holding forth?"

Shannon pointed to a hillside just west of the Italian chapel.

"Omigosh!" he exclaimed. "That slope must be covered with people! Let's get back to the car."

They drove up a series of switchbacks to reach the summit, where they were waved into a vast, impromptu parking area with hundreds of cars. "Please try to remember where we parked," remarked Jon, while locking their Peugeot. They walked southward along the hill's crest, past the inevitable concession stands, and reached the outer perimeter of a vast crowd blanketing the hillside below them. Loudspeakers had been set up, over which Joshua Ben-Yosef, in a clear, authoritative baritone, was holding forth in Hebrew.

"At least Jesus didn't need loudspeakers when He preached here," Jon commented.

"Quiet, Jon, and tell me what he's saying."

He squinted at the remote figure on the dais far below, as if trying to read his lips—a manifest impossibility at that distance. After a few moments he commented, "Well, that's a surprise! He's using a very classical kind of Hebrew—no local accents or twangs. No contractions. No slang!"

Jon listened on attentively while Shannon stared at the speaker, wishing she had brought binoculars and feeling a little jealous at Jon's command of Hebrew.

"Amazing!" said Jon. "I just don't hear any modern, synthesized Israeli words, no concessions to popular idioms. Heck, his Hebrew is almost . . . biblical in flavor."

"So please spare me the oratorical details. What's he saying?"

"It's a remarkable commentary on living the good life in today's world, both in relation to God and in concern for people. He seems to—"

Suddenly Jon was cut off by deafening cheers and prolonged

applause. Ben-Yosef had finished his address and was waving his appreciation to the vast throng before walking off the dais. Shannon, however, was frowning in frustration.

"Not to worry, dear," said Jon. "You can hear for yourself at four o'clock, and in English, no less. Though I wonder if he can really do English without smothering us in a thick Israeli accent."

They walked off to the concession stands, where Jon ordered a frosty bottle of Goldstar, the local brew. Shannon, however, drank only Perrier. "I don't want my wits dulled in the slightest," she explained. "I've been looking forward to hearing this man again!"

"Ah, but a beer on a warm day only sharpens the mind of a German-American like me," Jon assured her. "In moderation, of course."

When he and Shannon returned to the natural theater, to their surprise they found an even larger crowd seated on the grassy slopes. They had expected a complete change of audience, as between features in a movie theater, but many Israelis were apparently staying on for the English version.

"What dunces we are!" said Shannon, peeved. "We should have gotten closer to the front between Joshua's presentations. But here we are in the rear again, thanks to His Thirstiness!"

"No, I want you here in the back," said Jon with a smirk. "You're much too interested in this fellow!"

She chuckled, "You're a real nut case, Jon! Do you know that?"

Further chatter was cut off by a trumpet flourish calling the crowd to order. As the brass notes faded, Jon had a faint recollection of having heard similar music before.

When he was introduced, Ben-Yosef regaled his audience with several delightful pleasantries—always the way to get a crowd's attention wherever the place, whoever the speaker, whatever the language. But Jon and Shannon were not smiling at all; in fact, they were thunderstruck. They were expecting Ben-Yosef to speak English with the heavy guttural accents and swallowed *r*'s so familiar from radio and television interviews of Israeli statesmen or generals. This man spoke perfect English without any foreign accent whatever, and in a version that seemed to be a cultural cross between American and British English.

"Beyond belief!" whispered Jon. "I'd swear this guy could be broadcasting right out of NBC studios in New York!"

"Extraordinary!" Shannon agreed. "How can anyone speak both Hebrew and English without an accent in one or the other?"

Ben-Yosef clearly could. His message was directed across the board to all classes of hearers. He talked first to the disadvantaged, the handicapped, the hungry, the troubled, the suffering. Not many such were in the audience, apparently, but he was singling out individuals who seemed distressed, and they looked especially touched and helped by his words.

Next he addressed the common people—the farmers, fishermen, and blue-collar workers—not so much with words of comfort, but with challenges to stop self-defeating habits and add deeper meaning to their lives. "I ask you," he said, "isn't your life worth more than screaming at athletic events? Isn't it better to add to your family resources than to waste your wages on lottery tickets and leave your wife and children hungry? Isn't it better to drink in moderation than to become drunk every weekend? Isn't it better to improve your minds by reading Scripture and other great books than to spend endless hours in front of your television, being hypnotized by fantasies?"

"I'm beginning to like this guy," Jon whispered.

Ben-Yosef continued, this time targeting various echelons of hearers: "How blessed are you laborers who truly are worthy of your hire, who give an honest day's work for your wages. How blessed are you employers who honor the dignity of labor rather than exploiting it. How blessed are you merchants and tradesmen who keep your thumbs off the scales. How blessed are you office workers who will not steal even one paper clip from your employers."

"See what I mean, Jon?" whispered Shannon.

Ben-Yosef continued in his flawless English: "Blessed are you brokers who sell your clients stocks that reflect the true price-earnings ratios of honest corporations, as well as bonds that don't have a large, hidden markup. Blessed are you doctors who continue in your medical research and are more interested in curing your patients' illnesses than in collecting fat fees—from them or from their insurance companies or from the government. Blessed are you noble peacemakers who want to break the cycle of violence in this Holy Land: Israelis who have sympathy for displaced Palestinians, Palestinians who have sympathy for innocent Israelis maimed and killed by terrorists. Both of you are driven by a desire for peace with justice, and your reward will be great, both on earth and in heaven.

"But watch out, you lawyers who overcharge your clients and turn them into victims! Watch out, you financiers who help build monopolies to stifle competition and then raise prices to exorbitant levels. Watch out, you crooked executives who will lie about the lofty profits of your corporations to balloon the price of your stocks, only to sell it to innocent buyers who then have their pension plans ruined when your fraud is exposed. In view of the terrible suffering you have caused to so many, life imprisonment is too good for you. Watch out, you auditors who can't seem to discover fraud when it stares you in the face, and also you corporation boards of directors who receive large salaries while blindly endorsing all the lies of management. You will have your rewards!

"Watch out, you corrupt clergy—you false priests and pastors who have disgraced your high calling by preaching morality on Sundays and then sexually abusing those entrusted to your care during the week. Watch out, you bishops and archbishops who knowingly have perverted justice by shuffling such predators around so that they can infect other parishes. You will certainly have your reward!

"Watch out, you narrow-minded religious leaders who so legalistically remove the joy from life with your man-made rules and so many endless restrictions that you stifle divine grace and misrepresent our Lord and our land.

"On the other hand, watch out, you hazy, radical revisionist 'theologians,' so-called, who poke fun at God's Word or even deny His existence entirely. Watch out, you biblical 'minimalists' who wrench sacred history to suit your own, misguided imaginations, who blast holes in the biblical record, only to fill them in with your arbitrary maunderings. God is preparing *your* reward!"

The multitudes on the hillside were sitting in rapt attention, broken only by much head nodding, smiles of agreement, and mutual poking in rib cages to convey the message: "Right on target!"

"What do you think, Jon?" asked Shannon. "Is this man a spell-binder or what?"

Jon shook his head slowly in amazement. "I can't believe it," he said. "I actually agree with most of what he's saying!"

And now Ben-Yosef was concluding: "Resist religious extremism of every variety, dear friends! Extremism is a satanic curse that turns believers into blasphemers, devotees into devils, and the sane into insane. Jewish extremism led to the destruction of Jerusalem by the Romans in the ancient world. Christian extremism led to witch-hunts and pogroms in the Middle Ages. Muslim extremism leads to terrorism, war, destruction, and death in the modern world.

"Never measure success by what you have totaled up in the bank, in your portfolio, or in the size of your property. The genuinely wealthy are not those who have the most, but those who need the least. The truest measure of success is what you have done to help others. That will bring a satisfaction, a supreme and exuberant joy far greater than wealth, fame, or power can ever provide!

"And finally, my colleagues in this extraordinary experience called life, celebrate every magnificent moment of your days! Think of what God has given you: you are the only beings in the entire universe who are created in His image. Only you can think and rea-son, communicate and speak, create and love! Therefore live your lives in gratitude to God and in love for one another. Thank you, my dear friends, for spending this time with me!"

The hillside rose collectively in applause and cheering. Everyone seemed to jabber exuberantly as the meeting dispersed, including Jon and Shannon. While walking back to the parking area, she said, "So, I'll ask it again, Jon: what do you think?"

"Ordinarily I'd say that he's the most effective inspirational speaker I've ever heard. But . . ." He paused.

"But what?"

"Isn't it clear, Shannon? This all happened on the Mount of the Beatitudes, where Jesus most probably delivered His Sermon on the Mount. And Ben-Yosef's address is actually a modern parallel to that sermon: the 'blesseds,' the comforts, the warnings, the ethical advice. But, more than that, there's this mysterious personality, a man who can speak Hebrew as if he were born in Jerusalem, yet hold forth in English as if he came from Chicago."

"So?" she wondered.

"This man is a . . . a *Jesus wanna-be,* Shannon, a Jesus wanna-be! But why? And who is he really?"

They drove back to the Plaza in Tiberias, trying to make sense of the day's events. After dinner in the hotel's vast dining room, they decided to pass on dessert and take an evening stroll instead. No town in Israel came to life more exuberantly when the sun set than the seaside resort of Tiberias. Multicolored lights twinkled in strands over the main street as Jon and Shannon took in the sights. Music of every sort was blaring out of discos, while honky-tonk piano bars invited them inside—especially since it appeared that they had shekels to spend. Shops lining the streets offered them everything from *objets d'art* to tattoos.

Stopping at a newsstand, they noticed again the big play being given Joshua Ben-Yosef in the Israeli press—something that evidently had been going on for some weeks. To stay in touch with the home front, Jon bought a copy of the latest overseas edition of *U.S. News & World Report* and thumbed through it as they continued walking through Tiberias's version of the Great White Way. When he reached the religion section, he stopped abruptly.

"I don't believe this, Shannon: look, here's a big article on Ben-Yosef. Now he's hit the U.S. press too!"

Moving under a street lamp, he studied the photograph accompanying the story. "Hmmm, so that's what he looks like, up close and personal."

Shannon grabbed the magazine from Jon and tried to read the article. But bands of young people were parading through town, serenading the night and jostling bystanders—some in outlandish garb that suggested they were either skinheads or an Israeli version of Hell's Angels.

"Let's get out of here," said Shannon. "I've had enough of the local nightlife."

"How about a little nightcap along the Sea of Galilee?"

"Great."

Sauntering down to the waterfront, they found an open-air restaurant overlooking the lake. Because of the eardrum-shattering cacophony trying to pass for music inside the eatery, they chose a table at the far end of the restaurant's pier, which was illuminated by tiki torches. After a waiter took their order, Shannon read the article in *U.S. News*, passed it back to Jon, and said, "Well, Ben-Yosef's no longer just local news. Several American church leaders drop quotes in this article, including Martin Marty. He seems to agree with you: he calls Ben-Yosef 'an interesting contemporary parallel of sorts to Jesus.'"

Jon nodded, finished reading the article, then tucked the magazine away. He looked at Shannon—so excruciatingly lovely in the candlelight—and reached over to clasp her hand. Even though they had been married for many months, there was still an electric tingle, a tactile shock when he felt her hand. *I can't believe this radiant creature is really mine,* he told himself, while carefully caressing each of her fingers.

She responded by opening again a treasure trove of memories they had shared along that miraculous body of water. Then she stopped, blushed, and said, "I want to go straight back to our hotel, Jon."

"So do I, darling. But we did order drinks out here. And here they come."

Behind the approaching waiter Jon noticed a small group of men walking out onto the pier. After clinking his glass of Carmel red wine with Shannon's, he saw that the men had reached the end of the pier and were looking out over the Sea of Galilee. Suddenly he whispered, "Shannon! That tall one there: that's Joshua Ben-Yosef!"

"Where? . . . Oh!"

Ben-Yosef turned around and looked at them. He had a tanned face, square-cut features, and a generous mouth that was opening into a smile. His intensely blue eyes seemed to pierce theirs, a nice complement to his well-groomed thatch of dark hair, the hair-line proving that the man could not have been over thirty. He cupped his slightly bearded chin, walked over to them, and said amiably, "Excuse me, but I do believe I have the honor of speaking with Jonathan and Shannon Weber! Blessings, this evening, to you both!"

Jon and Shannon sat transfixed, dumbfounded that Ben-Yosef should have known their identity. Her jaw sagged open, with nothing by way of response. Jon, however, said, "We . . . we heard your discourse this afternoon above Tabgha, Mr. Ben-Yosef. Brilliantly done!"

"Well, then, there's a coincidence: you also know my name."

"I do think it's more remarkable that you should have known ours. Might I ask how that is possible?"

He laughed and said, "Not know the name of the man who has written the best life of Jesus to date? Several weeks ago, Professor Weber, I was pleased to attend one of your symposia at Hebrew University. Yes, I'll admit that I sat in the back of the auditorium and wore sunglasses to avoid recognition. Recently, this has become a problem. And everyone knows that you married the winsome daughter of the famous archaeologist Austin Balfour Jennings." Turning to Shannon, he bowed slightly and said, "You are far lovelier than even your charming photographs, Mrs. Weber."

Shannon blushed and thanked him, almost timidly.

"Your precepts this afternoon on the Mount of the Beatitudes were very eloquently expressed," said Jon. "I think they're almost what Jesus of Nazareth would say, were He to address us today."

"You give me too much credit," Ben-Yosef responded. Then, turning toward several in the group accompanying him, he called out, "Shimon! Yakov! Yohanan! Come over here: I want you to meet Professor and Mrs. Jonathan Weber!" Three men, about the same age as Ben-Yosef, walked over and extended cordial greetings. All were dressed, like Ben-Yosef, in clothing that might be styled Israeli casual: open-necked sport shirts, khaki slacks, and leather sandals.

"Anything you'd like to know about first-century Judaism, my colleagues, here is your man!" said Ben-Yosef, again in accent-free and even idiomatic English. "You'll recall how I advised you to read his book."

"Professor Mordecai Feldman told me that he's invited you to speak at Hebrew University," said Jon. "I do hope you'll favor us."

"All in due time," he replied. "I trust you'll be staying in Israel for the whole academic year?"

"I will indeed."

"Then I do hope our paths will cross again soon. Blessings to you both." He turned and walked off the pier with his associates.

Jon studied the group carefully as they headed back toward the restaurant with the blaring music. Shannon, on the other hand, overflowed with excitement and said, "This was *some* nightcap! Hear an internationally-known figure this afternoon, and then have him stop by our table this evening—and know who we are!"

Jon said nothing, but sat there tapping his fingers on the table with slightly wrinkled brow.

"What's wrong, Jon?" she wondered.

"Can you guess how many men were following Ben-Yosef onto the pier here, Shannon?"

"Haven't the faintest."

"I counted them as they left. There were twelve, Shannon. Twelve! Does that ring a bell?"

"Why should it?"

"Let me give you a hint: do you remember when Ben-Yosef called three of his friends over here? Their names were Shimon, Yakov, and Yohanan."

"So?"

"Shimon, Yakov, and Yohanan . . . that's modern Hebrew for . . . Simon—as in Simon Peter—James, and John!"

Shannon looked startled and said, "Omigosh! Peter, James, and John? Jesus' Big Three?"

"Exactly! You might say the executive committee of His twelve disciples. And what about the name Ben-Yosef? That's simple Hebrew for 'son of Joseph.' As if that weren't enough, his full name is Joshua Ben-Yosef? Joshua, of course—actually *Yeo'shua* in Hebrew—is simply their version of the name we anglicize as Jesus."

Shannon shook her head in silent bewilderment for some moments. Finally she asked, "What do you think's going on here, Jon? Is this science fiction and we're in some kind of time warp?"

Jon said nothing.

She persisted, "You . . . you don't suppose this could be a twenty-first century version of Jesus, do you? Or a Jesus returning again before His final coming?"

"No. I can't buy that. Probably he's just—"

"I mean, who else could speak different languages so perfectly? Or say to multitudes today what Jesus would say if He actually came back?"

"Probably he's just an extremely clever impersonator, Shannon."

She thought for some moments. "Well, if you're right, why on earth would he do this, Jon? What's really going on here?"

Jon gazed out onto the open waters of the Sea of Galilee. A full moon was floating up over the Golan Heights on the eastern shore, sending a shimmering silver spear across the placid waters. But Jon's mind was bending the spear into a question mark.

"We'll have to find out, Shannon," he finally replied. "We'll simply have to find out."

SIX

When Jon and Shannon returned to their apartment in Jerusalem the next day, the phone was ringing. Propelled by some universal human instinct, Jon made a flying leap to reach it before it stopped ringing, knocking over a chair in the process.

"Hello!" he said.

"Is this Professor Weber?" a male voice inquired.

"Yes?"

"Jeffery Sheler here, *U.S. News and*—"

"Hi, Jeff! No identification necessary! Calling from D.C.?"

"No, I left Washington last week. I'm here in Jerusalem."

"You are? What in the world brings you over here?"

"Joshua Ben-Yosef."

"Figures!" Jon nodded. "So he's getting big coverage also in the States? I saw your article in last week's issue."

"Big and getting bigger. Several days ago, your friend Merton announced to the media that Ben-Yosef could very well be the returning Jesus, just as promised in that cyberevent."

"Naturally." Jon laughed. "Who else is first to open his mouth? And whether that mouth spouts fact or fiction seems to make little difference to Merton, just so it's first. By the way, Jeff, I forgot to thank you for the accurate coverage of Merton's lawsuit against me. No one does a better job of reporting than the esteemed religion editor at *U.S. News.*"

"You're much too kind, Jon. Any chance we can get together soon? I'd like to tell you what we're up to."

"Great! How about dinner? Would this evening work for you?"

"Sure. Where and when?"

"Let's say . . . the Seven Arches. Know where it is?"

"Mount of Olives. When?"

"Say . . . 7 P.M."

"I'll be there."

Jon looked forward to seeing Sheler again. His religion features in *U.S. News* had always been meticulously researched and well balanced, not veering off in thrall to the radical, revisionist critics nor, on the other hand, in any way captive to the right-wing evangelical block. He was very much his own man.

When Jon arrived at the Seven Arches Hotel with its panoramic view of Jerusalem to the west, Jeffery Sheler was already standing in the lobby with his trademark pleasant smile and outstretched hand. During their dinner together, however, he looked over his shoulder several times and conversed in low tones.

"Okay, I admit," Sheler explained, "this may look a little cloak-and-daggerish. As usual, I'm merely trying to scoop *Time* and *Newsweek*. We're planning to do a cover story on Ben-Yosef, and I'm here to do the spadework."

"You think he's that important?"

"I have my doubts. But America's starting to go ape over this fellow. We're talking instant celebrity here, especially because a sort of messianic fervor is building back home. What you call the prophecy pack are partially responsible, of course, but there's a real apocalyptic element curdling the present climate. Ever since 9/11 and the terrorist attacks, the nation's been on edge, as you know. Then came that cyberthing on the world's computers. Ben-Yosef's appearance seems to play into that, and overnight he's attracting a following that makes the young Billy Graham phenomenon look like a small, preliminary event."

"But the whole darn thing is probably a hoax, Jeff! Or, to be fair, Ben-Yosef himself might even be sincere, a kind of . . . latter-day ethicist modeling his career after Jesus'. But a real Jesus II? I can't buy it."

"Agreed. But here's the point: either way, we have a story here— a very big story. If he's a fraud, we plan to unmask him and do the world a service. But if he's genuine . . ."

"Jesus, you mean?"

"Then," Sheler said with a smile, "*U.S. News* wants to be the first in line to welcome Him back!"

Both chuckled. Sheler now grew serious and said, "I'd like you to keep this confidential, Jon, but I'm not the only one here from our magazine. Mort Zuckerman has committed three of our best investigative reporters to assist me. He's sure this is going to be a major story either way, and I think he's right."

"Who's covering what?"

"I can't reveal any names yet, but one of our people is checking out Ben-Yosef's background. This man seems to have no past . . . or not much of one! Any decent Messiah—genuine or fake—should have a past."

"True enough!" Jon laughed.

"Another of our men, with medical credentials, is checking out Ben-Yosef's supposed cures. The third is interviewing friends, relatives, and associates."

"Good plan, Jeff. But how can I help? Or do you even want or need my help?"

"Affirmative! You can help us in at least two ways. One, I'd love for us to get together from time to time and exchange information. I'll supply what we learn, and I'd much appreciate your returning the favor—all in confidence, of course. After all, you've spent many months in Israel and have lots of contacts here."

"No problem. What's two?"

"No one on this planet knows more about the original Jesus of Nazareth than you, so I want your historical-theological response to this phenomenon, especially when more information comes in."

"While disclaiming the first part of that, sure—count me in. In fact, why don't we start now?"

"Great!" Sheler smiled. "Want to go first?"

Jon nodded, then proceeded to tell Sheler of his contacts with Ben-Yosef: Shannon's early reports, Feldman's observations, their trip to Galilee, hearing Ben-Yosef hold forth on the Mount of the Beatitudes, then seeing him close-up on the pier at Tiberias, where he had even greeted them by name.

Sheler's eyes opened wide.

"Find that unusual?" Jon continued. "Then try this: Ben-Yosef had twelve men in his entourage out there on the Tiberias waterfront. He called three of them over to meet us, and their names were . . . Shimon, Yakov, and Yohanan."

"Shimon . . . as in Simon? Oh, no. Simon Peter, James, and John?" Sheler's eyebrows formed a pair of arches.

"Exactly. And that's the sum total of what I know. What do you have so far?"

"We've checked with the Israeli authorities, of course," Sheler confided, "but they haven't been as forthcoming as we'd like. Frankly, they're trying to fight shy of any involvement. They just don't want to wade into matters religious, especially in view of their own problems with the ultraorthodox and all the small religious parties that have so much disproportionate leverage in Israeli politics."

"Yes, there's Shas, of course. Mafdal and Aguda, too—all tails trying to wag the dog. Oh, oh, that's not a very graceful—"

"It's okay, Jon, I won't report you to the orthodox chief rabbi here." Again Jeff looked around, then commented *sotto voce*, "We don't have much, but I'll lay out what we know. Joshua Ben-Yosef was apparently born in Bethlehem around 1973, and—"

"Born in Bethlehem, you say? The one here, or the one in Pennsylvania?"

He smiled. "The one here. I thought that might get a rise out of you!"

Jon tapped his fingers together, then thought out loud. "It's one thing for an impostor to plan his ruse to run parallel with Jesus' career and try to bring it off. But infants have very little control over where they're born."

"No kidding. But if you find that a little . . . unusual, consider where Ben-Yosef grew up."

"And where was that? Up in Galilee, I suppose? In Nazareth!" Sheler nodded.

"Oh, come off it, Jeff!" Jon replied, face darkening. "You're putting me on."

"No, I'm not. We're still sifting the details, but his parents seem to have settled in or near Nazareth when Ben-Yosef was very young."

"And I suppose his mother's name is Mary? We know from 'Ben-Yosef' that his father is Joseph. They must still be alive, no?"

"We don't know anything about his parents yet. There seems to be some problem in the records."

"What are the odds here, Jeff? Twenty centuries later, someone acts the part of Jesus, which he can control, yet was born in Bethlehem and raised in Nazareth, which he could not control!"

Sheler spread his arms, hands upturned. "I'm only reporting what we have so far, Jon. And that's it, to date. We just got here last week."

Drumming his knuckles on the table, Jon thought for some moments, trying to make sense of it all. "Well, we both have something to work on," he commented, "and I'd like to be more proactive than passive in this thing. It's a blooming mystery, all right, and it has some wild implications. Have you or any of your people been to Bethlehem yet?"

"No."

"Or figured out how a Jew could have been born there, when the place is totally Arab today?"

"No."

Jon thought for several moments more. "Okay then," he said, "why don't you let me do some spadework in Bethlehem? I always like to start at the beginning."

"Excellent!" Sheler beamed. "Even better than I'd hoped! Meanwhile, our people will follow up some leads in Jerusalem and Galilee."

"While I, like the wise men of old, wend my way from Jerusalem to Bethlehem."

There was no star to guide Jon in his quest, but rather complications the Magi never had to face. Only a scant five or six miles south-southwest of Jerusalem, Bethlehem lay beyond the borders of Israel in an area now controlled by the Palestinian Authority. Jon took Shannon along for several reasons: her loveliness never failed to distract officious border guards, he would look less the solo "spy," and, most obviously, life was always better with Shannon around.

Because of Arab-Israeli hostilities and the terrible siege of the

Church of the Nativity in 2002, the road to Bethlehem was heavily guarded with troop emplacements, barbed wire, not-so-hidden guns, and parked tanks. The border gates, painted in red and white, were down across the road as their Peugeot braked to a stop.

An officer of the Israel Defense Force peered into their window, requested the usual identification papers, and asked what they planned to do in Bethlehem. He spoke in English, correctly assuming that Jon and Shannon were foreigners. Jon was about to reply in Hebrew—he loved to flaunt that wherever possible—but then realized that it could raise suspicions: why was someone who knew Hebrew going into Arab territory?

Shannon saved the moment by announcing, "We're researching a book on the Church of the Nativity in Bethlehem." Surely that sounded more innocent than declaring, "We're checking out the shadowy past of one of your new Israeli celebrities." The IDF trooper returned their papers and waved them through.

Continuing through sixty yards of no-man's-land, they stopped at the Palestinian checkpoint. A frontier policeman in black-and-white *kaffiyeh* glanced through their papers, asking the usual questions about destination and intentions, also in English. Jon nodded to Shannon: her explanation worked once, why not twice? After she gave it, the gendarme returned to his guardhouse, checking their names against a master list of undesirables.

When he returned and was about to probe further, Jon added, "I used to bring busloads of tourists to Bethlehem. We're also trying to see how we can revive tourism here after all the hostilities." Immediately the guard smiled and waved them through.

They drove up to Manger Square, where Jon let Shannon out at the Church of the Nativity. That would look good in case they were followed. He drove on across the square to Bethlehem's city hall and located the records office on the second floor. Standing behind a long counter was a clerk who could have been Yasir Arafat's brother, since he had the same strained features under a black-and-white headdress.

"I'm trying to find the birth record of someone born here in Bethlehem around 1973," Jon told the man. "Would you be kind enough to help me?"

Faux-Arafat looked at him with a trace of suspicion and asked in accented English, "Why do you want this information?"

"I'm writing a book on the Church of the Nativity, and this person may be involved."

"The person's name?"

Jon wrote "Joshua Ben-Yosef" on a slip of paper and handed it to the clerk, hoping that, as an Arab, he would not recognize the name of the Israeli celebrity.

Apparently he did not. The man now did a computer check on the live births in Bethlehem in 1973, but found nothing matching the name. Jon asked if he'd be kind enough to broaden his search to cover all births from 1965 through 1975. Surprisingly compliant, the clerk did so. After some minutes, he shook his head and said, "No, nothing. Nothing by that name. Maybe he went by another name, yes?"

"Not that I know of."

"Do you know the names of his parents?"

"Unfortunately, I don't, although the father's first name would seem to be Yosef. I had hoped to learn the names from your records here, or maybe from his birth certificate."

"Well, he must be Jewish with a name like that. Is he Israeli? Or American?"

Jon was on the spot. Should he concoct some further cockamamy reason for his inquiry that would not prevent an Arab from telling the truth about an Israeli to an American, maybe by adding to the innocent fib about the book on the Church of the Nativity? Or, speaking of the truth, why not try it? Truth expressed in the vernacular, however.

Jon now switched to Arabic and confessed, "Yes, this Ben-Yosef *is* an Israeli, and we're trying to track down his background. But I myself am an American, not an Israeli."

A broad smile bloomed on the clerk's face. "Aha, you know Arabic! And you speak it well!"

"Not as well as you handle English."

It was enough. Score one for truth. The official was now a model of cooperation. Leaning over the counter, he confided in quiet English, "There were others born here about that time for whom we have no records. When the Palestinian Authority took control in

Bethlehem, names of the few Jewish families living here were deleted from the records, but not by our staff. Some of our young radicals who ransacked the place wanted to 'prove' that no Jews had ever lived here."

Jon thanked the man for his candor and said, "Here's my card. If ever you come across any records with the name Joshua or Yehoshua Ben-Yosef, would you be kind enough to contact me?"

"Indeed, Doctor . . . Webair," he said, reading the card. *"Salaam!"*

"Salaam alaikum!" Jon responded.

Jon picked Shannon up at the Church of the Nativity and they started driving back toward Jerusalem on Manger Street. Near the edge of town, he noticed a store across the street and suddenly wheeled a sharp left into its parking lot.

"What's *that* for?" wondered Shannon.

"Let's see if Afram and George are in. Remember the Nissan brothers? You met them a couple of years ago."

"Oh, yes. They sent us a Christmas card last year, didn't they?"

"Right. That pair are information central when it comes to what's happening in Bethlehem. Gutsy guys! The Arab-Israeli violence stopped tourism to Bethlehem, of course, and almost ruined them. But they always seem to bounce back."

Jon and Shannon walked into the establishment under a large sign—"Bethlehem New Store—Nissan Brothers"—and found themselves in a merchandise mecca. There were display cases and shelves full of mother-of-pearl items, gold and silver jewelry, gleaming brass candlesticks, shish kebab skewers, tourist trinkets, and sacred souvenirs of every variety. The overriding specialty, however, was carved olive wood used for every conceivable purpose: crèches in all sizes, Jesus at the Last Supper and other biblical scenes, as well as Bibles with olive-wood panels glued onto their covers.

Jon ignored the two clerks who descended on them, since he saw the sturdily framed, lightly jowled chief proprietor himself at the back of the store.

"Afram!" Jon called out.

The leathery, tanned face of Afram Nissan was cut by a vast

smile. "Yonatan! Is it really you?" he called back, displaying a set of gleaming teeth as he rushed forward to welcome them with arms spread wide. "Ahhh," he sighed, "I see you have brought a magnificent mirage out of the desert with you! Welcome, Miss Shannawn . . . as I recall."

"You have an excellent memory, Mr. Nissan," she replied.

"No, no, no: Afram, Afram! And of course I should remember you: I once offered your father twenty camels for your hand! Ah, but he refused, I am sad to say."

Amid their laughter, Afram shouted, "Achmed! Ali! Bring us tea." Turning to Jon and Shannon, he said, "Please to follow me."

Inside his modestly cluttered office, Afram Nissan apologized, "Do pardon this mess. I'm only sorry that my brother George is in Ramallah today. He'll be so sorry he missed your visit."

"Do give him our best," said Jon. "And congratulations, Afram, for continuing to make this the number one tourist emporium in Bethlehem. I can only imagine what you've been through. You and everyone around had planned so long for the great bimillennial celebration of Jesus' birth."

"Ah, yes . . . our huge dining room for tourists next door—"

"Its ceiling spangled with stars," Shannon recalled.

"I remember showing it to you and Yonatan." Afram smiled. "But when those terrible hostilities started with Israel, no more tour buses to Bethlehem, no more festivals in Manger Square. And, of course, we had to stop building on our hotel."

"All that, and then the siege of the Church of the Nativity two years later!" said Jon, who was now ready to conclude introductory small talk. Courtesy, especially in the Near East, demanded that one approach the object of any visit somewhat obliquely. But courtesy had been served. Jon now went on to explain what he and Shannon were doing in Bethlehem.

"Afram, have you heard about this fellow Joshua Ben-Yosef?" he asked. "And the excitement he's causing in Israel?"

"Oh, yes indeed," replied Nissan.

"But did you know that he was born here in Bethlehem?"

"He was? Amazing! No, I didn't know that. When was he born?"

"Around 1973, I understand. I checked for his birth registration at the town hall in Bethlehem, but his name doesn't show up in their records." Jon gave further details about his visit with pseudo-Arafat.

Nissan raised his right index finger and grabbed a phone. While hot tea was being poured for them, he unleashed a torrent of Arabic into the phone, all of which left Shannon baffled. Jon, however, heard his friend talking to the interior minister of the Palestinian Authority, urging that a general search be made of all birth records in the whole West Bank, if necessary, for a Joshua Ben-Yosef, born around 1973. Afram listened for some moments, assured the interior minister that it *was* that important, nodded several times, and then hung up the phone. "It is done," he announced. "They will call me."

Jon thanked his friend, although he cringed just a bit at how his "private" investigation had suddenly become quite public indeed. On the other hand, what real harm was there in that? Afram now pressed Jon for more details on Ben-Yosef. Jon opened his bag of growing information on the Israeli, including the detail about Jewish names being expunged from the Bethlehem records.

"Yes, it was a bad time," Afram sighed. "A plague on both our hotheaded young people and the Israeli 'settlers' building new villages on our territory. The Israelis seem to be the American-style homesteaders, while we are the Indians who are losing our lands. Still, I doubt if our young radicals made much of a difference: many of the names they deleted, I understand, were returned to the public records in Bethlehem later on."

Afram rolled his knuckles on the green blotter atop his desk, lost in thought. "Ben-Yosef, Ben-Yosef," he murmured. "And why was there no record . . ." He stood up and opened a file cabinet, hauling out a large black ledger that served as a company record of operations from the decade of the 1970s. Whipping through its pages, he stopped at an entry and read intently for some moments. Then he nodded several times, smiled, and said, "I just wonder . . ."

Silence followed.

"Wonder what, Afram?" asked Jon.

"I think I may have it. I knew I had heard that name before. It was toward the end of 1973 . . . an Israeli professor came here. His name—can you believe it?—was Yosef Ben-Yosef! That's why I finally remembered it. Anyway, he was driving from Galilee to the

Negev with his pregnant wife, but when they came to Bethlehem, she suddenly went into labor. She started delivering near Rachel's Tomb—that's just several blocks north of here, you know.

"Well, the husband—the professor—badly wanted shelter for his wife, so they stopped in front of our store. Our clerks shouted for me to come to the door. When I saw what was happening, I told the crowd inside our place to stand to one side—yes, we had crowds then!—and we brought the couple downstairs into the basement. We have our olive-wood factory down there, so they could have privacy. Then we phoned the Bethlehem hospital to send a doctor immediately. He came just in time to deliver a baby—a boy, I think. I don't remember what they named him, but . . . could that have been your Joshua? Who knows?"

Jon shook his head in wonder. "An amazing story, Afram! The extraordinary circumstances could explain why there's no record of his birth here. But think hard: are you sure you can't recall what they named the baby?"

"No. If they did tell me, I've forgotten."

Then his eyebrows arched upward. "Well now, I think . . . I think that the couple sent me something later . . . in appreciation. But what was it?" He put both hands over his eyes and thought deeply. "This was thirty years ago."

Suddenly he got to his feet, startling Jon and Shannon. "I know where to look," he cried. "Please to come with me . . ."

They followed him into the hall. Just outside his office door an archaic wooden cabinet stretched from floor to ceiling. Jon whispered to Shannon, "That thing must have been built by one of King Solomon's craftsmen!"

Afram opened the door, revealing shelves packed with dusty old trophies, fading pictures, tarnished plaques, ancient awards, and other memorabilia. He searched shelf after shelf, then gave a cry of delight as he pulled out an alabaster paperweight with a little inscribed gold plate across its face. Reaching for a cloth, he wiped dust off the thing and read the inscription aloud:

With thanks to the Nissan Brothers
at the birth of our son Joshua

Mariam and Yosef Ben-Yosef
December 1973

Afram chuckled triumphantly. "Well, Yonatan, there is your birth certificate for Joshua Ben-Yosef!"

Jon merely shook his head in utter astonishment. "And his mother's name *is* Mary. Or nearly so!"

Back in Jerusalem that night, Jon had the weirdest dream of his life. At breakfast he told Shannon about it before it faded from memory. Jesus was born in a basement olive-wood factory. Overhead, it was not angels but tourist shoppers singing hymns of appreciation to the Nissan brothers for sheltering the holy family. He and Shannon were among the shepherds who had left their flocks to hurry, crooks in hand, to Bethlehem for the great event. Down in the olive-wood factory, craftsmen were carving their images for use in future crèches.

"And what about the wise men?" asked Shannon, almost choking on her toast in glee.

"Well, there was only one of the Magi—not the usual three—but he *was* a wise man: an Israeli professor who was also the baby's father! And he presented a gift of gold—a golden paperweight, in fact—not to the baby, but to Afram Nissan!"

Shannon chuckled even louder. "I wonder what was in that falafel you ate last night after we got back from Bethlehem!"

On his way to Hebrew University, however, Jon's humor turned serious as he ruminated over the dream. No, he was not getting biblical about dreams as regular conduits for divine revelation, but even his smattering of elementary psychology all but shouted what was happening: the parallels between Jesus and Joshua were starting to get to him. In each case, a baby named Joshua or Jesus was born in Bethlehem—under extraordinary circumstances, and in a subterranean place. And his parents were named Yosef or Joseph, and Mariam or Mary—parents who had left Galilee and traveled to Bethlehem.

After his morning lecture at Hebrew University, Jon picked up the phone, called Afram Nissan, and asked, "That couple of yours and the baby in the basement—do you know what happened to them afterward, Afram? They didn't . . . perhaps . . . travel on to Egypt, did they?"

"Sorry, Yonatan," Nissan replied. "I totally lost track of them."

"Hmmm. Thanks, Afram. Do let me know if you recall anything further."

"Yes. Surely."

"*Salaam,* my friend!"

With or without Egypt, Jon mused, the Joshua-Jesus congruence was astounding. Was God really playing some sort of joke on the human race? Jesus couldn't *possibly* have returned . . . could He?

SEVEN

Comments and questions about Joshua Ben-Yosef's persona and deeds now intruded into Jon's symposium at Hebrew University so often that he had to remind his audience, "This is a history seminar, not a conference on current events! Our focus is on the man who lived two thousand years ago, not on any contemporary." Duly chastened, participants returned to the straight and narrow—for perhaps fifteen minutes. Then another student, with due apologies, would volunteer a fresh report on what Ben-Yosef had or had not done in the past week and wanted the professor's take on it.

Nor was his public symposium the only forum for the Ben-Yosef mania. That afternoon, Shannon came home from a university wives' luncheon on Mount Scopus, breathless with excitement. One of the women had returned from a wedding celebration up in Galilee, to which Ben-Yosef and his band of followers had also been invited.

"Jon, they ran out of wine. Sound familiar? But Joshua blessed some water jugs in the kitchen, and from then on they had plenty of good red wine for the rest of the festivities! The woman who was there said she had never tasted a better vintage."

"Oh, great!" Jon huffed. "Now we're into party supplies! But Ben-Yosef seems to have delayed this one: water into wine was Jesus' *first* miracle up at Cana in Galilee."

"Do you have to be so cynical, Jon? Put the case that Jesus *has* returned in the form of Joshua—though I'm certainly not saying that He has. Surely there's no need for Him to repeat Himself in exactly the same ways twenty centuries later, is there?"

"That does it!" Jon announced. "Even you are starting to credit this guy! Well, one thing's clear: I've got to talk to him again. And soon!"

This was no easy task, since Joshua and his cadre seemed to be always on the move. With great good luck, however, one of Jon's students, who was related to a follower of Ben-Yosef, confided that Joshua and his Twelve had just arrived in Jerusalem to celebrate Yom Kippur. He thought that they would be gathering near the Garden of Gethsemane on the lower slopes of the Mount of Olives at noon the next day.

Jon and Shannon planned to be there also. He thought it at least predictable that Joshua and his followers would have chosen Gethsemane, since it was a favorite haunt of Jesus and His disciples twenty centuries earlier.

At about eleven-thirty they walked across the bridge over the Brook Kidron and turned northward into a grove of ancient olive trees, wondering if Joshua and his entourage would actually show up.

"Well, even if they don't," said Shannon, "this is a beautiful spot, and we can always enjoy a picnic lunch here. Thanks for carrying the cooler, Jon."

"I wonder if it was really necessary," he trifled. "Joshua could provide food and drink at the drop of an amen, couldn't he?"

Had he not been smiling, Shannon would have pinched him much harder than she did. Suddenly she hushed him and whispered, "Listen, Jon . . ."

They heard talking farther up on the Mount of Olives and walked over to investigate. There, in a small clearing within the olive grove, they recognized the sturdy figure of Shimon, whom Ben-Yosef had introduced at the Tiberias waterfront. The soulful brown eyes and the salt-and-pepper beard edging his benign features were unmistakable.

Shimon spotted them too. Waving them over, he extended a warm greeting and formally introduced them to his colleagues. "Yohanan and Yakov here, you may remember from our meeting in Galilee." Both nodded with a smile. "And now, please meet Andru."

"Your brother?" asked Jon, though he found little resemblance to Peter in his thinner face and hazel eyes.

"Why . . . yes indeed! How did you know? Do we look that much alike?"

Jon shook his head, almost resigned to what seemed inevitable.

"Not really," he replied. "There are other reasons, and I think you may know them."

Shimon emitted a hearty laugh and said, "I ask your pardon for making a little joke. Andru is not really my brother, only my brother in the faith."

Without responding to Jon's puzzled expression, Shimon continued his introductions. "Next to Andru is Natan'el. You'll really like him: a very open sort."

"'An Israelite in whom there is no guile,'" Jon answered, almost in refrain, referring to the Nathaniel twenty centuries in the past.

Shimon smiled knowingly and continued, "And to his left is Thom. He's something of a skeptic, but we think he'll come around."

As the retinue chuckled, Thom rejoined, "The only thing I'm skeptical about is our eloquent spokesman here!"

Even Jon and Shannon joined in the laughter. The introductions continued until they came to a swarthy figure in the back of the circle with knitted brow and piercing dark eyes. Later, Shannon would tell Jon that he looked very much like a terrorist.

Shimon introduced the figure as Yudas and added, "He's from Judea—the rest of us are from Galilee—but we're trying to civilize him."

Yudas's brow undid its furrows as he grinned and responded, "More like the opposite. I'm the cultured Judean, trying to teach these boorish Galileans some manners!"

When the chuckling subsided, Jon finally raised the inevitable question, "And where is Joshua Ben-Yosef? We had very much hoped to see him again."

"His many healings down in Jericho have delayed him, but he plans to join us tomorrow."

Jon could stand it no longer. If he had had a whistle, he would have blown it—shrill, loud, and clear—to ask for time out. He now spread his arms wide and said, "All right, gentlemen. It's more than obvious that all of you are directly imitating Jesus' disciples of two thousand years ago—to the point of using their very names and even their personalities. I know that the following question may sound abrupt or rude or offensive, but I just can't help myself. Please tell me: what sort of charade is this?"

Shannon touched his arm in a cautionary gesture as a negative rumbling arose from the group.

Shimon frowned and said, "It is *not* a charade!"

"No? Then tell me truthfully," Jon persisted. "Those names in your introduction: are those the names each of you were given at birth?"

Shimon now smiled, shook his head, and said, "Only in my case, by mere coincidence. But, no, the rest assumed those names."

"Why did they do that?" asked Shannon.

"In honor of Jesus' disciples, of course. Apparently, you and your husband have already assumed that."

The candor astonished Jon. "But why in the world are all of you doing this?" he asked.

"Well . . . isn't that clear?" asked Shimon.

"No, it's not. It's not clear at all!"

Shimon walked over to Jon and assumed a stance that gave "in your face" a new meaning. Since he was half a head taller than himself, Jon now expected the worst and started tensing his muscles. But Shimon just smiled serenely and said, "We're doing this, Professor Weber, because the Master called us, just as He did the Twelve twenty centuries ago. We merely took their names to honor their memories."

A cold shiver shook Jon as he tried to digest Shimon's meaning. At last, he responded, "Well, then . . . your master Ben-Yosef must be doing the very same thing."

"Oh, no," Yohanan interposed. "We are the imitators. But Master Joshua *is* Jesus of Nazareth, who has returned, thank God, just as He promised!"

Shannon covered her gaping mouth with a folded fist. Jon felt the electricity at his extremities. He searched for words and finally found them. "You . . . you all actually *believe* that?" he stammered.

"No, Professor Weber," Yakov responded. "For others it may be a matter of belief, but for us it is proven fact! In the past months, we have come to *know* that he is the Messiah, the Christ who has truly and physically returned, praise God!"

"But what . . ." Shannon gargled, cleared her throat, and continued, "What makes you so sure?"

"He teaches with divine authority," Yakov replied, in a tone of earnest conviction. "He is all-knowing. He speaks any language. He commits no sin. He has never made a mistake. His mighty deeds prove his claims—his healings, his wonders, his exorcisms . . . the list is endless."

Jon and Shannon were too overcome to respond.

"I know that this is very difficult for you to believe so suddenly," said Shimon. "For several months now, you've read the news stories and heard the reports and most probably doubted them. But we shall pray for you, Professor and Mrs. Weber . . . pray that Joshua Ben-Yosef will touch your hearts as he has ours. Because our Jesus has returned, thanks to Almighty God! Please—I beg you both—hear his words, witness his deeds, and don't make the mistake of those who rejected him twenty centuries ago!"

Jon and Shannon remained speechless.

"But now, if you will excuse us," Shimon added, "we must take our leave."

With that, he led the modern Twelve out of the olive grove and headed for Jerusalem. Jon and Shannon merely stood there looking after them, arms hanging down at their sides.

When they returned to their apartment, the voice of Jeff Sheler was on the answering machine, asking if they could meet at the Hilton for lunch the next day. Jon called back immediately, only to learn the somewhat disquieting news that Sheler was returning to the States.

"But why are you leaving so soon?" asked Jon, as they sat down at the far end of the Hilton's Garden Court.

"Have to get back now and finish the special on Ben-Yosef. We're advancing publication by three weeks, since the story's starting to explode across the world. Heck, we'll be lucky now to beat the other newsmagazines."

"I've got to know what you and your crew have discovered since our last chat, Jeff, but let me go first. I'm really full of this because of what happened yesterday on the Mount of Olives."

Jon now downloaded for Sheler all the fresh information on Ben-Yosef he had learned since their last meeting, including the strange circumstances of Joshua's birth in Bethlehem, the reports of his vintage contributions to the wedding festival in Galilee, his healings in Jericho, and the encounter with Ben-Yosef's Twelve at Gesthsemene. Sheler's eyes widened and narrowed repeatedly during the telling, but when Jon reported Shimon's statement that Ben-Yosef *was* the returned Christ, his jaw sagged, he seemed to blanch, and he shook his head slowly.

"You actually interviewed his crew?" he finally managed. "We've been trying to get to them for weeks but could never pin down their whereabouts."

"Blind, dumb luck, Jeff! But what do you have?"

"Well, our medical specialist interviewed some twenty or so people who were supposedly cured by Ben-Yosef. All of them showed no signs of disease or handicap. Then again, it was hardly scientific, since he hadn't seen them before their presumed cures."

"What sorts of illnesses were involved?"

Sheler pulled a pad out of his coat pocket and read off a list. "Two pneumonias, four cancers, three deaf mutes, two blind, two cardiac insufficiencies, a cripple, two AIDS, one STD, and several exorcisms."

"Were those psychosomatic cures or physical cures? Real or assumed?"

"I don't know. He's staying on here to dig deeper."

"What else have you learned about Ben-Yosef's background?"

Sheler looked about warily, then confided, "Hardly anything in Jerusalem, but a little more at Tel Aviv and Haifa. It turns out that Ben-Yosef was an only child—so there's at least one nonparallel with Jesus, unless the Catholics have it right with their teaching on the ever-virgin Mary. Later, he studied at the Technion in Haifa, where both his father and mother were on the faculty—both brilliant biochemists."

"Biochemists, eh? Love in the laboratory?"

Sheler smiled and nodded. "That's where they met, evidently. But their research focused on enhancing crop yields, so much of the year they lived near Nazareth to supervise botanical experiments in the Valley of Jezreel just below Nazareth. That's why young Joshua grew up there, specifically in a Jewish settlement in a modern part of Nazareth—a place called Nazareth Ilit."

"Good detail, Jeff! Did any of your people interview his teachers or professors?"

"Affirmative." He nodded. "The principal of his school in Nazareth remembers Joshua well." Again Sheler flipped several pages in his notebook and read aloud:

> We never had a student like him—before or since. What a mind Joshua had! Almost too many talents in one young lad. The boy was a living prodigy and regularly corrected his teachers on how they handled biblical Hebrew. When he was only nine years old, he won Israel's national television Bible quiz. At thirteen his parents took him to Jerusalem for his bar mitzvah. There, just after reading the Torah in front of the Western Wall, Joshua started to argue fine points of Jewish law with several rabbis nearby. They finally threw up their hands and stalked off.

"Just like the twelve-year-old Jesus in the temple? You're spoofing about the last, aren't you, Jeff?"

Sheler smiled grimly and shook his head.

"What about his higher education?"

"We're still trying to fill in all the details, but we do know that he enrolled at both the Technion and the University of Haifa. He took a brace of scientific and technology courses at the Technion, along with history, humanities, and literature courses at Haifa. His total class schedule each semester was almost twice the normal course load."

"Well, *that* was some kind of well-rounded education!" Jon observed. "Where did he get his terminal degree?"

"The Technion."

Jon stroked his chin in thought. Finally he said, "One thing's perfectly obvious: we've got to interview his parents, Professor and Mrs. Yosef Ben-Yosef. Are they still in Nazareth? Or Haifa?"

Sheler shook his head. "They were both killed years ago in an early terrorist attack, on the road past Netanya. Their car was blown up in a roadside ambush."

Jon clenched his fist and banged the table: a major source of information was now eliminated. Finally he asked, "Where was Joshua at the time?"

"We're not entirely sure, but it seems he was out camping with friends along the Dead Sea."

"Of course! Every prophet—real or imaginary—has to have his desert experience!" Jon observed sardonically. "What else do you have?"

"That's it so far. When I write the story, I'll send you e-mail copy before we go to press. Then would you be kind enough to compose a sidebar for us on the significance of it all?"

"Glad to, Jeff. Let's stay in touch . . . close touch."

Too much was coming together in a vector that seemed to point to the incredible, thought Jon. Here were twelve apparently sane people who were so convinced Jesus had returned, they changed their names and modeled their personalities on His original band of disciples. "Jesus the Second" was speaking and acting in direct congruence with the original, addressing similar concerns with similar language while authenticating his mission, evidently, through powerful demonstrations of the miraculous. He also had a background no Jesus wanna-be could ever have arranged: born in Bethlehem of Galilean parents—virtually named Joseph and Mary—and raised at Nazareth. Nor had he dropped out of the blue: the man did have a past, however sketchy.

But more! Jon had almost forgotten about the baffling cyber-announcements on the world's computers regarding the returning Christ and how extraordinarily they seemed to be in line with Joshua Ben-Yosef's sudden public fame. Just for a moment he tormented himself with the thought that Melvin Morris Merton could conceivably be right after all, but quickly cudgeled that thought until it was quite unconscious. But it was time, in any case, to get back in touch with Rod Swenson regarding the Jesus Bulletin.

He looked at his watch. It was 6:00 P.M. Israeli time. "Good," Jon told himself. "It's 11:00 A.M. in Cambridge. I should be able to catch him before lunch." Murphy's Law was in remission that day, and the strategy succeeded: Swenson's Swedish-American "Hello" was unmistakable.

"Oh . . . it's you, Jon," he continued. "I just sent you a fax detailing what we have so far on that cyberincursion a couple months ago."

"Thanks much, Rod, but the fax machine is in my office at Hebrew University. Could you summarize it briefly over the phone?"

"Well, it's pretty detailed . . . even though we simplified it for a layman like yourself!"

"I won't even take offense at that, Rod!" Jon laughed. "But a recessive Scottish gene in me says I shouldn't spend more phone money to hear your insults."

"A bonny plan, laddie!" Swenson continued in a fake Scottish accent, "An' do let mi know if ya dunna understan' mi fax."

The next morning, Jon read the fax twice:

Hello, Jon! Here's where we are on the cyberincursion.

Some sender's address is always indicated at the beginning of communications sent on the World Wide Web. In this way, messages can be traced back to their source. But nothing seems to have been usual in this case, since the sender's name and address on the Jesus Bulletin was simply "The Forerunner." We don't know how he got away with that. It's just one of many riddles in this case.

So we had to do a global search using a time grid instead. All web messages show the time that they were sent, so we collated the times that the Jesus Bulletin appeared in various countries. Interestingly enough, the second series of bulletins occurred at the same times and in the same orders, country by country, as the first.

Both times, Israel turned out to be the very first, time-wise. Other countries followed, including the U.S. Israel is very hi-tech, it's fully wired, and probably the only place in the Near East with the cyber-capability to bring something like this off.

As to the identity of the sender, even a secular Swede like myself remembers enough from his Sunday school days to see that someone is trying to play John the Baptist when he calls himself "The Forerunner." When we find the hacker, he'll probably be sitting in the desert, dressed in camel skin, girded with a big leather belt, and chomping on locusts. We may criticize the guy's diet, but boy, can he ever crunch numbers!

Stay tuned, Jon. We'll solve this yet!

Jon filed Swenson's fax in a special drawer he had created inside one of his file cabinets code-labeled "The Enigma Variations"—in honor of a favorite composer, Edward Elgar.

Two weeks later, Jon found the e-mail draft of Sheler's cover story on Ben-Yosef so accurate that he had to correct only a couple of Hebrew transliterations. He immediately wrote a sidebar for the article, as promised—or rather, rewrote it, since the first draft seemed hopelessly biased against any possibility that Ben-Yosef could be the returned Jesus. "True scholarship must be dispassionate," he told himself. The final draft was better balanced, carefully listing conclusions pro and con, along with their implications.

He saved the most powerful negative argument for the last, knowing well enough that this doomed any serious claim that Ben-Yosef could be Jesus in any sense. If this *were* the returned Jesus, he wrote, where were the other spectacular symptoms attending His Second Coming that are cited in the Gospels: the darkening of sun and moon, His arrival on the clouds of heaven "with power and great glory," the loud trumpet call, Judgment Day, and the end of time?

It was only after he had e-mailed the piece to Sheler that he had second thoughts about that final argument. Some of the more outspoken prophecy advocates, including Merton, had affirmed a prior "secret" or less obvious return of Jesus—in some connection with the Rapture—prior to His formal final return in glory after the Tribulation. That earlier arrival, of course, would not be heralded by heavenly clouds or loud trumpets.

Jon, however, did not believe in such a preliminary arrival: the Second Coming would be the final coming. He did not change his text. "Like Pilate," he told himself, "what I have written, I have written."

EIGHT

U.S. *News & World Report* scooped the other newsmagazines by one slender week. The cover showed a smiling, head-and-shoulders, full-color photograph of Joshua Ben-Yosef in a royal blue, open-necked sport shirt—an undeniably attractive figure with a pleasant, tanned face, piercing cobalt eyes, a generous mouth, and a closely cropped beard edging his squarish jawline. Perfect white incisors showed through slightly parted lips, while thick, brownish hair—carefully parted in the middle—fell almost to his shoulders. His nose, the feature that can so easily detract rather than enhance, rather gracefully did the latter. It was neither Semitic aquiline nor Gentile straight. Some called it "international" or "everyman." Around his neck was a small gold chain with cross attached, leaving no doubt as to his religious affiliation.

Shannon and Jon read the overseas edition of *U.S. News* just a day after it appeared on newsstands in America. Sheler had managed to garnish his article with a gallery of photographs he had evidently picked up from the Israeli press, which had been focusing on Ben-Yosef weeks before the West even knew he existed. One of the first pictures was a wedding photograph of his parents, which Jon studied for some time. Yosef Ben-Yosef appeared as a youthful, pleasant-looking groom, waiting to conquer the future, while Mariam was an Israeli woman whom anyone would call attractive, a poised bride with a shy smile and soulful eyes. Joshua's distinguished features, clearly, had not developed out of a vacuum.

The other photographs were equally intriguing. There was even a shot of the basement olive-wood factory at the Nissan emporium in Bethlehem, with an inset showing Afram and George Nissan arm in arm. Joshua's boyhood home near Nazareth looked comfortable and more than large enough for a family of three. The elementary school he had attended had been newly rebuilt of white stucco in Nazareth Ilit, and stock photographs showed the administration buildings at both the Technion and the University of Haifa, where Joshua had pursued his university studies.

Jon was astonished, however, to see photographs also of six of the Twelve: Shimon, Yakov, Yohanan, Andru, Thom, and Yudas. All portraits seemed to do the men justice, except—predictably—Yudas, whose frown showed that he was really throwing himself into the role of the "heavy" in this strange scenario. Clearly, Sheler's investigative colleagues had sent him some excellent fresh material and photos since Jon's last meeting with him at the Jerusalem Hilton.

A sidebar brought readers up to date on the worldwide cyberphenomenon that seemed to herald the appearance of Ben-Yosef. Was the incursion coincidental, or not? The investigation, thus far, had yielded no absolute results, although Rod Jensen was quoted at length regarding Israel as the source of the web event. A reward of one hundred thousand dollars had now been posted by the U.S. Department of Homeland Security for any solid information on the origin of the cyberepisode and how it was accomplished.

Jon's own views on the Ben-Yosef phenomenon formed another sidebar. At second reading, his comments seemed to have the balance he had tried to convey. While conceding some of the extraordinary elements in the Joshua phenomenon, he added enough cold sobriety to deflate the more excessive claims being made about Israel's new religious luminary.

After Shannon had finished reading the story and discussed it with him, Jon commented, "I really don't know if the world is ready for this. Or maybe it's *too* ready!"

"What do you mean, Jon?"

"Well, many in the Christian public had already been stoked to red-hot anticipation by the prophecy fanatics before anyone even heard of Joshua Ben-Yosef. Then the cyberthing happened. And now comes a serious article on the Jesus candidate himself, giving some substance to what had only been frothy conjecture before. If people went ape over fantasy, what will they ever do over presumed fact?"

"So you think Joshua may really be Jesus, then?"

"I hardly think so, Shannon!" He smiled indulgently. "But the masses may."

Jon proved to be a prophet himself on that prediction. The story in *U.S. News* provoked a tidal wave of reaction. Perhaps inevitably, the first phone call came from Hannibal, Missouri. His father was not in a jocular mood.

"Jon," he demanded, "what have you gotten yourself into *this* time?"

"Hello yourself, Dad! What seems to be the problem?"

"Well, the loonies are on the loose around here, telling everyone who will listen to prepare for the end of the world! *Jesus has returned!* And people are actually believing them, thanks to you and that magazine."

"What do you mean, *me?*"

"Jon, how could you have made *any* favorable comments about that impostor? You surely don't believe he's Jesus, do you?"

"Of course not, Dad. I was only trying to be as fair and objective as possible."

"Well, there's one big argument against any identification of this Joshua with Jesus," he huffed. "And I'm really shocked that you didn't mention it in your sidebar!"

"What's that, Dad?"

"Well, for goodness' sake, Jon, do I have to draw you a picture? Weren't you listening when I taught you in confirmation class? The magazine shows a picture of Joshua's *father!* But Jesus had no—"

"I know, Dad. Jesus' father was God. But even the Gospels some-times call Joseph the father of Jesus when referring to the holy family. And the only reason I didn't mention that in my piece was because I didn't want to introduce the virgin birth debate at this early a stage in our investigation. I wanted to save it for later on, maybe as the clincher."

"Hmmm. Well . . . I guess that makes sense . . . just so you don't forget it."

"I won't. But hey, how about cutting me a little slack, Dad? I do think I was on the side of the angels on this one, don't you?"

"Well . . . yes, Jon. You did show that many of the other signs of

Jesus' triumphant return at the end of time are not present in the case of this Ben-Joseph. Good boy!"

"Well, thanks! And do tell Mom not to sell everything she has and put on a white robe to spruce up for Judgment Day, okay?"

"Heh heh. I'll do that. Bye, Son."

The phone rang again almost immediately. It was an operator at the Vatican in Rome, asking if Dr. Jonathan Weber were available. Soon he was on the line with a friend he had not seen for several years: Monsignor Kevin F. X. Sullivan. Both had been Harvard undergrads, and both had gone on to graduate studies at Johns Hopkins, after which their parallel pathways parted. While Jon returned to teach at Harvard, Kevin went on to become a Jesuit scholar at the Gregorian in Rome. His brilliance there soon gave him entrée with the power brokers at the Curia, and he had been Jon's personal liaison with Pope Benedict XVI during the Rama crisis.

Sullivan began their dialogue in much the same way as Jon's father. "Okay, Jon, what in God's name—and I say that with no hint of blasphemy—is going on over there? And how did you ever get involved in this latest sacred sensation?"

"I was wondering when you'd ask, Kevin . . . I guess I was just in the wrong place at the wrong time."

"No, it's more like the right place and the right time where you are concerned, good buddy. So . . . what's the buzz? Should Ben-Yosef be called Ben-Hoax? He couldn't possibly be legit, could he?"

"Do you want the five-minute version or the fifty-five? It's your nickel."

"You'd best give me the longer one, since the Holy Father is very concerned."

For the next half hour, Jon gave Kevin a complete briefing on everything that had developed to date. When he had finished, Kevin gave a soft, low whistle and said, "I . . . guess I'm surprised that there's that much in his favor—the geography of his birth and youth . . . which he couldn't arrange, the man and his message, the healings . . . You know, Jon—but please don't quote me—as I see it, this is sort of the way Jesus *would* speak and act if He were to return again prior to His final coming."

"So? Does that mean that you, too, are joining the growing ranks of Joshua groupies, Kevin?"

"Not quite!" He laughed. "But the Vatican simply has to be in the innermost loop when it comes to something like this, for over-obvious reasons. The Holy Father now wants me to report to him whenever anything new develops in this thing. When he heard that you were on the scene there in Israel, he smiled and said, 'Then I know that this whole affair is in good hands.' He well remembers our crucial contacts during the Rama crisis."

"That was very kind of him. By the way, Kev, how's Benedict doing on the medical front? I heard he was in poor health. What was it—cardiovascular complications? Heart?"

"*Was* is the operative verb, I'm glad to say. He's watching his diet now, getting more exercise, and taking statins. His HDL/LDL cholesterol count shows a big improvement."

"That's great news! Do give him my best!"

"I will indeed—if, that is, you promise to stay in close touch."

"You bet."

"Do you still have my private phone number at the Vatican? And my cell phone?"

"Yes, but best to give me both of them again."

A group of newspaper editors once speculated over what the biggest story of all time would be, and the Second Coming of Jesus Christ won by a landslide. And it seemed as if a media landslide was indeed developing across the world after *U.S. News* provided the first in-depth coverage. Magazines in both hemispheres ditched the cover stories they had planned and switched to Ben-Yosef. Newspapers that had previously covered his doings on page four of section B now regularly accorded him front-page treatment. The broadcast networks sent a small army of cameramen to Israel in hopes of securing fresh footage or at least some strategic sound bites. CNN had a "Joshua Update" every day at noon, while the BBC did the same every evening at five. The coverage was considerably less, however, in areas without a sizable Christian population, such as the Middle East, India, China, and Japan.

USA Today commissioned one of its many polls, this one asking people if they believed Joshua Ben-Yosef was the returned Jesus Christ. Almost a third said yes. The prophecy sector of Christendom was ecstatic. Sales of the Left Behind series boomed once again, and even Hal Lindsey's aging titles took on new life. Airlines started scheduling extra flights to Israel for pilgrims who wanted to see and hear Ben-Yosef, or just catch a glimpse of him—the largest upturn in tourism since the El-Aqsa Intifada nearly terminated the Israel tour industry in A.D. 2000.

No one, of course, felt more triumphantly vindicated than Melvin Morris Merton and his associates. The latest newsletter of his *Points of Prophecy* television show, sent to all the faithful (with contribution envelopes, of course), featured a large photo of Jon on the front page under a header, bannered WRONG AGAIN! Marylou Kaiser sent him a copy with a cheery note attached, "Congratulations, Chief. Now you've *really* made the big time!"

Jon read the article aloud to Shannon. It began:

> Throughout Holy Scripture, those who attacked the true prophets of God came to a disastrous end. Who can forget what King Ahab did to the prophet Elijah, or how the other wicked kings of Israel mistreated Elisha and the other prophets? God smote them all mightily!
>
> Sad to say, the prophets are still being attacked—not by wicked kings, but by equally reprehensible scholars so-called, such as Professor Jonathan Weber, who libeled me some months ago and ridiculed my inspired predictions. In view of God's record against such, if I were a life insurance company, I would not sell Dr. Weber a policy! (He need not phone his lawyers: this is not a threat, but merely a prediction of perdition to those who "stone the prophets.") Mark my words and read my lips: the returning Jesus will vindicate me! But I shiver to think what He has in store for Professor Weber.

"Well, you get the drift," he told Shannon. "You can read the rest for yourself."

"Jon, this buffoon is threatening you! I *would* call a lawyer!"

He laughed off her concern and said, "But one thing about the article does surprise me . . ."

"What's that?"

"Merton was able to spell 'reprehensible' correctly."

A week later came another envelope from Cambridge, with another issue of Merton's newsletter and Marylou's note attached, "I really think you should subscribe to this exciting journal!" This edition declared that Merton Ministries was now busily at work planning a great, international celebration in Israel to greet the returned Lord.

"Count on it," Jon commented to Shannon wryly. "If there's a trouble spot anywhere in the world . . . or an opportunity for public exposure . . . Melvin Morris Merton will certainly be there."

"Promise you won't let Merton use us as parade trophies again, Jon?"

"I do solemnly swear and affirm. But this whole international reaction to Ben-Yosef is ridiculously premature. There's just too much more that we have to do by way of checking the man out. We haven't even had a chance to interview him yet."

"I tell you, Jon, we should have followed up with his twelve disciples that day in Gethsemane. Why in the world didn't we?"

"As I recall, we were both a little stunned by their claims at the time. But I'm sure we'll run into them again. Or him."

"I really hope so."

Jon shook his head. "I don't know. I just feel it in my bones," he said. "This has all the marks of big hype, big expectations, big letdown. If Jesus truly *were* returning, it just wouldn't happen this way, would it?"

"I don't know, Jon. Didn't they say the very same thing about Jesus the first time around? What if you were a nice modern parallel to the scribes, Pharisees, and other opponents of Jesus who couldn't believe that the Messiah actually *had* arrived?"

"Thanks a heap, Shannon! Sounds as though Merton is getting to you!"

"And you can bite your tongue on that one!" she shot back, with a slight scowl—or was it a slight grin? Jon wasn't quite sure how to decipher it.

Marylou sent Jon all press clippings and published responses regarding the Ben-Yosef phenomenon that reached his office at

Harvard. Some of the most interesting reactions fell into a file called "Non-Christian Opinion." The chief orthodox rabbi in Jerusalem called the excitement over Ben-Yosef "vastly overdone" and added, "Judaism does not recognize Jesus of Nazareth as the Messiah predicted in the Hebrew Bible, and certainly does not recognize the Israeli citizen, one Joshua Ben-Yosef, either as Messiah or as any reincarnation of Jesus of Nazareth."

Jon was surprised to see that the world of Islam was giving some unanticipated attention to questions about Joshua Ben-Yosef. In fact, a number of Muslim scholars were discussing the possibility that Joshua could indeed be the returned Jesus, whom Muslims call Isa. The *Qur'an* has a high opinion of Jesus as a great prophet— though not the Son of God—who is indeed expected to return to earth before the Final Judgment. The Ben-Yosef phenomenon, then, was starting to provoke unusual debate in Cairo, Baghdad, Tehran, Karachi, and other Islamic centers across the world. The mullahs in charge, however, carefully monitored the growing speculation, lest the Islamic faithful pay too much attention to one solitary Jew, whoever he might be.

"The Far East doesn't seem as interested," said Shannon. "But I suppose you can't blame a Hindu for failing to wonder if one Jew might be identical to another Jew twenty centuries earlier!"

"Yeah, although I'll bet it *is* a curiosity that'll intrigue some of them," Jon replied. "The same goes for Buddhists, the Dalai Lama for one."

"Jon, have you really tried to get through to Joshua? I mean, here we are in Israel—his own backyard. Why is it so difficult for us to find him?"

"Well, the newspapers don't publish his daily schedule or whereabouts, after all. And I'm sure that the Israelis aren't even sure how to handle Ben-Yosef. His last known address was somewhere in the Sea of Galilee area—near where we first heard him, I think. But Joshua and his following always seem to be moving from place to place, and the authorities apparently know his location only after he and his Twelve have been there the day before."

"Oh, come on, Jon: the Israelis aren't stupid, you know. I'll bet their secret police have tracked him for months!"

Shannon's comment caught him off guard. Jon cupped his chin for several moments, then replied, "You know, you may have a point there, Shannon. Good girl!"

"Hey, don't patronize me, chum! I'm not a girl, but a magnificent and ever-so-desirable woman, in case you hadn't noticed!"

Jon pulled her close. "Believe me. I've noticed."

At Hebrew University the next morning, Jon went to Mordecai Feldman's office and found the great man at his desk.

"Jon," Feldman said, before Jon could even say why he had come, "I've been meaning to call you. How goes your work on the Sepphoris mosaic?"

Jon's face took on a rosy hue. "If it's any consolation to you, Mort, my conscience has been throbbing on that one. The Ben-Yosef thing has completely sidetracked the work I should have been doing on the mosaic. But here's a promise: I'll be on it next week for sure."

"Good!" Feldman smiled.

"On another matter, Mort, I know you shun politics as the living plague it often is. But do you know anyone at the Mossad? Or Shin Bet?"

Feldman was taken aback. "Our Israeli secret police? Are you spoofing, Jon? Not a soul!"

"Thought as much," said Jon sheepishly. Then he brightened. "Wait a minute . . . I just recalled another contact, so please disregard my question. And don't worry, friend, it has nothing to do with the security of the State of Israel!"

"Well, that's reassuring!" Feldman replied, in mock relief.

The name of Gideon Ben-Yaakov had flashed into Jon's mind. Gideon was the director of the Israel Antiquities Authority and had been of major assistance in the Rama affair. In fact, it was a sad commentary on Jon's preoccupation with the Joshua phenomenon that he had not contacted Ben-Yaakov much earlier.

Planning to act as if they had arrived very recently, Jon called Gideon at the Israel Antiquities Authority.

"*Shalom*, Jon," his cheerful tenor voice responded. "At last you call! Naomi and I heard that you and Shannon were in Jerusalem. Why didn't you call us earlier?"

So much for pretense. "I really feel awful about that, Gideon: I no sooner arrived in Israel than I got caught up in this Joshua Ben-Yosef thing. Can you ever forgive me?"

"Of course!" he laughed. "But only if you and Shannon come over for dinner before the week is out."

"Great! I'll—"

"No, that's too late. Let's make it tomorrow evening. Can you?"

"How could we resist so warm an invitation?"

At six-thirty the following evening, Jon and Shannon arrived at Gideon's condo at Givat Ha-Mivtar in northeast Jerusalem. Jon rang the bell at their apartment and brushed the mezuzah on the right door frame out of habit rather than conviction.

The lovely, even sultry, tanned figure of Naomi Ben-Yaakov opened the door. She flew into Jon's arms as if she were his dearest sister, and then offered a similarly warm greeting to Shannon. Gideon, a natty, well-groomed fashion plate of medium size with ash-blond hair, joined the trio in a festival of reunion.

"So how is the world's most beautiful ceramicist?" asked Jon, holding both hands with Naomi. "Is that lucky husband of yours treating you properly?"

"He's still on probation," she chirped. "But I think he'll pass."

"And when are you coming back to *Eretz Israel* to dig, Jon?" asked Gideon. "Surely that's more fun than teaching! And you, Shannon! I've never quite forgiven Jon for taking you away from me!" He bent down to kiss her hand.

"Maybe I haven't either," she flirted. "But with so gorgeous a consolation prize as Naomi, I knew you'd never be lonely!"

"It's an honor to be your surrogate, Shannon!" Naomi said with a broad, incandescent smile. "But sit down, dear friends. We haven't seen you since that 'greatest of all weddings' in Hanna-bell."

Cocktails were followed by a dinner that Naomi prepared in a tasty fashion. Jon and Shannon exchanged glances. *We really should have visited them before this,* his wide eyes told her, and her slight nod replied, *Yes, what took us so long?*

As the four enjoyed dessert and brandy—no cigars, out of deference to the ladies—Jon casually broached the subject of Joshua Ben-Yosef.

"Oh yes, our twenty-first century Jesus!" Gideon responded with a smile. "It seems he's come back from the dead—again!" Gideon was not a Christian, so both Jon and Shannon took it as the innocent, jovial comment Gideon had intended.

"But what do you make of him, Gideon?" asked Shannon.

Gideon shrugged his shoulders. "Another Billy Graham, I suppose: Israeli version."

"Know anything more about him?" Jon pressed.

Gideon shook his head. "I really haven't followed him that much. How about you?"

Although he hadn't planned to do so, Jon now dumped a truckload of data about Joshua without first asking his hosts if they wanted so great a pile in front of them. Both Gideon and Naomi seemed interested, however, and Jon's apology for having gone into such detail was brushed aside.

"So that's our general information on Ben-Yosef," Jon concluded, "except for this post-script. Gideon . . . this may seem like a dumb question, but do you know anyone at Shin Bet?"

He nodded. "Sure. Why do you ask?"

"Well, I've just *got* to get in touch with Ben-Yosef—there's special interest at the Vatican also. But no one seems to know where to find him."

"You mean, you'd like to know where he is now?"

Jon nodded.

Gideon reached into his pocket for his cell phone, punched in a number, and then spoke in rapid Hebrew. *"Ken . . . ken . . . ken,"* he responded, nodding repeatedly.

Even with her limited knowledge of Hebrew, Shannon translated this as "Yes . . . yes . . . yes."

When he had finished, Gideon reported, "They do have a file on Ben-Yosef, although they're not very concerned about him. None of his mass meetings have been unruly, and he doesn't seem to be preaching against the government or leading any sort of radical movement. If he were some sort of prototerrorist, it would be a different story, of course. They had a tail on him for a while, but took it off in the name of boredom."

Gideon paused, took a sip of brandy, and said, "According to Shin Bet, here's the bottom line, as you Americans put it: the Israeli government doesn't like to get involved in religious issues. It's all we can do to keep peace between our religious parties as it is. But if Ben-Yosef's following gets any bigger—and reports are that a huge influx of his followers is expected—then the tail goes back on. But meanwhile, in answer to your question, Joshua and his men were spotted on the Jericho-Jerusalem road several days ago, heading uphill. They're probably here in Jerusalem even as we speak."

"All that in one phone call?" Shannon enthused. "What a man you are, Gideon!"

"But not quite man enough, my dear, as you yourself demonstrated several years ago!"

Chuckling, Jon and Shannon took their leave with copious thanks.

NINE

One morning, after Jon's public symposium at Hebrew University, a student came up to the dais with a letter in hand. "Excuse me, Professor Weber," he said, "but I was instructed to hand you this."

Jon looked at the envelope, which was addressed to Professor Jonathan P. Weber, Hebrew University, with no return address. "Who gave you this?" he asked.

"I don't know, sir. I was sitting in the back of the hall, taking notes, when a tall, bearded fellow leaned over my desk and asked me to give you this at the end of the lecture."

"Fine. And thank you, Mr. . . . sorry, I should know your name, but I don't call roll."

"No problem, sir. It's Schmidt, George Schmidt."

"You're an American, aren't you? Where are you from?"

"Topeka, Kansas, sir."

Jon took a good look at the lanky young man with the distinctive red hair. "Aren't you the one who spoke up during my opening lecture? The Christian?"

"Yes, sir."

"How's our symposium going for you, George? Have I shaken your faith in any way?"

"Well . . ." He hesitated. "You've certainly given me a new appreciation of how fascinatingly complex Jesus studies can be. But no, you haven't shaken my faith."

"I couldn't ask for more." Lifting the envelope, Jon said, "Thanks for delivering the mail, George."

"No problem, Professor Weber."

Jon tore open the envelope and read the following message in attractive, flowing script:

Dear Professor Weber,

I understand from my colleagues that you would like to converse with me while I am in Jerusalem. I would be delighted to have such an opportunity. Lately, as you may be aware, it has become difficult for me to appear in public without attracting undue attention, so if you don't mind, I would be glad to welcome you to our abode in Bethany at 8:00 tomorrow evening. The address and directions are enclosed, as well as our phone number in case you are unable to come. The peace of God be with you!

Joshua Ben-Yosef

Smiling broadly, Jon read the letter again to make sure he had it right, and then almost sang a *Te Deum* for joy: his elusive target had zeroed in on him instead!

Shannon badly wanted to go with him the next evening, but since she had not been included in the invitation, Jon thought it best to go alone. Driving around the Mount of Olives to Bethany, Jerusalem's southeastern suburb, Jon muttered wryly, "Of course it would be Bethany: whenever Jesus stayed in Jerusalem, it was at the home of Mary, Martha, and Lazarus in Bethany!"

Since he had plotted his course ahead of time on a detailed city map, Jon had no trouble finding the address. It turned out to be a large, though not ostentatious, house constructed of typical grayish-white Jerusalem limestone, its windows framed with dark green shutters.

While locking the car, he was bothered that his pulse was accelerating. He had vowed a steely calm for his dialogue with Ben-Yosef, but apparently his heart had not gotten the message.

The door opened quickly to Jon's knock, and the robust figure of Shimon filled the doorway. "*Shalom*, Professor Weber," he said. "We're so glad that you've come!"

"*Shalom*, Shimon. Were you the gentleman who was kind enough to deliver the invitation to a student in my class?"

"I confess," he said with a grin. "The Master awaits you on the veranda upstairs. Please follow me."

While climbing the stairs, John was awash in a riptide of emotional crosscurrents. Was he foolishly alone in the headquarters of a cult? Was he venturing into a Jerusalem version of Jonestown, Waco, or Rancho Santa Fe? Or was he part of a harmless pageant in which the scene of Nicodemus visiting Jesus by night was being replayed? Or again, in the *least* possible scenario, could this all conceivably be authentic: that he was being given the incredibly rare privilege of dialoging with the returned Jesus?

Shimon brought him out to a spacious terrace and then returned downstairs. Although it was late fall, nights were still warm enough in Jerusalem, and the outdoor veranda had a splendid view of the Jordan Valley. Ben-Yosef stood up from the chaise lounge on which he had been reclining and extended a warm hand of greeting.

"I can't tell you how much I've looked forward to our meeting, Professor Weber," he said, again in perfect English. "Please take the other lounge chair."

While replying in kind to Ben-Yosef's courtesies, Jon studied firsthand the features that were now appearing in the world's newspapers and magazines. Undeniably, the man looked very much like traditional paintings of Jesus.

After exchanging brief small talk, Ben-Yosef came directly to the point. "By now, Professor Weber, you may well be puzzling between various alternatives as to who I might be. I'm quite sure you're debating the options: Ben-Yosef is a possibly dangerous cult figure. Ben-Yosef is a harmless mountebank, reenacting scenes from the life of Jesus for whatever reason. Or . . . he may be more than that."

Jon was speechless.

"Well, my friend," Ben-Yosef continued, "which is it, if I may ask? What's your opinion at this point?"

Jon replied evenly, quoting directly from John's Gospel: "'Master, I know that you are a teacher who has come from God. For no one could perform the miraculous signs you are doing if God were not with him.'"

Ben-Yosef shot a penetrating stare at Jon. Then he smiled, chuckled softly, and said, "You don't really believe that, do you?"

"No."

"But it was an apt quotation—Nicodemus's response to Jesus in John 3—a situation very much like ours this evening."

"I must commend you, a Jew, on your knowledge of the New Testament."

"But I'm a Jewish *Christian,* certainly, so this is hardly unusual."

"In any case, might I be bold enough to ask why you gave me the privilege of this conversation, when so many others—especially in the media—are screaming for interviews but don't even know how to reach you?"

"Well, that's very simple, Professor Weber—or may I please call you Jonathan? And you may call me Joshua, of course."

"Certainly. But make it Jon."

"As I told you out on the pier at Tiberias, in all of the centuries of Jesus scholarship, no one has come closer to capturing the true essence of who Jesus was than you. Your book *Jesus of Nazareth* penetrates deeply and accurately into the very Jewish soul of your subject, almost as if you had been His thirteenth disciple."

"You are very generous, sir! But to offer comments like that, you must obviously be a very accomplished Jesus scholar yourself."

"As well I should be," said Ben-Yosef with a slight smile.

Again Jon's pulse quickened, and the words were out before he could restrain them: "I . . . don't understand the 'should be.'"

"Isn't it obvious, Jon?" said Ben-Yosef, apparently staring through Jon's eyes into the innermost recesses of his mind. "But I should not presume."

Again, cold electricity tingled in Jon's extremities as his thoughts raced to deal with the impossible. No, he decided, it was not yet time to ask the ultimate question. Instead, he changed the subject and asked about Ben-Yosef's youth.

Jon expected vague information about a shadowy background, but Ben-Yosef was very forthcoming, providing a host of fresh details about his parents and ancestry that easily fit into the puzzle of his past. The sleuthing that Jeff Sheler and he had conducted proved accurate enough, including Joshua's birth in a Bethlehem basement and his youth near Nazareth. Almost modestly, however, Ben-Yosef said little about his prodigious intellectual feats as a young student, and he had tears in his eyes when telling of the deaths of his father and mother.

"But enough about me," said Ben-Yosef. "Now let's talk about your background, Jon. You were born in Hannibal, Missouri, of parents named Erhard and Trudi Weber. Her maiden name was Becker, as I recall. What a fine man your clergyman father is, and how proud he has always been of you and your accomplishments! At your confirmation, he gave you a motto verse from 1 Timothy 6:12: 'Fight the good fight of faith! Lay hold on eternal life, to which you have been called, and have professed a good profession before many witnesses.' And how you have fulfilled that verse in so many ways, Jon! You resisted the usual temptations of youth at Harvard and Johns Hopkins, thanks to your conservative Lutheran upbringing, and you didn't despair when your lovely wife, Andrea, was tragically killed in that Swiss avalanche near Davos. The Institute of Christian Origins you set up in Cambridge has been doing excellent frontier scholarship on Jesus and Christianity. And then, in becoming God's instrument in saving the faith, you met Austin Balfour Jennings and his beautiful daughter, Shannon, who also overcame the tragedies involving her mother in Ireland."

He paused, ignoring Jon's dumbfounded stare, then smiled and continued, "One of your rare missteps took place while your father was marrying you and Shannon in Hannibal, and you tried to assume the status of deity in your wedding vows! But you quickly returned to humanity, and you've both been very happily married ever since."

Jon sat riveted to the lounge chair, too stunned to speak.

"But these are only some of the highlights. I'd be glad to go into much greater detail about any year in your life, Jon, or in the lives of your parents. But that's hardly necessary." He laughed. "Obviously, you already know them!"

Jon started to reply, but he had to clear his throat to defeat the slight croaking that had seized his larynx. "That was very impressive, Joshua," he finally managed. There, he had called Ben-Yosef that name at last—intentional bravado to cover his stupefaction, Jon knew.

"Impressive, Jon? You will see greater things than this."

"Another biblical echo. All right, Joshua Ben-Yosef, the time has come to ask you the paramount question, which, of course, is this: *Are* you the reincarnation of Jesus of Nazareth—the Jesus who has

returned? Or are you not?" Jon could hardly believe that this surreal conversation was actually taking place, or that he would even
ask such an awesome—or inane—question.

Ben-Yosef smiled. "Thanks for putting it so directly," he said, moving his legs off the lounger onto the veranda floor. Sitting upright,
though bending toward Jon just a bit, he put his hands together,
faced Jon directly, and asked, "Put the case that I *am* indeed Jesus of
Nazareth who has returned: why would you have such trouble
believing this?"

Jon easily had the answer to *that* query. It was the one overriding objection anyone who knew anything about the Second
Coming of Christ would share. "It's very simple, Joshua, as you
must know," he replied. "Christians believe that the Second
Coming of Jesus will mark the end of time, the end of the world as
we know it: Judgment Day, no less! As Jesus told the high priest
Caiaphas at His hearing before the Sanhedrin: 'You will see the Son
of Man sitting at the right hand of God and coming on the clouds
of heaven.' Where are those celestial clouds, Joshua? I don't see
any of that in your own version of the Second Coming. Nor do I
hear any trumpets!"

Joshua nodded several times during Jon's statement. "Exactly
correct, Jon, and very proper theology. What's more, every syllable
of what I—what Jesus—predicted will come true."

Again Jon felt tingles of shock at his use of the first person singular. "How, then, do you reconcile the two pictures?"

"Jesus will certainly do exactly as He promised *at the end of
time.* This is not the end of time."

Jon was perplexed, thought for a moment, and then asked, "Do
you mean, then, that Jesus would stage, say, a . . . a sort of intermediate return to earth before His final return?"

"That's precisely what I mean."

"But . . . why?"

"Our Father, in His great mercy, has seen the perilous condition
of Christianity in the world today. The faith is under attack on all
fronts: Islam now has half as many believers as does Christianity,
and its militancy grows. Christians who should be defending the
faith have become lukewarm or listless due to attacks on biblical

truth by radical theologians. And this at a time when the pervading malaise of secularism hangs over a society that sneers at anything smacking of the spiritual. In the name of multiculturalism and political correctness, the Christian elements in world culture are being excluded, Christian holidays robbed of their original religious values, and the cultured despisers of the faith often in control of government and society."

Joshua stopped, a more serious, even mournful look clouding his features. "Just one local example," he resumed, spreading his arms wide. "Here, in our beloved Holy Land—the very cradle of Christianity—our faith is now only a tiny, diminishing fraction of the population. Our heavenly Father simply *had* to intervene."

Jon stared just over Joshua's right shoulder at the moonrise over the Dead Sea, trying to comprehend what he had just heard. Then he shook his head in puzzlement and said, "This may . . . all be very true, Joshua. But what's your role in all this? What do you propose to do about it?"

"The Intermediate Return, as you put it, is intended not only to firm up the faithful, but it will advance the kingdom of God very powerfully, as you will see very soon."

Ben-Yosef's rationale, Jon reflected, was cogent, even awesome. For the first time he saw some logic behind a returning Jesus. But was it all true? *No! Impossible! How could it be?*

He now issued another challenge. "How come, then, that the New Testament says nothing about an intermediate return or coming?"

"Easily answered, Jon: *most* things that have happened to our faith across two thousand years have not been specifically predicted in Scripture."

"But something supposedly as important as *this?*"

"Never make the mistake of trying to bind God through any formulas in which He 'should have' or 'would have' or 'might have' done this or that. If the Intermediate Coming had been spelled out in detail in Scripture, imagine how many would not have taken the faith seriously until proven by Jesus' next appearance. This way, the world has a further revelation, a new opportunity to receive and celebrate God's infinite grace in Jesus Christ before His final return and judgment."

"You can't be serious. God is giving humanity a second chance, then?"

"Yes, and isn't that marvelously merciful of Him!" Joshua smiled. "Although I'd hardly use the expression 'second chance,' since God has always given repeated chances for people to accept or reject His grace, even if the Intermediate Coming *is* an extraordinary instance."

Their astonishing dialogue continued far into the evening, far beyond the tea and cakes that Yohanan brought up to them on the veranda. Jon fired a fusillade of fresh queries at Joshua, all of which he answered patiently and in detail. Many of them were pointed and bold, Jon knew, but they had to be asked, and apparently Joshua was not at all offended in answering them.

"Are you the only—presumed—reincarnation of Jesus?" Jon wondered. "I know your band of twelve don't claim to be the original disciples. But are there others who will make their appearance? Like John the Baptist, perhaps?"

Joshua shook his head and said, "It's only I. This time, John's function was achieved electronically."

"Then you *were* behind the worldwide computer incursions!"

"Of course!"

"But . . . but how did you ever bring it off? The world's best cyberexperts still don't have an explanation."

Joshua smiled broadly and then laughed, the first time Jon had heard him go beyond a chuckle. "You still don't get it, do you, Jon? Remember what, ah, Jesus said, 'Having eyes, they see not. Having ears, they hear not'?"

Jon shook his head in silence for some moments. Then he asked, "In this presumed . . . replay of Jesus' great ministry, is there a cross waiting for you also?"

Joshua shook his head. "One great sacrifice for the sins of the world was sufficient. Anything more would detract from it."

Jon stooped over, propped his jaw up with forearms resting on his knees, and nodded. Finally, he asked two withering questions that should easily, he thought, puncture all of Joshua's pretenses.

"If Jesus *were* returning in any Intermediate Coming, Joshua, why wouldn't He just reappear as a grown man, rather than going through the whole babyhood and youth bit?"

"Good thinking, Jon. He might indeed have done just that. But the almighty Father, in His great mercy, arranged many parallels with Jesus' first coming in order to help authenticate His mission during His subsequent return. And you will see many more congruences than these. Now what is the other issue of concern?"

How did he even know there was another issue? Jon wondered, before asking, "All right, then. Here, I think, is the problem that dooms your campaign, Joshua: your mother, Mariam, works fine as the parallel for Mary, the mother of Jesus. But your father is Yosef Ben-Yosef. Jesus, of course, had no earthly father."

"Nor do I," said Ben-Yosef evenly.

Another stab of shock skewered Jon. "Come again?" he asked.

"I have no earthly father either."

"Would you like to . . . unpack that a bit?"

"Yosef Ben-Yosef was my distinguished *foster* father, but I always called him my 'father,' just as people supposed that Joseph was Jesus' father at His first appearance."

"How, then, were you conceived? Who was your true father?"

Joshua looked at Jon for several long moments. Then he replied, "Do you really have to ask that, Jon?" He looked upward toward the starry sky overhead and said softly, "I think you know the answer."

"But . . . but . . . how did your mother respond to this . . . this modern version of the virgin birth?"

"As Mary did of old: in humble, grateful acceptance."

"*What?* I thought your parents were Jewish, not Christian."

"I would remind you that the two are not mutually exclusive, Jon. Again, consider what happened in the case of Joseph and Mary two thousand years ago."

Jon nodded. Then, dizzying at the extraordinary revelations, he tried a new tack. "The miracles of healing attributed to you: are they physical or merely psychosomatic?"

"Some who come to me do have emotional and mental problems, which I easily cure. Twenty centuries ago, as you know, this was called 'casting out demons.' But in other cases, true physical healing certainly does take place, and not mental games. Do cancers vanish in response to any . . . voodoo psychology?"

"Well, the faith healers claim they do. But I don't believe them, of course."

"Nor should you."

"Well, then, what about the . . . ultimate miraculous sign. Have you ever raised anyone from the dead?"

"No. Not yet."

"Does that mean that you plan to?"

"That will be up to our heavenly Father."

"All right, then, but we hardly need so extraordinary a sign. Why not try a simple one?" Jon pulled a pen out of his shirt pocket, laid it on a small table between them, and said, "Would you be kind enough to make that pen disappear?"

Joshua shook his head sadly and said, "I'm a little disappointed in you, Jon. I thought—"

"Agreed! I apologize!" Jon quickly broke in, embarrassed at the naïveté of his challenge. "I was harking back to my freshman year at Harvard, when my roommate told me why he had lost his faith. He said, 'One day I got down on my knees and said, *Please, God, if you exist, make this pencil disappear. I won't tell a soul, and then I'll become a believer for the rest of my life!* But the pencil didn't vanish: *ergo,* there is no God.'"

"Ah yes," said Joshua, "the old put-God-to-the-test-to-see-if-He-passes challenge! Well, we may laughingly dismiss the pencil proof, but there's nothing wrong with understanding the miraculous as the true sign of God's presence." He smiled and looked directly at Jon. "Therefore, dear Professor Weber, let's go back to your freshman year at college: would you really like to see your pen disappear?"

While Jon fumbled for a reply, Joshua picked up the pen and said, "But that's a gilded Mont Blanc you have here, and they're expensive. If I made it disappear, you'd be out about $250, wouldn't you? Foolish! So, how about this . . ."

Ben-Yosef placed the pen back on the table, pointed to the wall of the house, and said, "On your way . . ." The pen shot across the veranda, hit the wall, and dropped onto the tile floor.

The small hairs at the back of Jon's scalp bristled.

"Now, Jon, go pick it up. Isn't that better than losing so valuable a pen?"

Jon's head was whirling. He stood up to retrieve his pen and then paced the veranda, locked into deep thought. He could find nothing theological or even logical to contradict the possibility that Joshua was genuine, that Joshua was Jesus. Still, he was not fully persuaded—the claim was just too bizarre for that—but his respect for Joshua had increased dramatically.

It was now very late and time for him to leave. As they walked down from the veranda, Jon could not resist another biblical quote. He thanked Joshua for their time together, looked directly into his sapphire eyes, and asked, "So then, *are* you He who should come, or do we look for another?" John the Baptist had told his disciples to ask that very question of Jesus.

Jon knew, of course, what Joshua would say. With a smile and penetrating stare, he replied: "Tell Jonathan Weber: The blind receive sight, the lame walk, the deaf hear. *Don't be faithless, but believe.*"

At their apartment that night, Jon reported everything to Shannon, having first turned on a tape recorder so that he would not forget a syllable of the most extraordinary conversation he had ever had in his life. Her eyes opened progressively wider in the telling, her hand covering her mouth when it came to the pen episode.

When he had finished, she shook her head and said, "Jon, unless you've taken leave of your wits, I think it's high time for you to get over your skepticism. I really think—I truly do—that Joshua most probably *is* the returned Jesus!"

Sleep eluded Jon for a long time that night. Shannon's comment ricocheted around in his mind. What if she were right? Then his "Nicodemus call" on Joshua Ben-Yosef was not merely a nocturnal chat, but a visit with ultimate, even cosmic significance. Still, if that were the case, how come everything seemed comparatively ordinary in his conversation with Ben-Yosef—well, certainly not ordinary, but perhaps not extraordinary enough? Where were the trumpets? The clouds of heaven?

Then again, like most Christians, he was likely expecting too much, and the celestial fireworks were hardly necessary if this were in fact an intermediate coming. No trumpets had sounded the first time around either.

Sleep finally approached after Jon made one safe decision; namely, to make *no* decision on Joshua—to postpone even the beginnings of any decision to a future as remote as possible. It was escapist, of course, and not very heroic. But it was soporific.

His last memory before falling asleep, however, was of a flying pen. Beyond all debate, this did seem to be a token of the supernatural. And he did not have to rely on possibly garbled reports. He had seen it with his own eyes.

TEN

The next morning, Jon's first thought was of a flying pen. Had he really seen that weird phenomenon? *Was* it a crossover from another dimension, a sign of the supernatural? Absent other explanations, possibly. Did it prove that Joshua was Jesus? According to Shannon, quite probably. And he?

Jon got out of bed and walked over to the dresser. There it was, the traveling Mont Blanc, lying unobtrusively next to his keys and wallet. He picked up the pen a little gingerly, as if the thing were somehow radioactive. The gold crown on the cap now had a slight abrasion on it—as might result when a flying pen hits a wall.

An entirely new vector of thought suddenly seized him. There was the supernatural, and then again, there was the supernatural. It all hinged on the cause. And that cause? Was it divine . . . or, perhaps . . . demonic?

Jon hated to go down that route: Joshua as satanic. For one thing, it was such a hackneyed theme in American novels and movies, whether for the secular or the religious market. You want a best-seller? Then simply invoke the demonic supernatural. *Rosemary's Baby* or *The Exorcist* or the Stephen King novels had their even more exaggerated counterparts in Christian fiction, especially for the evangelical market. Involve demons by the thousands or millions, as in the Left Behind series, or one by one, as in the Frank Peretti books, and your readership will instantly materialize. A multitude of readers, obviously, love to be terrified, a masochism of the masses that makes the satanic-scare books thrive. But this was reality, Jon mused, not fiction.

On the other hand, successful fiction often reflects fact, he knew well enough, and just because some authors involved the demonic in their novels was no reason to discount the possibility that the demonic did in fact cause the supernatural in Joshua Ben-Yosef's case. The scare writers could be right after all, especially since Jesus Himself predicted that there would be satanic imitators of Himself, and there were gospel references to the devil appearing as an angel of light. Joshua Ben-Satan? Jon shuddered at the direction his thoughts were taking him.

Before the flying pen, Jon had never personally witnessed anything incontestably miraculous. Would he now have to craft new tools of logic in dealing with the supernatural?

Grappling with all the options, he finally managed to isolate one clear conclusion: he found it extremely improbable that the first potential breakthroughs from the supernatural dimension into his own life should have come from the negative rather than the positive source. He recalled how, in his childhood, he had comforted himself after seeing a horror movie at too tender an age: the cross would always stop Dracula in his tracks, he had told himself.

Later on, in more adult terms, he had reasoned that while the demonic should never be denied, any miraculous incursions from that quarter should hardly be expected. For if they did take place, Satan would have defeated his own campaign by proving that a supernatural dimension existed after all. And whether or not it did was the most basic issue in religion or philosophy.

Moreover, if Joshua's healings were genuine and miraculous in fact—and the jury was still out on that—could something as positive and helpful as these be ascribed to the demonic? Jon knew that some would say yes: satanic imitators might try to deceive the faithful by such means. Yet there were no real instances in the Old or New Testament of this actually happening: satanic trickery was always exposed. And since the devil was not some second god on a par with the first, but very much "God's devil," as Martin Luther put it, anything supernatural with a positive result—like true miracles of healing—should have a divine origin. If Joshua's miracles were genuine, then he could hardly be Satan's minion.

What was he, then? A deluded Jesus imitator, like someone who believed himself to be Napoleon and went about acting the role? An outrageous liar, carrying out some demonic plan for his own evil purpose? Or, on the other hand, an ethically motivated leader, trying to do good in imitation of the Christ he admired? No, that wouldn't work: an ethically motivated Jesus imitator would never have presented himself as the personally returned Jesus.

So Jon was back to the three clear alternatives so starkly presented by C. S. Lewis: Joshua, like Jesus, was either a crazed delusionary, a perverse liar . . . or precisely who he claimed to be: the returned Jesus of Nazareth.

Jon was hunkered down with a magnifying glass, examining a half dozen copies of the Sepphoris mosaic spread out across his desk in various sizes and contrasts, in both black-and-white and color. On the left side of his desk was a lexicon of ancient Hebrew, which he consulted from time to time. To the right lay a pad of yellow legal paper, festooned with writing, lines crossed out, arrows, and blotches. *I've almost cracked this,* he thought, *but the Hebrew lettering uses several abbreviations I'm still not sure about.* His apprehension building, he planned to meet with Mordecai Feldman early the next day.

In Feldman's office at Hebrew University, Jon said, "This has been fun, Mort, a very pleasant change of pace—my first real chance to get away from this Joshua business!" Then he laid three items atop his desk. One was a sharp color photo of the mosaic, the second was his reconstruction of the text:

ו יְמֻת וְהוּא וַיחוה
יְחוּר וְהוּא יִשׁוּב
שְׁתִים כְּעמים דוד אַל הֲנוּכב

The third was a computer version of that text in conventional Hebrew lettering:

י ימות והוא יחיה
יסור והוא ישוב
שתים פעמים דוד אל הכוכב

Feldman studied the three documents carefully. Then he nodded and said, "I think you've got it, Jon. Have you translated it into English yet?"

"I'm close, but I'm still working out a couple of words. The last nut to crack, of course, is the calligraphy and its era, which will tell us whether or not the mosaic is contemporary with the synagogue, although it certainly looks as if it is."

"The problem here is the mosaic vehicle, of course," said Feldman. "If this were a normal inscription, the shape of the letters wouldn't be forced by the geometry of the tiny stones, the . . . the . . ."

"The tessera," Jon offered.

"The tessera, yes." Feldman now pulled over a ladder and climbed to an upper shelf in the fortress of books that enclosed his office from floor to ceiling on three sides. Pulling out a large tome and blowing the dust off its top, he said, "So let's see if Wassermann will help us."

"Oh-ho, you have Wassermann? Splendid!"

Hebrew Mosaics in the Ancient Near East—300 B.C.E. to 500 C.E. by Isidore Z. Wassermann was nicely divided by chapters into eight centuries, as suggested in the title. The text was full of mosaics from synagogue floors, private homes of the wealthy, public buildings, and tombs. Jon held a photograph of the Sepphoris inscription next to all mosaics with lettering while Feldman slowly turned the pages. The task was not as arduous as Jon had feared, since not even 10 percent of the illustrations contained lettering of any kind.

After wading through eight hundred years of Jewish artistry with tiny tessera, they returned several times to specimens from the first century B.C. and first century A.D. as the closest parallels to the Sepphoris inscription. Feldman finally looked up and said, "All things considered, don't you find a 100 B.C.E. to 100 C.E. horizon for our mosaic appropriate?"

"I do indeed, Mort. Note the similar shapes of those *yods* and *alephs*. Besides which, most of the other mosaics at Sepphoris also date from that time frame, when Antipas rebuilt the city. And, of course, the mosaic was found at the same elevation as that first-century synagogue floor."

"I'd say that's a double indication that our piece is about two thousand years old."

"Well, our puzzle is partially solved, then," said Jon, "except, of course, for the meaning of the text."

"Exactly. There's no subject! Do let me know what it says."

Jon's public symposia at Hebrew University were now so cluttered with questions about Joshua Ben-Yosef that he did something unprecedented. Opening his lecture one morning, he said: "I regret to make an announcement that I never thought would be necessary. In fact, it's against all principles of the free inquiry on which academe thrives. But I have no choice: in order for us to complete this symposium, I will entertain no further questions or comments about Joshua Ben-Yosef, only those relating to the historical Jesus of Nazareth."

A drone of discussion filled the hall, but enough hunching of shoulders and raised palms among students to demonstrate that they understood. Privately, however, Jon exempted himself from his own restriction. He had many—too many—questions about Joshua. He would continue asking them and continue seeking answers.

There were so many queries he should have raised with Joshua in their meeting in Bethany, he now realized. Why had he not gotten details on how the worldwide cyberincursion was accomplished? Or asked about Joshua's future plans, or hundreds of other items? One evening supplied only so much available time, of course, but he must see Joshua again, if possible.

When he returned to their apartment on French Hill, Shannon declared, "I just learned that Joshua is coming to Jerusalem again tomorrow morning, and I want to go out and see him. And Jon, whether you like it or not, I'm going!"

"By all means!" he replied enthusiastically. "I'd go myself if I didn't have to teach."

Barely a mile from Jerusalem, Shannon intercepted Joshua and his entourage as they rode donkeys—yes, donkeys—up the valley road from Bethany. Cheering crowds were lining the roadsides. They were not on the main route to Jerusalem, but on the lower trail through the Kidron Valley that finally reached a site below the southeastern walls of the Old City known as Silwan. Here Joshua and his twelve followers dismounted.

Shannon ran up to Shimon, hoping he would remember her, and asked where they were heading. Before he could reply, Joshua himself walked over to her and exclaimed, with his blazing blue eyes and serene smile, "What a pleasant surprise, Mrs. Weber! Please join us as we wade through Hezekiah's Tunnel!"

"Are you . . . are you really going to do that?" she stammered, not really caring how banal her query sounded.

"Why not? There's less than a foot of water at this time of year, and you can carry your sneakers."

"Well . . . I'd be delighted!" she enthused, while thinking, *How did he ever know the word* sneakers?

Shannon recalled that the tunnel was the only site in Jerusalem that looks exactly the same today as when good King Hezekiah constructed it 2,700 years ago. The king wanted to supply Jerusalem with water from the Gihon Spring in the Kidron Valley, the very place where Solomon had been anointed king to succeed his father, David. Here it was that Hezekiah constructed his remarkable 1,750-foot tunnel with workmen chiseling the watercourse out of solid rock at both ends to meet somewhere in the middle.

Shannon took off her shoes and waded into the cool waters just behind Joshua and the Twelve as they trudged through the tunnel to the Pool of Siloam on the other side—the reservoir into which the waters of the Gihon spilled. While sloshing through the still-flowing stream of water, she couldn't resist the thought: *Wait till I tell Jon about this! For once I got there first with the best!*

Halfway through the tunnel, they came to the place where Hezekiah's two teams of workmen, tunneling from both ends, met each other. With their primitive yet effective engineering, they were off only five feet laterally. *Not bad for the 700s B.C.*, thought Shannon.

Joshua himself threaded his way back to make sure Shannon noticed how the pick marks of the two teams of workmen cut the rock at different angles that intersected just at the dividing point.

"I'm not sure I see where that is. Here?" she pointed.

Joshua took her finger and moved it fourteen inches to the left. "No, here," he said.

"Oh . . . I see it now. Thanks for pointing that out!" she said, tears of excitement filling her eyes that Joshua had showed her such attention. He smiled briefly, his eyes meeting hers so pleasantly, and then he returned to the head of the procession.

Finally they reached the ancient Pool of Siloam. Again Joshua seemed to be a paragon of solicitude, making sure that his entourage recognized the spot where Hezekiah's famous sign, the earliest Hebrew inscription of any length, had originally been placed.

"Unfortunately," he explained, "the inscription stone has been pried out of its niche, as you can see. It's now in the Archaeological Museum at Istanbul. Someday, it really must be returned here."

He made sure his group was listening—as if that were any problem—and smiled again when he saw Shannon. Once more his azure eyes seemed to penetrate hers. Her pulse was wildly aflutter, and she could not forget the delightful tactile shock when he had touched her finger in the tunnel. It seemed wrong to her, of course: she remained totally committed to Jon. But this Israeli—quite apart from any superior credentials—was far more than what any American teenager would call a hunk. Not only was he a superb demonstration of the male species, but he seemed also to exude a unique magnetism that cast a spell on anyone in his presence. Begin with this, but then ask, what if he were all this and *more* than a man? Shannon still had trouble truly comprehending the latter, though it was always at the edge of her horizon.

The group paused for a moment around the muddy waters of the Pool of Siloam, the famous reservoir where Jesus had cured the blind man, and continued climbing up a stone staircase toward the walls of Jerusalem. Shannon hoped that the waters of Siloam in Jesus' day were a little cleaner and bluer.

At the street circling the south wall of the Old City of Jerusalem, Joshua's cavalcade turned left and continued upward toward the Dung Gate. Along the roadside, and dangerously close to oncoming traffic, sat a beggar on a soiled green blanket he had spread out on the sidewalk. He was croaking out a plaintive song as he accompanied himself on an ancient lyre, a pathetic musical performance for which he awaited contributions from anyone within earshot. But the dish in front of him contained only two coins. He turned toward Joshua's advancing group with a glassy stare, eyes milky and pupils rolling upward aimlessly.

"He's been begging here for the last seven years," an Arab street merchant told Shannon, over a cart laden with soft drinks, candy, and curios. "The poor guy is blind as a bat." Clearly, tourists must have taught the vendor American jargon.

Joshua now stopped in front of the beggar, greeted him, and asked, "Do you know who I am?"

The man turned toward the voice and seemed puzzled. Finally he replied, "No, sir. I can't see you."

"Perhaps you shall," said Joshua. "Do you believe that our Lord God is able to cure your blindness?"

For a moment the man was speechless. Then he wheezed, coughed, and finally mumbled, "Well . . . well . . . I guess so. God . . . He can do anything, can't He?"

"Just so," said Joshua. "Now go down to the Pool of Siloam and wash your eyes."

"Wha . . . why should I do that?"

Joshua smiled patiently and replied, "It's really quite simple, my friend: do you wish to receive your sight? Or remain blind?"

Shannon saw the beggar's jaw drop, almost in tandem with her own. A little more dialogue was necessary to convince the beggar that this could be for real. Finally he rose shakily to his feet. Shimon and several others in the entourage supported his arms and guided him as the group now walked back down the stairs to the Pool of Siloam.

Eyes tightly shut, the beggar was led to a spot at the edge of the pool, where he knelt down. "Ah . . . what am I supposed to do now?"

"Wash your eyes," said Joshua gently.

The man thrust two tremulous hands into the water and splashed it across his face and eyes several times.

Moments passed. Someone gave him a towel to dry his face. No one said a word.

"I . . . I can see nothing!" the beggar finally cried.

A loud murmur filled the crowd. All eyes switched from the beggar to Joshua.

"It would help if you opened your eyelids," Joshua advised, with a modest grin.

Slowly, the blind beggar popped one eye open, then the other. He shook his head rapidly from side to side. An instant smile bloomed across his face. He looked left, right, up, down, and shrieked, "I can *see*! Bless God, I can *see*!"

He stood up, laughed, heaved with exultation, and twirled about with arms spread wide as if he were a teenage ballerina. Then he stopped abruptly and looked around. "Who?" he stammered. "Who did this for me?"

"Joshua Ben-Yosef," several replied, pointing him out.

The beggar stared, walked over to Joshua, and asked, "Are you . . . you are the one?"

Joshua nodded, smiled, and said, "Give God the glory!"

"Rabbi, Rabbi!" he said, brimming with joy. "What can . . . what can I say?" Then he stooped down and wrapped his stubby hands around Joshua's ankles. "You . . . you are the Holy One of Israel!" he gasped. "I . . . I thank God! I thank *you*!"

Joshua gently lifted him up with both hands, cradled an arm across his hunched shoulders, and said, "Go your way. Bless the Almighty! Your faith has made you whole."

Shannon could barely breathe. She felt lightheaded and giddy, dizzy with awe. The people surrounding Joshua began praising him, many on their knees, some singing hymns, a symphony of waving arms and shouts of admiration. "It is the Lord!" many cried. "It is the Lord Himself!" The once-blind man, no longer bereft of sight, was embraced by everyone within reach—most with tears cascading down their cheeks—as he continued whooping with delight.

It was too much for Shannon. She, too, fell to her knees, hands clasped, head bowed in reverence, eyes brimming with tears. Joshua stopped, walked over to her, laid his hand on her head, and whispered, "You, too, daughter, will be free of your problem. Those dark dreams of yours . . . they will cease." He caressed her cheek lovingly and moved on.

A feeling of incredible peace came over Shannon, a soft feather-bed of faith displacing the demons of doubt that sometimes tormented her. She was not even surprised that Joshua knew about her occasional nightmares, although a month earlier she would have responded, "*What?* How in the world did you ever know that!"

Now she looked up through blurry eyes to see Joshua and the crowd moving back up the stony flight of stairs. She had an indescribable yearning to follow them and suppressed it only with extreme effort. It was late in the afternoon, and Jon would be wondering "where in blazes" she had been.

While returning to where she had parked the Peugeot on a road leading up to the Old City from the Kidron Valley, she shook her head slowly and asked, "Did this really happen?" No one answered her. Finally she smiled, nodded, and replied, "Yes . . . it did happen! And this is the day that changed my life!"

When she let herself into their apartment, Jon stormed out of his study and demanded, "Just where in blazes have you been, Shannon?"

She only smiled serenely and replied, "I . . . I don't quite know how to tell you this, Jon. And I don't want to shock you, but . . ." She stopped and groped for words.

"But what, Shannon?"

Twice he had called her "Shannon" in demanding tones—the first time in their marriage—rather than "Shannon dear," "darling," "sweetheart," "honey," or some other term of endearment.

"Okay," she said, fighting for composure against the emotional maelstrom building inside. "I spent the afternoon with . . ."

"With *whom*?" Jon barked.

"I . . . I spent the afternoon with . . . with our Lord and Savior, Jesus Christ." She started sobbing, but her tears seemed born of happiness, not grief.

Jon simply stared at her for a long moment, eyes bulging in disbelief, mouth agape. Would he ever even speak again, she began to wonder.

"You did *what*?" he finally bellowed. "Should I look in the yellow pages for a psychiatrist? Are you okay, Shannon, or have you lost it?"

"Come, darling, sit down, and I'll tell you the whole story." While a mask of shock continued to warp Jon's features, Shannon gave a detailed report of all that had happened at the Gihon, Hezekiah's Tunnel, and the Pool of Siloam.

Jon seemed to take it all in with something less than sympathy. His eyes narrowed when she told of Joshua touching her, but he seemed most interested in the blind beggar who had regained his sight.

"Who was that fellow, Shannon? What was his name? His address?"

"I . . . how do I know?"

"Well, you should!" he snapped. "If we're going to claim another miracle here, let's check it out! Why didn't you get a handle on his background? Was he really legit, or maybe Joshua's stooge, faking blindness so that he could be 'cured'? Maybe this was an Israeli version of those wonderful healing services in the Bible Belt: 'cripples' carrying their crutches through the back door of the auditorium to avoid being seen earlier, then hobbling pathetically on them until the altar call, when they get healed and throw away their crutches in triumph!"

"This was no fake healing, Jon."

"But how do you know that? See, this is why I wish you'd gotten into that fellow's background."

"*Look,* Mr. Unreasonable, I didn't know that I was assigned as a detective in this case! I suppose I should have gotten the guy's fingerprints, blood type, DNA, social security number, and sexual preferences!"

"Ah . . . okay, Shannon. Sorry. I—"

"But I did learn from a vendor on the sidewalk next to him that the fellow has been 'blind as a bat' for at least seven years."

Jon paused for a moment. "You did? Hmmm, that could be a break for us."

"For you maybe, not for us. I'm convinced by what I saw, Jon. How in the world could Joshua have known about my bad dreams, for example?"

"I . . . don't really know, Shannon. But then again, everyone has bad dreams at times . . ."

"Okay, Doubting Thomas. But add what I saw today to all the other reports of Joshua's miracles and healings. Then also add the other impossible things Joshua has done—his fantastic linguistic abilities, his total knowledge about you, about us. And again, the final clincher is that he could never have staged all this: born in Bethlehem, raised in Nazareth, et cetera. You know the list: we've been over it many times. What in the world does it take to convince you, Jon? For sure, your confirmation verse should have been: 'You have eyes to see, but you see not.'"

"Well, I don't think—"

"Exactly! You don't think! Here something . . . cosmic is taking place right under your skeptical nose, and you're blowing it! If I were Joshua, I wouldn't have any more patience with you. You're blinder than the man Joshua healed today!"

Angrily Jon started to retort, but then he stopped abruptly. He walked over to the sliding glass door to their balcony, shoved it open, and stepped outside. A warm southern breeze seemed to waft up from the galaxy of lights in Jerusalem below, a beautiful sight to anyone not wrestling with a dilemma. Jon hoped the fresh air might clear his thinking.

Shannon was about to join him on the balcony but thought better of it. There are times when a man has to be alone. Instead, she bowed her head and prayed to the man who had changed her life that afternoon, asking him to cure the blindness also of her husband.

Several times in recent weeks, Jon had in fact dealt with the possibility that Joshua could be the returned Jesus. The mounting evidence, after all, was very powerful. Each time, however, he had fought shy of going down that path. And why was that?

Several honest reasons, but among them was one that pained him deeply. What's more, it showed him to be petty and unprofessional in the extreme. It was this: if Joshua were Jesus in fact, then the "prophecy pack" was right after all, including the dimmest bulb in their manic marquee, Melvin Morris Merton. After a hundred miscues, could the man have it right at last? The law of averages almost demanded it.

Jon clenched his fist, pounded the metal railing of the balcony, and went back inside the apartment.

Shannon hurried over to him. "I'm sorry, darling. I shouldn't have been so rough on you. I promise to—"

"No, that's okay, Shannon. You . . . had reason enough. But would you at least come with me tomorrow morning and point out where the blind man and the merchant spoke on that sidewalk? I want to ask a few questions."

"Of course! Why not?"

Jon did not teach on Tuesdays and Thursdays, and it was on a bright and crystal Thursday morning that Shannon drove him over to the southern wall of the Old City above Silwan, parking their car near the Dung Gate. They walked downhill on the sidewalk to the spot where the blind beggar had sat.

"Well, this is the place," said Shannon, pointing to the open sidewalk. "But he's obviously not going to be sitting here begging, now that he can see again."

"Yes, but where's the vendor with the cart full of trinkets and soft drinks?"

Shannon shrugged her shoulders. "Not here either, it seems."

"Dang!" muttered Jon. "Show me again where everything happened yesterday."

"You mean you want to slosh through Hezekiah's Tunnel?"

"No, no, not that. But let's take the stairs down to the Pool of Siloam."

When they reached the bottom of the stone staircase, Shannon re-created the scene for Jon, showing him where Joshua and the blind man had stood, as well as where she had observed everything. "You really should have been here, Jon. It was the most moving experience of my entire life."

Jon frowned, shook his head, and said, "But why couldn't Joshua simply have cured the man on the roadside above? Why have everyone trudge down here to the Pool of Siloam—unless this muddy water is magic?"

"I can think of two reasons."

"And they are?"

"If you are a biblical scholar, Jon, I think you know them both. One, it's a parallel to what Jesus did in healing the blind man of John 9—and you know how many parallels are showing up between Jesus' ministry and Joshua's."

Jon nodded.

"And two, just like the prophets in the Old Testament, Jesus also used physical items quite often in His ministry. Water for baptism, bread and fish in feeding the five thousand, a fish to deliver a coin for taxes, bread and wine for the Last Supper, some—"

"Okay, point taken. The Pool of Siloam falls into that category, I guess. Well, let's get back to the car."

While walking back along the south wall of Jerusalem, Shannon suddenly cried, "There he is! The street vendor!"

"Great!" Jon grinned. "It must be warm enough to sell beverages."

They ambled over to the street merchant, who was busily laying out cans of Coke, Sprite, Seven Up, Schweppes, and orange juice onto his aging cart. Under a white canopy emblazoned with blue lettering declaring that this was "Saladin's Store" were shelves full of chewing gum, candy bars, toiletries, watches, and, of course, T-shirts and other tourist bric-a-brac. When the darkly tanned, walrus-mustachioed proprietor had finished opening his portable warehouse, he clapped a dark red fez onto his balding scalp and rubbed his hands together. Then he smiled at Jon and Shannon and said, "So, my friends, I'm ready for business, may Allah be praised! What do you like?"

Shannon was about to plunge ahead with questions, but Jon gently touched her arm. There was the matter of proper protocol and the necessarily oblique approach.

"Are you *the* Saladin of the South Wall here?" This, Jon thought, was more diplomatic than "the Dude of the Dung Gate."

"Well, yes, s*ayyid*," he replied. "But—"

"You're something of a legend in Jerusalem. Been selling here for years, have you?"

"Oh, yes, yes. Over ten years," he said, proudly.

"At this location?"

He nodded. "The best in Jerusalem: tourists have to go through Dung Gate to get to the Wailing Wall—most of them, anyway."

They purchased a couple of Cokes and casually explored Saladin's wares. With wicked humor, Jon held up a ghastly velvet drop cloth embroidered with the image of a literally openhearted Jesus. "This might be a nice present for your dad," he said.

Since her father was an agnostic, Shannon merely glared at him.

Repaying him in kind, she pointed to a mother-of-pearl model of the Dome of the Rock—one of the holiest sites in Islam—and suggested, "Wouldn't this look great on your father's desk in Hannibal!"

"Oh," said Jon, ignoring her. "Here's a T-shirt for our next archaeological campaign." He purchased two shirts, white with orange lettering reading "I Dig Jerusalem."

Finally he winked at Shannon, who picked up the cue and asked, "By the way, Saladin, I think you were here yesterday when Joshua Ben-Yosef talked to that blind man, weren't you?"

"Oh yes, yes . . . now I remember where I see you before. You wanted to know about the blind man, true?"

"Yes. I'm amazed that you remember that. There were so many people in the crowd."

"Oh, but so few . . . beautiful people," he said, whipping off his fez and bowing gallantly.

"Well, *shukran,* kind sir," she replied with a little blush.

"How long have you known the blind man, Saladin?" Jon could now put it directly.

"Oh . . . he begs here for the last six or seven years. At first I didn't want him around. He's Jewish, after all, and even if he were Arab, who would want someone like that next to you? Bad for business."

"What changed your mind?"

Saladin smiled. "I . . . in the name of Allah the Merciful and Compassionate, I finally took pity on the poor man, blind and all. And his singing and his playing were so bad that people stopped and stared at him. They'd toss him a couple of coins and then notice my shop here!"

They chuckled. Jon then grew serious again and asked, "Are you sure he was blind, Saladin?"

The vendor looked puzzled. "I . . . I not understand . . . don't understand your question," he said.

"I mean, how do you *know* he was blind?"

Still, Saladin looked bewildered. "He *had* to be blind, sitting here and begging all those years. Oh, I understand. You wonder if he could have told a lie about blindness in order to get sympathy from people?"

"Exactly."

"I also thought about that when he first came here. But those milky eyes of his, his stumbling, running into things . . . once I had to pull him out of the road to save his life. There is no question."

Shannon looked knowingly at Jon, who avoided her stare.

"You say that he was a Jew, Saladin?" asked Jon. "Isn't that unusual? A Jew begging in the Old City of Jerusalem, which is mostly Arab?"

"Maybe. But Jews are here, too, of course, and—I tell you again—this is best spot in Jerusalem for tourists."

"Do you know his name?"

"Schmuel."

"Schmuel what? What's his last name?"

"I never call him anything but Schmuel. But I did know his last name once. And what was it . . . ?" He thought for some moments, then shook his head.

"Do you know where he came from?" asked Shannon, to Jon's smiling approval.

"He wasn't from Jerusalem. He was Israeli from—where was it?—Haifa, I think."

"Did you see him after Joshua Ben-Yosef talked to him?" Shannon continued. "Do you know what happened down at the Pool of Siloam?"

Saladin nodded and grinned. "I never saw anything like it in my life! First there is this big crowd shouting blessings to Ben-Yosef! And then comes Schmuel: he could actually see now! Oh, how he was laughing and singing—better this time than when he was blind."

"Did he walk over and thank you for attending to him all these years?" Jon wondered, hoping to expose the beggar's chicanery.

"No, he didn't. That got me angry at first," replied Saladin, "after all I did for him. Then"— he laughed—"I forgot he had been blind! So I run after him and yell, 'Hey, Schmuel! Don't you say hello to an old friend?' He stops and turns around. 'Saladin?' he calls out. 'Saladin, is that really you?' When I tell him yes, he puts his arms around me and has tears running down his face. I . . . I admit it: I was crying too! So great a wonder it was! Then he thanks me for the years I took care of him. He even promises to make it up to me somehow."

"Well . . . what do you think happened to your friend?" asked Jon. "How did he get his sight back?"

"Who knows? It had to be . . . Joshua Ben-Yosef somehow. Oh!" He suddenly brightened. "I think I remember something about Schmuel's last name now. It had something to do with helicopters."

"Helicopters?"

"Yes, every time one flew over, he'd hear it and say, 'I wonder if that one was made by my relatives.' He told me the name of the company, but I've forgotten it."

"Was it Bell? Or Grumman? Boeing?" asked Jon.

The vendor shook his head.

"How about McDonnel? Bristol? Sikorsky?"

"That's it . . . that last one, Sikorsky—Schmuel Sikorsky."

"Excellent," said Jon. "Do you know where he lives?"

"No. No. Not at all."

"Well, if you do see him again, please find out where I can reach him. Here's my card . . . please get in touch with me. I'm a writer, and I'd love to do a story on how a blind man could see again." Along with his card, Jon slipped a twenty-dollar bill into Saladin's hand.

"*Shukran*! I thank you, *sayyid!*" he responded enthusiastically. "Most surely I will do that! *Salaam!*"

ELEVEN

Nothing was really the same anymore, Jon mused, as he fought to keep up with communications in his office at Hebrew University. Things were both better and worse. Even technological progress, like the e-mail he was answering, turned out to be two-edged. To be sure, e-mail was immensely handy—how many overseas seminars had been arranged for him without lifting a phone, pasting a stamp, or spending a penny? But at what cost? E-mail now drained an extra hour or two from each working day, and that was with a secretary in Cambridge and another in Jerusalem weeding out the spam, the ads, the free offers, the virus warnings, the virus warning retractions, the endless anecdotes, and the inevitable jokes—however well intended.

And the mail list in his in-box never seemed to go away: always, always a stack to be answered when he had the time.

Travel was not the same anymore either, thanks to Osama bin Laden and Al Qaeda. Security personnel—some of whom seemed to have come from another planet—responded woodenly to computer selections for further screening of passengers. How often at airports he would see a frail old lady, hobbling on a cane, asked to spread her arms for additional wanding, while burly males in the prime of their lives breezed past, thanks to political correctness and the sin of racial profiling. Never mind that nineteen out of nineteen hijackers who assaulted the United States on 9/11 came from the same racial-ethnic origins.

Nothing was the same anymore in Christianity either. While world terrorism had an ecumenical effect in drawing various faiths closer together, it polarized others—like Jon's own Lutheran Church—Missouri Synod. That conservative church body had one of its biggest intramural fights ever over whether or not it was proper for one of its clergy to offer prayer in Yankee Stadium on the same platform as representatives of other faiths. Those with a rigid mind-set claimed this act had betrayed the faith, but Jon thought any Christian should have the right to pray anywhere under any circumstances.

But far more significant issues were rocking the ship of the church. Roman Catholics had the horrendous problem of priest pedophilia to surmount, while Protestants wrangled over the role of women in ministry, what forms of liturgy to use, how to deal with homosexuality, the charismatic movement, those fixated on prophecy, and the like.

But nothing split world Christianity more than the Joshua Ben-Yosef phenomenon. Jon now saw that the faith, like ancient Gaul, had divided itself into three parts: a strong and growing third was convinced that Jesus of Nazareth had truly returned, a middle third thought Joshua an impostor, and the final third was undecided. A fissure was opening even in his own marriage: Shannon was living with a new joy that Jesus had returned, while he himself was somewhere between the skeptical and the undecided.

The trends, however, indicated that the division into thirds would soon break down. From public opinion polls, religious magazine surveys, and theological conferences, the army of the convinced was growing—at the expense of both the "undecideds" and the "Joshua-impostor" segments. To his dismay, Jon found himself serving as something of a spiritual lightning rod for the entire issue. Much of the Christian world trusted him because of his quasi-heroic role in the Rama crisis, and he was now absolutely unable to handle the volume of correspondence, e-mails, and faxes pouring into his offices in both Cambridge and Jerusalem.

Rod Swenson of MIT saved the day by establishing a web site for Jon that was constantly updated with the latest information on Joshua. "It's the least I can do for not yet solving the Jesus Bulletin incursion, Jon," he told him, using something so primitive as a transatlantic phone call. "Just feed us your information as you want it to appear. We'll take it from there and continually update your web site."

"Thanks much, Rod," he replied. "Do you suppose we could do

this thing on, say, two levels? Most would get the general information, but a very select list would get additional—and very confidential—detail, such as yourself, Jeff Sheler at *U.S. News*, another friend who has the pope's ear at the Vatican, and, of course, the members of our ICO?"

"Easily done. Just send me a list of your special URLs and e-mail addresses. What's your ICO, by the way?"

"The Institute of Christian Origins."

"Oh, yeah, I remember now. The big theological think tank that handled the Rama crisis, right? The spiritual geniuses who helped you save Christianity?"

"All correct except the final verb, Rod. And thanks, good friend!"

After hanging up, Jon pondered the ethics of involving only one media editor in his select list, rather than the entire coterie. But Sheler had been the first to cooperate with him in the early stages of the Joshua affair, and they had been exchanging information for months. Jon was sure he could rely on Sheler whenever he imparted something truly speculative or confidential: he knew it would not be published. Later, it might indeed show up—with Jon's permission—in a book Sheler was already writing on Joshua Ben-Yosef.

For several months now, Sheler had been reporting to Jon on the intelligence his colleagues had been gathering in Israel, especially on Joshua's youth and background, while Jon had reciprocated in sharing his and Shannon's eyewitness encounters. His Nicodemus visit, for example, made Sheler almost want to hop the next plane to Israel.

While he did not make that particular trip, hundreds of thousands of others were preparing to. For those convinced that Joshua was Jesus, this ultimate pilgrimage seemed almost mandatory, a once-in-a-lifetime—no, once-in-a-millennium opportunity to see God in human form and receive His blessing now in time, and certainly for eternity. If the Creator was gracious enough to grant humanity an intermediate coming of His Son, it would be eternal folly to pass up this opportunity—extraordinary, immense, unparalleled, and cosmic as it certainly was. To see Jesus Himself—people would die for the chance!

At first, the international travel industry rejoiced over the tourist bonanza developing for Israel, a perfect antidote to the many months of terrorism and bloodshed between Palestinians and Israelis. Soon, however, that same industry threw up its collective hands in dismay. Despite the precarious nature of the peace that seemed to have descended on the Holy Land, all flights to Israel on regular carriers were booked solid for the next five months, and hotel reservations were filled even beyond that, since many Europeans decided to drive to Israel when they couldn't book flights.

Jon was not surprised, then, when he received an urgent call from Ehud Olmert, the mayor of Jerusalem, asking him to attend an emergency meeting of the Israeli cabinet on the morrow. Jon turned his symposium over to a grad assistant and appeared at the Knesset in West Jerusalem at 9:00 A.M.

Not a member was missing, in view of the gravity of the situation.

"I should like to introduce Professor Jonathan Weber to our conference," said Israeli premier Daniel Cohen. A graying sage of impressive stature with the air of a commander-in-chief, Cohen continued, "Dr. Weber hardly needs an introduction, since he has been here before under, shall we say, unusual circumstances. His is the voice we respect in any matters dealing with Christianity in Israel.

"As we all know, great international attention has focused on one of our Israeli citizens named Joshua Ben-Yosef. Many consider him to be the returned Jesus of Nazareth. Others, of course, do not."

All eyes now seemed to shift to Jon, as if searching for some reaction that would betray his own personal opinion. Jon's poker face, however, was less than cooperative.

"Thus far," Cohen continued, "the State of Israel has tried to distance itself from any involvement in this case. As Jews, of course, we do not believe that Ben-Yosef could possibly be Jesus, since that extraordinary Rabbi died two thousand years ago. Nevertheless, we do respect the beliefs of Christians, who have looked for His return throughout that period of time."

Cohen stopped, sipped a glass of water, and resumed. "Now, however, nothing less than an army of Christians is approaching Israel—something that will put our whole infrastructure to a tremendous test. The logistics alone have forced us to limit this new wave of tourists to a rate we had not anticipated until 2050 C.E.

"There are also security dangers: with our entire police force and even sectors of the Israel Defense Force involved in handling the huge crowds that we anticipate, what if the Palestinians choose this as the moment to resume suicide attacks?" Cohen now stood up and strolled pensively along the conference table. Then he stopped, looked over toward Jon, and asked, "Or what about Joshua Ben-Yosef himself? What if all this massive acclaim turns his head and he becomes . . . political? What then?"

Loud murmuring swept across the cabinet. Jon felt a churning in his stomach as he thought to himself, *Oh, no, not again! Please, not a twenty-first-century parallel to the Jewish Sanhedrin!*

Cohen smiled briefly and added, "Pure speculation and extremely unlikely, but the idea was first raised by several members of Shas and their representative here in our cabinet, Isidore Schornstein."

Schornstein was frowning, apparently a bit miffed by Cohen's slighting reference. Shas, Israel's strongest religious party, had only 17 out of 120 seats in the Knesset, but its clout in Cohen's cabinet was out of all proportion to its size. Cohen's Labor government would have fallen to the Likud without their support.

"In any case," Cohen concluded, "we all have questions about Ben-Yosef. Professor Weber, what's your opinion? Should the government be concerned? Or are we overreacting?"

Jon sat up straight in his chair. "Well, honored members of the cabinet, Ben-Yosef, as you know, is puzzling the entire world. I've personally seen the man only four or five times, and nothing he has said or done seems any threat whatever to the establishment. He is, of course, a stringent critic of the evils in society—much like the prophets in the Hebrew Bible—but I've heard nothing at all that's subversive in what he has to say. The man has remarkable charisma, of course, and his following is most enthusiastic—and growing. But they haven't caused any demonstrations or riots anywhere in Israel, have they?"

Cohen looked to Judah Meir for a reply. A stocky specimen with ruddy skin, Meir was interior minister and the man to whom Shin Bet, Israel's version of the FBI, reported. He cleared his throat and shook his head. "No . . . although we have resumed putting a tail on Ben-Yosef." He stopped abruptly, looked at Jon, and asked, "Be kind enough to keep this confidential, Professor Weber?"

"Of course," Jon replied.

"Over the last weeks, our agents have followed him and his group to and from Galilee several times. There were large crowds everywhere, but we never heard him say anything against the government."

"What about his so-called healings?" asked Cohen. "Did you see anything like that?"

"Sure. Plenty of them. At least the people thought they were healed, but we've had 'faith healers' before, haven't we?"

"Back to you, Professor Weber," said Cohen. "What's your opinion on the healings, so-called?"

Carefully, Jon responded with a condensed version of everything he knew about Joshua's therapeutic activities, concluding with Shannon's experience at the Pool of Siloam and their apparent verification the next day. Cabinet members sat wide-eyed and silent. Some moments ticked by before one mumbled comments to the next and a general din of discussion ensued.

It was too much for Schornstein. Almost angrily, he turned to Jon and asked, "So, Professor Weber, do you Christians really believe that Mr. Ben-Yosef is the returned Jesus of Nazareth?"

Jon now reported the latest world opinion poll among Christians; it showed 41 percent affirmative, 31 percent undecided, and 28 percent negative, with the usual error ratio of plus or minus 4 percent.

"And what about your theologians?" Schornstein inquired.

Jon smiled and said, "Predictably, they're totally divided on the issue, which is what one would expect of theologians."

The room tittered, while Schornstein seemed less than amused. He probed further. "And what about that theologian whose opinion we evidently value very highly here in Israel? How does Professor Jonathan Weber regard Joshua Ben-Yosef? Is he, or is he not, the returned Jesus, in your estimation?"

Again a sudden hush blanketed the room, and all eyes were on Jon.

"A fair question, Mr. Schornstein," he replied, "even if I'm a historian rather than a theologian. I can only be candid: my own wife, Shannon, now believes that Jesus has indeed returned in the person of Joshua Ben-Yosef, and that this is His intermediate coming to sustain Christianity before His final coming at the end of time. As for me, I've seen an extraordinary number of indications that this *could* be true in fact—for reasons that would take the rest of the day to explain. And there are an astonishing number of parallels between the words and deeds of Jesus and Joshua. However, I've tried very hard to maintain neutrality on this issue as I continue searching for the truth."

Again, silence commanded the chamber. Finally Schornstein banged his fist down on the table and shouted, "So, my colleagues! Here we sit and quietly discuss whether or not a renegade Jew making a preposterous claim to divinity is or is not the same as another renegade Jew who also disturbed the peace two thousand years ago, and has caused endless suffering to the Jewish people in the twenty centuries since! This is madness! Absolute *madness!* You claim, as you sit here, to be good Jews, yet you dawdle away while letting our embattled state serve as the womb for a second monstrosity that this time could destroy Judaism in general and Israel in particular. And this time it won't be the Romans who conquer us and destroy our city, but the armies of Christian tourists—probably followed by real armies in a twenty-first-century version of the Crusades!"

When Schornstein paused, several colleagues tried unsuccessfully to calm him down. A quick gulp of water and he continued, looking to the left and right. "And so, you genial liberals in this cabinet, just do nothing while the *goyim* out there prepare another attack on our monotheism with their so-called doctrine of the Trinity! Perhaps, with Mr. Ben-Yosef, it will now become a Quadrinity and—"

A negative roar filled the room, interrupting Schornstein's tirade. Premier Cohen banged for order, looked to Schornstein, and commented sharply, "Perhaps our worthy representative of the ultra-orthodox might refrain from introducing religious racism into this discussion?" Then he turned to Jon and apologized for Schornstein's outbursts.

"No apology necessary," said Jon. "None at all. After the Holocaust—after Dachau, Buchenwald, Belsen, Treblinka, and all the other horror spots—I can fully understand any extreme opinions among Jews anywhere in the world. At the same time, I'd like to remind Mr. Schornstein that the main thrust in Christian theology for the last century has been to abhor anti-Semitism in all its terrible forms, to recognize in Judaism our mother faith, and to foster optimal relations between Christians and Jews."

"Hear, hear!" and other assenting comments greeted Jon's statement.

"And your scholarship in particular has been most helpful in this regard," said Cohen. Then he turned to Schornstein and asked, "We certainly don't wish to ignore the opinions of Shas in this matter, and so we must ask: what do *you* think we should do, Mr. Schornstein, in the case of Joshua Ben-Yosef?"

Schornstein thought for a moment and then replied, "I think Ben-Yosef should be arrested." Then, in a louder voice, "In fact, I would urge that he be arrested."

"Yes, and how about *crucifying* him after that?" shouted Moshe Breitenstein, the Israeli minister of tourism, as he slapped the table. "Let's make a martyr out of Ben-Yosef!" he shouted derisively. "That will turn him into the returned Jesus for sure!" Glaring at Schornstein, he continued, "On every issue raised in the cabinet or in the Knesset over recent months, you, Isidore, have chosen the path of suspicion, paranoia, legalism, restriction, regression, and repression. You reject everyone or everything that fails to support your excruciating narrow-mindedness! Human progress would be impossible if people like you were in the majority!"

"Now, see here, I—"

"You represent only a fraction of the Israeli public, and yet your half ounce of weight tips the scales into a precarious majority for our prime minister in this land of a dozen political parties. And look at your record! Look at Shas's record! You've managed to keep the orthodox wing of Judaism in charge of our entire religious life here—never mind that the vast majority of American Jews who support us are conservative or reformed.

"You've prevented full religious freedom here—just ask Christians in Israel about that. You've tried to prevent our great national airline, El Al, from flying on the Sabbath. You've protested our hotel swimming pools where—perish the thought—women might show up in bathing suits. Our hotel elevators must work automatically on Saturdays, since pushing a button on the Sabbath is somehow working, according to your tortured definition. And our buses—"

Schornstein pounded the conference table with both fists, stood up, and bellowed, "I will not tolerate these insults to our party and to me personally! Shas herewith withdraws from the government! I will introduce a motion of no-confidence in Premier Cohen at the next meeting of the Knesset on Thursday!"

Brushing aside all attempts to dissuade him, Schornstein furiously stuffed papers into his attaché case and stalked out of the room. Before closing the door, however, he had to endure the most exquisite insult of all: a round of hearty applause. The irrepressible Breitenstein had started it, and the rest of the cabinet quickly joined in.

Kol Israel and Israel Television broke the story later that afternoon, and the world media covered it that night. A stunning reaction followed, an unanticipated minirevolution occurred in world Jewry, which apparently had had enough of the minority domination of Israeli politics by the various religious splinter parties. Communications flooded into Israeli political party headquarters and to members of the Knesset, with variations on the theme: "Support Cohen! Oppose religious bigotry!"

But when Isidore Schornstein stood up in the Knesset the following Thursday to introduce his motion of no-confidence in the government, he had a slight smile of satisfaction brightening his usually austere features. He had calculated the votes of the various political parties, called in political favors, and held a series of intense strategy meetings with Shas, Mafdal, Aguda, and the other religious parties. He had just enough votes: Cohen would fall.

When the voting took place, however, he was shocked to see defections from his own list, political favors *not* repaid on the part of "ingrates," and members of the Knesset voting their consciences rather than the party line. Cohen and his Labor Party coalition received enough votes to more than compensate for Shas's defection. The premier would survive indeed, and without the help of the ultraorthodox—the first time this had happened in Israeli politics for some years.

And, in a way, we might thank Joshua Ben-Yosef for that, Jon thought to himself. Still, Jews hardly had any monopoly on polarizations like those that surfaced in the Israeli cabinet, he knew.

Every religious system, every government, every institution on earth had its liberals, moderates, neutrals, conservatives, and reactionaries—the too-open minds, the open minds, the centrists, the narrower minds, the closed minds. Israel was simply the world writ small. Perhaps he should discuss the human mind the next time he saw Joshua Ben-Yosef—if there was a next time.

Indeed there was, though without opportunity for any philosophical dialogue. Just after class one morning, several students returned to the auditorium and exclaimed, "Ben-Yosef's teaching down in the Kidron Valley, Professor Weber!"

Jon left the hall and walked outside to a promenade overlooking Jerusalem to the southwest. From that vantage point he saw a large crowd gathered on a hillside below the walls of Jerusalem, listening to a figure who was speaking at a spot next to the Brook Kidron.

The Kidron, the most famous brook in history, he reflected, *never mind that it now looks like a glorified ditch.*

Around 700 B.C., pious King Hezekiah had cleaned out the Jerusalem temple—*good*—but had the trash dumped into the Kidron—*bad*. On the Thursday of Holy Week, Jesus and His disciples had crossed the Kidron in order to reach the Garden of Gethsemane.

"I wonder if Joshua will try to claim old memories of that brook," Jon muttered to himself, in a skepticism he would not have shared with Shannon.

A brisk, ten-minute walk brought him to the edge of the crowd, just in time to hear the close of Joshua's discourse, in contemporary Hebrew. He turned on his pocket cassette recorder so he could later translate for Shannon's benefit:

"And so, my friends, all of you are burdened with concerns and anxieties of every sort. You worry over the past, but how foolish is that? You worry over the present, but only complicate your situation. You worry over the future . . . but then find that your problems have vanished! Learn from the very birds flying overhead, chirping away without fears of any kind: your heavenly Father protects them—He will protect you. Be concerned only that you ask God's forgiveness for your sins—and forgive others theirs—and then resolve to improve your lives with His help and His blessing. Now . . . go in peace, and serve the Lord."

Slowly, apparently savoring a spiritual feast, the crowd started to disperse. But Jon now had the opportunity of witnessing what went on after one of Joshua's presentations. For some reason, he decided to watch it all from behind a nearby hedge, feeling suddenly uncomfortable about confronting Ben-Yosef directly at that time and place.

As Joshua and his associates tried to leave, a handful of people who apparently needed help remained after his teaching and detained them. Patiently, Joshua laid his hands on each, and most smiled exuberantly as a result of what seemed to be healing, many kneeling before him in grateful joy and adoration.

But the quasi-biblical scene was suddenly interrupted when a large, apparently deranged creature came loping up on all fours to the small dais. Clad in a tattered maroon shirt and ragged, dirty jeans, the husky man had froth or spittle drooling out of his mouth. He reared up before Joshua and spoke to him in a Hebrew that ranged from whispers to raving shouts.

"So, you think you're back, Nazarene, aye?" the madman snarled and muttered. "And after all this time! Well, surprise: *we're back too! And stronger than ever!* Aha-ha! Aha-ha-ha!" He coughed and hacked.

"What's your name?" asked Joshua, interrupting the man's ghastly monologue.

"My name?" he mumbled. "It's not *my* name . . . it's *our* name. Our name is Multitude, *because we're a whole army!*"

"No, my friend, your name isn't Multitude . . . it's Solomon."

The man stopped his raving and looked thunderstruck. "How'd you . . . how'd you know that?" he muttered, in apparently his first coherent response, which was quickly lost in the raving that followed: "Jesus once, Jesus *twice* . . . come to drive us out again, are you? *Well, to hell with you, Ben-Yosef!*"

With that, he raised both arms and made a lunge for Joshua that nearly knocked him over. Shimon and the others quickly sprang to his assistance and fought to restrain the man, who resisted fiercely. It finally took at least six of them to subdue the demoniac and pin him to the ground.

Joshua now stretched his hands over the man and said, "Hear me, you demonic forces who hold this man in bondage: in the holy name of God, I command you to leave him at once! Be gone . . . *now!*"

The man shook, uttered a horrifying shriek, and stopped struggling. The men carried him over to a grassy spot along the brook where he rested briefly. Then he must have opened his eyes—Jon assumed, from the distance of his vantage point—and now he sat up and seemed to smile. Jon could not hear his first words, but later they were clear enough: "Thank you, thank you, Lord!"

"You're feeling better, then?" asked Joshua. "You are restored?"

"Yes, *yes*, Master! For the first time, I feel . . . I feel as if I am in control of my life again, rather than those . . . evil . . . awful spirits!"

"You are truly healed, my friend. Have no fear: the forces of darkness will not return. Now go in peace, and give God the glory."

"I will. I will indeed! Blessed be the name of the Lord!"

Joshua's associates gathered round to congratulate the man and renew their obvious admiration for their Lord and Master.

"Come, have dinner with us, Solomon," said Joshua.

And they all walked off.

After they left, Jon emerged from his botanical hideout, totally struck by what he had seen. Clearly, Joshua was playing to no galleries this time—not trying to impress anyone with spiritual sleight of hand. Only a few stragglers had witnessed this event and the setting, clearly, was far more objective, not staged. In many ways, what he had just seen was far more impressive than the flying pen.

Perhaps, too, that was the reason for his hiding, Jon finally told himself: it added to the credibility of the episode that Joshua was not performing the exorcism for his benefit either. But if Joshua were the returned Jesus in fact, he would have known all about his hiding in the first place, much as he knew the madman's name. Yet Joshua had not called him out of the hedge as Jesus had called Zacchaeus down from the sycamore tree.

This, of course, proved nothing one way or the other.

Would anything? Jon wondered.

TWELVE

Jon thought it interesting that Shin Bet was tracking Joshua again, after first disclaiming interest in doing so. Previously, he had wondered if they might share intelligence with him as to Joshua's whereabouts. That, however, was no longer an issue. To deal with the hordes of Christian pilgrims arriving, the *Jerusalem Post* now published a daily column called "Joshua Jottings." This listed places or events where Ben-Yosef was scheduled to hold forth in Judea or Galilee, along with whether his appearances were open to the public or private. If private, local police would help make them so.

"I think 'Joshua Jottings' is too flippant," Shannon opined. "The editors should show more consideration."

"Shannon, we're talking about the most prominent Jewish newspaper in English in the State of Israel," Jon reminded her. "I hardly think they're reverent Christians! Would you prefer, say, 'The Redeemer Report'? Or maybe 'The Savior's Schedule'?"

"Knowing you, that's even worse, Jon," she said with a frown. "Keep your incorrigible skepticism to yourself."

That little exchange was merely the tip of the iceberg—a chilly, growing mass of disagreement that was slowly wedging itself between them. It was the first real problem in their young marriage, which thus far had been something of a textbook case of marital joy and serenity.

Usually, to be sure, they were able to set aside their differences and enjoy one another to the fullest. Sex—that wild, unfathomable accoutrement to love—easily thrived. Each was "closest friend" to the other. There were delightful excursions on donkeyback to Petra in Jordan, the "rose-red city half as old as time" with its incredible facades carved out of living rock.

141

During a semester break, they flew to Cairo and climbed the Great Pyramid at Giza, an extraordinary concession granted by the Egyptian Department of Antiquities, which had banned tourist climbs for decades. At the summit of the pyramid, which had originally tapered down to one pointed capstone, there was now a nine- or ten-foot square of stones, thanks to many centuries of sandblasting by winds off the Sahara desert. After a rather exhausting climb, Jon and Shannon lay down on the apex, shielding their eyes from a noontime sun blazing overhead.

Jon now sat up in the lotus position and started chanting, "*Ohm . . . ohm . . . ohm . . .*"

"Has the heat gotten to you, Jon?"

"No, darling, I'm just getting in touch with my inner being so that it may better respond to the great oneness of the universe. *Ohm . . . ohm . . .*" Then he broke down in laughter and said, "At this moment, you and I are the envy of every New Ager in the world. They'd give up their favorite crystals, tarot cards, medicine wheels—their whole collection of psychic bric-a-brac, in fact, just to be where we are."

"Why is that?"

"Haven't you heard about pyramid power, my dear? We're sitting here at the very convergence of earth's forces projecting heavenward. Can't you just feel the invigorating stimulus?"

"No."

"Hmmm. Neither can I." He lay back down and said, "Guess we're just not cut out for the New Age."

Moments later, he edged over and started stroking her cheek softly, another idea in mind. "Wouldn't it be fun to make love up here, sweetheart?" he asked. "At the very pinnacle of the ancient world?"

She gave him a look. "You're totally whacko, my love!"

He was silent, letting his fingers reply instead.

"Jon!" she said, seizing his probing hand in a grip of iron. "Somebody will see us!"

He roared with laughter. "And just who might that be—here at the top of creation?"

"Quit that, you naughty man!" she exclaimed, with a blushing smile.

"Aw, I think you ought to call for help, Shannon!" he teased. "Of course, it would take the help a couple of hours to reach us . . . provided they even heard you scream in the first place."

She laughed lightly and sat up. "This is awesome, Jon!" she exclaimed. "What a tremendous view!"

He stood up, swept his arms around, and said, "Grandest view on earth, darling! You can see why Egypt is *not* the northeastern notch of Africa, as the maps have it. It's only a marvelous green snake of vegetation that runs north and south along both banks of the Nile. The rest is desert."

"Impressive! But . . . gosh, this is high up!"

"Look to the south: see the Step Pyramid down there at Saqqara? The pharaoh buried there is Djoser. His architect, Imhotep, designed that. It's the first —"

"Jon . . . later with the history lecture, okay? I . . . I just don't feel well. It's *scary* up here."

Putting his arms around her, he said, "Only a slight touch of acrophobia, my dear. Nothing to worry about."

"Jon . . ." It was the whimper of a very frightened little girl.

"Well, okay, then, let's go back down. But don't *look* down, Shannon; just look around at the magnificent scenery on the way."

He moved off the top platform to show Shannon how to manage the descent. Jon knew well enough the reason for Shannon's growing panic. Although the pyramids may look like equilateral triangles that provide an easy, pleasing climb upward, the view downward from the summit is positively intimidating. The nice, gradually sloping pyramid gives way visually to a cruel and much-steeper isosceles triangle. This optical illusion is one reason that climbing the pyramids was forbidden, since some tourist climbers had previously panicked, lost their balance, and fallen to their deaths.

Abandon hope, all acrophobes! should have been painted in huge lettering at the base, Jon thought. He was also cursing himself silently for not having known about Shannon's fear of heights.

Shannon looked down in dread. Her face turned white and she froze. Her hands dug into a seam between a row of stones, and she started sobbing.

"Shannon!" Jon cried. "I told you not to look down!"

"I can't help it, Jon!" she screamed. "It's terrible! I'm so scared!"

Jon himself had to fight down a tinge of terror, knowing that they had gotten themselves into potentially mortal danger with not a speck of help anywhere on the horizon. Perhaps it was time for "tough love."

"Stop whimpering like a little schoolgirl, Shannon!" he said firmly. "We're going to reverse things now: I want you to turn and face the pyramid head-on. I'll guide your feet each time we get to the next row of stones!"

"I . . . I can't, Jon!"

"*Yes, you can!*" he insisted. "You remember how great it was going up: we're just reversing the process on the way down!"

She turned toward the pyramid, slowly, timidly. He climbed down two rows of stones and grasped both of her ankles, now at his shoulder level.

"I've got you, sweetheart!" he assured her. "Now, one leg at a time. You just keep facing the pyramid while I place your left foot one row down—now drop your leg . . . yes . . . that's it. Okay, your foot's in a fine, firm place and you can put your weight on it. Good girl! Now do the same with your right leg."

Slowly, excruciatingly slowly, they descended. Jon's gentle coaxing seemed to gain credibility when they reached the halfway point and she was surprised to find herself still alive. Soon there were only fifteen rows of stone to go, and Shannon took heart, now a little ashamed of her performance at the summit. When they finally jumped down off the bottom row of huge stone ashlars, Jon hugged her.

"Way to go, darling!" Then he added what he thought was a helpful comment: "Remember what pilots do after surviving a plane crash? They go right up again to avoid the fear of flying. Shall we go for it?"

Shannon glared at him and snapped, "I do hope Cairo General Hospital has a psychiatric ward, Jon. I'm sure you'll be a model patient!"

He laughed, threw his arms around her again, and said, "I can think of better therapy than that: let's do a Nile River cruise from Luxor to Aswan! Are you game?"

"Is the pope Catholic?" Shannon beamed and nodded enthusiastically.

On all these jaunts, Jon tried to forget about Joshua Ben-Yosef and how that figure seemed to have monopolized their lives. Shannon, however, did not forget. She had resumed her bedtime prayers with a certain eagerness and regularly invited Jon to join her. Once, when she chided him for his wooden involvement, he said, "It's just that I don't know where to face in prayer, Shannon: toward heaven above, or toward Joshua's latest whereabouts in Galilee."

Like a legion of couples in mixed marriages—Jewish-Christian, Protestant-Catholic, Lutheran-Methodist—Jon and Shannon let their love bridge any denominational gaps. Theirs did not involve any disagreement over whether Jesus was or was not truly present in the Sacrament, or how much water to apply in baptism and at what age. Theirs, instead, involved an alternative of infinite significance: Joshua the Impostor or Jesus the Returned.

Soon, Jon reasoned, he *must* find proof one way or the other. Without telling Shannon, he now read "Joshua Jottings" on a daily basis, deciding when and how to intersect with Ben-Yosef. Without telling Jon, Shannon now read "Joshua Jottings" on a daily basis also. Neither, then, was surprised when Jon announced one morning, "Next Sunday, Joshua is holding forth again up in Galilee, at what seems to be his favorite spot. Shall we?"

"Oh, yes! Yes, indeed!"

Jon's friend at the Vatican, Kevin Sullivan, called from Rome that night. "I just can't hold off any longer, Jon," he said. "The Vatican is absolutely swamped with inquiries from the faithful all over the world, and you know what the question is."

"Sure. It's 'why can't priests get married?'"

Sullivan groaned. "Not a time for levity, Jon."

"Sorry, Kevin. The pressure's strong here too. Just trying to keep a sense of humor—and therefore my sanity."

"Thanks for the steady stream of information you've been sending me over that specially secured web site. It's been extremely helpful in keeping the Holy Father abreast of developments. But now he's dispatching me to Israel so that I can see for myself."

"Long overdue. When are you coming?"

"I land at Ben-Gurion day after tomorrow. The Archbishop of

Jerusalem will be meeting my plane, and I'll be staying at the Sonesta. When can we get together?"

"Hmmm. This could be great timing! Shannon and I are planning to drive up to Galilee this coming Sunday to hear Joshua at the Mount of the Beatitudes. Need a ride?"

"Fabulous! Just fabulous!" Kevin called into the phone. "I wondered if I'd even get to see Ben-Yosef while I was in Israel."

"I'll pick you up Sunday morning at the Sonesta at, say, seven? Then it's off to our place for breakfast and the drive up to Galilee, okay?"

"Made in heaven! Oh, I forgot to tell you, Jon: the Holy Father sends you his warmest personal greetings, but with a very modest request . . ."

"Which is?"

"To quote directly, 'Please solve this puzzle for Christendom as well as you did the last one.'"

"Oh, fine!" Jon commented wryly. "I was afraid he'd ask something really difficult! But do give him my very best in return."

"That I will, Jon. See you soon!"

Jon and Shannon again found elements of déjà vu on the drive northward, although this time the weather was even more delightful than on their previous trip.

"I'm sure Joshua arranged that," Shannon commented happily.

Jon flashed a wan smile to Sullivan in the backseat, but said nothing. Why resume The Argument on such a lovely day? For his part, Kevin, a ruddy-faced, dark-haired, Irish-American who could have led the band in a Saint Patrick's Day parade, returned the smile and also said nothing.

Their conversation quickly focused on Benedict XVI. "What a man, the present pontiff!" Jon enthused. "He's the best since John XXIII, of blessed memory. Benedict is one pope who knows how to guide the church through some difficult narrows—like those awful clergy pedophilia scandals. The American Catholic bishops did well in setting up a zero tolerance policy for abusive priests, Kevin—and was that long overdue!"

"It was long overdue," Kevin concurred.

"But what about the bishops themselves, the ones who shifted known child abusers from parish to parish and then refused to resign? Thank God for Benedict XVI! Did that man ever roll bishops' heads in the process of cleaning up the church!"

"I think the final count was twenty-eight bishops, nine archbishops, and five cardinals. I think you have to go back to Gregory VII in the 1070s to beat those stats," Sullivan agreed.

"Still, I don't think Catholicism's completely out of the woods yet, much as I wish it were."

"Not by a long shot, chum!" Sullivan agreed. "There's still our acute priest shortage . . . a delightful group called the 'Lavender Mafia' are partially responsible. I just cringe at the number of seminaries dominated by homosexual faculty and students. That's a huge turnoff for any straights wanting to study for the priesthood."

Jon always admired how deadly honest Kevin was. Never in their student days together did he tell even a white lie. When they double-dated at Harvard, Jon would occasionally try to impress his date with a slight shading of the truth, but Kevin? Never. After one such evening, Jon turned to him and said, "Kev, I really think you are the *only* person since Jesus who has never sinned." Kevin had laughed and said, "That's right, Jon, and I'll pray hard for your scurvy soul!"

As their conversation drifted on to other murky scandals, Kevin looked anxiously at Shannon. "Thank goodness she's asleep," he said, "I wouldn't want her to hear any of *this* dialogue."

"Oh, she's a big girl and could handle it," Jon assured him. "But enough of this cursing the darkness, Kev. Who's going to light the candle?"

"It could well be Benedict XVI. This is confidential, Jon, but the Holy Father will have much more to say on these problems in an encyclical he's preparing."

"He *will* . . . he *is*?" Jon's eyes brightened. He thought for a moment and asked, "Kevin, will you have any influence on the formulation of that encyclical?"

"Perhaps a little. Others in the Curia will have more, I'm sure."

"Hmmm . . . well, this is out of line, of course, but . . . couldn't you and the Vatican please consider reopening the question of clerical celibacy . . . on the possibility of a married clergy? Sure, celibacy is a great option for those, like yourself, who have the gift. But what about a wonderful Catholic kid, with the light of heaven in his eyes, who swears to celibacy on his way to the priesthood. But at prep school or seminary, the hormones really start flowing. Then he's at a crossroads about what to do, and neither option seems right."

"Yes, I know the arguments, Jon. And I wonder if I, myself, really have the gift of celibacy, as you assume. I'd call it more the *sacrifice* of celibacy."

"I knew you were a hetero back in Harvard days, Kev: we always tried to date the same beautiful girls from Radcliffe!"

Kevin laughed, then turned serious. "I'll do what I can, Jon. I . . . really mean it."

"I'll make a prediction: by A.D. 2030, there will be general priestly marriage in Catholicism."

"No, I don't think so," said Sullivan.

"Why not?"

"I hope it's more like 2020!"

Jon laughed and then switched the conversation to Joshua Ben-Yosef, giving Kevin a full debriefing. The eyewitness flavor of Jon and Shannon's experiences impressed Kevin far more than the many web communications, and he fired salvo after salvo of questions. Time and again, comments like "incredible," "beyond belief," "boggles the mind" erupted from the backseat.

Sullivan finally summed it all up. "Jon," he said in low, deliberate tones, "if we really have to take Joshua's claims seriously, then all of Christendom is faced with a problem far more excruciating than anything we discussed earlier."

"Well put, Kevin. And true."

"Okay, fellas," said a sleepy voice. "Are we there yet?"

"Funny you should ask, Shannon," said Jon. "Yes, in fact, we are."

THIRTEEN

Amid mounting traffic, they drove up the switchbacks on the Mount of the Beatitudes and reached the parking area at the summit. Aluminum grandstands now crowned the crest of the hill to augment the natural theater, adding another two or three thousand seats. There were more poles with loudspeakers and floodlights, a more impressive stage area, and two newly planted groves of Mediterranean pines lining the edges of what seemed to be a permanent outdoor theater. An array of television cameras on tripods lined the upper perimeter, all connected to vans ready to beam their signals to a receiver/transmitter tower temporarily erected at the summit of the mount, as well as to an array of satellite dishes scattered across the crest of the hill.

"I wonder what's going on here," Jon remarked to Shannon and Kevin. "Is this going to be Ben-Yosef's regular venue? His outdoor temple? An Israeli version of Oberammergau . . . or maybe Branson, Missouri?"

"Quiet, skeptic!" said Shannon. "I asked an usher, and he said this is going to be the Galilee Theater for musical and cultural events."

"Oh."

They arrived early enough to get middle seating in the alfresco theater. Kevin stared at the stage through binoculars, waiting for the luminous personality who was challenging and changing the religious world to appear.

At all of Joshua's recent public appearances, the themes of his presentations were announced in advance. Today it was to be "Parables." At exactly 3:00 P.M., a trumpet flourish silenced the crowd for the English program.

149

"Look to the left, Kevin," said Jon, pointing. "Here come Joshua's twelve associates." He still refused to call them disciples.

While they seated themselves in a row, the dominating figure of Shimon walked to center stage to welcome the crowd.

"That's the Peter figure," Jon advised Kevin, in what became a running commentary.

"May El-Shaddai, the Mighty God, extend His blessings to all of you!" Shimon announced in a commanding bass voice. "Whatever your backgrounds, whatever your beliefs, you are all welcome to hear the Master. Many of you know who the Master truly is. Some of you do not. All we ask is that you listen carefully to his words, and only then draw your conclusions. May the Spirit of God attend your hearing, as well as your response. And now, by divine grace, it is our humble yet blessed privilege to introduce that person who, by his words and deeds, stands closest to God Himself: Joshua Ben-Yosef!"

Deafening applause broke out, as well as some frenzied cheering. Joshua appeared—not dramatically from behind a curtain into the glare of a spotlight, but as a white-robed figure who climbed up to the dais from an area just below the stage, where he had been ministering to those in need. It was the first time Jon and Shannon had seen Joshua clad in biblical attire rather than the contemporary Israeli apparel he had worn previously.

"Yes, that's more like it," Shannon whispered.

Jon glanced over to Kevin, but he was still glued to his binoculars.

The applause continued loudly and incessantly for some minutes. Finally, Joshua held up both of his arms and the crowd stilled to a reverent hush.

Almost softly, he began, "A very wise and just king once established an ideal state with a perfect society, in which all citizens could live and thrive in endless bliss. But instead of enjoying their extraordinary happiness, the people grew jealous of their generous ruler who had given them all this. They rebelled against him, each somehow hoping to become like the king himself. Their rebellion, of course, failed. Saddened, the king gave up on his plan for a perfect society and simply let the people be what they had already become: a jealous, unruly, defiant, suspicious, and malicious brood, who plotted against one another or maimed and killed each other in their madness, for they were unable to vent their rage against the wise king himself. Whoever has ears to hear, let him or her hear!"

Joshua stopped speaking. Silence blanketed the theater for some moments. Then he asked the many thousands assembled on the hillside, "Who is that wise and just king?"

Nearly half the crowd shouted back, "GOD!"

"Yes, indeed!" Joshua responded. "The almighty King of the universe! And who are the rebels in that realm?"

Mingled shouts of "People," "Us," "Humanity" rattled across the hillside.

"Correct again, my friends! You easily understood my parable. Remember, again, that a parable is a parallel, a story that is easily understood and readily applied to something that happens in fact and not in fiction. Two thousand years ago, Jesus, you will recall, used parables regularly in His teaching. I use them also."

"This is incredible!" Kevin whispered to his hosts. "Ben-Yosef has no accent of any kind! The man speaks English better than I do!"

"Not that difficult, Kevin," Jon whispered back, "in view of your Boston Irish accent!"

"Jon, would you please!" Shannon groused. "We said exactly the same thing the first time we heard him, Kevin. And he can do this in a dozen or two other languages also. No ordinary man could ever bring that off. I don't know about you, gentlemen, but that alone convinces me."

Joshua was continuing with another parable, then a third, then a fourth, each beautifully crafted to convey a lesson with brilliant logic and ready application. People were mesmerized, sitting ramrod straight in their seats to be ready to answer the questions Joshua was tossing out. The audience seemed to hang on every word that he uttered in his rich baritone.

"I've never heard anything like this," Kevin commented, in a tone of half-whispered awe.

"Nor I," Jon admitted.

"Yes! And didn't they say exactly the same thing about Jesus twenty centuries ago?" Shannon commented. "Remember their phrase: 'No man ever spoke like this'!"

Joshua began yet another parable. "Do you remember the story about the great and wise king and his rebellious subjects?" he asked rhetorically. "Well, that same king decided not to destroy his subversive subjects after all, but in his great mercy, to spare them. So he sent them an ambassador with a message of love and reconciliation to heal the fracture between himself and his people. But instead of receiving him, they mistreated him and then killed him. And that ambassador was no less than the king's *own son*! And now what do you suppose the king did?"

"Destroyed his subjects!" someone yelled loudly.

"No! In the greatest example of mercy and love ever shown, the wise king brought his son back to life and promised to forgive all who would now accept him and believe in his mission. Now, again, who is that king?"

"GOD!" rang out from the multitude.

"And who is that son?"

"Jesus!" "Christ!" "Jesus of Nazareth!" ricocheted across the crowd.

"Exactly! Well done, my faithful people!"

Kevin looked over to Jon and whispered, "Note that he's saying, '*my* faithful people'?"

"Par for his course," Jon whispered back. "Very similar to what he said to me in our Nicodemus visit. Get used to it, Kev!"

"And now, dear friends, for my final parable," Joshua announced. "Twenty centuries passed since that same wise king restored his prince to life. But once again, his subjects doubted that the king had actually sent his son to reconcile them, or that he had even raised him from the dead. In fact, they went so far as to doubt that there ever was a prince, or even a wise king in the first place. And so, in his infinite mercy, the wise king proved that he did indeed exist by sending his own son into the world a *second* time—two thousand years after his resurrection."

Joshua paused, and life itself seemed to pause for the many thousands in the audience, who were sitting in a kind of vacuum outside the time-space continuum, waiting for his next words.

Joshua now raised his voice. "And that son has indeed come into the flesh again in order to reconcile the world to himself, and to give everyone on earth another opportunity to believe in him. One last time, he will show the world the way to salvation."

Another dramatic silence descended on the multitude. Jon, Shannon, and Kevin looked at each other with wide eyes. Then Joshua asked the now-almost-ritual question: "And who is that wise king?"

In unison, the people again responded, "God!"

"And who is that king's son?"

No one said anything, until a loud voice at the top of the theater yelled out, "JOSHUA BEN-YOSEF!"

The vast throng erupted in echo. "JOSHUA BEN-YOSEF!" "JOSHUA IS JESUS!" accompanied by wild cheering, a cacophony of shouts and hymns and prayers, all serving as counterpoint to the drumbeat of "JOSHUA BEN-YOSEF!" "JOSHUA IS JESUS!" repeated over and over again.

Terrified seagulls deserted the pine trees fringing the theater and fled screaming out over the Sea of Galilee. Denizens in nearby forests fled in fright. The whole multitude grew electrified, ecstatic as the rhythmic chant continued.

Nor were they the only ones. Since the event was being carried live on international radio and television networks, untold millions across the world—glued, boggle-eyed, to their TVs—were sharing in the emotional firestorm. Simultaneous translators, sitting in booths high atop the natural theater, had tears in their eyes while trying to convey what Joshua and the crowd were saying. Media directors in their headsets, perspiration dripping to their chins, were barking camera cues and angles to their crews.

"Do a full zoom-in on Joshua!" And the world saw a look of apparent divinity in his face as he raised his hands to God on high.

"Pan out to show the crowd!" And millions across the globe saw a forest of waving arms raised either toward Joshua or toward heaven.

"Cut to that old woman in the healing area!" And viewers saw a figure, radiant with joy, clasping hands pointed toward Joshua.

"Okay, now zoom out to show that chorus of children to the right of the platform!" And there they were, praising God and His Son, Joshua-Jesus, with cherubic enthusiasm.

Then there was a zoom-out to achieve a bird's-eye view of the entire multitude from a camera with a wide-angle lens at the crest of the hill. Another, with a telephoto zoom-in, happened to catch Shannon, Jon, and Kevin staring at one another in utter amazement.

And then it happened. A massive voice suddenly broke into the warm afternoon in tones that would make "stentorian" seem like a whisper. It was as if a thousand James Earl Joneses were perfectly enunciating their profound, mellifluous bass at the same time in a reverberating speech chorus that actually shook the entire theater: "THIS IS MY BELOVED SON, IN WHOM I AM WELL PLEASED! HEAR HIM! FOLLOW HIM!"

People collapsed into their seats at the sound waves. Several media amplifiers went up in smoke. If there was high emotion before, there was sacred pandemonium now. Some had been standing to cheer, but no longer. Like many in the crowd, Shannon fell to her knees in tears. Jon and Kevin were slumped over, holding their heads with both hands. For one long minute, the multitude seemed to sit suspended between time and eternity.

It was Joshua who broke the silence. "I thank You, Father," he said, arms raised toward heaven, eyes closed and a smile of serenity on his lips. "I thank You for having—so graciously—revealed Your Son to the world! This time, may the world correct its ways. May people everywhere begin to doubt their doubts and truly believe that You have sent me to give the world a new opportunity to receive Your grace! We pray this in my name, O blessed Father! Amen!"

Again, moments of sepulchral silence followed. Then it was the chorus of children who began singing the Common Doxology, immediately joined by fifteen thousand other voices on the hillside, and perhaps two hundred million more across the world:

> *Praise God from whom all blessings flow.*
> *Praise Him all creatures here below.*
> *Praise Him above, ye heavenly host.*
> *Praise Father, Son, and Holy Ghost!*

Joshua raised his arms in parting benediction and then dismissed the multitude in sacred silence.

On the drive back to Jerusalem, Shannon, Jon, and Kevin were as quiet as they had ever been in each other's company. In fact, no one even said a word until they had reached Tiberias. It was there that Jon finally broke the silence. The comment was no sooner off his lips than he knew it was a case of very bad timing. "You . . . you don't suppose the 'voice of God' was . . . some sort of overamplified, prerecorded tape?"

"Oh, won't you please shut up, Jon!" Shannon shouted. "You can take those blasphemous doubts of yours down to the *devil* with you, for all I care! What does it take to *convince* you? You wouldn't accept the truth if it stared you in your bleeding face! You're just a—" She broke into a soft sobbing that cut off further comment.

Jon shook his head slowly in chagrin. He flashed a wan, apologetic look to Kevin in the backseat, but Kevin failed to return it. He was sitting with his head down, eyes shut, and hands folded. Was he deeply in prayer? Or deeply embarrassed at the scene in the front seat? If little had been said before, the Peugeot's interior now had all the ambience of an undisturbed tomb. It was a return trip that could have been measured only in degrees of ugly.

Just before reaching Jerusalem, Shannon suddenly announced, "Gentlemen, I'm . . . so sorry for my performance back in Galilee."

Both men immediately broke in with assurances that they fully understood the high emotional stakes involved, she need not apologize, and other comforting *et ceteras*. By the time they delivered Kevin to his hotel, things had even begun to approach normality.

Over the next days, Jon took Kevin to the Pool of Siloam and other sights and sites associated with Ben-Yosef's appearances in Jerusalem. One early, important stop was at the Israel Antiquities Authority, where Jon introduced his friend to Gideon Ben-Yaakov. He asked Gideon to close his office door and then related the entire Sepphoris development to both men. Opening his attaché case, he laid several color photographs of the site, the synagogue floor, and the mosaic on Gideon's desk. He followed this with an explanation of his reconstruction of the text on the mosaic and his preliminary translation. Both Gideon and Kevin stared at Jon with wide eyes at hearing the name of David, but also failed to catch the meaning of the inscription.

"Please, of course, keep this totally confidential for now," Jon cautioned.

"Obviously," said Gideon. "But where do you peg it chronologically, Jon?"

"All I can say for certain is that we do have a first-century provenance for the mosaic. Mordecai Feldman concurs that the lettering reflects a style most appropriate to the first century B.C./A.D. Interestingly, that's the same time a young Jesus could have frequented Sepphoris with Joseph."

Gideon shook his head and asked, "Do you mean that this mosaic might have some connection to Jesus?"

Jon held up his hand. "No, it's just that the time and place correlate with Jesus . . . but there isn't any evidence that Jesus is part of this discovery. I'm still working on it. Nothing's set in concrete here—whatever may be set in grout!"

As they stood up to leave, Jon added a postscript. "Speaking of grout, is there any chance, Gideon, that the world's loveliest ceramicist might do a laboratory comparison test of the grout on the synagogue floor and in the mosaic?"

Gideon smiled broadly. "I'm sure Naomi would love to do just that!"

"Great! Jim Strange is spending the winter in Galilee this year, and I'll set up the arrangements. I promised to get back to him anyway on the translation."

A week later, Jon drove Kevin to Ben-Gurion Airport. En route to Tel Aviv, Sullivan commented, "I'll be the first to say that we dare not give to any human being—let alone an impostor—the worship and praise that belong to God alone and His Christ, Jon. It is possible, I suppose, that the world is making a horrible mistake here. But . . . I don't think so. True, I haven't seen what you and Shannon have seen. But just from your reports on Ben-Yosef, I can rather easily re-echo John 7:31." He said nothing more.

Jon smiled and asked, "And how does that verse go, Kev? You've always had a much better *Lokalgedächtnis* when it comes to Scripture than I. I had to admit that even in our student days."

"'When the Christ comes, will He do more miraculous signs than this man?' So let's list those signs, Jon. Joshua is born in Bethlehem, raised in Nazareth—something the lad could not arrange. He's as brilliant as the twelve-year-old Jesus in the temple. He laughs at foreign languages and can speak them without any accent whatever. He knows people before they give him their names. He knows their whole backgrounds too. He does miracles of healing, gives hearing to the deaf, sight to the blind, and he does exorcisms. He speaks beatitudes and parables almost exactly as Jesus spoke them. He even indulges skeptics like yourself with minor proofs of his divinity—flying pens, no less!—or major proofs, like God Himself opening up the heavens to declare His Son, just as He did in biblical times."

Jon was silent as Kevin continued, "From what I saw on the Mount of the Beatitudes, Jon, I . . . I really think that Shannon may be right. Why do you still have problems with Joshua's authenticity?"

Jon flexed his fingers on the steering wheel. "I don't know, Kev," he replied. "A big part of me wants to join Shannon on her knees to concede the ultimate high: the Messiah has returned! Something cosmic is unveiling itself right before our eyes! How great that I chose my parents correctly so I could be born in *this* generation to see this—a divine drama unfolding in our very own theater! Who wouldn't be excited?"

"But . . . ?"

"But there's what I like to call the scandal of the immediate. How often you hear people say, 'If only I could have seen the Lord Himself back in biblical days, how easily I would believe!' But it's a little different when it happens right under your nose—or maybe inside your own family. Why do you suppose Jesus' half brothers had such a tough time believing in Him?"

"Good question. I never really had a proper answer for that."

"You have an older brother, Kevin, don't you?"

"Two, in fact."

"Well, suppose one day your oldest brother came home and said, 'Hi, Kevin, it's time for you to know my big secret: I'm actually the Son of God and Savior of the world!' What would you do?"

Kevin laughed. "I'd run to the yellow pages and check out the office hours of the best psychiatrist in town!"

"Exactly! So here we are. We meet a fellow who has no halo gracing his scalp—a very human being, who still claims to be God in the flesh. A little tough to digest, no?"

"Yes, except for the miracles."

As they drove up to the departure concourse at Ben-Gurion, Jon cuffed his friend on the shoulder and said, "I'll bet you'll have *some* report for Benedict XVI, good friend!"

Kevin smiled and said, "And that's an understatement! So long, sport! Let's stay in touch . . . *very* close touch!"

FOURTEEN

Several days later, after arriving home from the university, Jon returned to his translation of the mosaic. He was staring at it when Shannon breezed through the door.

"Jon, are you all right?" Shannon asked when she saw him. Uttering several grunts, Jon seemed to be in a totally different universe—a cosmos that did not include his wife.

"Hello there," Shannon said, her lips just inches from Jon's right ear. "It's Shannon Jennings Weber here, your beloved wife, you may recall."

"Oh . . . sorry, darling . . . I think I have the final version of the translation."

"Maybe you're forgiven, then, spaceman. What does it say?"

Jon read the three lines aloud:

> Y *dies, but he lives,*
> *He leaves, but he returns*
> *Twice David to the star.*

"Or two times David to the star," he amended. "Either way, that line makes little sense. And it would be *so* helpful to know who in blazes Mr. 'Y' is—one solitary *yod*—who was merely the subject of this piece!"

Both studied the three lines. Suddenly Jon's eyes narrowed and, in barely audible syllables, he said "I can't believe it."

"What is it, Jon? What are you thinking?"

"In just the first two lines—only two lines—you have the outline of a *very* famous life story."

"Oh? . . . oh . . . OH!—Jesus Christ!"

159

Jon nodded slowly. Only Jesus, Christians believed, had died, lived again, and departed—with a promise to return.

"And this, of course, finally explains who our mysterious 'Y' might be," he added.

"Yes! *Yeshua,* of course, Jesus' name in his own Hebrew language!"

"But who could have laid this mosaic?"

"Some follower of Jesus?" she offered.

"Maybe . . . if the mosaic was laid later in the first century. Then it would be a kind of early Christian creed in miniature . . . like the words we say in the liturgy every week: 'Christ has died. Christ is risen. Christ will come again.'" He shook his head slowly from side to side, whether in wonderment or skepticism was not clear. "But the synagogue floor is from early in the first century," he continued, "when Sepphoris was reconstructed by Herod Antipas in—"

"Wait," Shannon interposed. "Weren't Joseph and maybe even Jesus involved in rebuilding the city?"

"Quite a few scholars assume that possibility."

"Well, then, Jesus could have laid that mosaic Himself."

Jon frowned. "It *is* an early first-century artifact, a time when there were certainly no Christians around . . ."

"But if Jesus wrote it, why didn't He use the first-person singular?"

"Oh, Jewish sages often used the third person rather than the first in referring to themselves." Jon paused, shook his head, and resumed, "Still, to think that this lad could predict His own death and resurrection by playing with tessera—maybe during a lunch break at Sepphoris—really strains all logical—"

"In the case of any other boy, Jon. But this one was Jesus, after all."

"But what about the third line? 'Twice David to the star.' That's still a puzzler."

"Could it have some kind of chronological significance?"

He thought for a moment. "Hmmm . . . chronological meaning. Okay, twice David to the star . . . David to the star . . . star of David . . . two stars of David. David was king around 1000 B.C. but neither the Bible nor Josephus mention any star in connection with his reign."

"What if the star simply means the most famous star in history: the Star of Bethlehem? The birth of Jesus—and thus the star phenomenon—happened a thousand years after David. So twice David to the star would mean twice that period: hence, two thousand years."

Jon thought for some moments. "It still makes no sense, Shannon. Y dies, but he lives. He leaves, but he returns for two thousand years. Yeshua—Jesus—returns for two thousand years?"

"Unless . . . how about this: Jesus dies, but he lives. He leaves, but he returns *in* two thousand years. Which would be . . . just about now, right?"

The blood seemed to drain from Jon's face. He sat down and said nothing for some time as he pondered each startling detail again and again. King David, apparently, may not have been the star of the Sepphoris mosaic after all.

Jon had another semisleepless night. A new—totally unanticipated—vector of hard evidence was apparently buttressing Joshua's claims. *If* "Y" was in fact Jesus. *If* the mosaic was authentic.

The world reaction to the episode on the Mount of the Beatitudes was more formidable than ever. For months now, Joshua had been an almost daily feature in print and broadcast media, but this time much of the world had seen and heard him "live." Television cameras that day, many of them equipped with long, fat telephoto lenses, had zoomed in on him so closely that his distinguished, tanned features and fluorescent indigo eyes filled television screens in both hemispheres. When that booming bass voice—believed to be of God Himself—enveloped the theater at the close of the program, the TV cameras shook with it, the screen image of Joshua vibrating slightly as he lifted his eyes skyward in beatific gratitude.

With much of the world watching, bizarre reports were bound to surface. Some viewers fainted outright in front of their television sets. A small army of women across the globe fell instantly in love with Joshua and understood for the first time Mary Magdalene's plaintive song from *Jesus Christ Superstar*: "I Don't Know How to Love Him." Many reports of healings, conversions, and rededications followed the television special. Viewers now recalled the computer screen incursions months earlier that had announced the return of Jesus. Most now regarded them as additional proof that Jesus had truly arrived in the form of Joshua.

Clergy were bombarded with fresh queries, while seminaries scheduled new courses on "A Contemporary Christ?" Believers, of course, had to endure taunts and catcalls from agnostics, who suggested that Christians had to be addle-brained half-wits to identify Joshua with Jesus. But most of the believing faithful were too delighted that their Lord had returned not to turn the other cheek.

Travel agents now had a whole year's backlog of jammed pilgrim tours. But since the bad always seems to follow the good, scalpers started booking blocks of tour reservations and then reselling them to wealthy but impatient believers at outrageous prices.

Melvin Morris Merton, of course, was on the ground floor when it came to pilgrim tours. Prior to the Joshua phenomenon, the State of Israel had awarded him a golden Star of David plaque for having led ten sellout tours of adoring followers to Israel in recent years, and he now was basking in the afterglow of "victory" over such prophecy-doubters as Jonathan Weber. Hardly a month passed without his newsletter publishing another editorial denigrating Weber and everything he stood for.

The latest edition, faithfully forwarded by Marylou, was so full of braggadocio and bombast that the target could only chuckle instead. It began with a garbled biblical quote, partially from Exodus 15, Moses' Song of Victory after the Egyptian forces had been drowned in crossing the Red Sea:

> "How have the mighty fallen! The horse and his rider have been cast into the sea!" So Moses sang in triumph when he had vanquished Pharaoh's forces, and so we, too, can rejoice that the "mighty" scoffer, Professor Jonathan Weber, and his shameless attacks on prophecy-lovers across the world have now been silenced by none other than our returned Lord and Savior, Jesus Christ Himself! He who once held us up for ridicule is himself the object of derision! We who bravely predicted the return of Jesus are now vindicated by our Lord Himself! Pray and give, so that we can get His message out to everyone!

Which is where Jon stopped reading, tossed the newsletter into the nearest wastebasket, and said to himself, "I hardly think Joshua needs Merton's help to get his message out."

Though perhaps he did, after all? While reading the next morning's *Jerusalem Post*, Shannon put down her coffee cup and gasped. Then she handed Jon the paper. "I don't think you're going to like this, dear!"

Glancing at the lower front page where she was pointing, Jon read the headline: "MERTON RALLY TO FEATURE JOSHUA."

"Will I *ever* be free of Merton?" Jon fumed. "I had no idea he was even back in Israel."

Jerusalem, AP. The Reverend Dr. Melvin Morris Merton has scheduled a mass meeting this coming Wednesday afternoon at 3:30 P.M. just below the eastern slopes of the Temple Mount in the Old City. A friend of Israel who has led ten tours with some twelve hundred participants to our holy sites, Dr. Merton affirmed that Joshua Ben-Yosef has been invited to address an anticipated audience of some seventy-five to one hundred thousand.

"I will have the extraordinary privilege of introducing him," Merton told the *Post*. "But this is not for me. This is for Him, the man whom most Christians now declare to be God's Son, Jesus Christ, returned in the flesh as Joshua Ben-Yosef! Here, in Israel, we are witnesses to the greatest event in human history since God sent His Son into the world the first time twenty centuries ago!"

The article continued on page two with a complete rundown on all the reasons why, according to Merton, "a majority of Christians in the world" were now confident that Jesus had returned.

"I . . . guess you know what we'll be doing next Wednesday afternoon, Shannon?" asked Jon. "Or is that a rhetorical question?"

"It is. I know, I know: we'll both loathe the sight of Merton. But I'd never miss seeing Joshua again."

"But I can't understand why Joshua would ever lend respectability to a blowhard like Merton. This really shakes my opinion of him."

Nearly a hundred thousand people were indeed gathered on the hillside that sunny Wednesday afternoon. As the crowd faced eastward toward the Mount of Olives, an afternoon sun baptized the hill in molten gold against a sky of Kodachrome blue. Wearing sunglasses to avoid recognition, Jon and Shannon thought the view itself was a spiritual experience. Here was the very rise where Jesus, facing in their direction, had wept over the city of Jerusalem. Here was the hill down whose slopes He had entered triumphantly into the Holy City on the back of a donkey, to the frenzied cheers of people waving palm branches and crying, "Blessed is He who comes in the name of the Lord!"

Jon broke the reverie, reminding Shannon, "This, you'll recall, is also the place where Merton assembled the faithful several years ago at an Easter sunrise service, which he predicted Jesus Himself might attend."

"How could I ever forget that?" she whispered into his ear, giving it a soft kiss in the process. "Or the night before, when we were in the Seven Arches Hotel up there to the right."

He smiled exuberantly, nodding at the memory.

At 3:35 P.M., several musical fanfares broke into their conversation. A raised platform just before the Kidron ravine to the east was decked out in the blue and white colors of Israel, with a Christian cross superimposed. The ruddy, trapezoidal face of Melvin Morris Merton was clearly visible on the dais, even at that distance, Jon and Shannon regretted to see. And now that oily, self-styled "anointed" voice of his boomed out over the PA system: "Hallelujah! This is a most blessed day!"

Day, Day, Day echoed across the Kidron Valley.

"My fellow Christians—and any unbelievers out there! As you all know, I've long declared that our Lord and Savior, Jesus Christ, would be coming back again soon. *And so He has!*"

A tidal wave of cheering wafted up from the vast audience, and quickly the synchronized chorus broke out: "JOSHUA IS JESUS!" "JESUS IS JOSHUA!"

"Oh, blessed, *yes!*" Merton answered. "Joshua *is* Jesus indeed! And He has returned, bless His holy name, just as He said He would! Soon you will see Him in person! Can anything be greater than *that?*"

A thunderous, rolling wave of cheering split the afternoon air. A praise band and chorus now held forth in a favorite contemporary

Christian anthem: "Majesty." Other praise hymns followed, with their inevitable reiterations of God being *glorious, glorious,* and *glorious.* Jesus, in turn, was *wonderful, wonderful, wonderful,* while the Holy Spirit was *awesome, awesome, awesome,* and even *awesome,* depending on how many identical verses followed.

Jon turned to Shannon and muttered, "Not my favorite music. The songwriters compose one or two lines, and the rest is repetition. Where, oh where, is Johann Sebastian Bach when we need him?"

"Okay, Jon, Bach obviously has the best music. But this is what gets through to the younger set."

"Yeah. Sure. Maybe. Nothing against contemporary Christian music, mind you, but some of it is really seedy!"

"And much of it is not, Judson Judgmental!"

More and even louder music filled the valley. A sea of arms waved back and forth, apparently to lend additional impetus to the prayers and praises wafting up to God in His own Holy Land. A Christian rock group came onstage to generate throbbing, earsplitting music amplified even more by PA system engineers, who had apparently lost their hearing earlier in life.

Holding his own ears, Jon told Shannon, "Generation X or Y— or whatever—will soon be known as Generation *Deaf!*"

"What's that?" she said, smiling. "Couldn't hear you, Jon."

But everyone—especially Jon and Shannon—wondered when Joshua Ben-Yosef himself would appear, at least to deliver them from what was now passing for music. Up on the dais, Merton was constantly looking at his watch and consulting with aides. Mercifully, he finally banished the rock group and tried to keep his audience alive with more traditional hymn sings, though with waning success. Lustily, he himself sang into the microphone, "I come to the Garden alone . . . ," expecting the throng to join in. Alas, he seemed to be walking alone indeed, since only a few in the older set knew the lyrics.

Next he inflicted one of his trademark marathon prayers on the multitude, informing the Almighty of things He already knew and so obviously stalling for time that soon there were shouts of "Amen!" from the crowd, expressed not as enthusiastic agreement but as recommended punctuation. That was clear when a voice yelled out, "So *amen* already!" while Merton was still addressing the Lord. Merton heard and heeded at last. His own "Amen" was followed by cheers. Or were they jeers?

Before he could announce what was next on a program that seemed dead in the water, scattered shouts of "Where's Joshua?" "Where's Jesus?" broke out. Then a gigantic chorus seemed to reecho those queries: "WHERE?" "WHEN?" "WHERE?" "WHEN?" The now-rhythmic calls grew louder and louder.

Waving his hands for order, Merton advised the throng, "We do expect Him shortly, my friends! Please be patient!"

The deteriorating situation was hardly saved when a fresh combo of gospel guitars, theological trombones, and Christian coronets tried to serenade the increasingly restless crowd. People started leaving the hillside in droves.

Then Jon noticed someone bringing what looked like an envelope to Merton. He tore it open, read something, reddened, and shook his head angrily. Then he stood up to the microphones and announced, rather lamely, that there must have been some mix-up regarding Joshua's appearance. They hoped to have him appear on another day.

A frustrated and irate mass of humanity grumbled their way off the hillside, many not even staying to hear Merton's benediction. Jon, however, flashed a big, broad grin as he and Shannon returned to their Peugeot.

When he saw the rear bumper of the car, he bent over in laughter. Some wag had plastered many of the parked bumpers with this slogan, printed in gaudy red: COME THE RAPTURE, MAY I HAVE YOUR CAR?

Joshua's no-show was big news across the world that evening. Speculation bloomed that he was sick, apprehended by authorities, or even dead. The Arab press suggested that Joshua's disappearance most likely had something to do with Israeli scheming, while Jewish media, in turn, blamed Islamic fundamentalists—until they were called off by the Mossad, who evidently knew more.

It was the *Jerusalem Post* that solved the problem, which, as it happened, was no problem at all. An investigative reporter they had assigned to the case located Max Griswold, one of Merton's top aides, in the bar of the Jerusalem Sonesta Hotel. Griswold had been drinking heavily—against company rules, of course—and now had a loose tongue. Up to that point, many had thought he would be Merton's eventual successor. He had the same freewheeling over-confidence, the same flair for the dramatic, the same bravado and all-around bluster. More than that, he was a visionary whose ideas often worked, though some worried that he was a loose cannon.

It was Griswold who had hatched the concept of inviting Joshua to appear at Merton's rally. In written form, however, Joshua had courteously declined the invitation. Yet before anyone could open Joshua's letter, Griswold grabbed it and reported a dream he'd had the night before.

"The letter is a test of faith," he declared to Merton and his associates the next morning. "If we confidently assume that Joshua said yes to our invitation—and do not open the letter—he will come. But if we waver and open the letter instead, he'll decline."

Never mind that this made no earthly sense whatever: Merton's associates got on their knees, prayed about it, and felt moved to agree that Griswold had indeed received a sign from heaven and that Joshua would come.

On the dais that disastrous afternoon, Merton had finally demanded the envelope, torn it open, and read it—just a bit too late to save the day. That evening, he fired Max Griswold from Merton Ministries. When the *Jerusalem Post* reporter found Griswold at the Sonesta bar, he was seeking liquid consolation for a shattered career.

The *Post* broke the story the next day. No one laughed more heartily at the report than Jon. He read every delicious syllable aloud to Shannon and commented: "Good for Joshua! If he *had* shown up at Merton's bash and lent his good name to that mountebank, that alone would have been proof enough for me that he's not Jesus."

"Exactly, Jon. But, as you may recall, he did not show up. Ergo, your conclusion, sir?"

Jon grinned, thought for a moment, and replied, "Nice logic, my dear, but too fast a jump to any conclusion."

Shannon merely shook her head and said, "Jon, Jon. What will it take to get you to see the light?"

It was long overdue. The biennial meeting of the Institute of Christian Origins in Cambridge, Massachusetts, had been postponed for two months because Jon, its president, was in Israel, heavily involved in the Joshua phenomenon. Because its elite, by-invitation-only membership consisted of world-class scholars on Jesus and early Christianity, the general secretary of the ICO, Richard Ferris, had been able to consult his specialists and answer many of the calls, cables, e-mails, and media queries that had deluged the Cambridge headquarters ever since Joshua appeared. Crucial issues regarding Ben-Yosef, however, only Jon could address, and ICO members, too, were looking to him for answers. Even his secured web site was not providing enough of them. Bottom line: Jonathan Weber had to return.

"I'll rely on you to monitor Joshua's activities while I'm gone, Shannon," said Jon, kissing her good-bye at Ben-Gurion Airport. "But don't join his gaggle of groupies!"

As with Jesus, a coterie of women followers had indeed materialized to assist the mission of Joshua and his disciples.

"Worry not, Jon: you're still the man in my life!"

"Good-bye, darling! Let's keep it that way!"

A nasty surprise awaited Jon after his jet landed at Logan Airport and he filed past security. Word had leaked about his return to the States, and his path to the baggage claim area was jammed with reporters, radio stringers with mikes, and network cameras. Twenty simultaneous questions were fired at him, causing a bewildering word salad of nonsense as he tried to make his way out of the concourse. Finally, the head of security at Logan ran up to him and asked breathlessly, "Sorry about all this, Professor Weber! But would you be kind enough to hold a quick press conference downstairs at a room we've cleared near the baggage carousels?"

"A press conference? Well, no, of course not! I had no idea—"

"Please, Dr. Weber! We had to allow the media inside here because it's a free country. But now there are just too darn many, and it's becoming an awful security risk. Please? For the good of the nation?"

"Well—put that way—all right."

The security official now grabbed an electronic megaphone and boomed out: "Dr. Weber will meet you downstairs at a room we've arranged next to Carousel H. Please clear this area at once!"

An impromptu dais and a portable PA system were quickly set up in a room used for overflow baggage at the ground level of Logan. Bare cinder-block walls surrounded them, and ugly fluorescent lamps hung overhead from a ceiling jammed with pipes and conduits. But such amenities failed to discourage the media people, who crowded into the room.

"I've seen nicer facilities in a prison!" muttered Donovan Whimpole of Reuters to Katie Couric of NBC. She smiled and quite agreed.

Jon barely made it to the dais, since the aging box that was supposed to be a step up to the podium broke apart the moment he put his weight on it. This served as a fine prelude to the PA system, which howled fiercely with "mike wash" when he first tried to speak into it. It took fifteen seconds of ghastly yowling, punctuated by a series of earsplitting screeches, before the electronics finally calmed down.

Feeling petulant and put-upon, Jon nevertheless tried to disguise his mood when he stood up to the microphone. "Clearly, I have no opening statement, ladies and gentlemen, since I had no idea you or I would even be here. I only hope this can be brief, since I'm due in Cambridge for dinner at six. Now, how may I help you?"

Fifty hands shot up. Jon nodded to Paula Zahn of CNN, who came right to the point. "What about Joshua Ben-Yosef, Dr. Weber? Do you think he is Jesus Christ?"

Jon smiled and said, "While some extraordinary events have been associated with this remarkable individual, I've not yet come to a definite conclusion."

"But which way are you tending at this point?" she wondered.

"Sorry, no further comment on that. Yes?"

"David Van Biema, *Time*. Does Joshua really heal people, Professor Weber?"

"A remarkable number claim to have been healed. I know firsthand of an instance in which a blind man apparently regained his sight."

"Did you actually see that?"

"No, but my wife, Shannon, did. The next day we checked out

the circumstances, and the episode seems authentic. I, personally, did witness a successful exorcism."

Surprise swept through the media crowd, and a dozen more hands shot up.

Jon recognized another familiar face.

"Richard Ostling, Associated Press. They say that Joshua sounds almost biblical in his discourses. Is that true? Have you heard him personally?"

"Yes to both questions. I've heard him speak on several occasions and he's . . . very impressive indeed."

"How so?"

"It sounds trite, but he holds his audiences spellbound. He can speak over a dozen languages without an accent of any kind. His message is a basic Christian ethic that attacks the evils of society and blesses those who do good. He also speaks in cadences and on themes quite parallel to those of Jesus."

"Have you ever seen him make a mistake? Say something incorrect? Do something wrong?"

Jon thought for a moment, then replied, "No, not that I know of."

"Well, have others seen or heard him make a miscue?"

"I can hardly speak for others. Yes?"

"Eric Gunderson, *Boston Globe*. What about Ben-Yosef's background, his youth, his earlier career before he went public?"

"I think most of those details have already appeared in newspapers and magazines. More will be forthcoming, I'm sure. Now, I really must—"

"Is there any chance that Joshua will get crucified?" Gunderson asked. "Like Jesus?"

"I hardly think that it will come to that! Crucifixion is now passé, I'm glad to say. I once asked Joshua that very question, and he replied something like: 'One cosmic sacrifice for the sins of the world is enough. Another would detract from it.'"

"So! Joshua *does* identify himself as 'the returned Jesus,' then?"

"Yes, at first a little indirectly, but lately all his comments point in that direction. Yes?"

"But why 'indirectly'? Oh, Bill O'Reilly, Fox."

"You'd have to ask Ben-Yosef that, although I do find a dramatic parallel there: most of the time Jesus only indirectly claimed to be the Son of God, though, at other times, more definitely so. Now it's time to—"

"I understand that you returned to the U.S. for a meeting of the Institute of Christian Origins in Cambridge," O'Reilly persisted. "Will that group decide whether or not Joshua is Jesus?"

"Not a chance!" Jon said, smiling. "That's not up to the ICO. But now, thank you, ladies and gentlemen. We'll issue a communiqué after the conclusion of the ICO meeting."

Additional questions rang out in that cramped basement room at Logan, but Jon ignored them. He retrieved his luggage, made a broken-field run for the exit, dodging a gauntlet of microphones in the process, and hailed a cab for Cambridge.

FIFTEEN

Nearly all thirty members of the ICO were present in the J. S. Nickel Center at Harvard University when Jon entered the conference room, looking fairly well recovered from his overseas flight the day before. As chair, he opened the meeting with predictable apologies for its tardy convening until Heinz von Schwendener—New Testament, Yale—genially cut him off.

"Stow that, Jon!" he said. "We certainly understand." A playful gnome whose mouth was often in gear, von Schwendener had gray-silver hair that had forsaken his now-bald pate and migrated southward to a rich stubble covering his cheeks and chin.

"Thank you, Heinz," responded Jon. "If any of you have a feeling of déjà vu, we all know why. Several years ago, in this very room, we were all reacting to the Rama crisis over Jesus. Now we have to respond to the *Joshua* crisis over Jesus, and this time we have *more than a skeleton* on our hands!"

Bemused smiles and head nodding accompanied several "Hear, hear!" comments offered around the huge mahogany conference table.

"I didn't have time to prepare a formal agenda," Jon resumed. "But if you don't mind, I think the usual three-part division will do fine. First, in pedestrian terms, will be the 'I ask you' segment. Then comes 'You ask me.' And finally, the section I've elegantly titled, 'What, if anything, should the ICO do in all of this?' But please don't tell anyone that I put it in these simplistic terms, or we'll all lose our reputations as scholarly sorts!"

"With grade inflation, you Harvards have already lost your reputations," the irrepressible von Schwendener retorted, with a beaming smile.

"As if you Yalies don't have a similar problem!" Jon shot back with a grin.

"Point taken," said von Schwendener, holding up hands in surrender.

"So, getting back to the main stream here. Is my 'carefully thought-out agenda' acceptable?"

After smiles and no objections, Jon continued, "All right, then, first off, how is America responding to Joshua Ben-Yosef? We won't bother with agnostics and non-Christians, since we know that they think anyone identifying Joshua with Jesus is a blazing idiot."

"Yes, except for Islam—among the non-Christians, that is," said Sally Humiston—archaeology, Berkeley. "On the West Coast, some Muslim clerics are wondering if Jesus actually *has* returned, as the *Qur'an* predicted He would. If Ben-Yosef weren't an Israeli, I think Islam would take even greater interest in him."

"East Coast too," said Brendan Rutledge—theology, Princeton. "Ben-Yosef is really stirring up some interesting thinking outside-the-box, and from the least expected quarters."

"All right," said Jon. "Let's inch away from the fringes. What are the liberal theologians saying?"

Katrina Vandersteen—semitics, Johns Hopkins—held up her pencil. "Well, our old friend Harry Nelson Hunt claims—very much like the agnostics—that any thought of Jesus physically returning is just as impossible as was His physical resurrection in the first place. In other words, 'Jesus wasn't God—He just shows us the way to God. He was a nifty, noble prophet, to be sure, but only a man who died, and that's the end of Him'—except, of course, for His massive subsequent influence."

"Predictable," said Jon, "though he may not reflect all liberal theologians in that regard. But now, I think, things will get more interesting. What does the Christian center say, Katrina?"

"Well, they, too, have some problems with Jesus actually returning under these circumstances. Not that they doubt He could: that's all but called-for in the Creed. It's just that they'd hate to, shall we say, back the wrong horse here. Well, that's not the best choice of—"

"Understandable," Jon commented. "Do continue."

"In many ways, I think this is the central point in the whole issue: what if Joshua actually *is* the returned Jesus? If we doubted it or denied it, then we'd be no better than those who rejected Jesus two thousand years ago. On the other hand, what if this truly is *not* Jesus at all but an impostor? Then, if we regarded him as Jesus, we'd be guilty of idolatry, blasphemy, folly, and a dozen other deadly sins! It's . . . just an incredible dilemma."

Silence reigned around the table. Then, applause actually broke out. No one had put it more succinctly than Katrina Vandersteen.

"Well done!" Jon commented. "That certainly is the nub of the issue. But I've heard that this broad center is leaning heavily in the direction of agreeing that Ben-Yosef equals Jesus."

"True enough."

"All right, then. Going farther across the spectrum, what about the center-to-right wing, the evangelicals?"

"Oh ho ho!" yelped the young, crew-cut pundit who was Richard Ferris, the ICO's general secretary. "You can't believe how divided they are! Half of them not only are sure that Jesus has returned in His intermediate coming, but they want to tell the world about it 'in these last days.'"

"Hold it, Dick," Jon interrupted. "How do they reconcile 'intermediate' and 'these last days'?"

"Many of them virtually equate the two: they think that 'intermediate' begins the end-times scenario. Anyway, this group—and it's big—is held in thrall by the prophecy preachers, and everything Joshua does over there is some kind of fulfillment in their book."

"And the other group of evangelicals?"

"Well, they and the Archies are against the very idea that—"

"Hold it!" Sally Humiston called out. "Who in the world are the Archies?"

"Oh! Sorry! The archconservatives. They're just next door to the Fundies, and they're all—"

"Wait a minute!" she again inquired. "Just who are the Fundies?"

"Oh—sorry again: the fundamentalists. In any case, both groups deny that Joshua could ever be Jesus, because the biblical signs heralding His Second Coming aren't there—the trumpets, the clouds of heaven, and the like."

"They don't buy the concept of an intermediate coming?" asked Jon.

"Never. To them, it's not part of Scripture and, therefore, not valid."

"So, put the case that Jesus actually *has* returned. They'd still deny it—on the basis of the Bible?"

"Right. He could do a miracle in front of their very eyes, but they'd doubt their own eyes before they'd doubt the Bible. In fact, were He to 'cast them into outer darkness,' they'd still be pointing to their Bibles on the way down to perdition, crying, 'It doesn't say that here!'"

Amid general laughter, Jon now called for the latest polls on whether Joshua was Jesus. Although no reliable worldwide sampling had yet been taken—a difficult project to bring off in any case—several ICO participants hauled out clippings from polls that both the *Christian Century* and *Christianity Today* had taken among Americans of all beliefs over the last month. Interestingly enough, the results of the surveys were within two percentage points of each other.

Jon read the statistics, then typed out the number averages via PowerPoint onto a screen at the end of the conference table:

Q: Do you think Joshua Ben-Yosef is the returned Jesus of Nazareth?

A: Yes: 54%; Undecided: 21%; No: 25%

"Incredible!" said Jon. "So more than half the country believes Jesus has returned?"

"And can you blame them?" asked Mark Noll, one of the country's brightest evangelical scholars. "I've taken reports from the media and your own web site, Jon, and made a list here of the extraordinary items associated with Ben-Yosef. May I read it?"

"Sure."

"Okay, but please tell me if I have anything wrong:

• Born in Bethlehem, raised in Nazareth.

• Parents: Joseph and Mariam, later claimed as Mariam only, with Joseph as foster father.

- Prodigy in school.
- A worldwide cyberphenomenon announces his return.
- Addresses crowds with great authority and eloquence.
- Uses beatitudes, warnings, parables very similar to those of Jesus.
- Linguistic genius: speaks many languages without accent in any of them.
- Apparent omniscience: seems to know the past history of everyone.
- Signs and wonders similar to those of Jesus—miracles, if you will—including healings, sight to the blind, and exorcisms, not to mention party supplies at a Galilee wedding.
- Indirect and later direct personal claims to be the returned Jesus.
- Endorsement by a presumed voice from heaven.

"Is that about it?"

Jon nodded slowly, then stopped and shook his head. "No," he admitted, "there are other items for your list." He went on to tell of the Sepphoris mosaic, his Nicodemus interview with Joshua by night, and anecdotal reports of Joshua's activities that he or Shannon had heard about but not witnessed. The ICO members were astonished and a bit amused by the flying pen episode, but totally mystified by the Sepphoris mosaic.

"You mean that young Jesus, working with Joseph up at Sepphoris, knew even then that He would die and rise again?" asked von Schwendener.

"Perhaps."

"No, wait; even more—that He would return twenty centuries after His resurrection?"

Jon nodded and said, "That's what the Sepphoris mosaic seems to suggest . . . if, that is, the Y abbreviation indeed refers to Jesus. The Israel Antiquities Authority is in the process of checking its authenticity to be sure no hoax or 'plant' was involved."

Silence and wonderment hung over the room like a low morning fog. Suddenly it evaporated into a babble of discussion, followed by a veritable hail of questions rattling onto Jon at the head of the table.

Clearly, the conclave had lurched into phase two. ICO members wanted exhaustive detail on all the items cited on Noll's list. Then, when Jon recalled further particulars not on that list, it evoked another cavalcade of questions that he fielded as best he could. Except for lunch, this consumed the rest of the afternoon.

Just before breaking for dinner, an interesting puzzler reemerged that had been asked earlier in the impromptu press conference at Logan Airport.

"Jon, in all your associations with Joshua, or from all reports," asked Brendan Rutledge, "did you ever note an occasion in which he made a mistake—did something wrong, got something wrong, or made an error or miscue of any kind, however minor?"

Jon sat back, rubbed his forehead, and pondered the query for some time, rehearsing all the points of contact he or Shannon had had with Joshua over the past months. Finally he shook his head and said, "No, not once that I can recall. Others may have, of course, but I've heard nothing of the kind to date."

A renewed buzz of discussion followed. It was now five o'clock, and they had not even reached segment three. They adjourned for dinner and were back at the conference table by seven-thirty.

When Jon reconvened the meeting, he announced, "Thanks for your patience, all! We're now at the last phase, namely, 'What, if anything, should the ICO do in all of this?' I remind you again: we're not obliged to do a darn thing. This is no Vatican Council— just a scholarly think tank that proved helpful in the Rama crisis. At that time, you'll recall, our suggestions were warmly received. So . . . the floor is open."

No one said anything for some moments. Then Rutledge volunteered, "I wonder if we should take a poll among ourselves. I mean, with all this evidence, shouldn't we be able to come to some sort of . . . provisional opinion on the question of Joshua's authenticity?"

The suggestion was met with furrowed brows. Then von Schwendener responded, "Yeah, I guess we could take a straw vote, but what in the world would that prove? The press could get hold of it and set us up as believing or denying Jesus Himself, for gosh-sakes, and we don't need that sort of publicity. Look out the window . . . see the reporters there? They'd water at the mouth if they learned about our poll."

Jon now weighed in on the proposal. "Whether or not we take a poll has no relationship whatever to the facts in the matter. Joshua could be Jesus even if we voted against it 100 percent; he could be an impostor even if we voted unanimously *for* his authenticity. Maybe we should avoid the mistakes of the Jesus Seminar and their stupid votes on whether or not Jesus could have said or done something."

"Hear! Hear!" The response was instant and enthusiastic.

"All right, then, colleagues: do we take any action?"

After some silence, von Schwendener stirred in his chair and said, "We have a heckuva lot of 'proofs' that Ben-Yosef is genuine, a really incredible amount of extraordinary signs! But we also have a big bundle of natural or even logical doubts that this could ever be, or at least be the case in this way or at this time. Someone has said, 'The greater the wonder, the greater the proofs necessary to substantiate it.' Hey, I believe that! And I'll admit: my favorite apostle in Jesus' group is Thomas! He's the scientist in that bunch. He was good for the first century, and I think he's good for us now."

Silence greeted von Schwendener's statement, until Sally Humiston asked, "And how is Thomas good for us?"

"Well, it was Thomas who said of the risen Jesus, 'Unless I put my finger in the print of the nails or touch the gash in His side, I will not believe!' I think we need a smoking gun here. We need the strongest possible proof of the suspension of natural law from Joshua. Lofty claims won't do, nor will charisma or eloquence, since we've had all these before. No hearsay cures either, nothing psychosomatic, but clear, obvious proofs of the supernatural dimension penetrating our natural order via things that we can see, hear, weigh, measure, and touch."

"What sorts of proofs?" asked Jon. "My wife and I have actually seen some of these very things."

"You may have, but I haven't! Mind you, I'm not in any way

impugning your powers of observation, Jon. But what if the wonders that you and Shannon saw were accomplished by some natural means? Even if I saw such things myself, I'd still have to ask that question."

"I agree. But again, what would qualify as an absolute proof?"

Von Schwendener said nothing. He only tapped his right forefinger on the writing pad in front of him while looking out the windows at the sky over Cambridge, with stars starting to pierce the violet of dusk. Finally he curled his fingers into a fist, banged the table, and said, "Christianity itself is founded on Jesus' resurrection—on life after death. And I guess it would take something like that—resurrection—as the ultimate sign."

"Has Joshua ever done that?" asked Mark Noll. "Raised someone from the dead?"

"I asked him that very question on the rooftop at Bethany," Jon replied. "He said, 'No, not yet.'"

"Does that mean he intends to raise someone in the future?"

"I don't know. He said he'd leave that to the will of his Father. You realize, of course, that if he does not do a resurrection, this in itself would not disprove his claims?"

"Of course. But what other parallels between Jesus and Joshua do you think might occur? Do we, say, look for Joshua's arrest by the Jerusalem authorities? Can we expect another crucifixion—or some such other ugly termination?"

"No, although I also asked him that question."

"What did he say?"

"He said that one sacrifice was enough. Anything more would diminish the original one, which was all-sufficient for all time."

"Hmmm, good theology," said Noll. "Which, I might add, we'd expect if our source is authentic!"

When the chuckling subsided, Jon tried to wrap things up. "All right then, colleagues," he said. "It's high time to get practical here, and so I ask again: What, if anything, should the ICO do in response to Joshua Ben-Yosef?"

The members of the Institute of Christian Origins wrestled the rest of the evening for an answer. It had seemed comparatively easy to assign the various investigative panels in the case of the Rama crisis several years earlier. Then, the evidence was static, but now it was dynamic. They were trying to focus on a moving target that itself was generating more evidence by the month, the week, the day. Because everything was so provisional, therefore, the ICO decided not to issue a statement of any kind.

The members did, however, authorize Jon to try to get federal help so that medical scientists could check on Joshua's therapeutic activities in Israel. Perhaps, too, the CIA or FBI could assist Israeli security in combing through Joshua's past. Some in the ICO who were nearly convinced that Joshua was genuine found such measures "distasteful, but probably necessary in the current climate of skepticism."

At home in suburban Weston that night, Jon called his parents in Hannibal. The phone was answered by a firm voice that had apparently escaped the ravages of time: "Erhard Weber here, proud father of the famous Jonathan Weber who saved Christianity. May I help you?"

Jon was momentarily taken aback, then he burst out laughing. "Dad! When did you get caller ID?"

"Heh heh." Erhard chuckled. "Had to, Jon. You wouldn't believe the number of calls I get simply because I'm your father! Where are you calling from?"

"Home. I made a quick trip back to the States for an ICO meeting in Cambridge. I return to Israel tomorrow."

"Well, tell me, what's the latest on Joshua? He's all we talk about at St. John's."

"Yes, and in a hundred thousand other churches across the world. You remember the big theological objection you had to Joshua: Joseph as his father?"

"Surprise, surprise! He wasn't after all, was he?"

"So Joshua claims. Shannon's now convinced that he's Jesus, back again after two thousand years."

"Hmmm. Is she now?"

"And what about you? You're in touch, Dad. You read widely; you've seen the media reports—what do you think?"

After a moment of silence, he replied solemnly, "Well . . . Trudi and I think . . . that Christ has truly returned, Jon."

"Quite a different response from the first time you called me about Joshua."

"Yes, but that was before I fully understood His intermediate coming. What do you think, Jon?"

"I'm on the verge, Dad. I'm on the verge. You've finally gotten a computer, I understand?"

"Yup. Good one, too! They finally dragged me, kicking and screaming, into the twenty-first century!"

"Great! And you're also on-line?"

"Of course, Son. We even have electricity here in Hannibal! Horseless buggies too!"

"Now that's progress! Okay, I'll keep feeding you our best information on Joshua via the web. You'll get special, inside info—more than what we send out over the usual web site. Just click on 'reply' to respond in each case, whenever you like."

"Fine. Thanks, Jon. And if Joshua does prove to be Jesus, Trudi and I want to fly over there as soon as possible. You'll have to pull some strings for us, since over at the Mark Twain Travel Agency they tell us we'd have an eleven-month wait!"

"Will do. Where's Mom?"

"She's off at a Lutheran Women's Missionary League meeting."

"Hope the coffee, cookies, and green Jell-O are good! Do give her my love."

At Logan Airport, just before flying back to Israel, Jon pulled out his cell phone for an important call he should have made several days earlier. Reaching into his wallet, he pulled out an old card on which President Sherwood Bronson had written his private number during the Rama crisis in his first term. That number was supposed to bypass the White House switchboard.

In view of all the new area codes since then, Jon wondered if the number was still good. He punched it in and heard a repeated ringing tone. Good: at least there was no annoying intercept. More ringing. Rats! Either the president was out, or the number was worthless after all.

Then a voice came on loud and firm, "Hello! Woody Bronson here."

"Mr. President! This is Jonathan Weber—you may remember me from the Rama crisis several years ago?"

There was silence. Then a mystified tone asked, "The *Rama* crisis, you say? How do you spell that? And who gave you this number?"

Jon's heart sank. "Well, you yourself did, sir. Remember that archaeological find in Israel that set the world on edge?"

"Oh, oh, oh, *yes,* Professor Weber! Yes, of course I remember you! How could I ever forget the man who saved Western civilization?"

"Oh-ho! Hardly that!" Jon laughed.

"Or at least Christianity itself," the president persisted. "What's up, Jon? Remember, you gave me permission to call you that!"

"I did indeed, Mr. President. It seems we now have another crisis on our hands, and I was—"

"Yes, and I'll bet I know what it is . . . it's about Joshua Ben-Yosef, right?"

"Exactly. I was—"

"Fact is, I've been meaning to call *you* about Ben-Yosef. That man is so Jesus-like! My pastor over at Foundry Methodist declared from the pulpit last Sunday that our Lord has most probably returned. The whole country's excited, even that hotbed of cynical expediency called Washington, D.C.!"

"But first, I think—"

"Yes, but there's a real downside, too: people are leaving their jobs in droves, assuming that the last days are finally here, and they actually want to cash in on their accumulated sick leave before the world ends! Can you believe it? Already the economy's affected. So, what do you think, Jon? Is Joshua for real? And if he is, what should the nation and I do about it?"

"First, of course, we have to answer the authenticity question, Mr. President, and that's the reason for my call. You said the whole country is excited, so I do think it's in the national interest that we know the truth one way or the other, and as soon as possible. If Ben-Yosef's an impostor, we mustn't be deceived any longer. But if he's genuine, we shouldn't be dragging our feet in recognizing that."

"Absolutely! I agree with every syllable! So how may I help, Jon?"

"More than anything else, we have to know even more about Joshua's past—ideally, *all* the details of Joshua's past. If he's a fake, he will have screwed up somewhere along the line, and we can find it out. But if he's genuine, Jesus would make no mistakes. Bottom line: we need additional investigative help to coordinate with Shin Bet over in Israel in order to fine-tooth comb every trace left by Joshua in his thirty-plus years."

"Right! And you'll have it! No question that this is in the national interest, so I'll have both the FBI and the CIA send some of their best people."

Jon couldn't resist asking, "Do you think this time they'll . . . actually cooperate?"

Bronson released his well-known, Paul Bunyan-style laugh. "There will be no turf battles on this one, I can assure you!"

"That's excellent, Mr. President!"

"Where should they contact you?"

"At Hebrew University in Jerusalem, the Mount Scopus campus."

"Done! Good work, Jon! And thanks for . . . maybe saving our faith a second time?"

"Vastly overstated, sir!"

"And, Jon, do me this favor. As you can see, my private number still works. So use it, please, the moment you know one way or the other. I really want to be the first to know on this one."

"That's a promise, Mr. President!"

SIXTEEN

After a very bumpy flight across the Atlantic facing the winds of March—headwinds, strangely, where tailwinds were the rule—Jon was back in his office at Hebrew University. No fewer than 674 e-mails awaited him, as well as a five-inch wad of letters in his snail-mail box. Fortunately, the ICO's Richard Ferris had come to Israel on the same flight to help Jon with the correspondence load, and it was Ferris's eagle eye that spotted a very important envelope that could otherwise have been lost or delayed in the mail deluge. He handed it to Jon, whose eyes immediately widened. He had seen that elegant handwriting before.

This time Joshua was inviting Shannon and him to a very private gathering of "The Seventy" at a hillside resort overlooking the Sea of Galilee near Magdala. The Seventy, Jon and Shannon knew from the Gospels, was that larger group of Jesus' disciples entrusted with mission responsibilities. Apparently, numbers seemed to have changed little across twenty centuries, in the Jesus-Joshua economy.

The invitation enthralled Shannon and pleased even Jon, who was happy that the event would occur on the first weekend in April, when his schedule was free. Did Joshua somehow know that? Would he himself ever stop asking such questions? Why couldn't he, like Shannon, simply take Joshua on his own terms and be done with it?

Both he and Shannon knew more was at stake in this visit than in any previous. They could feel it in their very bones: things were building to a climax in the case of Joshua the Christ v. Joshua the Charlatan. Now they would have a rare chance to dialogue with the man apart from crowds and public address systems.

But why had *they* been chosen? Jon wondered. Surely Joshua

wasn't trying to commission them into the larger grouping of his apostolic band, was he?

They arrived at the hillside resort late Friday afternoon. It was a little-known retreat compound with a panoramic view of the Sea of Galilee immediately to the east. The central building was a spacious lodge, where all Joshua's guests were assigned rooms: The Seventy, as well as a slightly larger group that included Shannon and Jon. Shannon quickly recognized other women there who had assisted in Joshua's ministry. The amenities at the lodge stressed comfort rather than luxury, and the food likewise. The opening dinner on Friday evening was nutritious rather than gormandizing.

Since it was the first really warm spring weekend in Galilee, Jon and Shannon were dining at a table out on the veranda. "I wonder if this food was catered or created," he whispered.

Without the expected smile, she replied, "Please, Jon, try to enjoy a truly spiritual event just this once without your inane comments."

Trying to make amends, he carefully steered the conversation back to their storied romance along the Sea of Galilee below, pointing out several of their most exciting sites. After two "remember when's," Shannon was smiling again.

Now she pointed to Joshua, who was playing with several of the children in the group on the lawn below. The younger set seemed to love him, running up and hugging him around his legs before he made a forgivably tardy arrival at the dinner tables.

After supper, in what could have been called an orientation session, the group gathered in the great room of the lodge. Orange tongues of flame crackled inside a huge fieldstone fireplace, since evenings were still cool in the north country.

Joshua rose and stood next to the hearth. The man now looked more Christlike than ever, thought Jon. Blue fire seemed to blaze in his eyes. The determined, lightly bearded chin and square-cut features were the same, but his hair was longer, now almost brushing his shoulders. His usual sport shirt was partially hidden under a broad white sash draped down from his right shoulder, the white reflecting the flickering orange from the fire.

Joshua began with the standard Trinitarian invocation: "In the name of the Father, and of the Son, and of the Holy Spirit. Amen!"

Although he had heard and used that invocation on countless occasions, Jon shivered a bit this time with the thought that it could be the Son Himself who was offering it.

Joshua continued with an opening prayer. What struck Jon was not the idle question of whether Joshua could have been praying to himself—there was too much biblical precedent for Jesus praying to the Father—but, again, how very Christlike was that prayer. Like Jesus' "High Priestly Prayer" in the Upper Room, it was selfless, caring, comprehensive, and, above all, concerned about his followers. In almost divine cadences, Joshua implored God to renew and augment the faith in a secularizing and competitive world. It was, purely and simply, the most moving prayer Jon had ever heard. Often, especially in marathon litanies by long-winded clergy, he could hardly wait for the amen. This time he was almost sorry when it arrived.

"I can't believe it, Shannon," he whispered. "I actually wish he'd gone on and on!"

She nodded, tears in her eyes.

Smiling, Joshua now reintroduced The Twelve. "And yes, they will remain at twelve," he added. "Our prize renegade—whom we renamed Yudas, of course—has learned his lesson well and will not betray me."

Actual cheering broke out. A smiling Yudas stood up, clasped his hands over his head in appreciation, and even bowed slightly—a scene that was becoming totally surreal for Jon.

"He's also promised not to commit suicide," Joshua added, with a twinkle in his eye. "And since some of you have asked, no, I will not be arrested in this, my interim return. Nor will there be a trial or crucifixion. Once was *quite* enough!"

Joshua now introduced The Seventy and explained why each had decided to become his special emissary. "Still others of you," he continued, this time looking at Shannon and Jon, "are believers, doubting believers, believing doubters, or skeptics. I have invited you to attend also, because of the special stations into which God has placed you for such a time as this. Professor Jonathan Weber over there, for example, despite his doubts, knows more about my first coming than any other scholar on earth."

A jet of hot blood surged into Jon's head, less because he had been singled out and far more because Joshua now seemed to go beyond any oblique claims to identity with Jesus. That claim was now open, obvious.

"Soon," Joshua continued, "the purpose of my interim presence here will become clear to the entire world. After that happens, I will return to my Father, leaving you in this world as eyewitnesses to who I am and the truths I have imparted. I have chosen you for this extraordinary purpose because of your faith, your hope, your love—and your promise. You, in turn, will choose others, so that all generations to come before my final appearance at the end of time will know how God again rescued His people and His church from decline or even collapse."

The room was silent as a sepulchre. For most, heaven and earth had joined in a cosmic drama that had suddenly engulfed them. Jon and Shannon, holding hands so tightly that they hurt, were nearly in a trance. No one moved. No one spoke.

Joshua walked back and forth before the fireplace, casting kinetic shadows on the floor. "Of course you are all overcome with this awesome responsibility. In fact, if you were not, you would not be instruments fit for this divine purpose. But the Holy Spirit will enlighten and inspire you as He did the early Christians. You will then succeed beyond all expectations. But now it is certainly time for your questions. Feel free to ask them. Ask anything."

As befitted his Peter counterpart, Shimon raised his hand immediately and asked, "Lord, in your first presence among us twenty centuries ago, the four evangelists wrote their Gospels about what you said and did. Shouldn't we have such a record this time also?"

"Blessed are you, Shimon, for that suggestion. But I've already commissioned one of you twelve—Matthan or Levi, as he prefers—to do just that. In future Bibles, his will rank as the fifth Gospel, following the other four."

Shimon smiled and settled back in his chair. Shannon, however, looked troubled. She whispered to Jon, "Shimon doesn't look well at all, does he, Jon? His hand is trembling."

"You're right . . . and I thought he looked a little jaundiced at dinner."

Matthan now asked, "What about our Jewish brethren, Rabbi?

Why are so few of them your followers? What will you do—or what can we do—to win them over so that they become Jewish-Christians or 'completed Jews,' as we often call ourselves?"

Joshua shook his head sadly and said, "It is the greatest paradox in the universe. God's own chosen people—the very apple of His eye—should have recognized His Messiah. They should have formed the very leadership among all Christians, then and now. And yet, as John's Gospel put it, 'He came to His own, yet His own knew Him not.' This is the bad news, but here is the good: I have come to correct this, as you will certainly see in a short time."

"But how will you do that, Lord?" Matthan inquired.

"Trust God. Trust me."

Jon had no intention whatever of intruding into the discussion, but he could not restrain himself. His hand shot up. When Joshua nodded, with a slight smile, Jon asked, "Far and away, the greatest challenge to Christianity today is Islam. Now, since—"

"No, Jon. The greatest challenge to Christianity today is to reach out with the good news of salvation to over three billion people on earth who are pagan or have no religious beliefs whatever. Islam, with a billion believers, is the second greatest challenge to our faith. But please continue . . ."

"Correct indeed! Yet Islam—and its massive birthrate—continues to narrow the statistical gap between itself and the two billion Christians. How should Christians respond to this challenge?"

"As with all other challenges: not with bigotry or self-righteousness, but with love and logic. So often in your religious discussions here on earth, 'sweet reasonableness' is overlooked and fanaticism takes its place. Remember how I told you, 'You shall love the Lord your God with all your heart and soul and mind'? Whatever happened to the 'mind' part of that?"

"Exactly!" Jon exclaimed, since it mirrored his own thinking. "Now, please, might you apply that to our dialogue with Muslims?"

"Certainly. In all such discussions, which argument do they raise most often in opposing the faith?"

"That our Scriptures have been corrupted through recopying across the centuries."

"Indeed. Yet this is absolutely incorrect! The Dead Sea Scrolls version of Isaiah, for example, is almost exactly the same as the version in the Masoretic text twelve centuries later! With reason and gentleness, then, point out to your Islamic brother or sister that the most authoritative information about events in the first century must certainly come from first-century sources, not seventh-century derivative works like the *Qur'an*."

Jon nodded enthusiastically, along with the others.

"You might also add that the miracles I performed were truly such. Those credited to their prophet have a legendary quality, such as the moon splitting in two and its halves falling on either side of Mecca."

Shannon suddenly raised her hand, and Joshua recognized her with a warm smile. "But what, Lord, should be done about all the Arab-Israeli hostilities?" she asked.

"Another great paradox!" Joshua replied. "Here, in this holiest of lands, not even a thimbleful of blood should ever have been shed. Yet sin and pride have taken their seats at the negotiation tables, rather than statesmanship and conciliation. Both Arabs and Israelis have often preferred the treacherous path of fanaticism that leads to violence and the ditches of despair. Both sides know the true path to peace, how to walk that path, and how to maintain that path. I'll have much more to say to the world about this shortly."

"Including the problem of terrorism?"

"Especially including terrorism."

There seemed to be no end to the questions—queries regarding means of defending the faith, public moral issues, further probing into the end times, and a dozen other topics. They easily spilled over into the Saturday sessions the next day.

After a morning coffee break, Jon decided to venture, indirectly, a question regarding the Sepphoris mosaic, the most nagging and unresolved issue on his mental horizon. In a frame of reference that theoretically mirrored Shannon's new faith, he asked, "I wonder if you'd be kind enough to tell us more about your so-called 'hidden years' two thousand years ago, the time you spent growing up in Nazareth? And why do we have so little information in the Gospels about your youth?"

"To answer your second question first, the four Gospels comprised one scroll each. Obviously, scrolls were expensive in those days, since they were copied by hand, and they had only very limited space. Mark and John felt that they had to proceed immediately to my adult ministry, but all believers are grateful that Matthew and Luke thought to tell of the Nativity as well." He went on to relate entrancing episodes of his boyhood life in Nazareth two millennia ago, anecdotes that involved Joseph, Mary, his four half brothers, and two half sisters.

Still he had not mentioned Sepphoris. Jon probed further, "Did you and your foster father, Joseph, ever get to Sepphoris?"

"Of course we did!" He laughed. "Sepphoris was almost a second home for us, since we helped rebuild the city after the Romans destroyed it. Archaeologists will be digging there again this summer."

"What parts of the city did you help reconstruct?"

"We built part of the theater, several mosaic sidewalks, and—oh yes, the synagogue, of course." He paused, grinned, and continued, "I even put my stamp, so to speak, at one corner of the synagogue floor. I laid a little mosaic that summarized my future in the fewest words possible. It read: *Yeshua dies, but lives. He leaves, but returns— twice David to the Star,* meaning, of course, this return of mine two thousand years later."

Even though John and Shannon had worked with that hypothesis, they were now electrified to learn that it was true.

Joshua stopped, looked quizzically at Jon, and said, "It's interesting that your questions led me back to that mosaic. Has it been rediscovered?"

There it was, thought Jon, his heart racing—*a genuine error on Joshua's part. If he were Jesus, he should have* known *it had been discovered!*

A slight tremble in his voice, he asked, "Please don't think this impertinent, sir, but don't you *know* whether or not it has been rediscovered?"

Joshua thought for a moment, head downward, the thumb and forefinger of his right hand slightly pinching the ridge of his upper nose. Then he said, "Yes, of course. My mosaic *has* been rediscovered, and you had a major role in interpreting it. But now, lest you doubt divine omniscience here, Jon, I should remind you of an important statement in Christology that you once studied in dogmatics and even included in your book. You wrote, 'During His earthly ministry, Jesus did not always or fully use His divine powers.' Nor do I here, and for good reason. Even though I certainly could, I do not pry into private matters, for example."

Jon nodded and raised both hands in surrender, ashamed that he had not thought of the answer himself, yet astonished that Joshua could quote his own words so precisely and apply them so well.

"Had enough, Jon?" Shannon whispered. "Or do you want to go on asking silly questions and making a fool of yourself? And embarrass us both in the process?"

"You don't have to put it that way, Shannon," he muttered, with a little bite.

Questions by the dozens followed, in what was clearly the most extraordinary Q and A opportunity in history. Hands in the room were still shooting up when Joshua announced, "That's enough for now, my dear friends. Don't you think it's time for lunch?"

Jon and Shannon returned to a table on the outside veranda because of its commanding view of the Sea of Galilee, even though the sky now seemed to be darkening. Joshua wandered among the diners, exchanging pleasant small talk at each table. Between soup and salad, he stopped at Jon and Shannon's. A little tongue-tied after his previous dialogue with Joshua, Jon let Shannon have the first word.

"Thank you!" she exclaimed, beaming at Joshua. "Thank you so much for including us in this . . . incredibly distinguished group!"

"I, in turn, thank you and the other women for your help and support in our great mission," he replied.

"This is a magnificent spot," Jon observed. "Now I can understand why . . . Jesus chose to move here from Nazareth. I doubt if it's changed much since His day."

"It hasn't," replied Joshua, smiling. "If your American developers owned this area, the lake would probably be surrounded with hotels. But do enjoy your lunch." He moved to another table.

The moment he left, Shannon looked tenderly at her husband and said, "I'm sorry for what I said back inside there, Jon. Forgive me?"

He smiled and reached over to squeeze her hand.

Dessert arrived. "Aha!" said Jon. "Raspberries and *angel* food cake. How very appropriate! But no, Shannon, I won't make any dumb comments about whether or not Joshua brought the angel food along with him from any celestial bakeries."

"Fine restraint on your part, Jon! Angel food also happens to be made of egg whites: very healthy!"

By now the sky had turned ominously black, and a nasty squall blew in from the Mediterranean. Rain and hail started pelting the veranda, and everyone scurried inside, plates in hand, to finish dessert. Some minutes later, Joshua reappeared in the great room.

Opening the sliding glass doors to the veranda, he stepped out on the deck, faced the Sea of Galilee, and held up both arms. "*Shalom! Peace!*" he commanded loudly. "*Be calm!*"

Gusts of wind continued to plaster paper napkins onto the wooden railings of the deck.

Jon looked at Shannon with raised eyebrows and whispered, "Maybe he shouldn't have attempted *this* one."

"Have some faith, Jon."

Several moments later, however, the wind died down to a whisper. In less than a minute, the rain and hail stopped. Seconds after that, the sun reappeared, surrounded by a clearing sky in glorious Galilean blue.

Shannon looked at Jon, her face transformed. "What manner of man is this that even the wind and the waves obey him?" she asked, as had Jesus' disciples twenty centuries earlier.

A barrage of questions continued in the great hall after lunch. Patiently Joshua fielded them all, even some that were less than apt. Since he had never held a press conference and did not intend to, this was as close to one as this privileged group would ever get.

By midafternoon, someone in Jon's marginal category inquired of Joshua, "Which of the various divisions in Christianity comes closest to God's truth in their beliefs, Rabbi? The Roman Catholics, Eastern Orthodox, or one of the Protestant denominations? And, if the last, which one?"

A great silence descended on the room. Probably it was the one

question the world's two billion Christians most wanted answered—
each one, of course, assuming that his or her own church body's doctrine and practice came closest to what Jesus had taught.

Laughter suddenly pierced the silence, Joshua's laughter. "Do you
realize that if I answered that question by announcing some sort of
'winner,' the rest of Christendom would be deeply disappointed?
And the winner would be ruined by pride and arrogance in telling
everyone else, 'See: we've been right the whole time!'"

Joshua paused to let that sink in. Then he continued, "In His
great and permissive providence, our heavenly Father knows that
humanity is not a monolith. He knows that people will respond to
His revelation in widely different ways. Some believers are more
emotionally driven in their personalities and therefore in their worship. Others are more rationally attuned and value the head over
the heart. And so we must thank God that there are the various
Eastern Orthodox church bodies that stress the mysteries of the
faith and cultivate their unbroken link with earliest Christianity.
We must thank God that there are Roman Catholics who take their
statistical majority so seriously and value the traditions and litur-
gies of the church. We must thank God that there are Lutherans
who, like Saint Paul, accent the central importance of how God
truly forgives sins by His grace and through faith in Christ Jesus.
We must thank God that there are Anglicans who celebrate the historical leadership of the bishops, as well as their Methodist heirs
who specialize in sanctification. We must thank God for Baptists
and their zeal for missions, Presbyterians and Reformed for their
worship of the sovereignty of God. And so it goes—right down to
South Sea Islanders in grass skirts, beating their drums in reso-
nance to the Creator."

Silence reigned again. "Not that disunity is God's ideal," Joshua
continued. "In the Upper Room on that terrible Thursday night, I
prayed that you might all be one. And you *are* all one, at least
regarding the essentials of the faith. Greater unity will certainly
come before I return to the Father."

The rest of the conclave was devoted to practical directives as to
how the Seventy and others could missionize successfully in what
many were calling a post-Christian world. Finally, Joshua closed the

conference with a brief devotion and benediction that again held everyone in thrall.

It had been Jesus' way with words that had captivated crowds the first time around, Jon recalled. And it was Joshua's way with words that was doing the same thing now. It was, far and away, the most extraordinary weekend any of them had ever spent.

On the drive back to Jerusalem, Jon and Shannon did not converse much. She was smart enough to quit trying to bring him to a decision regarding Joshua. A nagging "Okay, you've seen all the evidence! How can you possibly doubt?" would hardly have been helpful.

For his part, Jon was starting to see his qualms being suffocated under massive layers of proof. At one point that weekend, he thought that he had spotted the chink, when Joshua had apparently not known about the Sepphoris mosaic being found. Yet not only had he explained that perfectly, Jon reflected, but everything would have been much less credible had Joshua immediately cited the mosaic in telling of his youth. In that case, he might conceivably have "planted" the piece as part of his delusionary scheming. Jon was no stranger to archaeological frauds. But it was he himself, not Joshua, who had brought up Sepphoris in their discussions.

When they reached Tiberias, Jon said, "Let's do the Plaza for dinner, okay?"

"Yes, darling!" She smiled. "More than okay!"

They drove into the hotel parking lot and exchanged a long, lingering kiss. Once again they recalled that dinner several years earlier when they had fallen so totally in love. The week that followed was a magnificent mélange of the greatest joy they had ever known.

In the dining room, Jon asked the maitre d' for the table at the northwestern corner, and he kindly obliged. "Have you been here before?" he asked, while lighting the candles.

"Oh yes. Yes indeed!" Shannon replied with a great smile.

As he picked up the menu, Jon looked at the wall and said, "I wonder what they did with the plaque . . ."

"What plaque?"

"The one that says, 'At this table, Jonathan Weber and Shannon Jennings fell hopelessly in love.'"

She reached over to caress the back of Jon's hand. "I have an idea," she whispered. "Let's do the Plaza for overnight too, okay?"

"More than okay, my darling!"

They ate dinner in haste, passing up dessert. Fortunately, a room was available so that Jon would not have to physically evict its occupants. Once inside the room, he enclosed her in a rapturous embrace—until she whispered, "Do you think Joshua will see us?"

He stopped, broke out laughing, and said, "If so, he'll be *mighty* jealous!"

"Jon!"

"Sorry, darling! Forgive the impiety?"

"I love you, Jon."

His kiss said the same thing.

SEVENTEEN

S am Rosenzweig, FBI," said the tall figure with dark glasses as he stood in the doorway of Jon's office at Hebrew University, flashing his identification.

"Sol Falkenburg, CIA," said the man next to him, a head shorter but just as quick with his credentials.

"Welcome, gentlemen! Come in, come in!" said Jon, closing the door behind them. "I'm Jon Weber, and this is Gideon Ben-Yaakov, director of the Israel Antiquities Authority." After a round of handshakes, Jon ordered a carafe of coffee and asked them all to sit down.

Turning to the visiting Americans, he said, "Thanks for flying over here so quickly, gentlemen."

"As if we had a choice?" said Falkenburg. "The president was quite insistent—command performance stuff."

"And for good reason," said Jon. "You're clued in to the general situation?"

"Sure, like much of the world, it seems," said Rosenzweig. "It's hard to believe that one of our people could attract so much attention—unless, of course, he's . . . the Christ Himself!"

" 'One of our people' is the key phrase," said Jon. "You're both Jewish, I hope? You both know Hebrew?"

"As well as English in my case," said Rosenzweig. "The CIA will have to speak for itself."

"Here too," said Falkenburg.

"Excellent. By the way, are you religious Jews or secular?"

"We're secular," said Rosenzweig. "Why?"

"Fine. Nothing whatever against Judaism, mind you. It's just that we don't want any anti-Semites down the pike complaining that the Joshua investigation was stacked with 'Jewish anti-Christians.'

We badly need you and Gideon Ben-Yaakov here for your linguistic skills: Hebrew in all its dialects, especially Ashkenazi and Sephardi, okay?"

All nodded.

"Fine," Jon resumed. "Now let's begin with confession . . . always good for the soul. We may have muddied the waters a bit in the early phases of this investigation. It started with my checking on the circumstances of Ben-Yosef's birth in Bethlehem and several investigative reporters from *U.S. News* doing the same for his youth and education up in Galilee. Still, I think we uncovered some rather important information, all of which is spelled out in these files you'll each receive.

"Dr. Ben-Yaakov here became involved when we wanted to determine if Shin Bet was doing any surveillance on Joshua, and he continues to be our link with Israeli security. And yes, Shin Bet has had a tail on Joshua over the past months, with little more to report than what we all read in the newspapers.

"Meanwhile, my wife, Shannon, and I have had some very significant personal contacts with Joshua. In all of them, we've found that the man is anything but subversive. In fact, he's one of the most extraordinary—no, *the* most extraordinary—individual we've ever met, a multi-faceted genius with incredible charisma and so many other positive attributes and skills that—"

"Pardon me, Professor Weber," Rosenzweig interposed, "but we're trained to go after spies, criminals, subversives, saboteurs. Why are we checking up on Mr. Wonderful?"

"Well, I think you know the answer. Quite soon, two billion people on this planet are going to have to decide if Mr. Wonderful is just some bright guy—or the returned version of Jesus Christ, whom Christians call the Son of God. And the other four billion in the world are going to be impacted as well. I'm sure President Bronson has filled you in on the rest and how our national economy got involved: people leaving their jobs, selling everything they have to pack up and come here as pilgrims, et cetera?"

Both agents nodded.

"Well, our investigation should try to get a leg up on the rest of the world and find evidence on Joshua one way or the other."

"I think we have the picture," said Falkenburg.

"All right, then. Gideon, you were brilliant in the Rama crisis. Let's hear your thoughts on how we should coordinate this investigation."

Gideon pulled the pipe out of his mouth—which he had been smoking near an open window, in deference to the others—and said, "Shin Bet will cooperate in any way we think best, Jon. They're ready to add personnel, if necessary, and more importantly, they'll put their labs at our disposal. I'd suggest that we convene a meeting of the *U.S. News* people—they're still here in Israel, I understand—together with Noah Friedmann, the director of Shin Bet, and all of us here. Then we can decide on our best strategy and mark off appropriate investigational vectors—who's in charge of which turf—that kind of thing."

Falkenburg nodded and said, "That's the best way to go. The CIA can provide additional manpower, if necessary, as can the FBI, I'm sure. Our best contribution could be to provide any exotic lab tests that may become necessary."

"Good." Jon nodded. "So the FBI and CIA will cooperate and share information? Pardon the question, but you do remember what happened before 9/11?"

"Who can forget?" said Rosenzweig, shrugging his shoulders.

"Fine," said Jon. "We're all in agreement, then. Where shall we hold our first meeting?"

"Not here," said Gideon. "There's always a bunch of media people."

"How well I know!"

"Why not meet in our Israel Antiquities Authority conference room at the Rockefeller Museum? That should confuse the media hounds, no?"

"Good!" Jon agreed. "Please give me your local addresses and phone numbers, gentlemen. I'll have my secretary call around for an optimal date and time. Meanwhile, I need not tell you how important absolute secrecy is in this matter. If the world learns that criminal investigative agencies are on the trail of the man many believe to be the holy, innocent Savior of the world, it would be a public relations nightmare!"

Their agreement was obvious.

"And more than that," Jon continued, "our own lives could also be in danger from fanatics—of which organized religion, unfortunately, has too many!"

Two days later, Jon's cell phone rang as he was walking to his university symposium.

"Jon? Naomi Ben-Yaakov here."

"Hello, lovely one! I hope you're calling about the grout up at Sepphoris . . ."

"Precisely. I asked two of Gideon's lab colleagues in the IAA to be part of the team, and our test results just came in."

"Great! What did you find?"

"Well, the mosaic seems authentic enough. I only wish we could have checked something organic up there: then carbon 14 could have been used, of course, to find the age of the mosaic. But stone is stone. Grout is grout. The assay comparison, however, went very well. We took small samples of the grout in the mosaic, as well as from the synagogue floor, and compared them in our laboratory here. We found the same gypsum/lime materials and very nearly the same ratios of materials in the mix."

"Okay, but what about the tessera themselves? Do they match those in the synagogue floor?"

"Yes. The same pale yellows, the vermilions, and the rest. Those on the synagogue floor are first cousins, if not siblings."

"And the shapes?"

"Same cuts. Same angles."

Jon was silent for several moments. Then he asked, "Well, no question then, is there?"

"None that I can see. The mosaic looks to be the real thing."

A jumble of staggering thoughts jostled one another in Jon's mind. Was it really possible, he asked himself again, that young Jesus was already so sure of His messianic role that He could predict not only His own death and resurrection, but also His next coming? And how completely Joshua had confirmed it—and, in fact, how had it confirmed Joshua?

"Jon? Are you still there?"

"Oh, sorry, Naomi: I was woolgathering. My . . . profound thanks to you and your staff!"

Jon skipped lunch that day for a solo stroll along the summit of the Mount of Olives. In a very real sense, the more the evidence piled up in support of Joshua, the greater the problem for him. He felt the acids of stress starting to sear into his very soul. For weeks now, he had tried what he admitted were various "alkalines of avoidance" to neutralize them, but without success. Joshua—sham or Savior, quack or Christ, guller or God? Decide he was Christ when he was not? That would be a devastating blow to his reputation, imprinting a haunting defect onto his scholarship and theology. Still, people can recover from their errors.

But decide Joshua was not Christ when he *was*? Here there were cosmic consequences. In episode after episode, the Gospels were not very supportive of those who rejected Jesus. It wasn't fair. Jesus' first time around, two thousand years ago, should have been enough. Now, it seemed, a double dose of faith was required of believers. Not fair. Not fair at all!

"God help me!" he said aloud, while walking back slowly to the university. It was not an expression for Jon. It was a prayer.

The first meeting of the investigation panel took place four days later. Aside from Jon and his associate, Richard Ferris, Jeffery Sheler was there with two of the other *U.S. News* personnel. They passed out several files of material to other panel members, asking only for first publication rights once the investigation was complete. Several more Hebrew-speaking CIA and FBI operatives had arrived from the States to join forces with Shin Bet and its representatives, including the director, Noah Friedmann.

Jon was particularly impressed with Friedmann, a well-built veteran of the Six-Day War who had lost an eye in combat and now sported a patch in the tradition of another Israeli hero, Moshe Dayan. With leather-tan skin, hair the color of gray steel, and a crew cut, Friedmann never had any trouble getting people to listen to what he had to say. Certainly he spoke for Shin Bet—Israel's FBI—but, most convincingly, he spoke for himself.

Three women were also present: Naomi Ben-Yaakov, to report on the Sepphoris mosaic; Shannon, to tell of her encounters with Joshua; and Esther Meir, Jon's office secretary at Hebrew University, who would take notes. Jon asked Gideon to chair the conference, because, as he said, "my own mouth will be too active for the objectivity and restraint necessary in a chairman."

Early in the conclave, Naomi asked what her test of the Sepphoris mosaic had to do with the Ben-Yosef phenomenon. Almost gingerly, Jon reported the meaning that he and Shannon had teased out. His words were met with gaping stares of incredulity.

Finally Gideon exploded, "Do you mean, Jon, that young Jesus, an apprentice maybe helping his father build the synagogue at Sepphoris, played around with tessera to predict His own death, resurrection, and return!"

"That's merely one option—admittedly, a wild one. All we can say for certain is that we do have an early first-century provenance for the mosaic."

Gideon threw up his hands. "All right, but I hope you'll pardon me if, as a non-Christian, I find that explanation borderline *bizarre!*"

"Of course!" Jon laughed. "I, as a Christian, find the very same thing!"

"Still," Shannon interposed, "according to Christian theology, the young Jesus could have accomplished exactly that, however weird it may seem. She now went on to report Joshua's response to the mosaic up in Galilee."

Gideon smiled a little indulgently and said, "Ah yes, we have our miracle stories in Judaism also."

The conference debate continued. One day, the transcript of those deliberations would form an intriguing chapter in Sheler's book. Now, however, it meant unpacking a crate-load of information on Joshua, sifting through it for evidence, and then evaluating that evidence. The conference became a two-day affair.

At the close, Jon wearily summed it up: "Obviously, our information is still spotty in places. We should have done a rundown on Joshua's twelve disciples as well, and that's the first order of business. Even at some points in Joshua's career, our data is thin, particularly his university years in Haifa. For both of these shallow spots, our Hebrew-speaking agents will be especially necessary. And, of course, anything new from Joshua's childhood and youth will be more than welcome."

"Fine, then," said Gideon in closing the meeting. "We've already agreed on who will cover what in this probe. I remind you again of our need for absolute secrecy. Happy hunting, ladies and gentlemen! We meet again in three weeks."

After dinner that night, Jon dialed Kevin Sullivan's private number at the Vatican. With great good luck, he heard an answer after only three rings.

"Jon! I've been waiting to hear from you! I thought maybe you'd gone down to purgatory or something!"

"That's exactly where I've been, Kevin. All your many friends down there say hello, by the way!"

Kevin chuckled. "What about those in limbo?"

"Same message! See, you could spare them all that if only you'd turn Lutheran!"

"Well, I'll give it some *serious* thought!" he said, in jest.

"Okay, more seriously, Kevin, a lot has happened since we last talked." Jon updated Sullivan on the most recent extraordinary events involving Joshua. Just reporting on the retreat with the Seventy along the Sea of Galilee took a half hour of trans-Mediterranean line charges.

"You mean, he actually turned off a storm!" Kevin exclaimed. "Just like Jesus did?"

"Well . . . with this difference: Jesus did it from a boat."

"No big difference! Oh, I forgot to ask: anything new on the David mosaic?"

"And I was just about to tell you! Got another fifteen minutes?" Jon took a deep breath and reported the new version of its meaning.

Kevin was so soundless on the other end that Jon thought their phone connection had broken. Yet when he did respond, Kevin's tone seemed to breathe faith rather than skepticism.

"What a beautiful, tangible proof something like that is! But, Jon, let me give you the picture here at the Vatican. It's borderline bedlam. Over half of the Curia are sure that Joshua is Jesus, the rest are undecided or deny it. They're all looking to the Holy Father for

guidance, but he, in turn, is looking to you! I really think he wants
to fly over there and meet Joshua himself, if possible. Think you
could arrange that?"

"Is he well enough to travel again?"

"Getting there."

"I'll see what I can do. Uh-oh, I forgot to tell you the latest, Kev."
Jon now reported on the joint investigation panel.

"Excellent," Kevin responded. "Overdue. Let's stay in closer
touch, Jon."

"For sure. *Ciao*, good friend!"

After they had hung up, Shannon, who had picked up on the
last, asked, "Don't you find all this a little distasteful, Jon? You
and the spooks sniffing out Joshua's tracks like a pack of blood-
hounds, especially after our magnificent weekend with him up in
Galilee?"

Jon hung his head and conceded, "Yes, darling. I'll admit it: I
really don't find this pleasant at all. By now I admire Joshua so
much that I really ought to take myself off the case due to conflict
of interest. I tell you true: I really hope we find nothing fake in his
background. In the long run, the world may even be grateful to us
for testing everything carefully."

"Okay. I can live with a bias like that."

Such partiality would shortly be justified, and in a way no one
could ever have imagined.

One morning, Jon picked up the *Jerusalem Post* and did a double
take. At the bottom of the front page was a medium-sized headline:
"Ben-Yosef Disciple Critically Ill." Almost knocking over
his orange juice, he called Shannon and read the story aloud to her:

Shimon Levine, whom many Christians regard as the Simon Peter
figure in Joshua Ben-Yosef's following, collapsed yesterday at Ein
Kerem in southwest Jerusalem. He had gone there to celebrate the
Christian festival of Saint John the Baptist and represent Joshua Ben-
Yosef, who is in northern Israel at this time and could not attend.

Levine was rushed by ambulance to nearby Hadassah Hospital,
where he is in critical condition with labored breathing from an

undisclosed illness. Efforts to reach Joshua Ben-Yosef have thus far failed, according to Shimon's associate, Yohanan Bihran, who is at Shimon's bedside.

"How very sad!" said Shannon. "Remember? He didn't look well at the retreat up in Galilee."

"Not at all. They'd better get through to Joshua pronto. If he ever healed anyone, he should do it now!"

"I've always liked Peter. He may seem burly and even threatening, but he's a kitty-cat inside."

Both were silent for some moments. Then she said, "Jon, why don't we drive over to Hadassah and see if we can be of any help?"

"I was going to suggest that very thing."

The Hadassah, on its new Ein Kerem campus, was Israel's most advanced medical center. When Jon and Shannon arrived, they saw that a sizable crowd had gathered on the lawn outside the hospital, including media trucks. Police were guarding the entrance. Jon walked up to a man who seemed to be the chief of security and identified Shannon and himself as close friends of Shimon Levine.

"You may confirm this with other followers of Joshua Ben-Yosef who are doubtless inside," he added.

The man studied Jon for a moment, then waved them through. They hurried to the reception desk and were told that Shimon was still in the emergency wing, Room 117. Hurrying there, they found Yakov and Yohanan on their knees in prayer beside the bed. Shimon himself was gray and sallow from lack of oxygen—despite the plastic tubing in his nose. His breathing was labored and crackling from the edema building in his lungs. An attending doctor shook his head as he left the room, promising to return shortly.

Suddenly Shimon opened his eyes and tried to focus on Jon and Shannon standing at his bedside. His lips parted, and he mumbled, "J-Jon?"

"Yes, Shimon! It's Jon and Shannon here!" Jon answered loudly.

"Good . . . so good of you to come . . ."

"Shimon, do you know where Joshua is? Why isn't he here?"

He shook his head slowly, quizzically, then shut his eyes.

Yakov answered in his stead. "The Master was on retreat some-where in Galilee. We haven't been able to reach him," he said sadly.

"He should be here!" Jon snapped.

Shimon suddenly opened his eyes wide and tried to lift his head off the pillow as he gargled loudly, "Believe in Joshua, Jon! You must . . ." His head dropped back into the pillow.

"He shouldn't have tried to exert himself," Shannon whispered. "He only weakened—" She stopped in midsentence, for Shimon had quit breathing.

The green line on the cardiac monitor ended its oscillation between peaks and valleys and became one flat line, while the monitor buzzed a code blue warning that brought doctors and nurses rushing into the room.

After all CPR methods were tried—repeated poundings on Shimon's chest, followed by electroshock paddles—they could only pronounce the patient dead.

Yakov and Yohanan wept as James and John would have wept twenty centuries earlier had Peter been taken from them. Shannon cried also, and tears welled up in Jon's eyes.

The death of "Peter" was international news that evening. Much of the world was asking the same question that Jon and Shannon, the now-Eleven, and the Seventy were asking: where was Joshua, and why didn't he heal his closest friend?

Joshua never even made it to the funeral and burial, which, according to Jewish custom, had to take place on the same day as a person's passing. Israel Schneider, a wealthy Jewish Christian in Jerusalem who was one of Joshua's Seventy, had a family burial plot on the Mount of Olives that included a small cavern with loculi—cigar-shaped cavities into which bodies of the dead were placed. It was one of the very few remaining burial sites on the Mount of Olives, the southwestern slope of which was a massive cemetery with many thousands of graves. Schneider offered his natural sepulcher as a temporary burial place for Shimon until the Eleven established their own final resting places, probably in Galilee.

Late that afternoon, units of the Israel Defense Force were necessary to control the crowds that gathered on the Mount of Olives to try to witness Shimon's interment. Television cameras on cherry pickers zoomed in on the bereaved, including Jon and Shannon, as they threaded their way up the hillside. Seven of the Twelve stood reverently with them around the burial site as Shimon, wrapped in a white sheet, was laid inside the sepulcher.

Yohanan uttered the customary Jewish prayers for the dead, though with Christian adaptations that focused on the great hope of the resurrection. As he spoke the final "Amen," a golden orb of sun dropped over the Western horizon.

After more tears, breast-beating, and much head shaking, the mourners slowly filed back down the Mount of Olives, barely comprehending what had taken place. All of them were overcome with grief, not only because Shimon was dead, but because Joshua, evidently, had been unavailable or even unable to help his closest friend. Joshua's ministry, his cause, his mission had received a devastating setback not only in Israel, but across much of the world.

And, again, where *was* Joshua Ben-Yosef?

The next morning, Jon phoned Gideon Ben-Yaakov. "Naturally, I know why you're calling, Jon," he said. "I've phoned Shin Bet and— would you believe it?—they don't know where Ben-Yosef is either!"

"How's that possible?"

"A stupid administrative screwup. Joshua and several of his men were spending the night at a hotel in Nazareth. The tail from Shin Bet was on duty in the lobby there until midnight, after which another agent was supposed to spell him. Some idiot in Jerusalem, however, had that agent scheduled twenty-four hours later. The agent who wasn't relieved got tired and left, assuming that his replacement would arrive shortly, and that Joshua's group wasn't going anywhere in any case so late at night. Poor guy got the book thrown at him! Anyway, Joshua and the others left very early the next morning for points unknown, no tail in their wake."

"Now that's off-the-wall!" sniffed Jon. "Well . . . Joshua had better show up soon, unless he wants to see his cause damaged even further. Do get back to me if you hear anything, Gideon."

"And vice versa. *Shalom*."
Another e-mail from Rod Swenson arrived that night.

Sorry I haven't managed to get over to Israel, Jon, as I had hoped. Washington has us working full-time to develop strategies against cyber-ter-rorism, which looks like Al Qaeda's new weapon of choice. Besides, you e-mailed me that Ben-Yosef admitted that he was behind it all. That's also borne out by the timing. We finally put together an exact timetable of when the incursions appeared, and the order was the same both times. Each announcement was separated by two minutes, the exact length of the message, as you'll recall. The combinations are clear from the languages involved:

Israel
United States
United Kingdom
Most of Canada
Spain, Hispanic Central and South America
France, Quebec, and Francophone Africa
Germany, Austria, and Switzerland
Portugal
and Brazil
Italy
Norway
Sweden
Denmark
Finland
Poland
Greece
Russia
Slavic lands

And the list goes on and on, but you get the picture. Okay, Ben-Yosef did it, but *how* did he do it—unless, of course, he's Jesus! So this problem isn't over by a long shot. Stay tuned!

Cheers! Rod

Jon printed out the e-mail and then called Shannon. "Hey, look at this, honey."

When she walked over to his desk, he asked, "What do you see?"

"Well, it's a cross, obviously. But what are the names of all those countries doing there?"

"The rest of the e-mail explains it. Evidently, Rod had his computer on automatic centering. He probably didn't even notice the cross!" Then Jon shook his head and said, "Just another tiny facet of this whole extraordinary, improbable puzzle!"

Peter's death provoked surprising reactions in the world's press, as Jon quickly learned from faxes sent him by Marylou Kaiser. The Western media were generally sympathetic to Joshua in his loss, although some editorials wondered in print why the person who had provided such extraordinary healing in so many lives could not have saved his chief lieutenant.

Columnists in the Afro-Asian block, however, raised that issue frequently and in the form of a complaint. The majority were non-Christians who were puzzled as to how to handle the Joshua phenomenon and had never before covered him in print. Now, however, their restraint seemed to evaporate, and even some anti-Christian sentiment appeared to surface. Jon found this front-page editorial from New Delhi typical:

So often we Hindus are faulted by those in the West for our belief in the gods and goddesses who lead us all to the blessedness of Nirvana. They speak disparagingly of our "purple-faced deities gamboling about in a spiritual never-never land." They characterize our beliefs as primitive polytheism and attack our caste system as evil.

Well now, is Christianity so much better? Christians claim to be monotheists, and yet they seem to worship three gods, who are known as the Father, the Son, and the Holy Spirit. They even believe that one of these gods became a man two thousand years ago, and, incredible as it may seem, many of them now insist that this god has just returned as a contemporary Israeli named Joshua Ben-Yosef. And although this man is supposed to do "miracles" of healing, he was not even able to save his own best friend, who just died.

So, then, who deals in the absurd: Christians or Hindus? Perhaps it is high time to hear less preaching from the West. Perhaps it is high time for the West to learn some wisdom from the East.

Another, in the *Cairo Telegraph,* Egypt's English-language daily, seemed equally helpful. It was written by Egypt's principal mullah, Muhammed Abu-Bakkar:

La illaha illa Allah! "There is no god but Allah!" This, the greatest cry in Islam, is also the call of the present moment. While some in our brotherhood have been playing with the thought that an Israeli Jew named Joshua Ben-Yosef might conceivably be the returned Isa of Nazareth, events have now proved this to be ridiculous speculation. Any supposed prophet who cannot heal his own chief associate is not worthy of belief.

Only one prophet is so worthy, and his name, of course, is Muhammad. Now Muslims everywhere have an opportunity, given by God, to enhance our numbers: one billion of us across the world today, two billion more tomorrow—if we can convince Christians of their errors. The future is ours, beloved brothers, if we keep faith with God and with the prophet!

Jon filed both editorials. Should he let Shannon read them? Later, perhaps. Not now—she was worried enough about Joshua and his cause.

If only the man would return.

EIGHTEEN

It was early. Jon didn't even hear the phone ringing, but Shannon picked it up and sleepily passed it over to her husband, who managed a barely coherent "Hello."

"Sorry to bother you at 6:00 A.M., Jon," said Gideon, "but you told me to do this. Anyway, he's back."

"Who's back?"

"Ben-Yosef. He arrived at their place in Bethany late last night. It seems that he and several of his men went from Nazareth to Mount Tabor for seclusion and prayer. He's often been known to do that, I understand."

"Um-hmm. Jesus also headed for the hills to pray. Any idea what their plans are?"

"Haven't the foggiest."

"Okay, Gideon, I'll take it from there. Thanks for the good word!"

After repeating it all to Shannon, they got up and ate a hasty breakfast. Both knew that they would be heading out to Bethany at once.

Much of Jerusalem, it seemed, had the same idea. Word of Joshua's return and whereabouts had been broadcast on *Kol Israel* since six-thirty, and they found the road to Bethany clogged with motor and pedestrian traffic. Soon their Peugeot seemed as imprisoned as a prehistoric bug in a cube of amber.

"Dunce! Dunce!" Jon shouted at the steering wheel. "What a dunce I was to take the valley road! We should have taken the high road over the Mount of Olives."

"Well, take it now, then," Shannon suggested. "There's a break in the oncoming traffic."

Jon spun the wheel all the way left, inched out of the lane of traffic, made a U-turn, and sped the other way back up to Mount Scopus.

"Made it, Shannon! Good thinking!"

A sharp turn to the right and they were driving southward along the top of the Mount of Olives. Where the road from Bethany intersected the summit drive, however, their way was blocked by a large crowd coming up from Bethany. Quickly they parked the car and jumped out, because in the center of the crowd they saw Joshua, dressed in his now customary white robe, walking with his inner circle of followers.

Upon joining them, they learned that Joshua was going to pay his last respects at Shimon's tomb. "I wonder if he'll tell us why he wasn't here in time," Shannon commented.

"Yes. He's almost a week too late."

Partway down the western slope of the Mount of Olives, hundreds of additional people were lining the sides of the pathway to the cemetery, some cheering and applauding as Joshua passed by with his entourage and then joining it once they had passed. When they reached the Schneider burial site, they broke ranks and formed vast perimeter circles around Joshua and his party.

"This is incredible, Shannon," muttered Jon. "Look, the TV cameras are back. Next it'll be helicopters overhead!" Almost on cue, they heard the *wiff-wiff-wiff* of a helicopter heading in their direction. Along with some of the Seventy, Jon and Shannon were admitted to the inner circle at the burial site.

Joshua looked weary and depressed. His now-eleven disciples flanked him on either side as he walked silently to the tomb, raised his arms, and placed both hands against it. His forehead followed, hitting the rock with considerable impact. For some time he remained in that position, a living portrait of dejection. His eyes were tightly shut while his lips moved in anguished prayer. Tears trickled down his cheeks.

Though neither dared to ventilate it to the other, both Jon and Shannon felt a parallel thought surfacing in each of their minds. But it was so extreme, so outrageous, so impossible that neither could voice it. They could only look on with compassion, mesmerized by the pitiful scene unfolding before them. The silence was intense, almost palpable, and it lingered on and on.

At last Joshua pushed himself away from the rock. He turned to Yakov and Yohanan and told them quietly, "Move that stone away from the entrance opening."

Jon grasped Shannon's hand tightly.

"But, Master," said Yakov, "it's been almost a week, and you know what that means. The body will have—"

"I said, move the stone to one side." Then he added, almost in a whisper, "Don't be faithless . . . just believe."

"As . . . as you say, Master."

The two pushed and tugged the stone to one side.

Perspiring heavily, Joshua now stood before the opening and bowed his head in prayer once again. Then he opened his eyes, held his head erect, and called out loudly, "*Shimon Levine! By the power of almighty God, arise and come out!*"

Nothing happened.

Shannon felt a trembling in her knees. She squeezed Jon's hand even more tightly.

"I said, *come out,* Shimon!" Joshua repeated.

Silence.

Jon shook his head and thought, *He's gone too far this time!*

"*Shimon!*" said Joshua, almost angrily. "*Do you hear me?*"

Finally a muffled voice called plaintively from inside the tomb: "Yes, Master. I would come out, but . . . I'm trapped in this sheet. I can't move!"

Shouts of excitement rose from the inner circles that heard the voice.

"Help him!" said Joshua, smiling at Yakov and Yohanan.

They quickly crawled into the tomb, and in a short time Shimon appeared at the entrance to the cavern, a look of confused wonderment on his face. Yohanan and Yakov escorted him outside and helped him stand up.

It was "Peter" all right, though a healthier version with skin ruddy tan rather than sallow yellow. Squinting in the brightness, Shimon walked slowly toward Joshua and fell to his knees before him, weeping in utter gratitude as he grasped his ankles.

Swept by a riptide of total shock, wonder, and elation, the entire crowd fell to their knees also, including Jon and Shannon. No one was left standing except the lone figure in white at the center of many concentric rings of humanity. The camera shots from the helicopter would fill world television screens that afternoon and evening—and for weeks and months to come.

The on-site audio would do the same. A torrent of prayer, praise, and adulation erupted, for any remaining doubts about Joshua's true identity had now been swept away by the ultimate sign. The shouts greeting Jesus on that original Palm Sunday in the first century now broke out in a dozen languages in the twenty-first: "*Hosanna to the Son of David! Blessed is He who comes in the name of the Lord! Hosanna in the highest!*"

The English-speaking segment in the throng vented their awe by singing a familiar hymn amid joyful tears. Jon and Shannon joined them. This time there was a powerful passion in each syllable that they had never experienced before in any church service:

> *All hail the power of Jesus' name,*
> *Let angels prostrate fall!*
> *Bring forth the royal diadem*
> *And crown Him Lord of all!*
> *Bring forth the royal diadem*
> *And crown Him Lord of all!*

Not to be outdone, Germans in the crowd sang "*Schönster Herr Jesu,*" the French, "*A Toi la Gloire,*" Hispanics, "*Lo Ores Dad a Cristo el Rey,*" and so on through a dozen other languages. At last the multitude found two words that long ago had been transliterated into all languages and could therefore be shouted in unison: "HALLELUJAH! AMEN!—HALLELUJAH! AMEN!—HALLELUJAH! AMEN!"

Shimon remained kneeling at Joshua's feet, shaking his head from side to side in consummate reverence. Apparently he had forgiven Joshua his tardy return to Jerusalem, and so did all the many witnesses. Joshua now raised his arms in benediction to the multitude.

That blessing by the now-serene and smiling Joshua-Jesus would become the most graphic and intense memory in the lives of all present. Photographic versions would replace all previous artistic renditions of Jesus. Film, after all, was more faithful to fact than canvas.

The raising of Shimon "Peter" may have been a local event in Jerusalem, but it had reverberations across the entire world. Christians everywhere—many of whom saw it "live"—understood it as God's gracious endorsement of His Son, Jesus Christ, and the final proof of Joshua's true identity. And they were ecstatic.

Not surprisingly, the resurrection of Shimon had a massive impact on the non-Christian majority in the world as well. Muslims were asking penetrating questions of their mullahs, and Jews of their rabbis. No more editorials with anti-Christian bias appeared in New Delhi newspapers, and even Beijing's *People's Daily* called for a new and more favorable relationship between the Communist government and Chinese Christians.

Skeptics across the world, however, did not retreat, even if many were now less vocal in their disparaging remarks about Christianity. But Harry Nelson Hunt of Philadelphia was not one of them. Calling Shimon's resurrection "an interesting trick," he demanded medical and scientific verification that Shimon had actually died, as well as a complete physical report on his present condition.

With Shimon's cooperation and approval, the Hadassah Hospital in Jerusalem supplied both to the world media a week later: absolute evidence of death from cardiac failure due to a chronic, hemolytic cancer, and absolute evidence of current excellent health in all bodily systems. His blood pressure, for example, would have made a teenager proud.

At last Jon had reached the point where any further questioning of Joshua's claims was useless. Had he been there, even Yale's skeptical von Schwendener would have been kneeling next to Jon and Shannon on the Mount of Olives, since Joshua had now filled Heinz's prescription for convincing proof: the ultimate sign had taken place before their very eyes. Gone were Jon's agonizing appraisal and reappraisal, the mental hand-wringing, the shuttling back and forth between faith and doubt. There was nothing, absolutely nothing, like peace of mind.

Above all, there was also peace with Shannon. They had never been happier in their marriage. Not only had his nagging qualms about Joshua been gloriously resolved and her faith rewarded, but they no longer had to fight with each other over the issue.

On the other hand, Jon had never been busier in his life. Just as he and his web site had been the clearinghouse for past information on Joshua, he was now deluged with inquiries about Joshua's future plans—as if he were his spokesman, which, of course, he was not. Communications of every sort—air, surface, electronic—swamped his office. Some church officials asked if he knew how long Joshua planned to stay on earth before returning to heaven, and would he be addressing the church in general? Laymen and -women wanted to know if this was truly the beginning of the end times, and were they preparing properly? Some letters, incredibly, inquired if Joshua were Catholic or Protestant. Archconservative clerics, with millimeter minds, wanted to know all of Joshua's doctrinal beliefs before declaring altar and pulpit fellowship with him!

Some of the responses were crucially important: Kevin Sullivan, for example, was calling twice a day from Rome, pleading for Jon to arrange a meeting between Joshua and the pope. At the opposite end of the significance scale was a letter from Third Baptist Church of Tucumcari, New Mexico, wondering if Joshua-Jesus might be kind enough to address their mission rally in the fall, provided he had not returned to heaven by then. They would pay his airfare, but the honorarium would have to be small in view of transportation expenses!

"Nothing against Baptists or New Mexico," Dick Ferris said, laughing, "but how do you spell *inept*?!"

Joshua helped dramatically in solving the economic and dislocational problems he had innocently created through his interim appearance. At noon one day, another pop-up message appeared on all the world's computers on-line, again with a trumpet fanfare, again in the vernacular depending on the country involved:

> *Blessed are you who celebrate my return:*
> *For your faith is now rewarded!*
> *Blessed are you who maintain your regular employment:*
> *For spending your time in idleness is a sin.*

Blessed are you who avoid false prophets:
    For they do not know when I shall next return.
Blessed are all who heed my words to the church:
    For they shall be heard shortly.
Blessed are all who believe in me:
    For of such is the Kingdom of God.

The computer in Jon's office was on-line at the time, and he himself saw the message scrolling through twice, as it had months ago. It would appear word for word on the evening news, and so reach those who were not at their computers at the time.

"Notice that he didn't even have to sign the message," Jon told Ferris. "Everyone knows who the author is, of course." Suddenly he slapped his forehead and said, "Now I know where I heard that trumpet fanfare before: it was the same as the one up in Galilee at Joshua's mass meetings. It's his signature theme, for goodness' sake! I should have paid more attention to that months ago."

"What do you think will be his 'words to the church'? And where will he deliver them?" asked Dick.

"I don't know, but I can guess." His thoughts flipped back to Kevin Sullivan's urgent messages. "Which reminds me that I have to call Joshua as soon as possible."

Only the Seventy and their closest associates knew Joshua's private phone number in Bethany. That select group now included Jon and Shannon. He had never called Joshua before—graciously, Jon had always been contacted instead—and he now punched the phone's buttons with slightly trembling fingers. After three rings, Shimon's familiar *"Shalom"* was heard. Jon replied in Hebrew, but Shimon immediately switched to English once he knew it was Jon. Yes, the Master was in, and yes, he would speak with Jon.

First, Jon expressed profound gratitude to Joshua for giving an ultimate sign to the world, and for halting economic chaos with his wise cyberadvice. Then—the reason for his call—he passed on the urgent request of Pope Benedict XVI that they meet.

"How very pleasant," Joshua responded. "I was about to ask *you* to arrange such a meeting, Jon, especially in view of your previous contacts with the Vatican."

"I'd be more than delighted. The Bishop of Rome would be happy to fly here at your convenience. Perhaps you could meet at that splendid retreat lodge overlooking the Sea of Galilee, where you so graciously invited Shannon and me along with the Seventy?"

"I think not. The Bishop of Rome, I understand, is still rather frail, and it would be better if I went to Rome instead."

"You . . . you'd actually do that, Master?" It was the first time Jon had called him that, he realized, and he did so gladly.

"Why not?"

"Well . . . if I were the pope, I'd probably reply in the words of the centurion of Capernaum, 'Domine, non sum dignus ut intres sub tectum meum'."

Joshua laughed and translated, "'Lord, I am not worthy that You should come into my house.' Yes, the bishop and his vast following use that phrase even when they receive Holy Communion, no?"

"Indeed."

"Well, that's fine humility, but not at all necessary in this case. I'll be glad to come to the bishop's 'house' and even happier that you will make the arrangements. But what I have in mind is broader than a little . . . tête-à-tête along the Tiber. In fact, it will fulfill what I conveyed in one of my electronic Beatitudes."

"Yes! I suspected that it might: 'Blessed are all who heed my words to the church, for they shall be heard shortly.'"

"Precisely. Tomorrow morning, Jon, I will send Shimon over with a list of suggestions for our visit to Rome. Please communicate these to Benedict XVI and get back to me if you have any problems, especially regarding the suggested dates involved."

"Excellent. Ah, this is a little awkward: should I also make travel reservations for you? I well realize that you hardly need a plane in order to appear in Rome."

"Jon, Jon, Jon: you keep forgetting the 'not always' and the 'not fully' when it comes to my use of divine powers! I will, of course, accommodate myself to the normal means of air transportation, particularly since the Twelve will be accompanying me."

"Fine. When the date is set, I'll make the reserva—"

"No. God will provide. Alitalia will provide. Thank you for your concerns, Jon, and for your assistance. And yes, also for your . . . *faith!*"

Shimon appeared at Jon's university office the next morning, fully disguised in turban and sunglasses in order to bypass the media. When he delivered a large envelope from Joshua, Jon asked him, "Would you care to sit down and chat for a bit, Shimon?"

"Of course."

"Would you like some coffee or tea? Orange juice?"

The genial, twenty-first-century version of "the big fisherman" removed his disguise, opted for citrus, and easily filled the large leather chair Jon offered him. Jon, of course, thought it would be, at the least, exotic to interview someone who had endured much more than a near-death experience, of which there were dozens on television programs, reporting the great white light at the end of the passageway and other assorted claims. Here, instead, was a man who had gone the whole way: he had actually died, been buried, and returned to life.

Jon led off. "You know, of course, that you are the most extraordinary human being in the world, Shimon—aside from Joshua, of course—in view of what happened?"

He nodded. "Yes, yes. It is . . . a great responsibility that I now have."

"Tell me about your family."

"Well, I do come from Galilee, but my father was a farmer, not a fisherman like Peter's. He was born up in Banias. My mother came from Safat. Both have now passed on."

"Any siblings? Any brothers or sisters?"

"Unfortunately, no. I wish I had them."

Jon thought for a moment, then asked, "What sort of illness caused your death, Shimon?" The reverberation of that question in his mind, of course, sounded like the echo from an insane asylum.

"The doctors say that it was a cancer of the blood. I just got weaker and weaker. I hoped that the Lord would notice this and heal me, as he did many others. But he did not." Shimon paused to wipe several tears from his eyes, then resumed. "Two weeks before I died, I finally asked him to make me whole again. He only said, 'Divine power will be demonstrated in your weakness, Shimon. Trust in God! You will be blessed.'"

"What happened at Ein Kerem?"

"At the celebration for John the Baptizer, I had trouble breathing even before my address to the pilgrims there. And that's the last I remember. Oh, except at the hospital . . . I think I saw *you* bending over me . . . but that didn't really happen, did it?"

"It did, Shimon: Shannon and I were there indeed. But tell me what it was like when you crossed over into death."

"I remember . . . nothing at all."

"No white light? No upward passageway?"

"No, nothing at all."

"What was your very next memory?"

"Well . . . I heard the Lord calling me. And it was . . . just like waking up from a very deep sleep . . . except that I felt a warm, a hot . . . what is the word, 'itching'? The thing you feel when an arm or leg has gone to sleep?"

"A tingling?"

"Yes . . . tingling, that's it. Then I opened my eyes, but I saw mostly darkness. I heard the Master call again and I tried to get up—the bed of stone was not very comfortable—but I just couldn't move because of the shroud. And then Yohanan and Yakov came in and helped me."

"When you stepped out of the tomb, did you realize what had happened?"

"No, not at first, though Yohanan tried to tell me. The light outside was so bright it confused me. And where was I? It didn't look like a hospital at all! And what were all those people doing there?"

"When did you finally realize that you were the 'Lazarus of the twenty-first century'?"

"When they helped me stand up outside the tomb, Yohanan said, 'Shimon, I tell you again: *you were dead!* The Master has given you new life!'"

Jon shook his head and finally asked, "What did you think at that moment? Can you describe it?"

"No . . . I just can't. Earth and heaven were mine again—and all because of our Lord and Master, Jesus Christ—Joshua Ben-Yosef!"

"Thank you, Shimon. It was very kind of you to tell me your . . . your great story."

"I have no choice! For the rest of my life, I will tell it to anyone, everyone!"

"You'll be accompanying your Master to Rome, I trust?"

"Of course. I must tell my great story there also."

"Yes, you must." Jon thought for a moment, then asked, "Was death a terrible experience for you, Shimon?"

"No . . . no, not at all. The hard breathing at the end was not very pleasant, of course, but fading into death was very much like . . . going to sleep."

"I think that should be part of your testimony too, Shimon: tell the world that death is not so horrible after all."

"No, it is not. I will, after all, have to face death again, and our Master would never put me through it twice if it were."

After Shimon left, Jon opened the large envelope he had delivered and read its contents. For the next fifteen minutes, Dick Ferris in the adjoining office heard him emote with the strangest comments. "Yes!" "Exactly!" "Oh-ho!" filled the air, along with chuckling.

When several more "Good!" "Excellent!" and similar affirmatives followed, he could stand it no longer. Hurrying inside Jon's office, he demanded, "Okay, what's going on?"

Jon handed Ferris the file, laughed, and said, "Read for yourself, Dick, my boy: you and I have some work to do!"

At home that evening, Jon let Shannon read the file as well. Now it was his turn to hear a stream of glad affirmations from her lips. Then he picked up the phone and called Kevin Sullivan.

After he had heard his *"Pronto?"* Jon said, "Your pleadings and your prayers have been answered, Kevin! In spades."

"Is that you, Jon?"

"None other."

"What do you mean? Will Joshua agree to meet with the Holy Father?"

"He will indeed!"

"Wonderful! When?"

"That depends on your schedule too. Ideally, within a month or two. Or three."

"Fabulous! Where in Israel will we meet?"

"Not here. We'll meet in Babylon instead . . ."

"*What?!*"

"Well, 'Babylon' as in 1 Peter 5 . . ."

"Oh, you mean Rome? Here in *Rome?*"

"Yup! Joshua was concerned that Benedict might be too frail to travel to Israel, so he'll come to Rome instead. Mighty gracious of him, I'd say."

"*Wow!* Made in heaven, *I'd* say! Fabulous!"

"But there are some strings attached . . ."

"Oh?"

"Not to worry: they're pretty delightful strings."

"Such as?"

"Too much to tell you over the phone, Kevin. E-mail won't work either: too much joint planning is necessary. In other words, I'll have to fly to Rome to work everything out with you and the Vatican—and as soon as possible. Can you check the pope's schedule and get back to me?"

"Sure! Excellent, in fact! Couldn't be better!"

"So I'll hear from you soon?"

"Tomorrow afternoon at the latest. But Jon, one last time . . . and I sort of hate to ask this, but—"

"I think I know the question. '*Is* Joshua Jesus?' Right?"

"Yes, that's the question, of course. So what's the answer?"

"How would you answer at this point?"

After a pause, he replied, "Yes, Jon, he is. His resurrecting 'Peter' removed my last doubts. The evidence is simply overpowering!"

"Same here, Kevin."

"It all seems just too surrealistic for words. Cosmic events are taking place right under our very noses, Jon, but they're happening in what seems to be a normal space-time continuum. I mean, who could ever imagine that Jesus Christ, the Son of God, is flying to Rome to converse with the pope?"

"That *is* a problem: I tried to have him fly to Saint Louis instead and talk with the president of the Lutheran Church–Missouri Synod."

After a long pause, Kevin whined, "Jon, at times your attempts at humor leave so *much* to be desired."

"Sorry, sport! It's a problem I'll have to work on. Actually, I'm just trying to keep us from going mad at the cosmic drama taking place in some sort of invisible nimbus surrounding us."

"Makes sense to me. I'll get back to you tomorrow morning. *Ciao!*"

NINETEEN

Jon breezed through security at Leonardo da Vinci, Rome's international airport at Fiumicino, and scanned the waiting crowd for Kevin Sullivan. He failed to spot him in the milling mass of expectant Italians, waiting to greet their friends and loved ones. Then he felt a tap on his left shoulder and was pulled into a friendly hug.

"*Benvenuto in Roma,* Jon! I thought I'd attack you from the flank!"

"Aw, you Cats have always had it in for us Lutherans! Hi, Kevin!"

"Any baggage, persecuted one?"

"No, just this carry-on and briefcase with laptop."

"Great! That'll save us time!"

They proceeded to the arrival concourse, where a black Mercedes limousine was waiting at curbside, fluttering yellow-and-white Vatican flags atop the front fenders. When they had climbed inside and sped off, Sullivan handed Jon a suggested schedule for his two days in Rome. "Here's your dance card, chum, subject to your veto, of course."

Jon read it through and nodded. "Fine with me. It's already two o'clock, so it's good you didn't schedule our meeting with the pope till tomorrow morning."

"The Holy Father's always at his best in the morning. This way we can run through what you have later this afternoon and into the evening if necessary. If it doesn't take too long, maybe we can do the Via Veneto tonight. Or Tivoli? Whatever."

While cruising up the Via Ostiensis toward Rome, Kevin filled Jon in on the latest Vatican politics. "There's no longer much division in the Curia over Joshua," he said. "The raising of Shimon was the last straw, so to speak. Only God in Christ could do something

225

like that. Oh, there are a few important diehards, of course, who deny everything—like Gonzales and Buchbinder—but they haven't had a new thought since the sixteenth century and the Council of Trent. We have our Fundies too, you know."

"How about Benedict XVI?"

"Now fully on the side of authenticity."

When they passed by the Basilica of St. Paul Outside the Walls, Kevin remarked, "Just happened to think: St. Paul made it to Rome, of course, but Jesus never did. Now He'll have His chance." Then he shook his head and said, "Several months ago, if anyone had told me I'd be using language like that, I'd have called him a blooming idiot!"

"I know, Kev. We're all responding in ways none of us could ever have imagined a short time ago."

"Here something . . . divine, something infinite is taking place right in front of us, and yet life seems to go on normally in apparently regular channels. It really rattles you!"

They drove through western Rome, along the Tiber, and then over the Tiber River bridge into Vatican City. "You'll be staying at the same digs as last time, if that's okay with you."

"Fine, Kevin."

"And here we are," he said, as the limousine braked to a stop. "They're expecting you inside. I'll come back around, say, four-thirty with a bottle of sherry under my arm, all right?"

"Entirely all right!"

"Any particular brand?"

"I'm no wine snob, Kevin. Just don't bring a five-hundred-dollar-a-bottle vintage."

The Sandoz sherry that Sullivan uncorked was well within the budget Jon had prescribed. After filling two crystal glasses, he asked to read the document Shimon had delivered to Jon.

"Okay, here it is. But, fair warning: some of Joshua's suggestions may startle you, and I hope you won't get hacked off. I'll supply any running commentary you'll need."

Sullivan smiled and started reading. Then his features turned neutral, and a mild frown or two appeared. At several points, his eyes bulged, but Jon's quick comments—and a second glass of sherry—proved palliative. When he had finished reading, Kevin laid the document down, thought for a moment, and said, "It's really all justified in the end, isn't it? I was surprised because I had envisioned a spiritual summit between two people, and Joshua has a much broader conclave in mind."

"You see, Kev, unless Joshua is Roman Catholic—and I know you'd like to claim that he is!—he'd be showing favoritism if he talked only with the pope. The rest of Christendom would demand similar conferences with all the bishops and presidents of other church bodies, which would be impossible. It's really the only way. And besides all that, I think you should spell his 'suggestions' as 'specifications,' yes?"

"True enough! But now this changes our agenda: we'll see the Holy Father in the morning, as planned, but then, pending his approval, we'll have to see both the pope and much of the Curia in the afternoon, since they'll have to be heavily involved in the new arrangements."

"Can they fit this into their schedules on such short notice?"

"Of course not! If we had to work with all their schedules, we wouldn't accomplish this until the month of May, three years from now!"

"Well, what are we gonna do?"

"I'll simply urge them to *clear* their schedules—for something as unparalleled as this. Have to run, Jon. I'm going to the Holy Father first, and then to the Vatican secretary of state. After that I'll come back here, though maybe as an excommunicate!"

"There's always room for you in Lutheranism!" offered Jon, with a nasty grin.

"'From this preserve us, heavenly Father!' In any case, we'll do dinner after that." Sullivan hurried off.

Jon marveled at his friend. Kevin had actually quoted from Luther's *Small Catechism* in his riposte. Jesuits were a bright crowd indeed!

The next morning His Holiness, Benedict XVI—Bishop of Rome, Vicar of Jesus Christ, Supreme Pontiff of the Universal Church, Patriarch of the West, Sovereign of Vatican City, and Servant of the

Servants of God—opened the windows of his papal apartment high over the Bernini colonnade in front of St. Peter's Basilica and breathed in the fresh morning air. On this, as on other mornings, he was wearing the simple white gown, caped at the neck, that marked what passed for a papal uniform.

The 265th incumbent of Peter's chair kept looking at his watch, for at 9:00 A.M., his friend from the Rama crisis, Professor Jonathan Weber, would pay him a visit, along with Monsignor Kevin Sullivan. Now the bells at the Vatican started tolling nine, and before their last shimmering echo, there was a knock on the door of the papal apartments.

When the pontifical steward presented Jon and Kevin, Benedict XVI embraced them both and said, "I cannot tell you how much I've looked forward to this meeting, dear Jonathan!"

"As have I, Your Holiness."

"Jonathan, Jonathan, at the time of our last visit, didn't we agree to using first names?"

"Yes, but I didn't wish to presume—"

"Ah, my good friend, presume at will! Have you two had breakfast?"

Both nodded.

"Still, I have some espresso or tea and cakes at the table here. Let's all sit down, shall we?"

Kevin led off. "Thanks, *Santìssimo Padre,* for adjusting your afternoon schedule in order to meet with the Curia."

"It is nothing. The cause is . . . momentous. Now, Jonathan, let me first thank you for having kept Monsignor Sullivan and me so very well informed about Joshua Ben-Yosef. As we all know, there can be only two options in his case: Joshua is either a deceiver, or he is the very Son of God visibly returned to earth. Can you possibly imagine any greater extremes?"

Both guests shook their heads.

"After months of studying that extraordinary individual, we have come to the conclusion that only God could accomplish the miraculous signs that Joshua has performed—especially the raising of his friend Shimon—and so we believe that he speaks the truth, and we are extremely eager to hear him."

He now turned and looked directly into Jon's eyes. "But before we do, I must ask you, Jonathan: are we being foolish in this matter? Or . . . are our conclusions justified?"

Jon thought for a moment at the immense freight loaded onto a question like that—and its answer. "I now believe that it's the latter, Your Holiness," he finally replied. "To be sure, we still have a standing investigation panel in Jerusalem, which has the task of searching out the past histories of Joshua and his twelve associates. Both the Israeli and the American governments are involved with their special agents, but they've uncovered nothing so far that would in any way undermine the integrity of Joshua or his claims.

"Accordingly, after a long and careful study of Joshua's words and deeds that we've conducted over the past months, our conclusions are . . . the same as yours."

He interrupted himself to haul out two fat tomes from his briefcase, which he laid on the table in front of the pope. "Our findings are summarized in these monographs, which run nearly five hundred pages each. Volume one contains transcripts or summaries of Joshua's major addresses, teachings, dialogues, and claims, along with information on where and when the words were spoken, and to whom. Volume two lists all the known occasions in which Joshua has demonstrated the supernatural, along with our commentary following. I'll leave these copies with you, and they may be reproduced for anyone in the Vatican hierarchy."

"Excellent! Thank you, Jonathan. We've also done something similar here at the Vatican—not as comprehensive, perhaps, but, since our theologians were involved, with far more commentary, I'm sure!"

That brought a round of laughter.

"In any case," Benedict continued, "it will be pleasant to compare the two research projects, and we will see that you have copies of ours as well. Now, may we see the document that lists Joshua's suggestions for our meeting?"

"Yes, indeed. But let me first tell you that he proposes something far more ambitious than a meeting of just you two, *Santissimo Padre*. Actually, it may be simpler for me to read aloud each item on the list and then offer an explanation for it. Would that be acceptable?"

"Yes, certainly."

"I'll begin, then, with the prologue. Please notice that I have two versions here: the Latin original and an equally original translation into English. His resurrected disciple, Shimon, delivered both to me. I find Joshua's Latin perfect and his English version equally so. Which shall I read?"

"The simplest, I believe, would be to use the English version," said the pontiff.

"I was truly hoping you'd say that!" said Jon, with a smile that easily spread to the others. He read aloud:

I thank the Bishop of Rome for agreeing to our meeting, and for supervising the necessary arrangements at the Vatican. I would hope that our conference could convene within approximately two or three months from today, subject to the schedules of all concerned. My suggestions for our conclave follow:

"I don't think this needs any comment. We can work out the dates later on, all right?"

"Yes, please continue," said Benedict.

1. My twelve associates will accompany me, as well as others in our party, including Professor Jonathan Weber and his wife, Shannon. He is serving as liaison between Jerusalem and Rome in arranging our conclave. We will make all flight reservations.

"I'm not really sure how Joshua will handle the last. When I asked him about it, he said only, 'God will provide. Alitalia will provide.'"

"I'm sure that I can interpret that," said the pontiff. "Our national airline will certainly feel honored to put an entire aircraft at Joshua's disposal, or one of its large corporate jets. At no cost, of course. Will you see to that, Kevin?"

"Certainly!"

Jon resumed reading:

2. As soon as convenient following our arrival in Rome, I would welcome a private meeting with the Bishop of Rome in his apartments or wherever he deems appropriate.

"Anyone have any problem with that? No? Fine, on to point three." *And here's where the fun begins,* Jon thought to himself as he read the following:

> 3. Soon after this meeting, I would welcome a similar private confer-
> ence with the Patriarch of Constantinople, who must also be invited
> to our conclave, at whatever lodging will be arranged for him.

Relieved to see that Benedict frowned only slightly, Jon commented, "This and the rest of Joshua's suggestions you will find
quite ecumenical, Your Holiness. He feels that if he conferred only
with you, the rest of Christendom would feel excluded and then
plead for similar meetings between himself and the major patriarchs, archbishops, bishops, presidents, elders, and other principal
church leaders across the globe. You see—"

"Enough, Jonathan," the pope interposed. "I understand perfectly. There can be no other way. Please continue."

> 4. After this, it is my desire to address the whole church universal
> through its representatives at an assembly that will include the presid-
> ing officers of all major Protestant denominations, all Roman Catholic
> bodies, all Eastern Orthodox national churches, and other Christian
> entities across the world. I envision this as a great ecumenical council
> for all of Christendom, which must be inclusive rather than exclusive.
> Details on the invitation list, capacity, location, and the like will be
> coordinated through Professor Weber and Monsignor Sullivan.

Jon was pleased to see Benedict not only not frowning, but actually smiling and nodding. "This suggestion, Your Holiness," he
said, "resembles very much what you yourself had envisioned after
the Rama crisis when you were talking about convening a 'Vatican
III' ecumenical council."

"Yes! Yes, indeed! Now we have the sublime incentive to do so!"

"Joshua now speaks directly to that concept in point five." He read:

> 5. This suggestion may seem presumptuous, but, in view of the pre-
> vious, it would be more appropriate that the ecumenical invitation

be issued in my name, rather than that of the Bishop of Rome. I have been saddened to see how some in both Eastern Orthodoxy and Roman Catholicism have harbored grievances against one another for nearly a thousand years—ever since the Great Schism of 1054! I have been saddened to see Protestants and Catholics killing each other in Northern Ireland and elsewhere! Let all Christendom, then, replace hate with love and know that the One who invites them has no favorites.

Commented Jon, "Joshua was distressed also at the rude reception your predecessor, John Paul II, had received from some of the Greek Orthodox in Athens."

"It *is* very sad," said Benedict. "Some continue to fight battles that are ten centuries old."

"Here's the next point—six of seven:

6. While naming our great ecumenical council should be the prerogative of the host, if the name "Vatican III" is chosen, let it be clearly understood by all invitees, in view of the previous, that this name reflects only locational and not religiously preferential considerations.

Before Jon could comment, Benedict waved him off and said, "No problem. Please continue, Jonathan."

"Here's the last suggestion:

7. Finally, let prayer arise throughout Christendom that everyone may hear and heed my words to the church universal, so that all may enjoy greater unity in promoting the kingdom of God in this world, and in preparing for the world to come. Amen.

"Who can quarrel with that?" asked Benedict XVI. Then he smiled and said, "Joshua's suggestions are simply inspired. In fact, I even find them another proof that he is indeed who he claims to be. We'll observe them all."

Jon looked at Kevin Sullivan with a glance that all but shouted, "How do you spell *relief*?"

"Well, my dear friends," said the pontiff. "We must now ask a very important question, and that is this: 'Where shall the Council be held?' The answer, I think, should take all of ten or fifteen seconds . . ."

"The Basilica of Saint Peter, of course." Jon beamed.

"Where else?" Kevin echoed.

"Agreed," said the pope. "And what shall we call the Council? This may take as long as twenty seconds . . ."

"I don't think so, *Santìssimo Padre*," said Jon, twinkle in eye. "Wouldn't you find the Third Vatican Council immensely appropriate?"

"What else?" Kevin laughed.

The Bishop of Rome smiled broadly and said, "Vatican III, Vatican III! It will actually happen, God willing, and in my pontificate after all!"

"Congratulations, Your Holiness!" said Jon.

"Jonathan, I fear that you have a physical handicap: you seem absolutely unable to pronounce the word *Benedict*!"

Chuckling, the three laid plans for the meeting with the Curia, which was set for one-thirty that afternoon.

Might all the thousands of members of the Curia—the working hierarchy of the Vatican—answer the hasty summons of the Vatican secretary of state, Augustin Cardinal Buchbinder, and be present that afternoon? Not a chance. Some were out of town; some were out of the country; some were not even alerted, since the summons was limited to those leaders of the Curia known as the *Famìglia Pontificia*—the "papal family."

But quite a family it was, as they all filed into Paul VI Hall, the Vatican auditorium for papal audiences on that steamy afternoon in May: the cardinals and bishops present in Rome at the time for their mandated visits to the Holy See, the higher Curia officials, the secretaries of the sacred congregations, the generals and procurators of the religious orders, consistorial lawyers, palatine prelates, and others. In view of the momentous issue involved, hardly anyone complained about skewed schedules.

The Curia, of course, had taken action on the Joshua issue several days earlier when the pontiff had called it into extraordinary session to report Joshua's gracious intention to come to Rome. Even though, according to canon law, the supreme pontiff did not require Curia approval for his conference with Joshua, the Curia had approved it anyway as a show of support for their bishop in his epochal encounter. Eighty-six percent of Curia members present had endorsed the meeting, 7 percent had abstained, and 7 percent had opposed it. The last explained to colleagues that they would never have opposed Benedict meeting with the true Jesus: they just could not bring themselves to believe that Joshua *was* Jesus. Whatever their opinions on the matter, this second meeting of the Curia was to learn of Joshua's suggestions for his conference with the Bishop of Rome.

As Vatican secretary of state, Cardinal Buchbinder now opened the meeting with invocation and prayer. Then he called on the supreme pontiff. In words of classical clarity, Benedict reminded the Curia of the purpose for their gathering on such short notice, after which he introduced Professor Jonathan Weber. Fortunately for Jon—otherwise one exotic Lutheran fish in a huge Catholic aquariumful—he continued to enjoy high credibility with the Curia because of his record at Rama.

Jon's presentation was simply a reprise of his morning discussion with the pope and his recitation of Joshua's list-cum-explanations. A large majority in the Curia responded as Benedict had, but a quite vocal conservative minority voiced qualms, opinions, and suggestions of various sorts:

- Monsignor Sullivan was admonished to award one of every two seats at Vatican III to Roman Catholics, as befitted their statistical majority in world Christendom.

- Representatives of non-Christian religions should not be invited to attend.

- None of the limited seats at Vatican III need be "wasted" on representatives of para-Christian sects and cults.

- The invitations to Vatican III ought to come from both Joshua and Benedict XVI.

- The Roman Pontiff should be accorded, if not equal time on the program, then his should be the sole other programmatic voice at Vatican III.

- Roman Catholics should always celebrate the fact that the returned Joshua-Jesus had chosen Catholic Rome as the venue for his address to Christendom.

- Any publications deriving from the conference should be edited and published only by the Congregation for the Doctrine of the Faith.

Jon winced as the list of restrictions grew, and he was particularly nettled at the last: what was now the Congregation for the Doctrine of the Faith was formerly the austere and legalistic Holy Office.

And Jon was not alone. Benedict XVI, too, grew restless as these proposals were offered. Finally he stood up at the dais and said, with trembling lips: "My beloved brothers in Christ, know this: I will *not* change one jot or tittle of the gracious suggestions we have received from our returned Master! Nor shall I add to them! Truly, Peter and the apostles said it well: 'We ought to obey God, rather than men'!"

He paused, took a sip of water, then continued. "On the other hand, several of your suggestions that do not contradict the Master's requests might be implemented, at least in part. Again, although I am not obliged to ask for this, I solicit your support for my acceding to Joshua Ben-Yosef's suggestions for Vatican III *to the letter,* while taking some of your other suggestions into consideration."

Buchbinder now called the question via voice vote. "All those endorsing the Holy Father's procedure in this matter, say aye."

A booming affirmative resonated in the chamber.

"Those opposed?"

Several rather anemic nays were heard.

"Carried. I will now call on Monsignor Sullivan to discuss the many practical matters that must be addressed in preparation for Vatican III."

Ever since Kevin had first learned that the meeting between Joshua and Benedict would become far more complex than a get-together between two men, his brain had been in a whirl of strategizing. Between his and Jon's meeting with the pope in the morning and the Curia session in the afternoon, he had gone to the Vatican library to look for a record of how the church had prepared, committeewise, for

Vatican II in the 1950s. That conclave had also had a strong, ecumenical aspect, with many non-Catholics present.

He quickly found the record and made a copy. Using it as a template, he crossed out names of committee chairs at the time and replaced them with names of members from the twenty-first-century Curia. So when he appeared at the dais, his presentation on structure and preparation for Vatican III looked as if he had been preparing it the whole previous month.

At the close, he reminded the Curia: "One enormous difference between Vatican II and III is this: we have only a little more than two months to prepare. For Vatican II, they had many. Accordingly, I would beg all chairs to organize their committees immediately. If anyone dislikes any committee assignment, please see me at the dais after we adjourn today."

"Your Holiness, will you be kind enough to close our meeting with prayer?" asked the secretary of state.

Benedict rose to the microphone on the dais and said, "Into Your hands we commend the Third Vatican Council, O sovereign Lord. You have stood with Your chosen people, Israel. You have sent Your own Son, our Lord and Savior Jesus Christ, into the flesh to suffer, die, and rise again on our behalf. In Your great mercy, You have undoubtedly sent Him again into our midst in order to refresh His body, the church. May we greet Him worthily! May we hear His gracious words at the Council and be blessed by them so that we can be united in the faith. It is in His holy name that we pray. Amen."

"Amen!" resounded throughout the hall.

Members of the Curia, touched by the prayer, left the chamber silently.

Only one approached the dais, and he was not complaining about committee assignments. It was Pedro Cardinal Gonzales of the Holy Office. Looking intensely at Benedict, Kevin, and Jon, he said, in a wavering voice, "I pray to God that you are right about Joshua Ben-Yosef. If you are wrong, I will pray to God for your very souls!" Then he turned and walked off.

That evening, Jon's last night in Rome, he and Kevin were enjoying an after-dinner drink at an outdoor restaurant overlooking the

Forum. While the Romanized Sullivan had ordered Campari and soda, the Germanic Jon insisted on Peroni beer.

"I've just had a déjà-vu attack, Kevin," said Jon. "We were at this very same restaurant ordering the very same drinks, no less, several years ago at the beginning of the Rama crisis."

"Almost true, except that you ordered Nastro Azzurro beer rather than Peroni."

"M'gosh, you're right! You must be some sort of genius, Kevin. Take your performance on the dais this afternoon in front of the Curia. When did you bone up on all that structural stuff? You stayed up all night working after we returned from the Via Veneto, right?"

"No, I did not. I really didn't."

"When, then?"

"Between our meetings with Benedict today."

"Impossible! We had lunch together."

"Yes, but there was a little time before and after."

"Not possible, Kev. You must have been preparing before I even got to Rome."

"How could I? I didn't know any of the strings that were attached to Joshua's visit before then."

"How in very blazes, then?"

"How shall I put it, Jon? Okay, I'll admit it: I . . . I fell into a trance and was inspired by God."

Jon paused several moments, then huffed, "You're a looney, lying leprechaun, Kev. Do you know that?"

They exploded in laughter before Jon finally wormed the truth out of him. Their small talk turned serious when Kevin asked, "What did you think of Gonzales's Parthian shot at the dais this afternoon?"

"Frankly, I'm a little surprised that there wasn't more of that. For most of the time I've been negative in this entire Joshua phenomenon, Kev, and for the same reasons we discussed on the drive to Rome. I really think it takes *less* faith to believe those wonderful biblical accounts that happened two thousand years ago and *more* faith to believe them when you see them with your own bloody eyes! The 'scandal of the immediate,' I call it."

"Yeah. I can see that."

"Kevin . . . put the case that—in some sort of wild reversal—
Gonzales is right after all, and we're all wrong, despite the tremendous odds against it. Do we have any sort of fall-back plan? Our
investigation panel is still sitting. Nearly all the wind was taken out
of their sails by the raising of Shimon, of course."

"I don't even know how a fall-back plan would work at this
point, Jon. Well . . . except, maybe, for this: in the next couple of
weeks, I'll have to work my rear end off in getting Vatican III to
fly. If anything—and I mean *anything*—comes up over there that
calls *anything* into question about Joshua Ben-Yosef, you've got
to get through to me and the Holy Father *pronto*. If you can't get
through on the phone, use e-mail. If you can't send a long e-mail,
cut it down to, say, one lousy phrase. Or even a Bible passage,
like . . . hmmm . . . like James 1:16."

"Which is?"

"'Don't be deceived, my dear brothers' . . ."

"Aha! Right on target! Better tell Benedict about that too. Once
again, you can quote the Bible as if you wrote it, Kevin! You know,
you're a remarkable fellow . . . one day, quite probably, you'll be the
first American pope! If so, please 'remember me when you come
into your kingdom'."

TWENTY

The announcement from Rome that there would be a Third Vatican Council ignited worldwide enthusiasm. Christians of all stripes were delighted at the broad ecumenical nature of the planned conclave, despite its Catholic-sounding name. The fact that Joshua-Jesus himself would be addressing the Council made for an additional frenzy of anticipation.

In Rome, Kevin Sullivan was flitting from committee to committee, his hot breath on the necks of all committee chairs. Nearby, the Sistine Chapel Choir started rehearsing the best in sacred music. Inside the vast reaches of St. Peter's Basilica, workmen were erecting huge risers along the sides of the entire nave of the basilica, as they had for Vatican II, increasing its seating capacity to a total of ten thousand. But with more than two billion Christians in the world, only one out of every two hundred thousand would be able to attend. As Joshua had directed, these seats would go to world Christian leaders on a proportional basis related to the size of their church bodies.

But the rest of the public would not be denied. Vatican III and its preparation dominated most morning, midday, and evening radio and television news programs in the scant weeks prior to its opening. The national and international TV networks also planned complete coverage of the ecumenical council, all of them promising viewers that they would air Joshua's opening address live.

Meanwhile, theologians everywhere were speculating as to what Joshua would say to Christendom, and just how he proposed to revive the cause of Christianity across the world. Might he conceivably summon his followers to arms? Would he meet the challenge of Islam by announcing a new crusade of some sort? Would he cut through the tangled knot of denominationalism and define, once and for all, what were "the true doctrines" of Christianity and condemn those that were in error? Would he spell out clearly whether or not infants should be baptized? And how much water is necessary in the rite? Or whether or not he was truly present in Holy Communion? Would he identify the best form of church government—episcopal or congregational? And, in particular, might he supply new hints as to when the end times would actually begin?

The religion coverage on NBC, CBS, ABC, Fox, CNN, and other networks increased exponentially in the short time available. On Sundays, as usual, there was good religious programming and there was bad. The Billy Graham/D. James Kennedy/David Mainse–style evangelicals supplied typically responsible fare, acclaiming what was doubtless the return of Jesus without trying to squeeze extra contributions from their followers "for this great celebration."

The bigots, however, were having their usual field day, with pulpit-pounding, chancel-prancing, redneck-revivalist divines declaring that Joshua "will soon denounce the pope as the Antichrist within his own idolatrous temple." Prophecy fanatics were announcing new interpretations of the book of Revelation by the day, among them, of course, Melvin Morris Merton. But he got so excited during one address that he passed out on the platform from hyperventilation and had to spend several days in the hospital.

Meanwhile, the authors of prophecy best-sellers were madly re-editing their previous works in order to correct mistaken predictions from the past and make them focus instead on Joshua-Jesus and his return. Worse, their publishers encouraged them in this mendacity! Clearly, such trivial items as ethics, honesty, and integrity went by the board where the corporate bottom line was concerned.

Israel, of course, was the very eye of the religious hurricane sweeping the globe, and, like its stormy counterpart, it seemed less turbulent. Some of the hordes of frustrated pilgrims, in fact, were now switching their destinations to Italy in hopes of seeing Joshua there.

The day after his return to Israel, Jon delivered to Joshua the pope's enthusiastic letter of response to his planned visit to Rome.

Quickly they established a date for the opening of Vatican III. It would begin on Sunday, July 15, with no closing date specified. Joshua planned to attend only the first week, after which he would return to Israel while delegates would pursue his directives over the following months.

Almost daily, Jon was on the phone with Kevin Sullivan, coordinating the arrangements between Jerusalem and Rome. Yes, Kevin had been in touch with Alitalia, and—just as Joshua had predicted—the Italian national airline was overflowing with joy at being privileged to supply all air transportation. Their corporate jets would not be large enough for Joshua and his entourage, so an entire Boeing 757 would be put at their disposal.

"Not bad, eh, Jon?" Kevin chortled on the phone.

"Nice work! Twenty centuries ago, the only free transportation Jesus got was a donkey, you'll recall!"

"Right! But I forgot to tell you: Joshua goes by air; you have to come by donkey. So you'd better saddle your a—ah, donkey and start out a month earlier."

"*Now* who spouts the bad humor?"

"Sorry, couldn't resist! But, Jon, guess what my two biggest problems have turned out to be in setting this all up."

"What?"

"The first is proper protocol, I mean, even in getting all the titles straight. Take the Patriarch of Constantinople, the Eastern Orthodox primate and spiritual leader of 350 million Orthodox across the world. You have to get his titles exactly right, of course: 'His All Holiness Ecumenical Patriarch Bartholomew II, Archbishop of Constantinople and New Rome.' And if you want more: 'The 271st Successor to the Apostle Andrew.'"

"Good to know, Kev," said Jon, with something less than conviction. "What's the other problem?"

"The screaming from those who didn't get invited! You can't believe the number of requests—even from the top hierarchies of the major denominations, for 'just three more reservations' and the like."

"Predictable. How are you handling it?"

"Wait: it gets worse—something we hadn't even thought of . . ."

"Atheists demanding equal time?"

"No, *political* representation at Vatican III, the heads of state and their retinue who want to attend! We didn't have that problem with Vatican II, but since the Lord himself will be there, everyone wants in! I learned that the hard way when the British ambassador to the Vatican stopped by my office and requested 120 tickets for Her Majesty, Queen Elizabeth II, and her party."

"Good Lord!"

"Exactly what I said, after picking myself up off the floor. 'Good Lord Waddington,' I said, 'this is a religious council, not a political one. Only churchmen are invited.' He then stood loftily erect, all six and a half feet of him, and said, in his marvelously dismissive Oxonian accent, 'Sir, I should like to remind you that Her gracious Majesty, Queen Elizabeth II, is and remains the Supreme *Head* of the Church of England!'"

"Oh, wow, Kev! Ninety-yard loss for you! What did you do?"

"What *could* I do? I told him I'd work hard to get the space and would get back to him. And then the other calls came in, once word was out that the queen would be invited. Every head of state wants room on the bandwagon. President Sherwood Bronson asked for sixty-five tickets for himself, the cabinet, and their wives. As the hosting government, the president of Italy demands a whole block of seats, and so it goes."

"Well, what's gonna happen? I hate to think that important Christian delegates will have their seats swiped out from under them."

"Me too. And so I think I've devised a solution, with the blessing of the Holy Father. We're going to seat people not only in the nave of St. Peter's, but also in the narthex, the side aisles with the chapel areas, the transept, and even the apse. We'll erect tiered seating at all these areas, with huge closed-circuit television screens. Mitsubishi Rome is glad to provide their Diamond Vision screens gratis for this 'sacred gathering,' as they put it. That gives us five thousand more seats."

"You're a blooming wizard, sport! How does 'Pope Kevin I' sound to you?"

"Oh, it has a nice ring to it, Jon. But it'll be a cold day in the warm place before my name gets Roman numerals. Any interesting data from your investigation panel, by the way?"

"Interesting? Yes. But important? No. We now have minibiographies of the Twelve and they're quaint, but . . . well, 'yawnsville' is the operative term."

"How's Peter doing? Is he . . . staying alive?"

"Healthier than ever!"

"Have to run. Carry on, O Papal Emissary!"

Kevin's mention of the investigation panel tore the scab off of a nasty little sore in Jon's conscience. Here he was, heavily involved in planning Joshua's visit to Rome, yet he was also heavily involved in checking up on him. It wasn't honest. It wasn't fair to Joshua. Jon had never been a duplicitous sort, and being a spook in any form was not in his genes.

But worse, it suddenly occurred to him that although the Judas figure among Joshua's associates had mended his ways, another Judas had taken his place who better resembled the original: he himself! What a disgusting, unforeseen role to have to play!

Should he simply inform Joshua of what he was doing and make a clean breast of it? Actually, did he even have to do that, if Joshua was the omniscient Jesus? The first time around, Jesus had had no trouble whatever seeing through Judas. Was the same thing happening now? Or was Joshua being selective in his omniscience— "not always, not fully" probing into everything? Or, the worst scenario of all: what if Joshua was nothing more than a man after all and couldn't possibly penetrate his mind? In that case, informing Joshua of the investigation would be rank idiocy. Once again, Jon found himself tightly affixed to the horns of a painful, even tormenting, dilemma.

Shannon seemed to be weighing similar thoughts, with the exception of the last: Joshua *was* Jesus, all right, and her husband was playing with fire in his double role. In fact, she had refused to attend any further meetings of the investigation panel at the Rockefeller Museum. Jon understood perfectly and made no attempt to change her mind. He finally muddled through to a provisional conclusion for himself: for now, at any rate, he felt that he had no choice but to continue his unhappy role as a spiritual schizoid.

The third meeting of the panel convened at 8:30 A.M. on July 8, three days before Joshua and his entourage were to leave for Rome. A depressive mood seemed to saturate the very air inside the IAA conference room at the museum, each member sensing the futility of their entire probe. The raising of Shimon had not only sucked the wind out of their sails, it created something of a reverse vacuum that tugged their precarious craft backward. Anyone who could raise the dead was hardly a target to be investigated!

A further complicating factor, of course, was the imminent convening of Vatican III. Now the panel had a pistol pointed at its collective temple, and the pistol came not from Colt but from vaudeville. You pulled the trigger, and a message scrolled down from the barrel that read: "Put up or shut up!"

To be sure, Gideon Ben-Yaakov tried hard to be a good host and a good chair—coffee was poured, Danish pastry distributed, pleasantries dropped—but the heart seemed to have abandoned the enterprise. Rosenzweig and Falkenburg looked bored, Shin Bet seemed to respond woodenly, and even Jon was a creature with two minds—a lovely collection of participants, all things considered.

Jeff Sheler and his *U.S. News* team, however, seemed to have a little life left in them. Since the last meeting, they had worked closely with Shin Bet at the University of Haifa and the Technion, where they had dug up additional names of Joshua's classmates, as well as snippets of further information from members of the faculty and administration there. Further probing at banks, restaurants, archives, and civic records at Haifa yielded nothing.

"You were asking about Joshua's classmates at the Technion, Jon?" Sheler inquired.

"Yes. What are the new names?"

"Actually, we have them all now—or at least all the members of his graduating class. Here's a photocopy of their commencement program—Class of 1994—from the university archives."

Jon flipped through the pages of the copy quickly, and said, "Hmmm. There must be some . . . seven hundred members in that class, all listed on the last pages of the program. And yup, there's Joshua Ben-Yosef's name. Nice work, Jeff!"

"No, I'm just amazed that we didn't find something like that earlier."

At the head of the table, Gideon said, "With your permission, I'll

have more copies made of that, as we have of everything else. ⟨
what fresh information do we have on Joshua's twelve associa
Anyone?"

Rosenzweig shifted in his chair, pulled out a file, and said, "Well,
let's see . . . Yohanan (real name, Ari Silbermann) was born in
Accho—don't think we had that before—and studied at Tel Aviv
University. Iacov (real name, Ezra Schechter) hailed from Hadera, and
studied way down at Beersheba, for some reason. Shimon (real name,
Shimon Levine)—nothing new on him. Yudas—that's the one who's
not a traitor this time, right? Anyway, his real name is Benjamin
Krupnik. Came from Ashdod, and never got beyond high school, I
understand."

Rosenzweig continued rattling off mundane bits and pieces of
information on the Twelve. After lunch, the lifeless recitation continued, and they were ready to adjourn by midafternoon. In closing,
Jon reminded the panel that he had to accompany Joshua to Rome
in the following days, and they would probably not return until the
last week in July. Their next meeting would be August 7.

At the end, Gideon reminded all panel members, "We've not yet
agreed to disband, ladies and gentlemen, however pointless our
prospects may seem to most Christians. So please continue your work.
Until August 7, then?"

When he returned to their apartment that evening, Jon poured
himself a generously ginned martini—*medicine for my conscience,*
he told himself. He offered Shannon the same, but she declined.

"Bad day at the office, dear?" she asked. "And doesn't that
sound like a Grade B sitcom?"

"Yes . . . to both."

"I can't understand you, Jon. This should be the greatest time in
both of our lives: we get to fly to Rome with Jesus Himself! What
could be more sublimely exotic than that? Yet here you are, down
in the mouth. What in the world is wrong?"

"So? You don't call him Joshua anymore. Just Jesus?"

"Oh, all right, all right. I'll call him Joshua if you prefer. And I
think I know what's bothering you, Jon: you and that silly panel are
still trying to undermine him, aren't you? What on earth does it take

to convince you skeptics? He raises someone from the dead, and you still call him a faker!"

"No, I don't call him that at all, Shannon. It's just that—"

"For the first time in my life, I begin to understand how people in Jesus' day could see His miracles and still not believe in Him. You're no better than the scribes and Pharisees in the Gospels, Jon! I'm *sick and tired* of your endless doubts!"

By now, Shannon was almost shouting. He tried to calm her, but to no avail.

"What's more, I'm totally *nauseated* at the double role you're playing! What in the world do you do for a conscience, Jon? Or should I call you Judas? Yes, that's it: Judas Iscariot Weber, the twenty-first-century edition! Well, you can go *hang* yourself as he did for all I care!"

She burst into tears, fled downstairs, and drove off in their car, tires screaming.

Jon poured himself another martini and slumped down into his favorite chair. Should he contemplate suicide, too, like Judas of old? No. In the present horrendous series of complications, that would be too easy a solution.

Would Shannon come back? he wondered. Probably. But when? If she chose to stay out overnight, their marriage could well be in danger, he knew. Should he call the police? With world attention focused on Jerusalem, that would be stupidity in the extreme.

The only way to climb out of a nasty situation, he had learned from previous experience, was to continue business as usual—however very *un*usual he might feel at the time. "Yeah, let's try that," he told himself.

He went to his desk, hauled out the new file from the panel findings that day, and read through them again. Once more he glanced through the fresh material Rosenzweig had supplied, then set it down and thought for a moment. Then he reached for a copy of the commencement program from the Technion and flipped through the pages until he reached the list of graduates. Because lists dull any reader, he tried to defeat boredom by paying forced attention to the names.

Alas, the force weakened, and he almost dozed off until he came

to an entry that jolted him awake. His eyes widened. Not
Joshua's name in the list of graduates, but the name of Shimu.
Levine was there as well. And there was a third name that started
his heart pounding so strongly that he could feel the pulsing in his
carotids up to his ears.

It was now eleven o'clock. No matter. Rushing to the phone, he
called Gideon Ben-Yaakov.

"Hi, Naomi," he said when he heard her *shalom*. "This is Jon
Weber. Dreadfully sorry to be bothering you at this hour. Is Gideon
in? . . . Oh, good Lord, he's *not*? . . . Just went to the convenience
store to pick up some bread? How glorious! Listen, please have him
call me here at home *the moment* he returns, okay? . . . Thanks,
lovely one!"

Jon paced the floor impatiently. Was he overreacting? Maybe,
maybe not. But if he made a mistake now, the world could change.
He walked circle after circle in his study.

At last, thank God, came the sweetest sound he had ever heard:
his phone ringing. Grabbing it, he said, "Hi, Gideon? . . . I've just
discovered something so very urgent that I . . . I plead with you to
drop everything tomorrow morning and come with me. Is that
possible? . . . It is? Fabulous! You and I will have to drive to Haifa.
Pick you up around seven, okay? . . . Just great! Better have had
breakfast, if you don't mind. . . . No, I can't tell you over the phone
what I've found . . . just too sensitive . . . And thanks, Gideon. Bye!"

Jon could hardly sleep that night. When Shannon finally returned
at one-thirty in the morning, he acted as if he were in a very deep
sleep. He just had no stomach for another argument. Besides, there
was much, much to do on the morrow.

TWENTY-ONE

Jon needed no alarm clock the next morning. His needled nerves took care of that. He checked his watch: 6:30 A.M.—perfect! Slipping quietly out of bed, he padded to the bathroom and brushed his teeth almost soundlessly. Getting dressed was also an exercise in silence. Heading for the refrigerator, he quickly drank some orange juice, microwaved a cup of coffee, grabbed a bagel and his attaché case, and slipped out the door. Shannon had not told him where she had gone. He would not tell her where he was going.

Fifteen minutes later, he was at Gideon's door. With hardly a word, Gideon climbed inside the Peugeot, and they drove across West Jerusalem and took the road to Tel Aviv. About five miles down the highway from Jerusalem, Jon finally opened his mouth.

"Thanks, Gideon. I'm really sorry about this ridiculously short notice, but here: please check the names on that graduation program Jeff Sheler gave us."

Gideon scanned the list of names. Then he commented, "Okay, Jon. I saw these earlier. There's Joshua Ben-Yosef, among the other B's. And your point is . . . ?"

"Look at the list again, Gideon. Try the L's."

He did so, then shook his head and said, "I still don't see what you're after, Jon."

"All right, check out the name Shimon Levine."

"Okay, I see it. Nothing unusual about it."

"Nothing unusual? Here, open the file on the Twelve and look under Shimon."

Gideon read for several moments and then his eyes widened. "That's right; Shimon Bar-Yonah's real name is Shimon Levine. Guess I haven't had my morning cup of coffee yet."

249

"We'll stop down the road a bit and take care of that."

"Still, we have no proof that it's the same Shimon. Israel has lots of similar names, and this one's fairly common."

"Maybe."

"But even if he is our Shimon, I think we knew that he also attended the Technion, didn't we?"

"Yet neither Joshua nor Shimon told us they were in the same graduating class. But what else do you see on the list that's a little unusual?"

He shook his head. "Don't see it."

"Look back at Shimon's name."

"Hmmm. There's another graduate on the list with the same last name: Baruch Levine."

"Exactly."

"That's not unusual, Jon. There are almost eight hundred names here, after all, and other duplicate last names. Some threes, too."

"True. But don't you think we need a little more information?"

"Do you mean: was it worth getting me up so early and canceling my schedule for the day?"

"Yes?" asked Jon, hesitantly.

Gideon was silent for several moments, staring out of his side window. Then he turned back, smiled, and nodded.

At the outskirts of Tel Aviv, they turned northward and took the coastal highway to Haifa. Along the way, they explored all sorts of scenarios involving the fresh information. By 9:45 A.M., the heights of Mount Carmel had loomed up to the right and they were at Haifa.

The Technion is Israel's MIT, its premier university for science and technology, with a handsome campus halfway up the northern slopes of Mount Carmel. As director of the Israel Antiquities Authority, Gideon had immediate recognition and entrée at the Technion. He and Jon went to the registrar's office in the university administration building, where Dr. Michael Grossman, the registrar himself, handled their inquiry.

"We'd like to ask you about several students who graduated from here in 1994, Dr. Grossman," said Jon, following appropriate introductions. "I hope you still have records of their registrations, identifying information, transcripts of their courses—that sort of thing."

"I'm sure we do, Professor Weber. But the Technion has a confidentiality policy. Only the student himself may have access to this information—unless, of course, criminality is involved."

"We can appreciate that," Gideon commented. "Probably no crime is involved. Still, I'd ask you to make an exception in this case and let us see the information. I can assure you that it's in the national interest."

Grossman seemed hesitant. "I enormously respect you, Dr. Ben-Yaakov. And the head of our archaeology department here will be very angry if he learns that I didn't service your request immediately, but—"

"I understand." Gideon pulled two cards out of his wallet and handed them to Grossman. "If you'll be so kind, please call Noah Friedmann, the director of Shin Bet in Jerusalem. After that, you may also wish to call the prime minister of Israel. That's his private number."

Grossman raised his hands in surrender. "Not necessary, gentlemen. Please forgive my reticence. Now, what are the names of the students in question?"

Jon handed him the copy of the graduation program, with the names of both Levines underlined.

"Oh! Class of 1994—Joshua Ben-Yosef's class, yes? And I . . . I begin to see how this may indeed be in the national interest."

And the international, thought Jon, but he said only, "I hope it won't be too difficult for you to locate the information."

"We transferred everything to computer some years ago, of course. Let me find our mainframe disk for 1994. Do make yourselves comfortable."

Jon and Gideon looked at each other, smiled, and sat down to wait.

When Grossman returned, he was wearing a frown. "I find this hard to believe, gentlemen," he said, "but that disk is missing. I have no idea why, but I've authorized an immediate search for it."

Again Jon and Gideon looked at each other, this time darkly.

But Grossman's frown was fading. "Not to worry, my friends," he said. "We'll send to the archives and get a copy disk. We have complete backup records of everything here at the Technion. Won't you join me for coffee while we wait for the disk?"

Twenty anxious minutes later, a gofer came through the door with a packet under his arm. Grossman opened it, smiled, and said, "Fine. First, of course, we have to make a complete copy of this disk, since the original is missing. Then we can look up the two Levines. While this is being done, perhaps you might join me for an early lunch?"

As if we had a choice, Jon felt like responding, while accepting graciously, of course. He limited himself to a vegetarian falafel, too preoccupied for anything more.

After lunch, Michael Grossman mounted the disk on the Technion's mainframe and pulled up the computer records from 1994. "Aha," he said. "Here we are . . . which Levine do you want first?"

"Shimon," replied Jon.

The registrar entered the name, and the screen quickly filled with everything the university knew about the man: name, address, phone number, birth date, identity number, transcript of classes, academic recommendations for employment, and alumni contribution record.

"Look, Gideon!" said Jon. "Look at Shimon's identity number—477286312. Ever see it before?" As with an American social security number, the Israeli version also had nine digits, but no dashes.

Gideon turned to Shimon's file, opened it, and read his identity number out loud: "477286312." He shook his head. "Is that one of your hobbies, Jon? Memorizing strings of numbers?"

"No, it was just late last night that I took some interest in that particular number."

"Okay, it's settled. It's the same Shimon." He gazed over the others' heads, lost in thought. "But I don't think this violates anything either of them told you, even if they didn't mention that they were classmates. In fact, in one of the transcripts—I think in volume one—didn't Joshua even state that he and Shimon were old friends? Wouldn't it be natural for him to choose a classmate as one of his associates?"

Jon puzzled for a moment, but then looked at the computer

screen of information in Hebrew and pointed to the upper left-hand corner. "That says birth date, correct? That box?"

"Yes," said Grossman. "May 31, 1973."

Jon rubbed his chin pensively. Then he said, "Please bring up the record of that other Levine in the class, Baruch Levine."

The screen filled with similar data. Jon grabbed Gideon's arm and said, "Look at that identity number! It's just *one digit different* from Shimon's!"

He looked further, squinted in shock, and almost shouted, "And *look at that birth date,* Gideon: May 31, 1973! They were born on the *very same day!* Now let's check out their home addresses!"

Somewhat startled at Jon's excitement, Grossman said, "Well, this fellow's home address, when he attended here, was . . . 8383 Herzl Avenue in Tiberias."

"And Shimon Levine's?"

Grossman exited his entry, keyed in the name of Shimon Levine again, and stared at the screen. "The other fellow's address was . . . 8383 Herzl Avenue in Tiberias."

"*Great God in the mountains!*" bellowed Jon. "They're *twins!*"

"Oh, yes—now that you mention it—I think I do recall the Levine twins," said the registrar. "Is that somehow significant . . . that they're twins?"

"Incredibly significant!" said Jon. "For two reasons. For one thing, it proves that Shimon lied to me, Gideon, when he claimed he had no brothers or sisters."

Gideon's eyebrows were arching.

"And the other?" asked Grossman.

"I . . . haven't completely thought it through yet," responded Jon warily, sensing that he had already said too much. "I would only plead with both of you distinguished gentlemen not to say a word about our visit or its results to anyone—not your wives, not your closest friends, not your colleagues. I know this sounds pretentious and entirely bombastic, but the fate of Western civilization could well be at stake here. I promise to explain everything later. But may I have your solemn pledge to secrecy?"

"Of course," said Grossman, while Gideon nodded.

"I don't wish to be presumptuous, Dr. Grossman," s

"but . . . in view of the gravity of this situation, could we have a printout of everything we've seen on the computer screens regarding the Levine twins, as well as all the information you have on Joshua Ben-Yosef?"

The registrar frowned and said, "One of the reasons I can easily agree to seal my lips on this matter is that I, too, don't want anyone knowing that I broke confidentiality on student records here. But if you really think it's in the national interest . . ."

"It is! It is!" advised Gideon.

"I'll print out the copies, then. But I must ask both of you for the same confidentiality that you asked of me."

"Agreed!" said Gideon.

"In all honesty, however," said Jon, "I should ask this: what if the day should come that these records had to be made public in order to avoid . . . what might be called an international cultural catastrophe?"

Grossman thought for a moment and replied, "I would then ask that you first contact me, listing the reasons for this urgency. I, in turn, would try to secure permission from the Technion's board of regents."

"Fair enough!" Jon smiled, extended his hand, and said, "Thank you for your . . . strategic assistance, Dr. Grossman."

"Glad to be of help!"

On the drive back to Jerusalem, Jon looked at Gideon and said, "Well, you certainly know the other reason, the one I didn't feel like exposing in front of Grossman."

"Yes, I certainly do, Jon. It was the wildest, most extreme of the scenarios—as you call them—that you and I imagined on our drive up here. I thought you were daft when you first suggested it—absolutely bonkers! But now . . . I promise not to comment on your sanity in the future—except, of course, to endorse it!"

Jon smiled. "Thanks for the vote of confidence, Gideon."

There was a long silence that persisted almost back to Tel Aviv. "What are you thinking, Jon?" Gideon finally asked.

"I don't know, my friend. It's just incredible how your entire horizon can shift so . . . so *dimensionally* so quickly. Until eleven o'clock last night, I thought I was a true believer. Now I'm boiling angry. Or potentially so . . ."

"Which means . . . ?"

"I don't have to spell it out for you, Gideon, since we're both on the same wavelength. In this wild, wild business, I wouldn't be surprised if maybe I ought to remain a true believer after all. There may be some valid explanation behind all this—even for Shimon's lie. Meanwhile, of course, I'll probably swing back and forth between the believer/unbeliever columns—like some crazed pendulum—about twelve more times before this is over."

"Can't blame you for that. But can you figure out any sort of motive for that wild scenario—if it finally turns out to be correct?"

"Not in my wildest, Gideon, not in my wildest! Joshua crowing, 'Lookee here, folks, at what I just brought off!' just won't cut it!"

By now they were climbing upward on the road to Jerusalem, again tossing off various options in finding a solution. They were trying to strategize vertically, horizontally, directly, obliquely.

"I do have one bit of advice for you, Jon," said Gideon.

"Which is?"

"Which is this: don't try to put yourself in harm's way again . . . the way you did in that Rama thing. You were a blooming fool then!"

"But I got to the truth, didn't I?"

"Yes, and we very nearly lost you in the process."

"As they say, a miss is as good as a mile."

"You won't always miss, Jon. The law of averages doesn't permit it."

"I'll be careful, Gideon."

"No, this time you have to be *more* than careful. Too much is at stake here. All spoofing aside, what are you thinking of doing?"

"Obviously, I have to confront Shimon again—and, of course, Joshua Ben-Yosef."

"Wrong, wrong, wrong, Jon! *We* have to confront them—you, I, Shin Bet and whoever. You can't do this alone. Not like last time."

"If we get too many involved, our targets might clam up or even claim persecution. Jews would be arresting Jesus again, and get a third of the world on your backs in the process. And, of course, we still don't have nearly enough answers. So much of what Ben-Yosef has done simply boggles the mind, and we haven't proved anything wrong in his case yet—however suspicious things look at this point."

"Well, at minimum, it should be you and I—and probably several from Shin Bet—at any confrontation. No more solo performances!"

"I'll go along with that, Gideon. But we've got to chase down more information on all of Joshua's associates, not just Shimon, and that'll take some time. I desperately wish we could bring it all off before Vatican III, for obvious reasons, but that's not possible now. So our confrontation will have to wait until we return from Rome. After all, we have to fly there in a couple of days."

"Good! I'll get to Friedmann and Shin Bet as soon as we get back to Jerusalem."

"Meanwhile, everything has to stay perfectly normal as far as Joshua and his entourage are concerned. If they should suspect anything, it would ruin our efforts. Darn! Again, if only we had more time before Vatican III to solve this thing: we'd probably be sparing the world a lot of grief—if, that is, our scenario is correct. But, as of now, it's still a big if."

Jon drove into their garage at French Hill around seven, dreading another confrontation with Shannon. Already he could hear their dialogue. *She* (in demanding tones): "Where have you been, Jon?" *He* (in tones of injured innocence): "I'll tell you if you tell me where *you* were last night!"

He had it wrong. Shannon met him at the door as if nothing had happened between them. In an upbeat mood, she smiled, hugged him, and said, "Oh . . . *so* glad you're back, dear! I tried to reach you at the office, but Dick Ferris didn't know where you were. Anyway, whatever you've got planned for tomorrow, you've got to drop it."

"Oh? Why?"

"Joshua is calling a final conference to prepare for our flight to Rome. His women's auxiliary, as you call it, is meeting at their place in Bethany. You men are joining him up at that retreat lodge along the Sea of Galilee where we were guests."

"Separating the sexes, eh? Sounds like Joshua has turned into an orthodox rabbi! What time am I supposed to be there?"

"Ten-thirty tomorrow morning. Oh, Jon, I'm so excited! I just can't wait to fly to Rome with Joshua. It will be a . . . a twenty-first-century recap of Jesus' triumphal entrance into Jerusalem on Palm Sunday!"

"Will Alitalia permit you to take palm branches inside the plane? And where will they stow the donkey?"

"You silly, silly cynic!" she chuckled, as she pulled his face down to her lips for a long kiss.

He had difficulty falling asleep that night. While his body was bone tired from a daylong trip across half of Israel and back, his mind acted as if he had just had his third cup of strong morning coffee. Why hadn't he asked Shannon where she'd been last night? Or better, why hadn't she volunteered the information? Then again, why hadn't she asked about *his* whereabouts that day, and why hadn't he volunteered the information? Tit for tat.

Trying to put the best construction on everything, he assumed that Shannon was probably too embarrassed at her outburst even to remind him of it by way of telling him she was sorry. But why, for the first time, was he keeping secrets from his wife? Why hadn't he reported to her the drive to Haifa and its potentially shocking consequences?

Tossing in bed, he quickly found answers to the last. He didn't want to spoil her joy—at least for the moment. If truth were told, he was probably a bit of a coward too: if Shannon had previously blown up at his Judas-like probing, how great would her explosion be at this latest twist in his "traitorous plotting"? He could just see her vaulting out of bed and demanding to know where he had put them. *What?* he would ask. *Your thirty pieces of silver,* she would reply.

Time for all that later. Time for sleep now.

He was finally drifting off when he heard a little girl's voice next to him.

"I'm so sorry about last night, Jon," she said softly. "Can you please forgive me?"

So much for assigning wrong motives to a wonderful wife.

"Of course, darling!" he said and kissed her softly. After which he kissed her again, with gathering dedication.

Twenty-Two

As Jon breezed northward to Galilee for the meeting of what he called the "Master's Men," he thought back to his Sunday school days and how wrong he had been about the geography of the Holy Land. Galilee was at the northern edge of those color maps in the back of his Bible, and he had always assumed that if Jerusalem were, say, Los Angeles, then Galilee would be up around Portland or Seattle. In fact, it was only a two-hour drive, more like L.A. to Bakersfield—so small was that sacred park called the Holy Land. And how fortunate, Jon mused, since he almost seemed to be commuting between the two regions.

When he reached Tiberias and drove up the hillside road above Magdala, with its magnificent view of the Sea of Galilee, he recalled Joshua's calming of the storm. He still had no explanation for that and many other wonders that Joshua had apparently accomplished, even if he and Gideon had perhaps solved one of them. Nothing in life had ever been so difficult as the belief/disbelief decision he had not yet irrevocably made. Somehow, Joshua himself would have to help in the solution—not immediately but shortly, after Rome and Vatican III.

Jon drove into the parking area behind the lodge, wondering why it was almost empty of cars. Had he come too early? He knocked on the door and was surprised when Joshua himself opened it.

"Welcome, Jon." He smiled in greeting. "Come in, come in!"

Jon was puzzled. No one else was in the great room.

"But where are the others?" he asked. "Shannon told me that all the men on our flight to Rome would be up here for a final briefing."

"They're coming at noon. I wanted some time alone with you before they arrive, Jon. That's all right with you, isn't it?"

259

f course."

hen let's sit down for a fireside chat—even if it's too warm for a fire."

Joshua made a small Gothic arch out of his hands and asked, "Now, is everything in order for our flight? They'll meet our delegation at the airport—the welcoming ceremonies, and all?"

"I've been over our checklist a dozen times. Everything's fine."

"Excellent! And thanks for the work you've done, Jonathan."

"It was a great honor to be of service, of course."

Joshua shifted in his chair, then focused his flaming sapphire eyes on Jon's, piercing, it seemed, into his very essence. "I think it best to come right to the point. Why are you still playing the role of skeptic, Jon?"

"Ah . . . how do you mean, sir?"

"You know very well. On the surface you seem to be one of my loyal followers. But behind my back, you have this 'investigation panel' looking into my past, yes, and into the lives of my disciples too."

Jon's heart started accelerating to a mad tempo. Deception or subterfuge would no longer work because somehow, Joshua knew. Instead, he steeled himself to reflect perfect calm on the surface. "I'll be glad to explain that," said Jon evenly. "But first I'd like to ask: how did you learn about the panel?"

"Jon, Jon, Jon . . . how long have I been with you, and you still ask questions like that . . . do you still doubt?"

"If you're referring to divine omniscience, why, then, are you using it to penetrate my privacy—something you promised not to do?" Again he was overwhelmed by the surreal nature of his own words.

"Aha!" Joshua chuckled. "Good response! Well, I did keep my promise after all, Jon. It was your lovely wife, Shannon, who came to me the night before last. She was distraught by what she called your 'blazing unbelief' and told me in tears how conscience-stricken she was to have served on that panel, and would I please forgive her."

Hot blood flashed into Jon's head, and he felt its pulsing pressure at his temples. But again he struggled to maintain a mask of placidity. "Well, good for Shannon," he lied, since the path of honesty seemed to be premature after all. "I certainly was going to inform you about the panel, but only after its work was completed. I thought that its results in finding your mission genuine would be accepted far more easily by skeptics across the world if you had known nothing about its activities beforehand. In that way, no one could claim any interference by you or your followers."

Joshua thought for a moment, then replied, "All right, that's plausible enough."

"And frankly, I think that's still the best course. I'd strongly suggest that you not divulge your knowledge of the investigation to any of your associates. Shannon and I will seal our lips also. The result will be much greater objectivity in the panel's findings. In the long run, your cause—our cause—will have much greater credibility before the world because there was a strong investigation in the first place."

Joshua nodded and was silent. For some time he continued staring hypnotically into Jon's eyes before he said, "I'd like to believe you, Jon . . . but I really can't. Yesterday, you and Gideon Ben-Yaakov drove to the Technion in Haifa, where you retrieved information on Shimon and his brother, Baruch, didn't you?"

Now the blood seemed to drain away from Jon's brain in total shock. His face turned ashen and he felt dizzy. For an instant he wondered: was this God in the flesh after all? "How?" he gargled, then tried again, "How did you know that?"

"With God, all things are possible!"

Some weeks earlier, he would have been frightened, terrified, or at least humbled by that phrase. But now he was boiling angry. He snapped back, "But with God, Joshua, some things are *not* possible, such as His supposed Son using a liar as His chief follower—a man who told me that he had no siblings!"

"But that was true, Jon: he had no living siblings because—"

"Because the one he had, Shimon Levine, was dead! Shannon and I even saw him die! And the fellow you supposedly resurrected on the Mount of Olives was his identical twin brother, Baruch! Now, I still don't know how you managed to bring off all the other wonders, but we were fortunate to be able to solve your greatest miracle first. I'm sure that's the capstone: remove it, and the others will collapse . . . crumbling away into the ash heap where they belong!"

Joshua shook his head sadly and replied, "Jon, Jon: how very sad! How close you were to the kingdom of God! Quite apart from the blasphemy involved, you—"

At the pious language Jon lost control completely. "Okay, let's cut the crap, Ben-Yosef! Let's both try the route of honesty instead and quit the pious palaver, okay? Let me ask you a few questions. And the first is this: what did you do with Shimon's body so that it wouldn't be inconveniently around when you 'raised' his twin brother from the dead?"

Joshua only stared out over the Sea of Galilee, silently, sadly.

A chill of horror rippled through Jon at what he had just said. His mouth, again, had run off in its own rogue direction without first consulting his brain. A large sector of that mind still stubbornly believed—especially in view of the many other signs and wonders Joshua had apparently accomplished for which he had no answers. If Joshua turned out to be the returned Son of God after all, he himself had just uttered the worst sort of blasphemy imaginable and could now look forward to burning in hell. His entire future—in this life, and in that which is to come—now seemed to depend on what Joshua said next.

But Joshua said nothing. He only smiled faintly at Jon and shook his head dejectedly. Finally he responded, "This is very tragic, Jon. I had really hoped that you would be my St. Paul—to systematize and teach and preach the revitalized good news after I return to my Father."

Jon was now at the very edge of the precipice. Should he recant what he had just said—at least until he had all the answers—and thus not jeopardize his soul's salvation? Or should he continue to press his case?

Before making the greatest decision of his life, he found that his mouth again seemed already to have done so for him. "I thought we were trying honesty, Joshua, not myths, fantasies, and fables. I ask you again, what did you do with Shimon's body?"

Again there was no reply for what seemed a young eternity. Joshua continued staring out at the Sea of Galilee. Every second that ticked by in time seemed an hour in suspense.

Suddenly Joshua's face darkened as he turned to Jon and said, "Baruch and I removed Shimon's body the night after his burial and placed it in an unmarked grave near Nazareth. Baruch, of course, crawled inside the tomb the night before he was 'raised,' and I wrapped him in grave cloths."

A terrifying, frigid chill spread upward and downward across the vertebrae of Jon's spine. He now had the truth, but the truth was awful, glacial, wintry. For months he had searched for the truth, but now that he had it, he hated it. He had trouble thinking clearly, a problem evidently not shared by his tongue, which seemed to continue independently. "Good, Joshua! Bravo for your honesty! Then, of course, you replaced the stone at Shimon's tomb. Were you and Baruch the only two in on the plot? Or were all of the Twelve involved?"

"No, just Shimon, his brother, and I. The rest know nothing."

"Did you kill Shimon . . . poison him somehow?"

"No! Although he would have been ready to sacrifice his own life for the cause. But he didn't have to: a cancer of the blood did it for him."

"The cause. What cause?"

"That's a long story. I may tell you later. Or I may not."

Jon shook his head in disbelief. "What about all your other so-called miracles, Joshua? How did you ever bring them off? How, for example, did you ever control the weather and stop the storm that day we were all up here?"

Joshua laughed and replied genially, "Oh, that was the simplest of all my signs! Just before returning inside here that day, I stepped out the back door, looked at the western sky, and saw a great band of blue chasing the line of storm clouds directly overhead. I knew the squall would be over in minutes. It was all a matter of timing."

"But what about calming the waves on the Sea of Galilee?"

"You got that from the Gospels, Jon, not from me. The waves were still choppy, but we were too high up to notice."

Jon shook his head slowly in amazement at how ready they had all been to accept the supernatural. "But what about all the healings?" he asked. "Some people actually *were* healed, weren't ⌐⌐⌐?"

"Of course they were! Some healings, to be sure, we⌐ apparent—like those claimed by your American faith hea⌐

tent evangelists. Others were purely psychosomatic. Still others I hypnotized over their problems. For others, again, plain good counseling did the job."

"Wait a minute: medical people checked out some of your cures, and they claimed that physical diseases were often involved."

"They were indeed. But I also know medicine very well and was able to make quick diagnoses in many cases: fevers about to break—that sort of thing. I can't tell you how often plain aspirin helped me out! The reports of my healings got exaggerated in the retelling, of course, and they took on a life of their own." He stopped, grinned, and added, "I was really amazed that all of you didn't do a more scientific job in following up on the healings."

"I agree. It was the weakest point in our whole investigation. But what about that blind man at the Pool of Siloam? Shannon swears it was a miracle."

"Schmuel Sikorsky? Oh, yes, he too was in on the plot."

"Hold it! I thought you said only you and the Levine twins were involved."

"We were the only ones involved among the disciples. Schmuel wasn't a member of the Twelve."

"Well, how in blazes many more are there?"

Joshua laughed and said, "I'd love to dazzle you with our numbers, Jon, but that's it. Since Shimon died, there are only three in this world who know the truth. Make that four, since now you know also."

While shuddering at the implications of the last, Jon said, "But how did Sikorsky bring off his supposed blindness?"

"Cleverly. In public, he put a neutral salve in his eyes to make them look rheumy and infected. What a noble sacrifice Schmuel made for our cause: feigning blindness and begging for years near the Dung Gate in Jerusalem to establish his credibility!"

"What is this cause, I ask you again?"

"Later, maybe—I tell you again."

"Well . . . how did you get Schmuel involved in your plot?"

"The Levine twins, Schmuel Sikorsky, and I were all members of the Class of '94 at the Technion."

"Sikorsky! I didn't notice his name in the graduation program. Bad slipup on our part!"

"Bad indeed! We used his versatile talents in many ways. His best act was to play the part of a madman, from whom I would drive out evil spirits. But you saw our performance that day at the Brook Kidron, didn't you?"

"How in the very devil did you know that?"

"Shimon saw you in the bushes, so we hauled out our big act just for your benefit. Nice of us, was it not?"

Jon merely shook his head. Even as he was firing his fusillade of questions, he asked himself, *Why is Ben-Yosef telling me all this? And what sort of danger am I in at hearing it?* But since truth was rolling out like a crystal stream, far be it from him to play beaver and build a dam to halt the flow.

"What about the water into wine at the wedding celebration here in Galilee?" Jon continued.

"Shimon had arranged that ahead of time. There was this huge jug full of real water, out of which the guests were served following my 'miracle.' But the spigot was connected to a tank full of wine— a magician's trick. We did several of those."

Jon nodded, then shook his head back and forth. "Oh," he said. "I almost forgot to ask: what about my flying pen on Nicodemus night at Bethany?"

Joshua laughed heartily. "Again, that was Shimon's idea. I thought we'd never get to use it, but you were putty in our hands. We had built a very strongly focused electromagnet into the wall at the end of the patio, and I simply flipped on the switch with my elbow."

Jon felt like a fool, though a worried fool who seemed to relish throwing caution to the winds. He shook his head ruefully, then said, "What about your apparent omniscience, Joshua? How, for example, did you know all those details about my past?"

Joshua held up his hands modestly and said, "That was nothing at all. When you became famous in the Christian world, Jon, I started building a big file on you, knowing that our paths were bound to cross one day."

"But what about your . . . incredible linguistic abilities? I know a lot of languages. But to be able to speak them all, and without an accent? No one can do that. How did you?"

"With the help of the devil, Jon," he said, looking directly into his eyes without the slightest trace of a smile.

"*What?!*"

Joshua nodded. "Only Satan could put such perfect speech into my mouth."

Jon merely stared at him.

Joshua then shook with laughter. "Only spoofing, Jon! Using the devil—that's for your American religious novelists, not I. Both of my parents were virtual geniuses in biochemistry. In their research, they were pursuing amino acid compounds to enhance brain function, especially memory. They arrived at a perfectly balanced formula that promoted the multiplication of neural axons and dendrites, which, as you know, are the basic units in how the brain is wired and communicates. It also enhanced the electrochemical transmissions within the nerves themselves. First, of course, they tried their preparation on laboratory rats. The results were dramatic!"

"Rodent geniuses?"

"Nothing less: one trip through a maze to find the food and they had it memorized. Then my parents tried it on themselves and found remarkably enhanced awareness and increased mental capacity with no side effects. What they didn't know was that my mother was pregnant with me at the time, and it had a much greater effect on my own neural development."

"So that explains your intelligence?"

"Yes, and also my enhanced sense of hearing. I've never understood why people who speak with an accent can't *hear* the differences in the way they speak. I hear it immediately and can mold my speech to the local dialect with no effort whatever. Languages, too, were a snap for me, including all the dialects and idioms—"

"Like the word *snap* you just used. Okay, and that also explains your phenomenal IQ as a child, your winning the Israel national Bible quiz at a tender age, and the like."

"Oh, you learned about that too? Good for you!"

This was becoming almost friendly, thought Jon, despite the underlying hazards involved. But part of his mind was already hard at work on his available options. With eleven of the Twelve about to arrive who were not part of Joshua's plot, they should be able to help him overpower Joshua, if necessary.

But for now he had to keep talking, so he asked, "Why didn't your parents prepare a scientific paper on their magnificent discovery and give it to the world?"

"Two reasons. First, does the world really need another Joshua Ben-Yosef, let alone the hordes of weird geniuses that would result?"

They both laughed. Jon actually appreciated his self-deprecating humor. "And the other reason?"

"My parents actually *were* writing a book on the subject, along with suggested safeguards to prevent the globe from hatching a corps of overgifted freaks. But . . . but they were both killed before they could finish the manuscript."

"Yes . . . that tragic terrorist attack near Netanya."

Joshua looked down sadly, shook his head, and said, "Well, no . . . that's the official story we put out . . . again, for the cause."

"So? What really happened?"

The muscles on Joshua's jaws tightened. "My father and mother were taking a vacation tour of Germany while I was at summer camp here in Israel. One evening, near their own camping spot in eastern Bavaria, they saw a huge bonfire burning into the evening sky. They went over to investigate and were horrified to see that it was a gathering of neo-Nazi skinheads celebrating some pagan rites that were a throwback to the Third Reich. Someone discovered them in hiding and they were dragged into the open. When those neo-Hitlerites learned that they were Jews and from Israel, no less, they held a mock trial and sentenced them to death. They were Jewish Christ-killers who had desecrated their sacred rites." Joshua's head dropped to his chest, tears in his eyes, as he added, "Then they . . . they hanged them . . . from a rope they had strung between two pine trees."

"How . . . utterly . . . *horrible!*" commented Jon, in shock. "I think I read something about that years ago. Well . . . there you have humanity at its very worst—except to call beasts like that 'humans' is to give them too much credit!"

Neither man spoke for some moments. Then Jon commented,

"Still, Joshua, I don't see this as a motive for what you're trying to do in revitalizing Christianity by your . . . interim return as a fake Christ. If you were going to attack the faith, then maybe I could see some indirect motive here, however twisted. But you—"

"I *am* going to attack the faith, Jon—or at least your Christian perversion of the *true* faith."

"*What?!*"

"Well, on second thought, I don't really like that verb *attack*. Better to say that I'll be *reforming* your faith and leading it to better ends. And what an event this is going to be! It will be the most dramatic moment in all of Christian history. This coming Sunday, with fifteen thousand leaders of all Christendom gathered inside St. Peter's Basilica to hear the words of their Lord and Master returned in person, I will announce that ever since the year 325 C.E. and the Council of Nicaea, Christians have had it all wrong. They have taken God's Messiah and turned Him into God Himself or even something of a second god. But now, no less than the Messiah Himself will disclaim all that. He will call it blasphemy and idolatry, a reversion to polytheism! He will ask all Christians everywhere to return to the mother faith of Judaism, the belief in one true God and the only God." Joshua quit speaking and merely smiled at Jon.

Jon was almost paralyzed with shock. He groped for words and finally found a few. "But . . . but Christians don't regard Christ as a second god, Joshua. They're monotheists, just like Jews, and—"

"Tell that to the Trinity, Jon, not to me."

"What you're planning at St. Peter's is just a warmed-over version of what Arius taught—the heretic who was condemned at Nicaea."

"I know who Arius was, Jon. And I'll tell you this: Arius was closer to the truth than what became orthodox Christianity. How did Arius put it in Greek? *Ein hote ouk ein*: 'There was a time when He was not'—when Jesus was not? Hence He was not eternal with the Father.

"I have a great dual goal, Jon: to return Christianity to Judaism, and to rehabilitate for Jews a very human Christ that they can appreciate and revere again once He is stripped of the divine baggage you Christians have loaded onto Him. In time, they'll start to separate the noble rabbi from the memories of horror Christians have inflicted on us Jews for the past twenty centuries. I know it can be done, Jon! And then, with a revived Judeo-Christianity, we can finally meet the Muslim challenge and overcome it."

"You can't be serious, Joshua! You're dreaming dreams that no one will ever follow."

"That's what they said about Abraham, about Moses, about Elijah, and about Jesus. As I recall, all their dreams turned into reality, didn't they? So will mine."

"All your objections to traditional Christology have answers, Joshua, and they're solidly based on the biblical sources. I could demonstrate the proofs of Jesus' divinity to you for hours, and that Nicaea only declared what the church has always taught. But let's debate theology over lunch. Right now, please unpack more of your motives for this . . . monumental hoax. Why in very *blazes* did you and the other three warp your lives so drastically in sacrifice for 'the cause'? Again, what cause could ever be important enough for that?"

"Well, that's a rather long story, Jon. But before I tell it, would you like some sort of refreshment? Coffee? Tea?"

"Kind of you, Joshua! Yes, I'd like some coffee if you have it. Black."

While Joshua went out into the kitchen to prepare it, Jon had a life-or-death decision to make, and less than a minute in which to make it. Having revealed so much, Joshua could never let him emerge from the lodge alive, he knew: that would scuttle everything to which Ben-Yosef had devoted his genius. Basic instincts of self-preservation yelled inside Jon to run for the door! Take the chance while Joshua was in the kitchen!

But there was *so* much more to learn about why this frenzied four had tried to dupe the world, so many other issues to probe. A little more dialogue, a few more secrets to pry out of Joshua . . . then he could make a dash for the door.

Twenty-Three

Joshua walked in from the kitchen with a tray and set it on a table between them. It was laden with two mugs, a silver carafe of coffee, several bagels, cookies, and sweets. *Why is Ben-Yosef doing this?* Jon wondered. *Why did he leave me unguarded?*

"All right, Jon. Let's pick up where we left off. You wanted to know more about our cause, correct?"

"Yes . . ."

"Shimon, Baruch, Schmuel, and I were all classmates at the Technion, as you know. One evening the four of us were sipping wine at a restaurant on Mount Carmel overlooking the Mediterranean. When the conversation finally wound its way around to religion, I brought up the statistical problem. I said, 'Gentlemen, we have a wretched, wretched paradox here: Judaism gave the world monotheism—a very precious gift! And yet the other two monotheistic religions, which have received this gift, vastly outnumber Judaism, the giver. There are two billion Christians in the world and one billion Muslims, but only sixteen million Jews. Is that fair, my friends? Is that in any way fair? Do you realize that there are 125 Christians in the world for every Jew?'

"They grumbled, of course, as I expected them to. Shimon suggested that medieval pogroms and the Nazi Holocaust had something to do with it, and that's when I told them about my parents. They were livid, and Baruch asked, 'What can the four of us do about this?' And that's when I started sketching the first outlines of our cause. It was motivated not just by the horror inflicted on my dear parents, but by the millions of other hells imposed on my people over the last twenty centuries, from the destruction of Jerusalem to the ovens of Nazi Germany. As Jews, we've been

271

treated with contempt, thrown into ghettos, victimized in pogroms, forced to convert, discriminated against, gassed, and then burned— by the millions! That 1– to –125 ratio shouldn't surprise anyone!

"First, of course, I studied every aspect of Christian doctrine and history to see where it was most vulnerable and where it had most departed from Judaism. The Levine twins, who were totally identical as you saw, agreed to provide the 'resurrection,' as it were. But which of them would have to die? They agreed not to decide that until later on in life. Either of them would have given his life for the cause, but, as it turned out, the Lord decided that for them—another sign that God sanctioned our cause! Schmuel, in turn, agreed to get 'healed' of many different maladies at various places. At Jerusalem he was the blind beggar only when tourists would see him. I mean, he didn't spend his entire life at the Dung Gate!"

Jon forced a smile at the pleasantry while disguising a clump of anxiety within. He suddenly realized that the Twelve and the other men would not take his side in overpowering Joshua after all: he would never be able to convince them in time that their Master was a fraud. In fact, they would probably join Joshua in overpowering *him*! Perhaps he should escape now, before they arrived. Why had he not told Gideon about his trip to Galilee? He struggled to maintain serenity at the surface, even as he was wildly scrambling for options.

"What are you thinking, Jon?" The penetrating voice interrupted the pause in their dialogue.

"Just this: in trying to run your scheme parallel to Jesus' life and ministry, there were some items you could not control. For example, your birth—in Bethlehem, no less—to parents named Joseph and Mary, as well as spending your early years in Nazareth."

"Pure coincidence, Jon! Pure, unadulterated coincidence! Earlier in my student days, I used to joke with my friends and say, 'Hey, you guys, I'm the Christian Messiah: I was born in Bethlehem and my parents were Joseph and Mary!' It always brought a big laugh. See, it's been over twenty centuries since Jesus was born, so, in that long a period of time, the law of averages just had to permit such a coincidence."

"And did that coincidence help give you the idea for your plot?"

"Of course it did! It was almost a blueprint from God. But notice, too, that there was no exact parallel, which would have been impossible. My mother's name was Mariam, not Mary. I was an only child, whereas Jesus had four brothers, two sisters. I grew up in Nazareth Ilit, not Nazareth, et cetera."

"Speaking of your youth, how did you bring off the Sepphoris mosaic?"

"Baruch's idea. He graduated from the Technion in chemical engineering, so it was no problem for him to play tourist at Sepphoris and retrieve some of the grout in the synagogue floor, matching it completely with the grout for our inscription. I thought the idea was hopelessly far-fetched when we planted the mosaic one night at the Sepphoris dig, but you people proved so cooperative in its discovery and interpretation."

Jon nodded, feeling like a wooden marionette on the end of Joshua's strings. Then he commented, "I won't even ask how you generated the voice of God at the Galilee theater: tape with multi-track recording, plus bass overmodulation and gross amplification, of course."

"Except we used a CD instead of tape. Of all my 'miracles,' that one, certainly, was the easiest to bring off."

"Oh, yes, one more of your wonders isn't explained: your famous Jesus Bulletin on the world's computers. The best web people in the world haven't figured that one out. They know it originated in Israel, but how in blue blazes did *that* work?"

"I love the cyberuniverse, Jon. If I hadn't had more important things to do, I could have designed computers that would have made Bill Gates and Microsoft look like they were dealing in abacuses! So when instant messaging came along with those annoying pop-ups on the screen, it gave me the idea on how to handle John the Baptist's role."

"Wouldn't an actual person have been less complicated?"

"Negative. Only four of us were involved in this great cause, and we wanted to keep it at that: the fewer the better."

"But how did you do the cyberthing?"

"For all its enormous spread, the World Wide Web is controlled by very few main server software vendors across the globe. I devised an almost dimensionally different way to penetrate the entire web through those software programs, a way no hacker would ever have thought of. The servers, in turn, infected the entire web with harmless worms that would program all computers on-line to respond to language-coded instructions from the mainframe server I have in the basement here."

"You have your own server *here*? You own this place, then?"

Joshua nodded, almost proudly.

Jon knew it was nearing noon, and the rest would be arriving imminently. Could he perhaps succeed in exposing Joshua before them, after all? Unlikely, and why take the chance? Might it come to violence with Joshua? They were rather evenly matched physically, and he was ready for a fight. But what if Joshua had a weapon hidden somewhere? Again, why take the chance?

Jon had been fingering the keys to his Peugeot in his right pocket. Fortunately, he had not locked the car: he would dash inside it, lock the doors instantly, and drive off. Jon knew it was a long shot that the old gimmick would work, but suddenly he jumped up, pointed with horror at the veranda windows, and shouted, "*Watch out!*"

While Joshua turned his back to see, Jon made a dash for the main door and flung it open. There stood the six-foot, four-inch frame of Baruch Levine, blocking the exit with both arms. Jon ran through the house to the back door. It was locked, apparently from the outside. He fought the knob and hurled himself against the door, but it wouldn't open. Wheeling about, he ran to the glass doors opening onto the veranda, but before he could slide them open or crash through them, six hands grabbed him tightly. Someone he had not even seen before held his lower legs in a tight armlock, while Joshua and Baruch clamped both his arms and pinned him to the floor. Shackles were clamped onto his ankles, while handcuffs were slapped onto his wrists. The three then lifted him back onto one of the couches.

"I . . . regret any unpleasantness here, Jon," said Joshua, smiling. "And do permit me to make the introductions. Baruch you already know, and our football 'tackle' here is Mr. Schmuel Sikorsky. Once he was blind at the Pool of Siloam, you may recall, but now—amazingly!—he seems to have regained his sight. Oh, and by the way, I didn't tell you how I knew that you and Ben-Yaakov had driven to the Technion. By great good fortune, Schmuel here paid an alumni visit to his alma mater the same day. He was at the administration building that morning, purloining the computer mainframe tape for 1994."

"Okay, Ben-Yosef," Jon responded. "This was inevitable, of course. But you've claimed only four people were in on your plot: one's dead; the other three are here. What will the rest of your cadre think when they get here and see me in irons? Or have you lied about that too?"

Joshua broke out laughing, and the other two joined in.

"Jon, Jon, Jon," said Joshua, "the others would indeed be shocked, since what I told you is true: only the people in this room know. But I do confess to fibbing about them coming. They have no idea we're even up here!"

A stab of horror pierced the very marrow of Jon's bones, but he swore not to let his captors sense it as he replied evenly, "Well, then, I'm dreadfully sorry to have upset your plans, Ben-Yosef. The best thing you can do at this point is to call the police, come clean with your entire operation, tell the world how you did it, and go down in history as having pulled off the greatest caper in the annals of humanity. You'll be famous for centuries, no, millennia to come!"

"Sorry, Jon. I just can't do that."

"Why not, Joshua? Believe it or not, up to this point—in your whole weird and wild conspiracy—I really don't think you've broken any laws . . . nothing for which they could send you to jail. Well, I guess I could sue you for false arrest here, but I won't press charges . . . if, that is, you release me immediately. After that I'll thank you for a most stimulating conversation this morning. To say it's been enlightening is to understate. In the extreme!"

Joshua said nothing but merely unleashed a low smile at Baruch and Schmuel.

"C'mon, Ben-Yosef, use that marvelous intelligence of yours and take the high road: no jail time, writing an international bestseller telling the world how you brought it off, and enjoy the rest of your life in luxury. So take these lovely bracelets off, since I have to get going now." He held up his arms. "Obviously, I won't be accompanying you and the others to Rome."

"No, that's true."

"So, then . . . what are your plans?" Jon was maintaining the air of insouciance as long as possible. "How long do I have to wear these lovely . . . iron accessories of yours?"

"Oh . . . just as long as it takes, Jon."

"Which means?"

"Shall we say . . . for the foreseeable future?"

"Fine. But what will Shannon say when I'm not on that flight to Rome?"

"You will have gone there a day earlier to help prepare for my arrival, Jon. I suggested as much to Shannon, so she'll not be concerned."

"What about the people in Rome?"

"I'll say that you were detained by urgent business here in Israel."

"And what happens when all of you return from Rome? Having fooled the world, you'll release me then?"

Joshua flashed him a wan smile and said, "You can't be serious, Jon, can you?"

He swallowed hard and said, "Your scheme is impossible, Ben-Yosef. You ought to know that! The government, the academic community, the press corps . . . everyone will be looking for me." He was about to add "Shin Bet also," but thought better of it.

Joshua took a long breath and said, "They'll quickly have a reason to . . . stop looking, Jon."

An icy shiver tickled his nerves. "And what is that?"

Joshua avoided his eyes, looked down, and shook his head. "Jon, Jon, why couldn't you simply have believed—like so much of the world? Again, you could so easily have become my prime apostle Paul—and Paul is even your middle name! But no." He threw up his hands and sighed. "All right, then, have it your way. I'm really . . . dreadfully sorry, Jon. But the cause is . . . infinitely more important than any one individual."

"Which means . . ."

"Which means that . . . when the authorities find your body, they'll stop looking for you, of course. It's as simple as that. Your suicide note will explain it all."

An emotional tornado blowing inside made Jon cough. He hated that. He wanted to betray nothing, however dread the situation. Mastering himself, he had only the slightest waver in responding, "So what will my suicide note say? And, by the way, I hardly ever write notes: I just type memos and initial them."

"Which will be very helpful for us. We'll type the note on your letterhead, and I've already practiced writing your initials."

"Where do you propose to get my letterhead?"

"We already have it. The day you interviewed 'Shimon' in your office—after his astonishing resurrection—he swiped several copies off your desk while you went out for coffee. Of course, he had no reason to suspect you at that time, but how very brilliant of you, Baruch, to see that all our bases were covered."

"Yes," he replied. "Some intuition made me do it." Then he pointed upward and said, "God."

"Well, that was clever, gentlemen," said Jon. "But why in the world would I ever want to commit suicide? Where's the motive?"

"The most frequent motive for any suicide," Joshua replied. "Grief and heartbreak over the loss of Shannon."

Jon's eyes blazed in fury. "If you do anything . . . *anything* to Shannon," he yelled, "so help me God, I'll—"

"Oh, no, no, no. I don't propose to hurt her in the least. Quite the contrary! I intend to have her fall in love with me, because I'm already deeply in love with her. She is simply the most exciting creature I've ever encountered, Jon. And that, you see, will be the reason for your suicide."

"You're totally crazed, Joshua, do you know that? You're whacko, off-the-wall! You're living in La-La Land! If Shannon's not suspicious before her flight to Rome, she certainly will be once I don't arrive there. On the flight back to Israel, she'll be in total panic."

"True enough. But our women's auxiliary, as you call it, will keep her busy enough in Rome. And we won't sedate her until her complaining about your absence gets obnoxious—if, in fact, it ever does. Once she returns here, of course, your body and suicide note will solve it all. If she claims that you had no reason to write such a note, the authorities will simply interpret that as a woman covering her tracks for an illicit affair with someone else. The other ladies will report her reverent love for me, and I, of course, will do everything I can to help her surmount her grief, believe me!"

"You're a fool, Ben-Yosef. And you're taking her for a fool too."

"I don't think so, Jon. Of course, if she fails to respond to my overtures in the months to come, or if she gets too suspicious about your suicide, well then—I deeply regret—hers must inevitably follow. Out of grief for you, of course."

Jon strained at his chains. Fury vied with fright for control of his psyche, and at this point anger held the upper hand. "Throughout this weird sham of yours," he seethed, "I've eliminated the satanic as in any way involved in your fake miracles, Ben-Yosef. But now, I think, it's finally time to involve the devil—not to give you any powers you don't already have, but to account for your own satanic intellect. You're a depraved, damnable monster, Joshua. You do realize that, don't you?"

Schmuel had been standing in the background, making no response whatever. Now, however, he snarled angrily. "May I please smash his face, Joshua, so that he shows you some respect?"

"Not necessary, Schmuel. Let's just take him downstairs."

They lifted Jon off the couch, Joshua carrying him at the shoulders, with Schmuel and Baruch at each leg. Jon twisted and jerked with adrenaline energy. On the stairs to the basement, he succeeded in shoving the three off balance, and they all slid most of the way down to the concrete floor. Jon got up first and tried to climb back up the stairs, but his shackles hobbled him, and he stumbled.

The others pounced on him and dragged him across the basement floor to a wine cellar. There they fettered his wrists to two three-quarter-inch wrought-iron chains embedded in the concrete wall.

"Why would anyone have chains in a wine cellar?" Jon asked, inanely under the circumstances.

Joshua replied, "We took appropriate precautions a month ago in case anything went wrong. Now, while Baruch and I fly to Rome, Schmuel here will keep you company. We certainly don't want an early suicide to detract in any way from the great event at the Vatican. Now we ought to—"

"I wonder if I shouldn't stay behind too," Baruch suggested. "If Weber escaped, everything we've worked for all these years would be doomed."

Joshua shook his head. "The world wants to see the man I raised from the dead. 'Peter' must certainly be present for our triumphal entry into the basilica named for him! You can handle this, can't you, Schmuel?"

"Of course! I didn't sit outside the Dung Gate of Jerusalem all those years to let this *goy* spoil it all!"

"Very well, then. Don't release him from his chains under any circumstances whatever! If he tries to scream, gag him. Then again, why bother? We're six kilometers from the nearest house. We'll lock the gate on the entrance road down in the valley. The place is surrounded by motion sensors, of course, and will buzz an alarm if anyone approaches. In that case, use ether on him immediately. The bottle's over there on the table."

Then he turned to Jon and said, "Schmuel will supply your food and drink."

"But what about entertainment?" Jon wondered, in a feeble attempt at humor.

"Hmmm. Oh, I have it, fellows: let's bring down the smaller TV set upstairs so that our friend here may enjoy our Roman holiday also! All right with you, my colleagues?"

"Fine."

"The day after we return from Rome, then, we'll reconvene here and offer Professor Weber a generous helping of wine, pasta . . . and, of course, potassium cyanide."

"Not my favorite dessert, Ben-Yosef," said Jon. "I think I'll pass."

"In which case, some force-feeding may be necessary, good friend. Then we'll take your body up to, say, Banias, and dump it at night into the headwaters of the Jordan. We'll leave your suicide note on a picnic table nearby, and then get back to Jerusalem before your remains are even discovered. How do those plans suit you, Jon?"

"They certainly suit a maniacal psychopath! And what else would one expect from a homicidal fraud who thinks he'll dupe two billion people?"

"Oh, I'll convince them all right."

"Your plan is full of holes, Ben-Yosef! I doubt if anyone would commit suicide using cyanide."

"Hmmm. You may have a point there . . . well, we could always fall back on barbiturates—sleeping pills, overdosed, of course. Thank you, Jon. You've been very helpful on that point."

"But I—"

"But you won't swallow any? Well, then, we'll put them into solution and use a catheter on you, I suppose."

"You're *crazed*, Ben-Yosef! Mad! Unhinged!"

"Ta ta for now, Jon. Enjoy the accommodations. See you soon!"

TWENTY-FOUR

The second week in July was almost ostentatiously beautiful. A limpid canopy of blue with a few cottony tufts of clouds hung over the entire Mediterranean basin, with fragrant southern breezes gently caressing all three of the great peninsulas on the north shore: the Balkans, Italy, and Iberia. Christians there knew well enough why the weather was superb: clearly, Joshua had arranged it for his historic reception in Rome.

An hour before Alitalia's special Flight 100 was scheduled to land at Fiumicino, all flights into and out of Leonardo da Vinci airport were diverted or grounded. The air was to be entirely clear for the arrival of the returned Messiah and his party. When their 757 left Greek airspace over the Adriatic and the peninsula of Italy came into view thirty-four thousand feet below, it was met by an honor guard of six jet fighters from the Italian air force that assumed a cruciform formation ahead of their plane for the rest of the flight.

"Alitalia 100, you are cleared to land on runway 16L," the tower radioed, and then added something not covered in flight manuals: "All Italy welcomes you in the name of the Lord!"

"His name be blessed!" responded Captain Domenico Guardini, who had top seniority among Alitalia's pilots. Crossing himself, he eased the 757 down the glide path and into an extremely gentle landing. While taxiing to the terminal, Shannon, who had insisted on a window seat, was almost beside herself with excitement. She stared out at what must have been the largest welcoming throng in the history of aviation. A double-broad red carpet had been rolled out, the 110-member Italian army band was holding forth with the "Grand March" from Verdi's *Aida*, and an official welcoming party stood on both sides of the red carpet, waiting for Joshua-Jesus to appear.

When the jet's doorway finally opened, there stood Joshua, clad in a robe of brilliant white and looking more biblical than ever. Smiling beatifically, he stepped out onto the deplaning ramp and raised both arms to bless the crowd. The people nearly went out of control. Hosannas, shouts, prayers, hymns, and exclamations roared throughout the tarmac—and across the world as well, since all the international radio and television networks were covering this totally unparalleled event.

When Shannon and the rest of the party had followed Joshua off the plane and down the aluminum staircase, they were ushered over to several rows of chairs and seated for the welcoming ceremonies. Dr. Luigi Bertoni, the president of Italy, faced a wide battery of microphones and said, in a voice quaking with emotion, "In the name of the Republic of Italy, we welcome our Lord and Master to the land He never visited in His first earthly manifestation, sending instead His two greatest apostles, Peter and Paul, who gave their lives for His cause in Rome. Now, however, you have seen fit to grace us with your own sacred presence, for which we thank Almighty God and say, in the words of the Latin Scriptures, 'Osanna filio David! Benedictus qui venturus est in nomine Domini! Osanna in altissimis'!"

As if rehearsed, which was not the case, the entire assemblage burst into all the vernacular translations of the Latin. Shannon heard the American delegation nearby reechoing, "Hosanna to the Son of David! Blessed is he who comes in the name of the Lord! Hosanna in the highest!"

Then, in carefully planned protocol, Pope Benedict XVI and Eastern Orthodox Patriarch Bartholomew II approached Joshua from the left and right respectively and knelt humbly before him. Joshua placed his hands on the head of each in blessing, then quickly raised them up, put his arms about them, and had them join hands with one another. They did so, with enthusiasm. And when Joshua's was the third hand to clasp the other two, a thunderous roar of approval filled the air. Not since the eastern and western churches had excommunicated each other in the Great Schism of A.D. 1054 had such a scene, with divine endorsement, been possible. The pope and the patriarch then embraced each other in tears as the Sistine Chapel Choir sang a principal theme from Vivaldi's Gloria.

Shannon, fully realizing that this was an incandescent moment in the history of Christianity, only wished she could have shared it with Jon. She kept looking through the ranks of dignitaries, hoping to see the distinguished visage of her husband, but evidently he was elsewhere in the crowd.

Next, the archbishop of Canterbury, the president of the Lutheran World Federation, the presidents of the World Alliance of Reformed Churches, of the Methodist World Council, of the Baptist World Alliance, and a score of other ecclesiastical dignitaries genuflected before Joshua and were rewarded with his blessing and his embrace. Ecumenicity ruled the day.

The heads of state then had their turn. Queen Elizabeth II of Britain, before whom thousands had regularly curtsied, did so herself before Joshua. The American president, Sherwood Bronson, gave him a powerful handshake, raising not a few eyebrows, but Joshua hardly seemed put off by the gesture.

When the world's political greats had paid their respects, Joshua stood before the microphones himself, looked heavenward, raised his arms, closed his eyes, and said, "I thank You, Father, for having inspired Your children who are gathered here to give me this magnificent reception. And now bless Your Son in His great mission to renew Your church, so that it may finally achieve my great intention to make disciples of all nations. I ask this in Your own blessed name. Amen."

A vast, full-throated "AMEN!" from the crowd endorsed the prayer. Joshua and his party were now escorted over to a row of Vatican limousines that had been driven out on the tarmac. A new and much larger "Pope-mobile" stood at the head of the cavalcade, on which Joshua would stand so that the crowds lining the highway to Rome would be able to see him clearly. Seated on either side of him were the pope and the patriarch. The first two limousines were reserved for the Twelve. Shannon was delighted to find herself directed to limo number three, and as she climbed inside, she half hoped to find Jon sitting there with open arms. But only empty seats of black leather greeted her.

While she did not see Jon, Jon certainly saw her. Fifteen hundred miles to the southeast, he was watching the entire ceremony on television in his dank basement prison. While his guard, Schmuel Sikorsky, was cheering along with the crowd at Joshua's triumphal reception, Jon was shaking his head and mouthing silent expletives at the improbable scene: world leaders in religion and politics being deluded by a diabolical con man. Each time the camera panned across the dignitaries and zoomed in on Shannon, he called out, "Please notice my absence, darling! And do something about it!"

"I doubt that she can hear you, Weber!" said Schmuel. "Besides, it looks like she's having such a good time that she's probably forgotten you by now."

"Bite your forked tongue, Sikorsky!" Jon snarled. "And see if you can't—even for a moment or two—wake up to reality. This whole weird charade of yours is going to crash on its face very soon now, and if you continue to do Joshua's dirty work, you'll be an accessory to attempted murder and spend the rest of your misguided life behind bars!"

"No, I won't, Weber. Finally we're going to do something about how horribly Jews have been treated across the centuries. We've been invaded, banished to ghettos, forced to convert, exiled, and brutalized in every way possible, not to mention the millions of lives we lost in the Holocaust. And that's one of the reasons for those disgusting ratios: 60 Muslims and 125 Christians for every Jew on earth!"

"But when your hoax is exposed, you're actually going to embarrass world Judaism by this . . . clumsy attempt of yours. Why not spare your people all that? Be a hero instead, and blow the whistle on Ben-Yosef! History will applaud you for your honesty!"

"You take me for a fool, Weber? You think I devoted half my life playing blind only to say the whole thing was merely a practical joke after all? Not a chance!"

"Then you're pathetic, Sikorsky! Half your life you *play* blind, the other half—or what's left of it—you *are* blind . . . blind to reality, stupidly going down that impossible rat-hole Ben-Yosef put you in."

Schmuel got up, hurried over to Jon, and slapped him hard on the left cheek. "Better watch it, man!" he spit out. "I might be tempted to use that ether over there after all, and accidentally hold it under your prying nose longer than necessary. Who cares if you die a couple days too early?"

Shannon was overwhelmed at the reception lavished on their cavalcade as it traveled slowly toward Rome on the Via Ostiensis, flanked by *carabinieri* on gleaming motorcycles. It seemed as if most of Italian humanity was lining both sides of the road, shouting, singing, and applauding, many waving palm branches in recapitulating Jesus' entry into Jerusalem on that first Palm Sunday. Standing majestically erect in the new pope-mobile, Joshua smiled warmly at the multitudes, hands extended outward in blessing as he turned from side to side with the light of heaven illuminating his features. Many were crossing themselves and breaking down in tears at a sight they had never expected to see, while some were so overcome that they fainted. Near Rome, outlying churches had their choirs assembled along the roadsides on portable bleachers, singing hymns of praise to the arriving Christ.

When they penetrated the old city walls of Rome at the Ostian Gate, the masses pressing onto the roadway were, if anything, even more enthusiastic. The white-helmeted city police had a very difficult time containing them.

Conversation inside the limousines was now impossible because of the joyful din outside. The Eternal City, which had seen many a triumphal parade by the Caesars in antiquity, had never witnessed anything like this. Only cameras with wide-angle lenses in helicopters overhead could begin to gather in the magnificence of the moment for the rest of the world.

Crossing the Tiber River bridge, they proceeded westward into Vatican City on the Via della Conciliazione, which was choked on both sides with cheering, black-garbed seminarians, neophytes, nuns, deacons, priests, bishops, archbishops, cardinals, bearded patriarchs, and every degree of clergy and administrative laity. Somewhere in that throng, Shannon assumed, would be Jon. She couldn't possibly know where he was, but *her* whereabouts were obvious, and he would soon be wrapping his arms around her.

The entourage halted in front of the papal apartments, where Joshua, the orthodox patriarch, and the highest of the world clergy would stay as guests of the pontiff. A broadly beaming Kevin Sullivan greeted the group and announced the logistical details for their visit to Rome, beginning with a great banquet that evening in the Sistine Chapel. Shannon, the Twelve, and the rest of the entourage would lodge very near the papal apartments in luxury accommodations arranged for VIPs visiting the Vatican.

Shannon wanted very much to ask Kevin where Jon was, but he was conducting Joshua and the highest prelates into the papal apartments. A large company of porters now descended on Shannon's group, each conducting guests to their respective quarters.

When Shannon's valet opened the door to her room, it turned out to be a lavish suite with elegant Louis XIV furniture, a king-sized bed, and a huge basket of fruit on a table, with bottles of red and white wine flanking two long-stemmed glasses. She asked the porter whose names were assigned to the room. He looked at his card and said, "*Professore Jonathan and Shannon Weber, Signora.* I bring your luggage when it arrives from airport, yes?"

"Thank you. *Molte grazie!*"

"*Prego. Arrivederci.*"

She looked around the suite and was both relieved and worried. She was glad that Jon was expected as her "roommate," but where in the world was his luggage, if he had arrived the day before? Putting him up at a different location his first night in Rome would have been stupid. She looked at her watch: three-thirty. By, say, five o'clock, she would phone Kevin Sullivan to ask about Jon—unless, of course, her missing husband walked in with flowers, champagne, and a great big "Surprise!"

He did not. At five she picked up the phone.

"*Pronto,*" the hotel operator replied.

"Ah . . . *parla inglese?* Do you speak English?"

"*Sì.* Yes . . ."

Shannon spoke slowly and distinctly. "I would like to speak to Monsignor Kevin Sullivan, who is in charge of arrangements for Joshua's visit here at the Vatican."

"Ah . . . *un momento, per favore . . .*"

She heard the endless ringing of a phone, but no answer. She hung up and told herself, "Oh well, I'll see Kevin at the banquet—and Jon too, surely!"

The great festivity that evening in the Sistine Chapel was unparalleled in the history of the Vatican. Ordinarily, the chapel was a magnet for tourists the world over because of Michelangelo's magnificent ceiling frescos. On rare, extraordinary occasions it also served as the place where the College of Cardinals, in solemn conclave, elected a new pope after the death of the previous. On this night, however, it became the site of the "Lord's Supper" in a quite literal sense. At the western end of the chapel, under Michelangelo's enormous portrayal of the Last Judgment, the high table was reserved for Joshua, flanked on each side by six of the Twelve, and, after them, the pope, the patriarch, and the world's principal religious leaders. Forty festively adorned banquet tables covered the rest of the chapel floor, where archbishops, cardinals, ambassadors, world heads of state, the Vatican diplomatic corps, and local Roman "glitterati" were seated.

Shannon, wearing a stunning evening gown of gold lamé, was happily surprised to find her place setting at table number five, just under Joshua and the head table. Next to her was a place card engraved with the name *Jonathan P. Weber, Ph.D.* in flowing script. Now he *must* appear, thought Shannon, her eyes darting in all directions to find him. The other guests at her table were members of the women's auxiliary who had accompanied Joshua to Rome.

At last she spotted Kevin Sullivan, who was darting to and from the head table. Pushing her chair back, she stood up, excused herself, and tried to accost Kevin when she heard the papal master of ceremonies banging his gavel, and all conversation in the lofty chapel stilled to a hush. Quickly, Shannon returned to her seat.

Benedict XVI now welcomed the guests and delivered a very moving invocation, made even more powerful by the presence of the Lord himself. Following the amen, an entire corps of waiters, colorfully dressed in medieval uniforms, filed into the chapel with huge trays of succulent appetizers. Shannon soon saw that the dinner would be Italian cuisine at its best: prosciutto with melon and pasticcio were followed by a broad pasta selection—she chose tortellini—while the soup, of course, was a particularly rich minestrone. As for the entrées, how the Vatican chefs were able to offer a selection for so vast a number of diners seemed another wonderment, she thought, as she chose pollo piccata.

When the food arrived, handsomely presented and garnished with piquant sauces, a string ensemble at the eastern end of the Sistine Chapel had just begun playing banquet music from the Italian Renaissance. A wine steward now leaned over with helpful suggestions as to the appropriate vintage to accompany her entrée. Still, she could hardly savor the feast, since her uneasiness about Jon's absence was now bordering on distress, and the small talk she was forced to make with others at their table hardly helped. Several times she glanced up at Joshua, who, each time, seemed to be smiling and looking at her. That was certainly pleasant enough, but why did he seem so unconcerned about the empty place next to her?

Just before dessert was served, Kevin Sullivan came to their table and sat down next to her on Jon's empty chair. "Hello, Shannon!" he said, patting her back amiably and innocently. "Where in the world is Jon?"

"*What?* You don't know either? You've *got* to know! He flew to Rome yesterday, for goodness' sake, as Joshua asked him to! Didn't he contact you?"

Kevin's face darkened. "No, he didn't. Not at all. That's . . . very strange!"

"I was so sure you knew where he was, Kevin. Now I'm really terrified!"

"Tell you what, please stay here right after the banquet, and we'll both talk to Joshua about it, okay?"

"Yes. By all means!"

Shannon ate her dessert, an Italian version of *Schaumtorte*, with a knot of anxiety in her stomach. What could possibly have happened to Jon? Kevin should have had all the answers, yet he had none. Still, she could relax a bit in the knowledge that the Master would soon solve the riddle.

Joshua arose after dinner and delivered brief but brilliant remarks about his great mission to Rome that would culminate in the opening session of Vatican III in just two days. There he would announce God's momentous plans for the church. His own fervent prayer for Christians everywhere was "that they might all be one" in a spiritual unity that would, with divine help, overcome many generations of differences in doctrine and practice among believers.

"And thank you for this evening's celebration," he concluded. "I consider it a preview of what Scriptures call 'the Wedding Feast of the Lamb' that we shall all enjoy in my Father's mansions at the end of time. And now, my beloved brothers and sisters, I have been asked to repeat what happened on that Thursday night in which I began the very painful process of achieving your salvation. Please, then, prepare the chalices and patens at the end of each of your tables and remove the fair linens covering them. My general blessing will suffice for all the elements on each table."

The entire Sistine Chapel stilled to almost mortal silence, an air of exquisite anticipation in the air. Everyone present knew the Words of Institution that Jesus spoke on Maundy Thursday evening at the first celebration of Holy Communion—words in the third-person singular. Now, however, they would hear them in the *first* person.

Joshua extended both arms in blessing to all assembled as he said: "*On the very night in which I was betrayed, I took bread, and when I had given thanks, I broke it and gave it to my disciples and said, 'Take, eat: this is my body, which is given for you. This do in remembrance of me.'*"

Joshua now broke a large circle of unleavened bread and passed it to his left and right, with each communing the next. He also broke off a chunk of regular (leavened) bread for the benefit of the Orthodox Christians in the room, who followed the Passion story according to John's Gospel. This ecumenical gesture all but shouted what remained unsaid: "Either form of distribution is acceptable to God."

He then continued: "*In the same way also, I took the cup after supper, and when I had given thanks, I gave it to them, saying, 'Drink of it, all of you: this is my blood of the new testament which is shed for you for the forgiveness of sins. This do, as often as you drink it, in remembrance of me.'*"

He passed chalices to the left and right, each, again, communing the next. When everyone had finished, Joshua again raised his arms and said, "My peace be with you always!"

"AND ALSO WITH YOU," came the general response.

"May my body and blood strengthen and preserve you steadfast in the faith unto life everlasting. And now, depart in gladness, and in the peace of Almighty God. Amen!"

"AMEN!"

Most now stood up from their tables and left the Sistine Chapel with heads bowed and remarkably little conversation. Shannon lingered on, her spiritual experience tinged with understandable concern. She looked around for Kevin. There he was, at the high table just behind Joshua, waving for her to come up. When most of the dignitaries had left the head table, she and Kevin approached Joshua to ask if he had any idea why Jon was not present in Rome.

For all his brilliance, Joshua had not intuited that Shannon and Sullivan might have been in touch, let alone that they even knew each other. His explanation must now satisfy both, and must also build on what he had previously told Shannon. Every cerebral advantage that his parents had bequeathed to him now worked overtime for an answer. Neuron clusters in his mind flashed hundreds of different options to each other until he seized on one of them.

With perfect serenity, he smiled and said, "Obviously you are both concerned about Jonathan, Shannon and Kevin, and I deeply regret that I didn't mention this earlier, but we've all had a hundred items to attend to, haven't we? Two days before our flight, I noticed on the list of dignitaries attending Vatican III—the one you e-mailed to me, Kevin—that the Greek Orthodox archbishop of Athens, Christodoulos II, was not planning to come to Rome. This deeply saddened me. So I got through to Jon by phone just after he landed at Fiumicino and asked that he take the next flight to Athens instead and try to convince the archbishop to attend. How could Vatican III be truly ecumenical without him? In any case, I'm sure they'll both arrive in time for the opening the day after tomorrow. Christodoulos once said that Jon's book on Jesus was the only one he respected in Western scholarship!"

"Oh, that explains it," said Kevin, since the information jibed ᵂⁱᵗʰ his list of names.

"Oh, thank you, Joshua, thank you!" Shannon added, tears in her eyes. "I was so worried."

"Understandably!" he said, giving Shannon a soulful look that threaded its way into her very being. "And now may the peace of God go with you both."

That evening, both Kevin and Shannon were a little nettled at Jon. Kevin thought he might at least have had the courtesy to phone him about the change of plans. Then again, if Joshua himself could have overlooked mentioning that change, a mere mortal like his friend Jon might well be excused.

Shannon, for the same reason, was disappointed that Jon didn't have the decency at least to phone her from Athens about the shift in arrangements. Then again, the parallel thought: if Joshua himself could have overlooked mentioning that shift in arrangements, a mere mortal like her husband might well be excused also.

The next morning, she was pleased to find some of the women in Joshua's entourage asking if she wanted to join them on a daylong excursion through Rome that Joshua had so kindly arranged for his "auxiliary." In the evening, they would take in the illuminated fountains at Tivoli. She happily agreed.

High in the papal apartments overlooking the city of Rome, Joshua relished a morning cup of espresso and said to the breezes from the south that ruffled the curtains flanking his window: "Excellent! No more tête-à-têtes between Monsignor Kevin Sullivan and Shannon Weber prior to the opening of Vatican III. Tomorrow will change the world. God grant me success . . . on behalf of His chosen people!"

TWENTY-FIVE

Early Sunday morning, the phone at Gideon's bedside started ringing at 4:15 A.M., Jerusalem time. Barely awake, he grabbed the phone and muttered, *"Shalom . . ."*

"Gideon Ben-Yaakov?"

"Ken. Or, yes, if you speak English . . ."

"Terribly sorry to bother you at this early hour! This is Kevin Sullivan in Rome. You may remember me from—"

"Oh, yes, of course, Monsignor!" Gideon replied, now fully awake. "Have you seen Jonathan Weber? He was supposed to call me before he flew to Rome, but I never heard from him."

"You didn't? That's why I'm calling: we haven't seen him in Rome either!"

"What? You mean he hasn't shown up in Rome *at all?"*

Kevin updated Gideon on how Joshua claimed to have sent Jon to Athens. "But I've been calling the airlines all evening, and Jon isn't on any of their manifests in the last forty-eight hours."

Gideon emitted a low whistle and then reported the suspicions about Ben-Yosef that had arisen on the trip to Haifa.

Sullivan gasped at the potentially poisonous tidings. "Do you have any . . . proofs for your suspicions?"

"Jon and I were going to try to find some after he returned from Rome."

"This is simply horrendous!" Kevin exclaimed. "At St. Peter's this afternoon, a . . . a *fraud* could be taking place?" Then he added, almost in a tone of despair, "Unless, of course, there *is* some explanation for all this. I should have checked on Jon much earlier, of course, but I've been up to my ears running the 'greatest show on earth' here."

"Shannon's there, isn't she? When was the last time she saw Jon in Israel?"

"I asked her that, of course. She told me it was when he drove off for a meeting of the men in Joshua's entourage up at their lodge in Galilee."

"Oh? . . . Well, well, well . . . we know where that is. Shin Bet has had the place under surveillance whenever Ben-Yosef is there."

"You'll be calling Shin Bet, of course?"

"Immediately!"

They exchanged cell phone numbers and promised to relay any information either of them uncovered. As he hung up, Kevin heard rumbles of distant thunder west of Vatican City. *Seems as if God isn't very happy about our crisis either,* he told himself.

Gideon quickly briefed Naomi on what was developing, then called Noah Friedmann's home. Fortunately, Friedmann was an early riser, which diminished the offense only a bit. Yet Friedmann would inflict the same on a SWAT team that he instantly organized, all twenty members of which were at Shin Bet's Jerusalem headquarters before the sun rose. Gideon was there also, on his own invitation, and asked to don commando gear like the others, though Friedmann declined his request. Ben-Yaakov, however, pouted, pleaded, and finally got his way.

Two troop transport trucks in camouflage paint now moved out and rattled through the empty streets of Jerusalem. Soon they were on the road down to Jericho, since traveling north from there on the military highway along the Jordan frontier was the fastest way to the Sea of Galilee.

Ninety minutes later they rumbled through Tiberias and set up a staging area several miles north of the city at the ruins of ancient Magdala on the lakeshore. It was now 7:00 A.M., and a golden yolk of sun was floating upward over the Golan Heights.

Friedmann spread out a large aerial photograph of Joshua's compound across the hood of one of the trucks so that all could see the target, and be assigned their respective sectors for assault. Then he had Gideon explain the purpose of their mission.

"I'm very embarrassed to have to tell you this, gentlemen, but

Professor Weber may not even be inside the central lodge here,"
Gideon said, pointing. "Or he might be inside, but held under guard.
Or he might even be dead—or in Rome. We just don't know."

"What we do know is this," Friedmann broke in. "While we were
driving up here, we phoned Ben-Gurion to do a search for his car in
all their airport parking areas. It's a white Peugeot, license number
53-417-04. But they didn't find it. So if it's in the lodge parking area
here"—he pointed—"we can assume Weber's inside. The whole
perimeter may be wired, so we'll advance with extreme caution. Half
of you will approach from the high ground on the western hillside,
the other half from below, here on the eastern side. We're all in wire-
less contact. Always wait for my orders. Any questions?"

"Wouldn't it be better to do an operation like this at night?"
asked Ehud Nimron, a veteran sapper who could strategize like a
general.

"Affirmative, of course. But we just can't wait that long. Oh . . .
Gideon, you stay next to me, hear?"

Gideon nodded, with a big smile.

A bend on the seacoast and some helpful terrain hid the staging area
from anyone in Joshua's compound who might be on the lookout, and
soon the command half of the operation crept along the upper hillside,
nicely hidden by the local scrub brush. Field glasses in hand, they
searched the parking area behind the lodge. Friedmann shook his head
and whispered, "No Peugeot . . . only a blue Mercedes."

"I'm not surprised," said Gideon softly. "Unless they're fools,
they would have hidden the car, wouldn't they?"

Friedmann nodded, then said, "Let's look through our field tele-
scope and see if anyone's home." He peered through a 75X field
scope, focused the lens, and then trained the scope on all the windows. Blinds were drawn in all of them. Then he added a doubler
eyepiece to the scope and looked again at the back door. Smiling, he
muttered, "Yes, I do think someone's inside . . ."

"How do you know?"

"Look."

Gideon peered through the scope—now at 150X magnifica-
tion—and saw the electric meter next to the back door. It was running at a fairly good clip. Suddenly the back door opened, and a

stocky figure took out what appeared to be garbage and dumped it into a brown plastic container. Then he went back inside and closed the door.

"Any idea who that was?" Friedmann asked Gideon.

Gideon shook his head.

"All right then," said Friedmann, "here comes the fun part. Ehud, you've got to sneak down to that large shed or garage and peek through the back window. Watch out for any perimeter alarm wire. If you find any, use our usual procedure to bypass it. Then let us know by phone: we'll see where you are and pass the word on to the rest."

Nimron crept downward toward the shed. Through binoculars, Friedmann's group watched him crawl to the back of the structure that was not visible from the lodge. Evidently he had not encountered any perimeter wire. Now he cautiously stood up and looked through the rear window for some moments. Then he hunkered down again, flipped on his phone, and reported quietly: "White 1999 Peugeot inside, license number 53-417-04."

Inside the lodge, Jon and Schmuel Sikorsky were not getting on very well. Schmuel watched most of the proceedings in Rome on a large-screen television set in the great hall of the lodge, but he would occasionally run to the open basement door and toss some taunt down to Jon in the wine cellar, who was watching on a smaller screen below.

"Ho, ho, Weber: look at all the fun they're having at that banquet in Rome," he had said. "See how Joshua is staring at your wife from the head table? He's really undressing her with his eyes!"

"Just shut up, Sikorsky!"

This morning, he opened his cheerful comments by calling down, "This is the big day, Weber. Everything changes from today on!"

"Time's running out for you, Sikorsky!" Jon called back. "It's your last chance to use your head and do the right thing!"

"You're just dead meat, Weber, as you Americans put it. I don't take advice from a dead man!"

A shrill buzzing suddenly filled the lodge. *A perimeter alarm?* Jon wondered. He heard Sikorsky running around upstairs, darting in various directions. Then, to his horror, he came bounding down the basement steps with a malicious scowl on his face. He headed for the table where the bottle of ether stood at the ready.

Jon breathed in and out vigorously to superoxygenate himself in preparation for the awful ordeal ahead. Sikorsky opened the ether bottle and saturated the cloth lying next to it. When he whipped about to anesthetize Jon, his elbow caught the bottle and it smashed to the floor, filling the wine cellar with the sickeningly sweet smell of ether. Ignoring the fumes, Sikorsky approached him, the cool, dripping cloth in hand. With a swift swing of his arm he tried to clamp it onto Jon's mouth and nose. Using all available slack between his two confining chains, Jon dodged back and forth in a frenzied struggle with his attacker. Each time he felt the chilly cloth slapped onto his forehead, cheek, or mouth, Jon clenched his jaw and twisted to avoid inhaling the evil fragrance. His eyes were now stinging from the ether and his lips were burning, but still he continued holding his breath doggedly.

"You're gonna inhale this stuff if I have to *kill* you, you swinish *goy!*" Sikorsky snarled. He finally caught Jon in a headlock. Hands shackled, Jon could not break free and finally had to gasp for air. But what he inhaled was hardly air. A suffocating dose of saccharine-sweet, aerosolized ether now saturated the air and filtered through the cloth clamped like a vise over all his breathing passages.

Light-headedness seized him quickly, and his balance was affected. His attempts to break free of Sikorsky seemed much harder now, though he was still rational enough to realize that his next breath of the stuff could be the end of all resistance on his part. Should he make a last great effort to break free? Of course! But his attempt to jerk his head away was so weak, so pathetic, that even in his fading consciousness he was ashamed of it.

"That's better . . . much better, Weber," crooned Schmuel Sikorsky, in the oiliest, ugliest voice Jon had ever heard in what seemed like a remote echo.

A deafening, explosive clap of sound knocked both of them over, immobilizing them for several moments. A shattering sound of smashing glass followed, and the rumbling tread of what seemed to be a small army upstairs, pouring throughout the lodge. Jon still had enough sense to turn his head away and take two deep breaths as Sikorsky made a run for the rifle he had left standing against the post of the basement staircase.

With supreme effort, Jon tried to yell out, "Basement!"

Whether anyone upstairs heard him or not, five of Friedmann's commandos were already storming down the basement steps, Uzis at the ready. Sikorsky aimed his rifle at Jon to kill the only witness who could defeat their grand plan. One quick blast from Ehud Nimron's Uzi, however, shattered Schmuel's right hand, and he collapsed onto the floor, holding his wrist in agony.

Noah Friedmann and Gideon rushed downstairs and saw that Jon was still alive. Several breaths from a canister of pure oxygen soon revived him, and he held up his shackled wrists to hint at the next step in his deliverance. Friedmann called for a pair of power hacksaws to cut him free of his chains.

"Sorry about our stun grenade," said Noah, "though it seems to have done the job." Then he looked around at the stacked wine bottles, sniffed the air, and asked, "What's the brand around here, Ether Valley?"

Jon grinned and replied, "More like Ernest and Julio Gallows."

"Bad, Jon, bad!" said Gideon, a glad twinkle in his eye. Then he shook his head. "You had to go do it again, didn't you—this solo sleuthing of yours?"

"Didn't intend to. Long story, Gideon." When both his arms were liberated, Jon rubbed his wrists and said to the assault detail, "*Toda,* gentlemen! *Thanks* for giving my life back to me!"

Jon, Gideon, and Noah left the Galilee compound in the Peugeot, since it could return them to Jerusalem faster than the trucks. The time was exactly 9:00 A.M., Sunday, July 15. Vatican III would begin at 3:00 P.M., exactly seven hours later, since Italy was in the next earlier time zone. That should be more than enough time to contact Kevin Sullivan and call off the opening ceremonies, Jon assured his colleagues. They quickly debriefed each other on everything that had happened prior to his deliverance from the Galilee compound. Friedmann called it the most clever, yet most diabolical hoax Shin Bet had ever encountered, although Gideon claimed equal honors ⸻he Rama crisis several years earlier.

At Tiberias, they decided to take the Mediterranean coastal highway back to Jerusalem, since phone communications would be better there than in the Jordan Valley depression. When they reached the Galilee plateau west of Tiberias, Jon pulled over to the side of the road and used his cell phone to call Kevin Sullivan in Rome. Despite repeated rings, there was no answer.

"Strange," said Jon, "though he's probably at Sunday morning mass in St. Peter's. They probably make them turn off their cell phones."

Twenty minutes later, he tried again. No answer.

After climbing through the Megiddo pass, they reached the Mediterranean coast, where Jon again tried to call. Still no answer in Rome.

An undercurrent of anxiety started swirling inside him. "Maybe it's my cell phone," he said. "Here's Kevin's number in Rome . . . why don't one of you try to call?"

Neither Noah's nor Gideon's phone raised anything more than the same endless ringing. By now they were headed southward on the Mediterranean coastal road. Again Jon pulled over, this time dialing the Vatican City operator. "I'll have him or her put out an APB for Sullivan," he said. Incredibly, however, he heard only the same endless ringing.

"Gentlemen, we have a terrible problem developing here," said Jon, now perspiring. "In less than six hours, Vatican III begins. Why can't we get through?"

"You drive, Jonathan," said Noah Friedmann. "I'll take care of the communications." He then called his second-in-command at Shin Bet in Jerusalem, asking him to find out from Israel's Communications Service Center why they couldn't raise the Vatican by phone.

Friedmann's phone rang six minutes after he had put in the call. *"Ken . . . ken . . . ken? . . . Lo! . . . Ken,"* Noah responded before hanging up. His face tensed as he said, "Well, friends, we do indeed have a problem: a fierce thunderstorm broke over Rome early this morning, and lightning knocked out two cellular communications towers on Vatican Hill. Somehow, the bolt also charged into the Vatican telecommunications network and must

have fried something there. They were supposed to have everything running again by now, but obviously they haven't."

"Good grief!" said Jon, glaring at the highway. "God must want
Ben-Yosef to bring off his scheme after all! What if Vatican communications aren't restored in time? What then?"

"Well, Jon," said Gideon, "isn't it obvious? Then you'd simply
have to expose Ben-Yosef some time after Vatican III gets under way."

"But I'd hate to have to go that route. If Joshua does preside at
the opening of Vatican III—and you know how masterfully he could
do that with the whole world watching—we might never be able to
reverse the damage. You can't believe the number who would
believe in him from that point on, despite any hard evidence to the
contrary. At the very least, it would split Christendom."

Two kilometers farther down the highway, Jon hit the steering
wheel and said, "I just thought of something even worse: Kevin
Sullivan, even if he gets our message in time, may not even be able
to stop something with such massive momentum as Vatican III.
He'd have only my message . . . no tangible proof to convince the
pope and the Curia . . ."

"Valid point," said Noah.

"True enough," sighed Gideon. "So . . . any other ideas, Jon?"

Jon said nothing for long moments. But then he nodded very
slowly. "There's just no other way, gentlemen. When I tell you what
it is, you'll suggest that I seek psychiatric help, of course. But here
it is . . . Gideon, you are my directly corroborating witness. You and
I have to fly to Rome on the very next jet out of Ben-Gurion. With
any luck, we'll find one. By the time we land in Rome—and if
there's a God in charge—Vatican telecommunications should be
back in service. At the airport or en route to the Vatican, we'll
phone Sullivan that we have some tangible proof—the latest documents there in my attaché case, including the printouts and graduation program from the Technion—as well as the whole litany of
what happened to me at the Galilee compound. Meanwhile, Noah,
you too have eyewitness proof for the State of Israel to swear out
warrants for the arrest of Joshua and Baruch Levine, as well as
extradition papers for them both. Fax the warrants to the Vatican
if you can't get them prepared in time for us to take along." He

paused. "Well, that's it, gentlemen. What do you call it? Madness? Or the only way we may be able to stop a horrible international fraud?"

Neither replied. Gideon immediately called Ben-Gurion for flight information, while Noah called Daniel Cohen, the prime minister of the State of Israel.

A cacophony of dual Hebrew conversations in two cell phones commanded the next kilometers. Gideon was the first to end his.

"Believe it or not, Jon," he said, "your insane scheme might work. KLM has a flight at 11:15 A.M. that arrives in Rome three and a half hours later at 1:45 P.M., since we gain an hour. When does Vatican III begin?"

"At 3:00 P.M. Book it, Gideon!"

At 10:40 A.M., they were racing through Netanya en route to Ben-Gurion, courtesy of a police escort for which Noah had again used his cell phone to good advantage. They still had not raised the Vatican by phone, but now there was hope. Noah arranged that Shin Bet would meet them curbside at Ben-Gurion with the legal documents and have them bypass security. Fortuitously, both Jon and Gideon had passports in their attaché cases.

Shin Bet would also contact their counterparts in Italy, who would meet the KLM flight at Rome's airport, whisk Jon and Gideon through customs, and speed them on to the Vatican. Any faulty link in this inane chain of events, of course, would doom it to failure.

When they reached the outskirts of Tel Aviv, highway traffic was getting more congested, despite the wailing sirens of their police escort. Checking their watches four times every minute, they saw that they were running behind. Ten minutes to takeoff, and they were still fifteen minutes from the airport. Constantly on his cell phone, Noah put pressure on KLM to hold the flight for them. KLM replied that airline policy was never to do this. Friedmann insisted that the request was in the national interest of the State of Israel. At that KLM agreed to hold the flight for ten minutes, but no longer.

"Make that fifteen minutes?" Noah bargained. "This is probably in the world's interest, not just Israel's. Why not have the pilots make up for time lost by advancing their cruising speed? Israel will pay for the extra jet fuel."

"Well, put it this way," KLM responded. "Our flight 705 will push back at exactly fifteen minutes following scheduled departure. If King David himself were to come a minute later, we'd wave good-bye to him on the way to takeoff."

"Agreed! *Toda!* Thanks."

At last, the brakes on their Peugeot screamed to a stop at Ben-Gurion's departure concourse. Shin Bet handed Jon and Gideon their boarding passes and whisked them through security. Both were now running to the departure gate, even though their watches had told them the bad news: they were seven minutes beyond the extension.

Still they pressed on, hoping KLM would relent. When they finally reached the departure gate, all signs for the flight to Rome had already been removed. The one remaining attendant didn't even respond to their question. She merely pointed out the window at KLM Flight 705, which was just taking to the air off runway 08-26.

TWENTY-SIX

The Third Council of the Vatican, as it was officially termed, was set to convene at 3:00 P.M. on this Sunday of Sundays, July 15. A fierce thunderstorm in the early morning hours pelted the Eternal City, but by noon the rains had passed eastward. Opening masses in St. Peter's Basilica had already taken place, and official council business would begin at midafternoon with an address from "God's own delegate," as Rome's *Il Tempo* put it, Joshua-Jesus.

The entire colonnaded piazza before St. Peter's was packed with humanity. Ordinarily, this would largely have been drawn from the Roman populace, in front of whom the pope would give his holiday blessings *urbi et orbi*—"to the city and to the world." This time, however, most Romans would have to settle for their television sets to view the event. The hundreds of thousands who stood around the obelisk in the piazza this Sunday had to have tickets even to enter the colonnaded circle. They were leading Christians from all corners of the globe who had not been given reserved seats inside St. Peter's, nor for the risers erected along the steps leading up to the basilica. To accommodate them, all principals in the opening ceremonies would process across the piazza before entering the basilica.

About two o'clock, the remaining clouds gave way to a halcyon sky, right on cue as background for the processional, which began along the Tiber at two-thirty and proceeded up the Via della Conciliazione into the Piazza San Piètro. Shannon and other privileged guests would see the procession from the top of the steps to St. Peter's, and then be escorted to reserved seats inside the basilica. Once again, she was very concerned that Jon had apparently not yet returned to Rome from Athens—unless, of course, he surprised her by already occupying the seat next to hers in the basilica.

The very air in Vatican City seemed saturated with anticipation. About two-thirty, Shannon saw the procession begin to enter the piazza, led by the Vienna Boys Choir singing Verdi's *Te Deum*. The scarlet-clad college of cardinals followed, after which the train of clergy turned black with bearded representatives from eastern Christendom, and then variously robed archbishops and the highest clergy of the other major denominations. Finally the pope, the Orthodox patriarch, and the Twelve preceded Joshua, who, like the rest, walked across the piazza to waves of worshipful adulation before ascending the steps to the basilica.

Shannon and others in her party were now ushered inside before the procession continued into the basilica. The sight inside St. Peter's nearly overpowered her. She had visited the basilica before, and just walking inside the immense interior of the world's largest church seemed to vacuum the breath out of her lungs. But on this day the effect was at least tripled. On the main floor of the nave, thousands were seated on eighteen rows of seats in rising tiers that ran the whole 615-foot length on both sides of the now-narrowed aisle at the center of this canyon of humanity. Additional rows of seating filled both balconies, while the thousands more sitting in the side aisles and chapels would be able to witness the proceedings via television, receiving the same feed that was now transmitted live to networks throughout the world. About three thousand churchmen had gathered inside St. Peter's for Vatican II, but almost fifteen thousand leaders of church and state were now awaiting the opening of Vatican III.

A mighty organ prelude resonated throughout the vast reaches of the structure as Shannon and all those who had flown in from Israel, but were not part of the procession, were conducted down the nave—almost two football fields long—until they finally reached the transept. Here at the basilica's focal point—the papal altar beneath Bernini's bronze *Baldachino*—they were ushered into the basilica's equivalent of box seats. Later Shannon would tell anyone who would listen that she had had the best possible view of everything that took place on that most extraordinary day.

And now the Vatican orchestra and brass choir trumpeted forth Joshua's signature flourish—the same fanfare that had accompanied his cyberannouncements and his mass meetings in Israel. Joshua had composed the music himself, as Jon and Shannon had learned, another token of his many-faceted genius. But now his entire score was heard for the first time, a masterpiece of brilliant, brassy themes interspersed with contrapuntal seraphic melodies that, unlike most music, pleased the ear the very first time it was heard. Later, music critics would compare it favorably with the best in Gabrieli or Bach or Handel.

Although silence was the best background for great music, this rule was violated when Joshua appeared at the end of the lengthy procession. Against general protocol, all in attendance stood up, applauded, and cheered as he passed by, blessing everyone on both sides of the nave. Many tried to kneel, but the cramped seating arrangements made this difficult. When Joshua finally reached a dais erected before the high altar, the Twelve fanned out to their designated seats while the pope, Joshua, and the patriarch sat down on three central thrones facing eastward across the nave.

In the north wing of the transept, the Sistine Chapel Choir sang the sublime *Gloria* chorus from Bach's *Mass in B Minor* to supplement the grand harmonics preceding. When the last tones had spent themselves, Benedict XVI stood up, crosier in hand, and announced in traditional Latin, *"In nomine Patris, et Filii, et Spiritus Sancti. Amen!"*

Then Patriarch Bartholomew also stood up and announced, in traditional Greek, *"Eis to onoma tou Patros, kai tou Huios, kai tou Hagiou Pneumatos. Amen!"*

The rest of the ceremonies, they had agreed, would be conducted in the world's international language—English—since the world was also attending St. Peter's on this day of days. The pope now took his place at the lectern and said, "My beloved brothers and sisters in Christ, it is my pleasure as your host, to welcome all of you—delegates and observers—to Rome, to Vatican City, to the Basilica of St. Peter, and to this Third Council of the Vatican. Despite its official name, this conclave far exceeds the bounds of Roman Catholicism, since its delegates have come not only from every corner of the earth, but from all major Christian denominations on earth. It is, then, in accordance with the directives of our Master, the first truly ecumenical council since late antiquity. The church universal is meeting here today!"

Wild applause and cheering erupted throughout the basilica, and it would not stop. Centuries of rivalry, mistrust, and even open hostility between Christian church bodies had always addled the consciences of dedicated churchmen, and Benedict's statement pointed the way to a better future. After seven full minutes of ovation, the pontiff pounded the floor with his crosier and continued.

"The church universal is not only meeting here today, but it is meeting under circumstances which our forefathers, our saints, our martyrs, and Christians of all ages have anticipated but never witnessed: the return of our Lord and Savior, Jesus Christ!"

Another massive wave of applause broke across the basilica, and it, too, abated only some minutes later after the determined pounding of Benedict's bishop's staff. He continued, "To be sure, there are some, even in our Curia, who deny that our Master could return in this form or under these circumstances, and others present here today may also harbor doubts that Joshua is Jesus in fact. But was not this the case also in Jesus' day? Even after His triumphant resurrection, Matthew tells us in chapter 28, 'Some doubted.'

"As a mark of his great mercy, Joshua has urged us all to treat such doubters never with coercion of any kind, but only with patience, love, and prayer. In this spirit, then, it is my extraordinary, my God-given privilege to present to you the man called Joshua Ben-Yosef, whom a large majority of Christians today hail as the returned Jesus of Nazareth! Like the father of the possessed son in Mark's Gospel, the church cries out to you, Blessed Joshua, 'Lord, we believe! Help our unbelief!'"

The multitude of churchmen and statesmen rose to their feet as if one person, cascading swells of deafening applause down the tiers of seating. This time Benedict's crosier seemed powerless to halt it, and the ovation surged on for ten minutes, despite Joshua's own attempts to curtail it. Another trumpet fanfare finally succeeded when all else failed, and the assembly sat back down in expectant silence.

His robe dazzling white in the lone spot of an arc light, Joshua took his time at the lectern, first bowing his head in prayer, and then looking out across his vast audience for several moments with a fire of determination in his eyes. Not once did he look down to any or notes before him, for there were none. When he opened his mouth, his words resonated across the distant reaches of the basilica and into its farthest galleries with authoritative reverberation.

"At the beginning of my first earthly ministry, twenty centuries ago, I was in the synagogue at Nazareth one Sabbath and was handed the scroll of the prophet Isaiah to read aloud. I read these words:

The Spirit of the Lord is upon me, because he has anointed me to preach good news to the poor. He has sent me to proclaim release to the captives and recovery of sight to the blind, to let the oppressed go free, to proclaim the year of the Lord's favor.

"Then, you will recall, I sat down . . . until I was asked for a brief commentary. I stood up again and said, 'Today, this Scripture has been fulfilled in your hearing'—and Galilee was never the same after that!"

Unscheduled titters of laughter actually surfaced.

"I should now like to adapt Isaiah's words for this solemn occasion and say: 'The Spirit of the Lord is upon me, because He has anointed me to preach good news to Christendom. He has sent me to proclaim release of the church from error and the recovery of its sight from blindness, to restore His oppressed people, and thus return the church to the Lord's favor.'

"And today, this Scripture *will be* fulfilled in your hearing!"

The international assembly sat in stunned silence, wondering how Joshua would apply his revised version of Isaiah. Archconservative Cardinal Pedro Gonzales—a.k.a. "God's Bulldog for the Faith"—furrowed his brow and exchanged worried glances with colleagues in the Holy Office. But Shannon and many others were hardly surprised, since Joshua had said no more than what many reformers inside Christendom had said for centuries. A church that had burned heretics and impeded science in the Middle Ages, or kept silence on issues ranging from the Holocaust to child sex abuse scandals in the modern era had its own catalog of errors. And wasn't this exactly how Jesus would score the sins of His people?

With stunning rhetorical skill, however, Joshua knew how to keep all hearers on his side, even Cardinal Gonzales. He now welded their attention to the problems and challenges facing Christianity today that had prompted his call for reform. It was not a pretty list. In colorful detail, he attacked the evils, external and internal, that were compromising the faith. Outside the church there was the spiritual indifference of the modern world and its relativistic ethics; the challenges from Islam and the Far Eastern religions; the cults and "their para-religious claptrap masquerading as rational belief"; governmental intrusion curbing the free practice of religion in some countries; the persecution of Christians and Jews in the Middle East, Africa, and the Far East; and, in particular, the pseudo-intellectual, sensationalist attacks on the faith and its biblical basis by radical, revisionist critics.

Again the entire assembly arose in prolonged applause. None of Joshua's targets were made of straw, delegates knew, and they had all contributed to something of a stagnation in the growth of world Christianity. It was a sad but true statistic: more babies were being born across the world than were getting baptized. Shannon only hoped that the entire address was being recorded, since these words had compelling power.

Joshua held up his arms for silence. "Now, my brothers and sisters in the faith," he continued, "we must turn to the *internal* evils that compromise our faith today, and this will be more painful. In the Upper Room on that bitter Thursday night, two thousand years ago, I prayed to the Father that you would all be one! And what have you done? What *have* you done? You have divided and subdivided, split and split again, separated and reseparated so that today there are hundreds of different church bodies. Is this a proper witness before the world?

"And some of you theologians, you shepherds of the flock, bear a heavy responsibility for warping the faith in directions that have suited your own fancies rather than reflecting my will for the church. You have introduced practices not warranted in Holy Scripture and then doggedly defended them.

"Sometimes you are hopelessly lax and open-minded in an 'anything goes' theology that puts our faith on an equal plane with other world religious systems. But more often you are hopelessly narrow and closed-minded, doctrinaire purists who, like the Pharisees of old, legalistically force your notions on the church and refuse even to pray with other Christians who don't agree with you on all points of doctrine. Still others of you higher clergy have tolerated horrendous immorality among your lower clergy."

Joshua paused, and this time a buzz of concerned whispering replaced applause. Many, however, like the Bishop of Rome himself, were nodding in agreement with Joshua's strictures.

"But even this is not the greatest problem facing the church today," Joshua continued. "I shall now tell you what it is." He stopped, looked up toward the ornate ceiling of the basilica, and then, with powerful emphasis, added: "It is for *this very reason* that the Father sent me into the world again!"

Not since it opened in 1615 had the Basilica of St. Peter been suffused with such instant silence. No one even moved, for fear of missing the next word.

"Seventeen centuries ago, the holy Christian church made a tragic error, an error that has been a festering wound in the body of truth ever since. And it must now be identified. It must now be cauterized. It must now be corrected!"

Many in the great basilica moved forward on their seats. Shannon cupped her ears lest she miss a syllable. Benedict XVI clutched the arms of his chair and exchanged glances of concern with Bartholomew II. Both knew well enough what had happened seventeen centuries earlier.

"This tragic error," Joshua continued, "occurred at the Council of Nicaea in the year 325, when I was declared 'God' and put on the same plane as the almighty Father. *This is not true!* I am the Father's special representative, to be sure—yes, His Messiah—but to say, as in the Nicene Creed, that I am 'God of God, Light of Light, Very God of Very God, begotten, not made, being of one substance with the Father' is *blasphemy*! All these many centuries, our Father's chosen people—the Jews—have been correct in proclaiming that God is *one* and one only, and so I have been commissioned by my Father to purge this error and unify Judaism and Christianity under His divine unity and supremacy. And then we will be able to meet the challenge of Islam and—"

"*No!*" a lone voice rang out, with the same intensity as Joshua's, and it reechoed *No No No* throughout the lofty galleries of St. Peter's.

"Joshua Ben-Yosef is a *fraud!*" the voice continued. *Fraud Fraud Fraud* echoed.

The voice continued inexorably in the stunned silence. "Don't believe this *hoax*!" *Hoax Hoax Hoax* . . .

Whose voice was it? Shannon knew, to her utter shock. The voice belonged to Jon! But where was he? Looking down the long nave of the basilica, she saw three figures walking briskly toward the high altar. When they were halfway there, a squad of fifteen Swiss guards in blue, red, and yellow medieval garb rushed in with their halberds, surrounded them, and held Jon tightly.

But the seized figure exclaimed, "This is Jon Weber, *Santissimo Padre*! I invoke James 1:16: '*Do not be deceived, my beloved brothers!*'"

Kevin Sullivan and Gideon Ben-Yaakov were standing on either side of Jon. Kevin had equipped Jon with a portable lapel microphone tuned to the basilica's public address system. Kevin now rushed up to the dais and whispered something to the pope in high agitation. Benedict turned ashen and started trembling. He stood up, shakily, and moved next to Joshua at the lectern. Pulling the microphone over toward himself, he commanded, in Italian: "*Che la Guardia Svizzera, rilasci immediatamente il Professor Weber e lo scorti fino alla predella!*"

The Swiss Guard obeyed at once, releasing Jon and escorting him up to the dais.

The many thousands in attendance sat stupefied. People of the world sat stupefied, disbelieving their eyes at what their television screens were showing them, not trusting their ears despite what they were hearing.

Shannon's relief that Jon had finally shown up was shot through with horror at what he was saying. To believers like herself, such an attack on the Messiah could only be followed by lightning from heaven, or, perhaps, the earth opening up and swallowing him as it did Korah and those who disobeyed Moses in the Sinai wilderness.

Joshua, meanwhile, had also lost color, but he quickly mastered his shock, pulled the microphone over, and, as usual, said the unexpected. A word of malediction? A dire curse on Jon, consigning him to the flames of hell? No. Joshua put his hands together, gazed heavenward with a look of sad serenity, and said, "Father, forgive him, for he doesn't know what he's doing!"

Bedlam broke out inside the sacred Basilica of St. Peter. The mind, theological or otherwise, can stand only so much. One moment, the faithful were listening to the words of their returned Lord and Savior, Jesus Christ. The next, that Savior was telling them that their faith was hopelessly flawed. Then, a world-class theologian was calling that Savior an impostor. Finally, the "impostor" seemed to have returned to the Jesus mode in forgiving his detractor, much as Jesus had forgiven His executioners at Golgotha!

Joshua held his arms up for silence and continued, "The Father warned me that during my mission into the world this time, the Judas Iscariot figure would come . . . not from the ranks of my faithful followers gathered on the dais here, but from someone in the New World who would usurp a place in the temple of God as the Antichrist. And that Antichrist from the New World, who will deny my mission, is now advancing to this very platform!"

A grand chorus of murmuring wafted up from the packed benches to the highest galleries of St. Peter's.

Jon stopped below the steps leading up to the dais, locked his own penetrating gaze onto Joshua's, and said, "If this is true, Mr. Ben-Yosef, then I ask you—in the holy name of God—to *blot this Antichrist out of existence here and now!*"

Joshua's classic, tanned cheeks took on a darker hue as he fired a ferocious scowl down at Jon and spit out the words, "No, you demonic enemy of the truth! I prefer to have mercy even on such a wicked blasphemer as yourself!"

"Now is the moment, Joshua! If you *are* telling the truth, and I'm the Antichrist indeed, then, for the sake of the church and for all believers on earth, I demand that you use your supernatural powers to annihilate me at once!"

"You, a mere mortal, *dare* to tell me what I should do?"

"I dare indeed, fellow mortal! The original Judas went out and hanged himself. So if I *am* the latter-day version, then please confirm your identity before this great assembly and before the world by terminating me at once! Untold millions of people are watching us at this moment, Ben-Yosef, and not one of them would ever doubt you again if you were able to cause my instant death!"

Joshua flashed a beam of pure, undiluted hatred at Jon. He had a momentary urge to leap down from the platform, encircle Jon's neck with hands of demonic force, crush his neck vertebrae into splinters, and strangle the very life out of him.

"Or is it that you have no supernatural power whatever to eliminate me, Joshua?" continued Jon, relentlessly. "And that all of your so-called miracles were tricks? Like raising not Shimon Levine from the dead, *but his identical twin brother, Baruch,* who is sitting behind you?"

While exclamations of shock and groaning rippled instantly throughout the basilica, the two continued to glare at each other, Joshua's genius working every neuron in his marvelous mind for a solution.

"Well, since you won't answer, Ben-Yosef, then I will," said Jon. "And the answer is this: no, Joshua, you do *not* have any *supernatural* powers, because you and your henchman Baruch there had planned to use very *natural* means to murder me about a week from now—namely, by forcing potassium cyanide down my throat!"

The basilica broke into an uproar.

"I had discovered your stratagems, you see, and so I had to be eliminated. I must now introduce Dr. Gideon Ben-Yaakov, director of the Israel Antiquities Authority in Jerusalem, who has been specially deputized by the government of Israel. He is also here as a second witness, should any of you doubt our mission."

Gideon, who had also been fitted with a lapel mike, stepped forward and held up two documents, one in each hand. "Joshua Ben-Yosef and Baruch Levine," he announced, "in my right hand is a warrant for both your arrests, issued by the State of Israel, on charges of complicity to commit murder. In my other hand is a formal request from the Government of Israel to the State of Vatican City and to the Republic of Italy for your extraditions!"

The immense basilica was jolted into a demonic chorus of shock and consternation. Shaking his head mournfully, Benedict XVI returned to the lectern, grasped it with trembling hands, and ordered the Swiss Guard to take Joshua and Baruch into custody.

The guardsmen clattered up the steps to the dais in tight formation and arrested them. Thirty thousand disbelieving eyes watched the messianic figure in white being marched off the platform, followed by the *faux* apostle whose *ersatz* name graced the vast cathedral. The dumbfounded eleven "disciples" remaining on the platform could only conclude that, once again, their Lord and Master was being taken into captivity by the Romans.

During the continuing near-chaos in the nave of St. Peter's, Jon huddled with the pope and Kevin Sullivan, planning urgently on how to deal with the awful crisis. Suggestions were voiced, options quickly explored. At last, all three nodded in agreement.

Jon now stepped up to the lectern and asked the assembly for permission to say a few words. When calm was finally restored, he said, "I deeply regret, honored colleagues in the faith, that you've been so profoundly shocked this afternoon. In view of time constraints, there simply was no other way to expose this deception. Christianity itself was at stake!

"Now, of course, you have many, many questions about Ben-Yosef, his apparent miracles, his motivation for attempting this colossal fraud, and the like. We plan to answer all of them in a general press conference that will be held tomorrow afternoon at 3:30 P.M. in the papal audience auditorium, Paul VI Hall. And now, our host has some parting words. Your Holiness . . ."

Benedict XVI stepped before the lectern and said, his voice trembling with emotion: "By the grace of almighty God . . . truth has apparently triumphed again . . . and the holy Christian faith is secure. But many of you may be thinking that now there is no reason to hold the Third Council of the Vatican. Nothing could be farther from the truth! Please do not even *think* of leaving Rome! We need this conclave now more than ever in order to enhance the unity of the church and equip it to meet the challenges of our day. Our first general session, which was to have been held today, will take place instead the day after tomorrow—again, here in the Basilica of St. Peter.

"And now may the grace of our Lord Jesus Christ, the love of God the Father, and the fellowship of the Holy Spirit be with us all!"

"AMEN!"

"Go in peace! Serve the Lord."
"THANKS BE TO GOD."

Jon remembered very little of the rest of that extraordinary day. He had been without sleep for the past thirty hours and almost fell on his face several times as he trip-walked out of the basilica and across the Piazza San Piètro. He recalled a passionate hug and kiss from Shannon, and he vaguely remembered that he had commended Gideon Ben-Yaakov into Kevin Sullivan's able hands.

Shannon shepherded him up to their opulent accommodations, where he nibbled a bit at the food she had ordered in, promising to answer all her many questions in the morning. Then he took a healthy sip of Lambrusco, passed out on the bed, and slept for twelve hours straight.

But sleep escaped Shannon for several long hours. She was enduring the most agonizing emotional clashes in her life, bouncing between utter happiness—her husband was safe—and utter depression: her returned Lord and Savior, Joshua-Jesus, on whom she had pinned her faith, hope, love, and trust, was evidently a colossal fraud. How could her relief and elation be mingled, at the same time, with chagrin, disenchantment, bewilderment, and sadness? However unlikely such a combination, it was happening to her.

TWENTY-SEVEN

M uch of the Christian world shared Shannon's bewilderment. While night's encroachment on the Far and Middle East postponed some of the bafflement until the next morning, it became the immediate central story throughout the Western world. Joshua's arrest in the Vatican hit the world news wires at 3:30 P.M., which was 9:30 A.M. in New York. An immense number had seen it all live, of course, but for those who did not, most other programs on radio or TV were interrupted with the momentous news. The old saw, "People would always remember where they were when—" was dusted off and used again and again.

Headlines in the American midday, special, and evening newspaper editions had all the obvious wordplay: JOSHUA NOT JESUS! was the most frequent, with FRAUD ON THE FAITHFUL, JOSHUA BEN-FAKE, HOLY HOAX! and A SCAM SAVIOR following. Editorial after editorial pompously excoriated the gullibility of the religious public, even though hardly any of the writers had previously predicted fraud.

While Jon and Shannon slept, massive responses were boiling up in all segments of society. Religious liberals and religious ultraconservatives—usually the very antitheses in spirituality—finally found common ground: both had, for different reasons, doubted or denied Joshua's claims, and both now felt vindicated. Although some trumpeted their I-told-you-so's as loudly as their voices would carry, most showed considerable restraint, especially when they saw the pain in the eyes of so many who had believed, with various intensities, that Jesus had returned.

Tom Brokaw, Dan Rather, Peter Jennings, and Jim Lehrer were already in Rome to cover the opening of Vatican III, and their evening news programs for NBC, CBS, ABC, and PBS respectively gave full reports on the high drama that had unfolded at the Vatican just hours earlier. Fox, CNN, CNBC, PAX and other cable networks had also sent their anchors to Rome, prompting one irate network executive to complain, "Is anyone left in the U.S. to cover the news?"

Though it was now night in Europe, the BBC, Radio-Television Francaise, Deutsche Welle, Radio e Video Italia, and all other European national networks replaced their usual fare with the urgent news from Rome. Jon's confrontation with Joshua before the high altar in Saint Peter's was translated into a dozen languages on the tube, and many European Christians got very little sleep that night.

Joshua's hard-core "true believers" in both hemispheres, of course, continued to believe. He had been called a fraud and was arrested, true. But wasn't that arrest itself further proof that Joshua was indeed Jesus? Before anyone even asked him, Melvin Morris Merton predicted that Joshua would "certainly" go to the cross—if not in Italy, then "certainly" in Israel, to which he would "certainly" be extradited.

Anti-Semitic elements in society started parroting that particular aspect of Merton's forecast. Not that Merton was an anti-Semite—quite the opposite was the case. But twisted bigots started mounting the following message on the Internet: Jews did it to Jesus once, now they'll do it to him again! Leaders of some fringe sects called one another and debated about somehow trying to rescue Joshua from his adversaries. One proposed that they change the Second Article of the Creed to: "I believe in Joshua Christ, God's only Son, our Lord . . ." as a first step in reestablishing his credibility.

Yet even their warped approach to reality required, after all, a little more information before any attempts could be made to rescue Joshua or his reputation. And the only one who could deliver that information was fast asleep.

It was the bells of Rome that awakened Jon. In the Eternal City, it doesn't have to be Sunday for the bells to ring one out of bed. The place is bell heaven: tinkling bells that sound like celestial, though castrated, chimes; marvelously matured midsized bells that carry whatever melody is intended by the tintinnabulation; and great bass monstrosities that mournfully—even threateningly—toll like mega-phones of fate.

"Hello, darling!" said Jon sleepily to the lovely elfin figure tip-toeing around the room. "Sorry I cut out on you last night."

"Hello, Your Eminence!" she teased. "How does it feel to be One Man Against the World?"

"Very lonely, now that you mention it. But let's cure all that: come on over here and let's do some serious snuggling."

She only chuckled. "With the whole planet waiting to hear what you have to say at the press conference? I don't *think* so!"

He glanced at the clock on a table next to their bed. "Oh . . . that was kind of you, Shannon," he said. "Taking the phone off the hook."

"Otherwise, you'd have had two hundred calls by now and not slept a wink."

"Yeah, probably. Is it really ten-thirty?"

"Yup."

"Okay. Let's do brunch before we face the press."

"Make that, before *you* face the press, Jon. If I could, I'd be out there in the press corps myself, ready to send two dozen questions your way! No, more like a hundred."

All sixty-five hundred seats in the auditorium for papal audi-ences—Paul VI Hall—were occupied a half hour before the press conference was set to begin. A thicket of television cameras and cables rimmed the rear of the hall, while a bulging cluster of micro-phones surrounded a speaker's lectern on which the papal coat of arms was emblazoned. The pontiff himself had been asked to open the conference, but he delegated that responsibility to Kevin Sullivan, while he sat with Curia officers and members of the col-lege of cardinals in the front of the auditorium. Ordinarily, he would have occupied the papal throne, but since the Joshua affair had engulfed the highest echelons of the church, it was thought best to proceed in this manner.

Promptly at 3:30 P.M., Kevin stepped up to the battery of microphones and welcomed the crowd. Then he identified two others who shared the platform with him: Gideon Ben-Yaakov and Jon, introducing the latter as "the man who played a major role in preventing the church and the world from making a terrible mistake."

Now fully rested and no longer tripping over everything in his path, Jon delivered an opening statement in words that he knew would be fiercely important in guiding world response to the Joshua affair and heading off a whole galaxy of misinterpretations. "I should like to emphasize at the very start, ladies and gentlemen of the media, that the Joshua Ben-Yosef episode does not and will not affect the credibility of the Christian faith in any manner whatever. Simply because Jesus did *not* return in the form of Joshua does not mean that He will not return in the future, according to the basic Christian creeds. While this may seem obvious to you— in fact, *over*obvious—please never underestimate the ability of people to get it wrong unless you make this point very clear in your coverage.

"I also think it is most important not to try to assign blame for this unfortunate episode beyond the four individuals who were directly responsible, one of whom is dead. Let's just for once deny the conspiracy theorists their favorite game of concocting weird, sensationalizing scenarios that have no relation whatever to reality— but have every relation to financial gain at the expense of the naive."

Jon now made a strong effort to intercept any wrongheaded reactions to the Joshua affair that could surface in the future. Since the perpetrators were Jews, bigots might try to foment anti-Semitism. "But that would be utterly ridiculous," he said. "It was a Jew—Dr. Gideon Ben-Yaakov on the platform here—who, with a small army of fellow Jews, saved my very life! Jews have been totally cooperative in every phase of our investigation, and it is the State of Israel that not only went to great expense to fly us here, but will see justice done in this case."

Jon knew that Christian church leaders might also be faulted as "gullible dupes" in the Joshua affair, but he tried to abort any such criticism by pointing out that some of the very best minds in all branches of Christendom were deceived, as was so much of the world.

He now finished his introductory comments on a note of surprise. "This may shock you," he said, "but I have something positive to say about Joshua Ben-Yosef that I could not have said yesterday. This man is a genius, in a very literal sense, and few people on earth have made a more careful study of Jesus or the Christianity that He founded. To be sure, he did this in order to deceive the world, as we all know. But in the process, so much of the thinking and spirit of Jesus of Nazareth seem to have rubbed off on him that nearly all of his public statements, as late as yesterday afternoon, have been amazingly Christlike—the very sorts of things we would expect a twenty-first-century version of Jesus to say.

"Perhaps, then, we might try to divorce the message from the man and take very seriously some of the important things he said to Christendom. Now, I'll be the first to admit how difficult this may be, considering the source, but truth has its own validity, no matter who expresses it."

A buzz of discussion wafted up from the front rows of church leaders with much nodding. Even Benedict XVI was smiling, though Pedro Cardinal Gonzales and several of his colleagues in the Holy Office exchanged renewed frowns.

"But now it's time for us to explain how we discovered Ben-Yosef's fraud," Jon continued.

For the next hour, the conference tried to absorb all the information as it cascaded down from the three on the dais. Most reporters used electronic devices of all kinds to record and/or transmit the data to their sponsors. Video cameras, of course, were covering it all both live and for rebroadcast in prime time.

After the explanations, Kevin Sullivan announced, "We'll now take your questions. Please identify yourself and your sponsor."

More than a hundred hands shot up. Kevin tried to recognize them as best he could.

"Victoria Chamberlain, *London Times*. Where is Joshua Ben-Yosef at the present moment? And his accomplice?"

"Both are under guard in the Vatican jail."

"What will happen to them?"

"Even though the Vatican has no formal extradition treaty with the State of Israel, Cardinal Buchbinder, the Vatican secretary of state, has assured me that both individuals in question will be returned to the State of Israel for prosecution."

"But what about Italy?"

"The Republic of Italy has promised to honor the Vatican's decision in this regard. Yes?"

"Gottfried Heim, *Berliner Zeitung*. Vot vill happen to zem in Israel? Maybe ze death penalty?"

"Perhaps Dr. Ben-Yaakov would be kind enough to reply. Gideon?"

Gideon walked to the battery of microphones and said, "Israel has no death penalty, except for Adolf Eichmann–type crimes against humanity. Besides, even though murder was planned in this case, fortunately, it was not accomplished. The State of Israel will charge Joshua Ben-Yosef, Baruch Levine, and their accomplice in Galilee, Schmuel Sikorsky, with conspiracy to commit murder."

"Und ze punishment?"

"This will vary. Generally it runs ten to fifteen years in prison. Yes?"

"Umberto Richi, *L'Osservatore Romano*. Who is Schmuel Sikorsky?"

"You may recall that he was the so-called blind man we mentioned earlier, the accomplice who guarded Professor Weber in Galilee."

"Ah . . . *si. Mi scusi!*"

"Yes?"

"Peter Jennings, *ABC Evening News*. Professor Weber, we now know how Joshua raised an accomplice from the dead, how he cured the blind man, and other facts. But what about his other wonders—calming storms or miraculous control of languages?"

The revelations Joshua had disclosed to Jon in the Galilee lodge Jon now summarized for Jennings, the press conference, and the world. A sea of smiles, shaking heads, "Aha" reactions, frowns, and looks of shocked incredulity greeted his words. After what became his longest response that afternoon, Jon recognized the next hand.

"Tadaki Yamauchi, *Tokyo Shinbun*. I still not understand *why* Joshua Ben-Yosef do all this. Did he ever tell you?"

"Yes. He and his three friends planned all this back in their student days as a way to vent their ire against mistreatment of Jews across the centuries, and to augment Judaism in a religiously competitive world. He thought he'd be able to co-opt Christianity for Judaism by excluding Jesus from deity—under orders from Jesus Himself, as it were. The resulting 'Christian Judaism,' he thought, would present a stronger response to the challenge of Islam. But that's only a brief summary. A complete version of this and many other items in the Joshua affair will be provided you in media handouts on the long tables in the foyer of this hall at the close of this conference. They'll be available in different languages. Yes?"

"Renee St. Laurent, *Le Monde*. Put the case that you had *not* discovered the fraud, Dr. Weber: do you think Joshua Ben-Yosef would have succeeded in his plan?"

Jon thought for a moment before replying, "I truly hope he would not have succeeded. Somehow, I think, he would have been found out sooner or later. I also find it hard to believe that the church universal would have demoted Jesus and abandoned the Creed it had developed at the first great ecumenical council at Nicaea. Yes?"

"Alex Hopkins, *USA Today*. You mentioned that the State of Israel flew you and Dr. Ben-Yaakov here at great expense. Would you care to explain that, and why did you both arrive so late at the opening of Vatican III yesterday?"

Jon looked at Gideon with a slight grin and shook his head, almost in bewilderment. Then he said, "Well . . . that's a subplot in itself, and I'm afraid it would shift the focus away from where it belongs."

"Oh, please: can't you tell us anything?"

"Suffice it to say that I wouldn't even be here if it weren't for superb detection and intervention by Dr. Ben-Yaakov here and a force from Shin Bet, the Israeli version of the American FBI. When we missed connections for our flight to Rome, the Israeli air force generously flew us here in two F-15 jet fighters. The rest of that story will also be available in the media handouts. I wrote copy on the flight to Rome, and the Vatican has been kind enough to reproduce it."

A huge din arose in the hall, and the next question had to be asked several times before order was restored.

"Morgan Davis, *New York Times*. Yesterday evening, on the Fox Network, Dr. Melvin Merton claimed that Joshua was most probably ᴊᴇᴏᴜs after all, and that you, Professor Weber, were very likely attacking the Savior himself. Would you like to comment on that?"

"Well, it would be a sad commentary, were I to make it. Please, simply, consider the source. Dr. Merton is always 180 degrees out of phase with anything I do or say."

"Boris Goldovsky, *Izvestia*. I haff a beeg qvestion for you, Doktor Veber. Becauss zees 'second Jesus' used tricks and people taught dey ver miracles, vot about da *forst* Jesus? Maybe da same teeng? Tricks den too?"

Jon smiled and said, "Now that's a question I thought would arise earlier. In comparing the deeds and wonders of Jesus with those of Joshua, Mr. Goldovsky, I see a very profound contrast: those of Joshua were derivative, poor copies of the originals that Jesus performed. Those of Jesus involved no tricks whatever, no twins, no stooges, no—"

"Vot means 'stooges'?"

"Sorry. For example, people with normal eyesight posing blindness so that they could later be 'cured.' Jesus' healings also had much greater variety, while those of Joshua were limited, contrived, psychosomatic, or done through sleight of hand. And, again, the medical findings are contained in the handouts."

"Doris Dinwiddie, Reuters."

Instantly, Jon rued his mistake in recognizing that particular hand, which belonged to his nemesis from previous press conferences. Always the most outspoken and provocative member of the press corps, Dinwiddie had for years been a White House correspondent—until her acerbic ways led President Sherwood Bronson to ban her from 1600 Pennsylvania Avenue. Others, however, admired the journalist's probing style and uncanny ability to cut to the bone on whatever issue she chose to explore, which was why Reuters had rescued her career. Jon now clenched his back teeth and prepared for the worst.

"Ah . . . Professor Weber," she said, "in your opening remarks you claimed that the Joshua caper had not done any harm to Christendom. I beg to differ. Despite your disclaimer, the high church officials in this hall have indeed been taken in as 'credulous dupes.' But very likely, 'credulous dupes' were also taken in during the first century by the first Jesus. So maybe the whole foundation of Christianity has cracked wide open, and Joshua was only doing us a service: helping usher it into the dustbin of history, one of many myths from the past that have no relevance today. And maybe—"

"Are you making statements about your own opinions, Ms. Dinwiddie, or asking a question?" Jon wondered, amid a rising murmur in the hall. "All you've done so far is to restate Mr. Goldovsky's question, though without the question mark, and preach to us in the process. So let me do some restating of my own: as I said previously, the Joshua fraud has done no harm to Christianity whatever—*for anyone with normal intelligence*," he added, under his breath.

Then he suddenly brightened and continued, "In fact, I think it may even have *helped* the credibility of the faith in confirming the prophetic powers of Jesus Christ Himself. Not only did He provide a deadly accurate prophecy regarding the destruction of Jerusalem—fulfilled to the letter less than four decades after He made it—but He also predicted that there would indeed be false Christs in the future. In Matthew 24, He specifically said: '*For false Christs and false prophets will appear and perform great signs and miracles to deceive even the elect, if that were possible.*' Obviously, Joshua Ben-Yosef, without intending to do so, has just fulfilled that prophecy to the letter!

"But now, patient friends in the media, it's time to draw this conference to a close, so please permit several final comments. And the first is this: God can indeed make the proverbial silk purse out of a sow's ear. This otherwise sorry episode has stimulated the church universal to come together at the Third Vatican Council. In terms of hopes for additional unity in the church, only great good can come of this! As you already know, Vatican III will indeed remain in session, and—no longer distracted by a master actor—it will draw from Jesus' true spiritual presence."

In closing, Jon extended gratitude to the pope and the Vatican for providing the venue for Vatican III and offered special thanks to Sullivan and Ben-Yaakov—and also to someone he had overlooked. "I should mention, too, that Jeffery Sheler and his fellow staffers at *U.S. News and World Report* were a great help to us in various phases of the Joshua investigation. Oh, I see Jeff out there in the audience, and I must say that he showed great restraint in not asking any questions this afternoon. Do stand up, Jeff!"

He was greeted with a warm applause.

"Many further details await you in our handouts. Thank you, ladies and gentlemen of the media, and good afternoon!"

TWENTY-EIGHT

Relief and elation percolated through the conversation of four supremely happy people as they dined that night at La Méla Segréta ("The Secret Apple"), a restaurant overlooking the Tiber. Jon and Shannon were on one side of the table, Kevin Sullivan and Gideon Ben-Yaakov on the other. Pinpoints of light speckled the scene, whether from candles plugged into old wine bottles at their table, fireflies cruising over the river, streetlights on the opposite bank, or a thousand stars overhead. A boat floated by with a gondolier singing *"O sóle mìo."*

"That guy's lost," Shannon commented. "He should be up in Venice!"

Jon, of course, was in a particularly rare mood. "It's amazing," he told the others. "Just yesterday I wanted to see Ben-Yosef roasting in the infernal regions, especially because of that cyanide cocktail he was ready to serve up for me. But now, I don't know . . ."

"Are you getting Christlike on us, Jon?" asked Kevin. "Forgiving your enemies?"

"It's just that . . . somehow, we ought to try to understand the man. Maybe he does need psychiatric help, especially after what happened to his parents. One thing's sure: we really should take advantage of that marvelous mind of his. Just letting him rot in prison seems stupid."

"You mean you'd want him released?" asked Gideon. "You won't testify against him in Israel?"

"I mean nothing of the sort. I just wonder if, somehow, we couldn't work on his moral sense—if indeed he has one, of course. That way he could do something positive for the world instead of misleading it."

"Like what?" Shannon wondered.

"Well, he's a polymath, thanks to his parents. Biochemistry and medicine could maybe get his cooperation in finishing their book—with safeguards, of course. The computer science people might tap his genius to build better firewalls against cyberterrorism. Psychiatrists, psychologists, and sociologists could study why the man had such powerful personal magnetism, even to the point of literally curing some people. Musicologists could encourage him to compose great symphonies, and then try to determine how his creativity was able to achieve them. I mean, the man has an intellectual Midas touch: whatever he undertakes in the arts or sciences could yield great things for humanity."

"I'm afraid you're dreaming, Jon," said Gideon. "The man tried to *kill* you!"

"On the other hand," Kevin observed, "there'd be nothing wrong in *trying* your approach, Jon. And here's one reason why: left to himself, brooding away in his dungeon, that prodigy mind of his might hatch something even more evil yet. Then he'd be a horrible menace when released, a real monster—'with attitude'—let loose on humanity!"

It was over their second glasses of Chianti that Shannon nearly caused a scene. Knowing full well that she might be speaking too loudly, she nevertheless demanded, "Enough of Ben-Yosef, gentlemen! I've been asking what happened during Jon's *dis*appearance ever since his *re*appearance. But all I get from you is 'We'll tell you over dinner.' Well, here comes dinner! When's the telling?"

"Okay, patient princess," said Jon grandly. "Here—at your invitation—is the story. Feel free to jump in wherever you like, Kevin and Gideon. Actually, all three of you people had a hand in saving my life, but you, Shannon, lit the fuse, so to speak. Why not start off at your end in Rome, Kevin?"

"Okay. Saturday night, when you returned from Tivoli with the ladies, Shannon, you had trouble getting to sleep and called Alitalia about Jon and his flight to Athens, right?"

"Yes. I was so frustrated. Alitalia claimed they couldn't divulge any names on the passenger manifests, so with that—and the language problem—I gave up and called you instead, Kevin."

"And thank God I was in," he continued. "Naturally, I called Alitalia and pulled rank—in the name of the Holy Father, no less—and they gave me their full cooperation! I spelled out Jon's name, and they did a search for it in the passenger lists of all their flights from Rome to Athens over a forty-eight-hour period straddling the approximate time he would have made the flight, according to Joshua.

"A half hour later, they called back to say they had drawn a complete blank. 'Maybe Professor Weber had chosen another airline,' they suggested. I then asked that they contact all other airlines flying planes from Rome to Athens at the time. I realized it was an outrageous request, but I told them that this was not only in the national interest, but—and then I really fibbed—that this came at the direct request of Joshua-Jesus himself. No argument with that! And so they went to work."

"Why didn't you simply call Joshua about it?" asked Shannon. "I certainly would have."

"I too. But it was now one o'clock in the morning, and I—"

"Oh, that's right. Go on."

"Around two-thirty, Alitalia called me back with word that Jon's name appeared on no passenger manifests of any airline for that route and time frame. Well, that shocked my socks off. My brain started spinning out some fairly dark thoughts, I'll tell you. You see, I thought it extremely strange that Jon hadn't contacted me at all after arriving in Rome."

"As I obviously would have!" added Jon.

"Fact is, that alone should have sparked my suspicions. But I was so swamped with last-minute preparations for Vatican III that my guard was down. Still, I gave Joshua one last chance for honesty, thinking that maybe Jon had flown to Athens by private jet. So, at three o'clock our time—four o'clock in Athens—I called the residence of the archbishop of Athens. To my horror, the great man himself answered the phone—yes, 'His Beatitude, the Archbishop of Athens and All of Greece, Christodoulos II' answered the phone! I introduced myself and had to beg his forgiveness for the hour at which I was calling, of course. Then I asked if Professor Jonathan Weber had arrived there to discuss Vatican III with him. '*Whaaat?*' he replied, angrily. 'I avv no idea *whaaat* you are talking about!'

and hung up on me. And so I guess I've merely set back ecumenical relations with the Greek Orthodox church for another thousand years!"

Pausing for their laughter, Kevin continued, "But now, of course,
I was deadly worried and very suspicious. Whom to call in Israel?
You, of course, came immediately to mind, Gideon."

"Yes, and good thing you did!" he replied. "Your call shocked
me into action. Then, of course, I feared the worst. I had warned
you to stay out of trouble, Jon, and not to go it alone—"

"Right," Jon agreed. "It was imbecilic stupidity on my part not
to tell you about my going to Galilee. I'll cheerfully grant you that!"

Gideon and then Jon detailed, from their separate vantage points,
the harrowing rescue at the Galilee compound. Shannon shivered at
the account, while Kevin looked tense and stressed—never mind
that they were all enjoying a night on the town. And when, in the
retelling, the KLM jet took off from Ben-Gurion *without* Jon and
Gideon aboard, Shannon threw up her hands in dismay.

After taking a long sip of Chianti, Gideon then related how they
had phoned the prime minister of Israel in desperation, and how
Cohen—to foil so horrendous a plot and "in the name of truth
itself"—ordered the Israeli jets.

"None of the fighters have three seats," Gideon explained, "so
two planes had to be used. They were McDonnell-Douglas F-15
E's—Strike Eagles. Fortunately, their base was nearby."

"And I'll tell you true," Jon broke in, "never in my *life* have I felt
such a sensation. Take all the thrills you've ever felt on that first big
plunge on roller coasters, add them up, and then you'll begin to get
the feeling. After we cleared the runway at Ben-Gurion and were out
over the Mediterranean, our pilots hit the afterburners for a while,
and I thought we were headed for the moon! We hit Mach 2—twice
the speed of sound—and peaked at sixteen hundred miles an hour
before they throttled back to cruising speed of only a thousand!"

Clearly, the air-minded boy was coming out in Jon, Shannon
noted. Later she would have to ask him how many model airplanes
he had built as a kid.

"Anyway," he continued, almost breathlessly, "we made the trip
in under ninety minutes—half the time it took KLM to fly the same

route. And what a great job the Mossad and Shin Bet did for us at the other end in greasing the rails with Italian security!"

"Oh, yes!" Gideon smiled. "That wild ride with the *carabinieri* and their screaming sirens on the way to the Vatican was almost as scary as the jet flight!"

"Why don't you pick up the story from there, Kevin?" Jon suggested.

"Well, at long, long last our Vatican repair crews restored communications after the big storm, so Jon was able to get through to me just after he landed. So here we were, all marching across the Piazza San Piètro, when my cell phone starts ringing, and others in the procession give me a very nasty look. I almost turned the thing off, but thank God I didn't! It was Jon, of course, filling me in on everything and throwing James 1:16 at me as if it were the only verse in the Bible! Obviously, it was too late for me to halt the proceedings—as if I could have done that in any case! All I could do was peel out of the procession and have portable lapel mikes ready the moment you and Gideon graced us with your presence!"

"I'll never forget the looks on the faces of those papal police when Gideon and I dashed up the steps of St. Peter's, you slipped on our portable mikes, and then signaled to the police that it was okay—we were not terrorists."

Kevin laughed and said, "I kid you not: if the captain of the *Gendarmeria Pontificia* hadn't recognized me as a . . . a rather reliable sort, we might be the ones sitting in the Vatican City slammer instead of Ben-Yosef and Levine!"

"Then, of course, came our triumphal procession down the center aisle of the Basilica of St. Peter," said Jon, with mock pomposity.

"And not too bad for a Jewish boy born in a kibbutz down in the Negev!" Gideon said with a wink, as they all chuckled.

The owner of The Secret Apple, a rotund, olive-skinned gourmet who put his pasta where his mouth was, stopped by their table and thanked them for their crucial services to the church in unmasking the false messiah. He had recognized them from the evening television news and now had a "Vesuvio Surprise" wheeled out to their table, with his compliments: brandy-saturated baked Alaska, which he ignited into a flaming volcanic dessert.

"Wow! Where are Nero and his fiddle while Rome burns?" asked Shannon. "I'm really glad we're sitting on the outside terrace here!" Then she added, "I still have so many questions about how Joshua brought it all off that I'd be sitting here until tomorrow morning if I asked them all. I need so much more detail, because now I feel like a simpering fool for ever thinking that he was Jesus Christ, no less!"

"Well, dear, so did much of the world," said Jon. "So you're in good company."

"All of us thought that, Shannon," said Kevin, "except maybe Gideon here."

Gideon smiled and said, "Ah yes, you must forgive this Jewish skeptic. But, then, my head is stuck in the past. In the Israel Antiquities Authority, perhaps I'm the chief antiquity."

"Anything but!" Jon laughed, clapping him on the shoulder. "And I'm sure the gorgeous sabra you married would agree with me! But, in answer to your . . . very understandable questions, Shannon, I promise to give you a total rundown in the days and weeks to come."

After the last, delicious portions of the dessert had found a new home in their stomachs, Jon thought of how many other bewildered Shannons there were, even among people he knew. Alitalia's jet full of cheated and possibly despairing followers of Joshua came to mind, especially the Twelve-minus-one whose faith had been so pathetically misplaced. Before they left the table, Jon turned to Kevin and asked, "What are we going to do about that planeload of believers in Joshua's entourage? Are they stranded here in Rome?"

"Way ahead of you on that one, sport," Kevin replied. "Alitalia had promised them a round-trip flight and they'll keep their word. The return flight goes day after tomorrow."

"Excellent. Why don't we get a message to everyone who flew here on that plane that I'd like to meet with them, as a group, tomorrow afternoon? Sure, we gave them all reserved seats at the press conference, but they're probably still reeling from the news. I'd like to help them, if I can."

"Good plan, Jon. I'll see that they're all contacted."

That night, nestled together in the huge, Louis XIV bed, Jon and Shannon reviewed the events of that second tumultuous day. At first, she seemed a little cool to his advances. It was nothing he had said or done. It was her own nagging conscience. She turned away from him and let some tears wet her pillow.

"What's wrong, Shannon?" he asked.

She just shook her head, face turned the other way and buried in the pillows.

"I'm not going to sleep until you tell me, Shannon."

Turning about, she said, "I feel like such a miserable worm, Jon . . ."

"What's that supposed to mean?"

"No, worse than that: what I said was an insult to worms! I'm the lowlife who betrayed you, Jon, who got you into terrible trouble. Just call me Judith—Judith Iscariot."

"That's ridiculous, Shannon."

"Oh no, it's not! Joshua would have known nothing about the investigation panel and your role in it if I hadn't blown everything wide open by crying on his shoulder that awful night in Jerusalem. It's the worst thing I've ever done in my life!"

"Well, what about me—taking off for Galilee without telling you? I'm just as much to blame."

"See, Jon: I really thought Joshua *was* Jesus, and I figured that he knew about everything anyway, and so I merely—"

"Enough, darling! The two of us are textbook examples of what happens when a couple of strong-willed individuals don't communicate!"

"I . . . guess so." She brightened and turned to face him. "We could fill a whole chapter in a marriage manual, I'll bet! Can you . . . really forgive me, then, Jon?"

"Of course," he replied, brushing her cheek lightly with the tips of his fingers. Then he smiled and added, "You know, your so-called betrayal was really about the best thing that could have happened under these wild circumstances."

"What? Why in the world is that?"

"Because it forced Ben-Yosef to show his hand in luring me up to his lodge. What if I hadn't gone up there? Joshua would have exploded his bombshell successfully at St. Peter's, and Christendom would have been reeling. After that, it could have taken months, maybe years, to unmask him and undo the damage—if indeed, we could even have brought that off. And then what would have happened to Christianity across the world?"

Shannon pondered that thought for some moments. Finally, she said, "You know, you have a wonderful way of comforting people, Jon."

"No, darling." He chuckled. "I have a much better way than that. C'mon over here: I'm just aching . . . aching to hold you!"

ABOUT THE AUTHOR

Paul L. Maier is a best-selling author of both fiction and nonfiction. A professor of ancient history at Western Michigan University, he graduated from Harvard (M.A.) and Concordia Seminary (M.Div.) before he took his Ph.D. *summa cum laude* at the University of Basel, the first American ever to do so. He has several million copies of his books in print—in twelve languages. His popular novels include *A Skeleton in God's Closet, Pontius Pilate,* and *The Flames of Rome.* He also penned the best-selling trilogy of books on the life of Jesus and earliest Christianity, now included in one volume, *In the Fullness of Time.* His translations of the first-century Jewish historian Josephus and the father of church history, Eusebius, are widely used. His children's book, *The Very First Christmas,* received the Gold Medallion Award in 1999, and was followed by *The Very First Easter* and *The Very First Christians.* Dr. Maier travels and lectures widely, appearing frequently in national radio, television, and newspaper interviews. He and his wife Joan have four daughters.

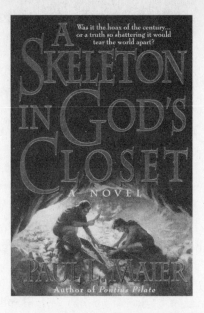

A SKELETON
IN GOD'S CLOSET

PAUL L. MAIER

In this #1 best-selling novel, Dr. Jonathan Weber makes a discovery so shattering it shakes the very foundations of Christianity.

Jonathan Weber, Harvard professor and biblical scholar, is looking forward to a sabbatical year on an archaeological dig in Israel. But a spectacular discovery—a skeleton almost two thousand years old!—will either shed light on the life of Jesus Christ or be the death rattle of the Christian faith. Meanwhile, Weber's interest in Shannon Jennings, daughter of the dig's director, proves to be an exciting complication.

Delving into the worlds of science, archaeology, politics, and religion, this fast-paced thriller explores the tension between doubt and faith and one man's determination to find the truth—no matter what the cost.

ISBN: 0-8407-3424-7